# A Heavenly Moose

THE CANDLES IN the trophy room guttered to cowering blue sparks at the base of the wicks. The cold draft got colder. I looked up. One of the moose faces had grown whiter, the snout shorter, the eyes sadder. "Sweet Jesus, Papa, but you look strange with antlers," I whispered.

The stove roared suddenly as if devouring a new log. "Sscat! Get out! Sscram—"

I set the candelabra back on the table, and faced the spectre. "For pity's sake, Papa, will you quit the macabre monosyllables? If you've something to tell me, come out with it."

"Nag, nag, nag," the fire snapped and Papa grinned a moose-wide grin.

As cold as I felt, I was soaking with perspiration. My head throbbed and my feet burned and here I stood arguing with my dead father, who was no doubt of even less use in spectral form than he had been in life. Just then the door flew open and I twisted to stare dazedly at an opera-caped Vasily Vladovitch.

My host stared at me as if I was insane.

"The water bucket!" he cried, and pointed. I picked it up and threw the contents into the fire, which blossomed into a wide explosive ball.

Suffocating black smoke filled the air. From within the stove, the choked flames sizzled themselves to death, hissing "crosses," and then "crusssscifixsss" as it died.

# THE
# GOLDCAMP
# VAMPIRE

····〉⊛〈 OR 〉⊛〈····

# THE
# SANGUINARY
# SOURDOUGH

*Elizabeth Scarborough*

**BANTAM BOOKS**
TORONTO · NEW YORK · LONDON · SYDNEY · AUCKLAND

# Dedication

THIS BOOK IS affectionately dedicated to Alaska and
the Yukon Territories, and to the lands, the people,
and the mosquitos thereof, the latter supplying the
inspiration for the vampire.

THE GOLDCAMP VAMPIRE
A Bantam Spectra Book / November 1987

Grateful acknowledgment is made for permission to reprint the excerpt from
THE ALASKAN GOLD FIELDS, Copyright © 1983, Alaska Northwest
Publishing, 130 Second Avenue So., Edmonds, WA 98020. Originally
published as The Alaskan Gold Fields and the Opportunities They Offer
for Capital and Labor, by Sam C. Dunham, in "Bulletin of the
Department of Labor" No. 16, May 1898, pp. 297–425.

ISBN 0-553-26717-5

Published simultaneously in the United States and Canada

PRINTED IN THE UNITED STATES OF AMERICA

O    0 9 8 7 6 5 4 3 2 1

# Acknowledgments

FOR CHRONOLOGY OF a Klondike quest in 1897, the weather conditions and sequence of historical events, as well as the posted notices at Fort Selkirk and in Dawson City regarding the *Bella*, I relied on *The Alaskan Gold Fields* by Sam C. Dunham, available from Alaska Northwest Publishing Company. Other historical references included: *Klondike Fever* by Pierre Berton, *I Married the Klondike* by Laura Beatrice Berton, *My 90 Years* by Martha Louise Black, *Magnificence and Misery* by E. Hazard Wells, edited by Randall M. Dodd, and *The Streets Were Paved with Gold: A Pictorial History of the Klondike Gold Rush 1896–1899*. I relied on these books for background information, color, and some idea of conditions in the Yukon in 1897. Except for the partial evacuation of the provisionless Dawsonites by the *Bella* and the destruction of an opera house by fire in Dawson City on October 27, 1897, all events in this book and all interpretations of actual historical events are purely imaginary. Of the people mentioned, Father Judge, Joe Boyle, Mr. Ladue, Captain Healy, Inspector Constantine, and Jack London were real people. To the best of my knowledge, Inspector Constantine never knew anything about vampires or werewolves in Dawson City and never set foot inside the Rich Vein. That Jack London wrote wonderful books about the North and animals, had bad teeth (due to scurvy), and was not a teetotaler are matters of historical record. All the rest of it, I made up. I thought he might enjoy it.

I would like to express my gratitude to Professor Mary Mangusso, Renee Blahuta, Bill Schneider, Dick North, Cam Sigurdson, Ursula, who gave me her map, Anne Marie Brochard, and M.S. Gates, Curator of Collections, Klondike National Historic Sites for Environment Canada Parks, for allowing me access to special reference material and providing information about what Dawson City may have been like physically (sans vampires) in 1897. Any possible historical accuracy in this book is to the credit of the above named people and works. All the errors, embellishments, and downright lies are my own. Very special thanks to Karen Parr and Al Rice for electronic rescue during the latter stages of the book.

And finally, of course, I am deeply indebted to Bram Stoker for writing *Dracula*, and for having had it originally published in exactly the right year to suit me.

# Cast of Characters

*THE INCOMPARABLE SASHA DEVINE:* A chanteuse with a heart of gold, former mistress of our heroine's dear departed papa.

*PATRICK HARPER:* Above noted dear departed papa.

*THE APPARITION:* Above noted Patrick Harper.

*THE WIDOW HIGGENBOTHAM-HARPER:* Sanctimonious surviving spouse of above noted Patrick Harper.

*WY MI:* Former drinking companion of Harper and reluctant childhood mentor of our heroine.

*JADE FAN:* Our heroine's landlady.

*VASILY VLADOVITCH BLEDINOFF:* Aristocratic entrepreneur and a sourdough of extremely long standing.

*FRANCIS DRAKE:* The comanchero villain of an adventure experienced by our heroine ten years before. An exploiter of helpless women and confused displaced Mexican dragons.

*ALONSO PURDY:* Sometimes referred to as "Dr." Purdy, a medicine show charlatan, rainmaker, former preacher, and current tinhorn gambler. Also involved in Pelagia's previous adventure.

*SERGEANT MALCOM DESTIN, ROYAL CANADIAN NORTHWEST MOUNTED POLICE:* A long-time veteran on the force and also the ancestral laird of a little-known Scottish clan.

*CONSTABLE FAVERSHAM, NWMP:* A young officer of little experience and a fatal aptitude for bureaucracy.

*DAG LOMAX:* A sourdough, a squaw man, a cat lover, and a landlubber yearning for the water.

*LOKI:* Lomax's cat.

*EGIL LARSSON:* Lomax's nephew, who set out to join him at his Henderson Creek claim. Egil was forever changed by his Yukon experiences.

*TAGISH TOM AND MARY:* Lomax's Indian brother-in-law and sister-in-law, siblings of his deceased wife, *Lucy*.

*MR. LANE:* The bartender at the *Rich Vein* Opera House.

*GIN-MILL GISELLE:* A New Orleans dance hall queen who should have stuck to dancing.

*BON-TON BUNNY, JEANNINE WITH THE LIGHT BROWN HAIR, MISS MILLIE THE ALABAMA FILLIE, NELLIE THE KID, AND MAISIE OF THE SEVEN VEILS:* The all-star revue at the *Rich Vein* and our heroine's erstwhile colleagues.

*CORAZON, THE BELLE OF BARCELONE:* Our heroine's nom de stage while incognito.

*STELLA THE STIFF AND LURLEEN:* Two working girls comprising the welcoming committee in our heroine's new neighborhood, Paradise Alley.

*JIM RINGER:* Owner of the Yukon Belle, a saloon.

*JACK LONDON:* Prospector friend of Dag Lomax. Another tiresome young would-be novelist seeking our heroine's advice about how to write anthropomorphic animal stories.

*VALENTINE LOVELACE:* Our heroine's nom de plume.

*PAT HARPER:* Our heroine's nom de guerre when she is incognito and disguised in gentleman's attire.

*PELAGIA BRIGID HARPER:* Our heroine's true name, whatever else she calls herself in the course of this narrative.

*THE BIOGRAPHER:* A stuffy historian who puts in her two-cents' worth by intimating that people who write books about living through an unusual experience don't know what it is they lived through.

# CHAPTER I

*•••••═╾╪◄◙┣ ┫◙►╪╼═•••••*

THREE DAYS AFTER my father's funeral, his former mistress summoned me to her place of employment and proposed that the two of us distract ourselves from grief by accepting a rather bizarre proposition. "Meet me backstage at 12:15 and you will, as they say, learn something to your advantage," her note read.

As very little had been to my advantage lately, I roused myself to accept.

It would be inaccurate to say I had been prostrated with grief. My father's death was hardly unanticipated—he had been deliberately drinking himself to death since the demise of my mother thirty years ago, and since his second marriage to the sanctimonious Widow Higgenbotham, he had speeded up the process appreciably.

Considering his inclinations, the manner and location of his passing were as he would have wished it. When found, he wore a blissful smile upon his face as if he had discovered some new and particularly potent elixir that had carried him straight to heaven—assuming that was his destination. I felt guilty when I saw him to note how pale and drained he looked, for I so despised his new wife that I had seen him very seldom. But his happy expression and the fact that he had died just outside his favorite haunt, the Gold Nugget Opera House, consoled me.

Nevertheless, I purposely averted my eyes and held my skirts away as I passed the spot where he had been found on my way to the backstage door.

With the mist creeping up to conceal the garbage and broken bottles, and the drizzle descending like unceasing tears, the alley was a depressing place to be. Even the pearl-handled derringer in my bag was cold comfort. This was a night the poet Poe might relish, except that ravens seldom frequented the alleys of San Francisco anymore. Pigeons perhaps. Pigeons with uncannily direct gazes, for as I turned back toward the lamplight flickering in from the main street, small eyes glittered down at me, then swooped aside. I grasped the knob of the backstage door and shoved.

The strains of the final chorus act met me even before I entered, but Sasha Devine's numbers were over for the evening. It was her policy always to "leave them wanting more." Her dressing room door was cracked open, for despite the midsummer fog and damp, the air was warm.

Sasha saw me reflected in her mirror even before I spoke. "Vahlenteena," she said effusively, twisting in her chair to face me. "How kind of you to come to see me in my bereavement. You alone know how very dear Patrick was to me. And you, my dear Vahlenteen, have always been the daughter I never had."

I would have been more moved by this declaration were it not for the fact that it was only since my novels began to sell that Sasha had learned my name—and at that she chose to learn my nom de plume, Valentine Lovelace, not my given name, Pelagia Harper. Although to be perfectly fair, I do recall that at times while I was in my teens, she was wont to refer to me as "Peggy."

"Because of this sentiment I bear you and your dear departed father," she continued, "and because you are a fellow artiste in what I understand are straited circumstances, I have selected you to be my traveling companion on my grand tour of the Klondike. Expenses will be paid, of course, but you must wait for your salary until we arrive."

My spirits rose immediately. I was, in fact, so elated by the chance to see the Klondike, that dazzling repository of gold of which everyone was speaking, that I failed to note Sasha's tone. It was identical to the one I had once heard her use when she parted my father from the subscription money that was supposed to support our newspaper for a month.

Instead, my previous caution vanished and I saw in her my

deliverance from my problems. No matter if Jade Fan, Wy Mi's grieving sister, sold her laundry—and my lodgings—and moved back to China. No matter if the Widow Higgenbotham refused to pay me the monies that Papa had promised me for the serialization of my latest saga in the *Herald*. No matter that the West was now all but won, and I had to dredge my dwindling memories of Texas for material for my popular-but-unlucrative epistles. No matter that I would never again see Papa slumped over his desk, or hear him singing as he stumbled from his favorite saloon. Long since he had ceased telling me the stories of Cuchulain and Maeve, and Wy Mi had not mentioned the Wind Dragons of his native China since I told him I'd met one. Life had become quite dull. And now lovely, kindly Sasha Devine, in all her beneficence, was going to take me away from all this.

My face must have betrayed my emotion. With a complacent smile, she turned away from me and began removing her stage makeup, smoothing the cream below the high ruffled collar of her dressing gown, which kept tickling her chin and threatening to get makeup and grease on its lace. I had never realized her complexion was so fair—pallid, one might even say. When she removed the whitening under her great green eyes, dark hollows appeared. When she turned back to me, her collar flopped away, revealing an angry insect bite on the left side of her still almost-perfect throat.

Even without the makeup, however, Sasha looked no older than I, though she had to be at least ten years my senior. Her hair really was that blond, but without the false curls of her fancy coiffure, it hung long and straight. She looked delicate when unpainted, rather like a fairy princess who might, with that sharp determined chin and those acquisitive green eyes, turn into a wicked queen with the least encouragement. Hadn't I heard a rumor somewhere that she was descended from the royal house of some long-defunct Balkan country?

"I have been working very hard, and your father's death has distressed me greatly," she said. "Also, until departure time, I must continue to fulfill my contract here. You will be in charge of the practical details, booking the passage for me, yourself, and Mr. Lawson's coffin . . ."

"Mr. Lawson's what?" I asked.

"His coffin," she said, slowly and distinctly, as if to the deaf. "Mr. Lawson is dead and requires one."

"Excuse me," I said. "Unacquainted with Mr. Lawson as I

am, his demise had escaped my notice. If he is dead, why does he require not only a coffin, but passage aboard a steamer to the Klondike?"

She turned again, her actress's eyes entreating me tragically. "Because Mr. Lawson's partner is a man not only of exceptionally good taste, as he is an admirer of mine, but also of considerable sentiment. He and Mr. Lawson worked their Alaskan claim for many years without success. Even when my admirer temporarily gave up mining for bartending in order to earn a further grubstake, Mr. Lawson, it is said, worked with commendable determination throughout the winter in an attempt to find the mother lode. To no avail. This earned him the cruel soubriquet of Lost-Cause among his associates. Finally, his partner insisted that he come to San Francisco to recuperate from exhaustion and the illness that consumed him as a result of his efforts. When the gold strike was made in the Klondike, my admirer abandoned his bar, after standing a drink for the denizens in order to get a head start on them, and headed for Canada. The day Mr. Lawson died, my admirer made one of the richest strikes in the Yukon. But he is guilt-ridden about it. His partner must at least see the wealth that eluded them both for so long, he feels. The gentleman in question remembers me fondly from a night—a performance—two years ago, and dispatched a message containing a retainer and promising that if I would see to it that his poor partner was escorted to the Yukon, he would make me owner of my own establishment, which is somewhat better than a gold mine."

"I see."

"And you, you will get the experience of traveling to the most exciting place in the world. Later, when I have earned my reward, you may be my agent to summon my girls to come join me."

"It's a very kind offer, Miss Devine," I said. "But I fail to understand exactly why you need me . . ."

"Because I certainly cannot be expected to do everything. You must see to collecting the body from the undertaker's, to booking the passage, to acquiring certain papers assuring Mr. Lawson's corpse of entry into Canada."

She rose and faced me, one hand extended dramatically. "Vahlenteena, I ask you because I know that you are a person of integrity, and in my line of work one meets all too few of those. Do you think I failed to see how you kept your newspaper running when dear Patrick was unable? You are rather young, of course, and a woman, but I thought you might be—"

She needed to say no more. I was hooked without hearing any of the particulars, which is, of course, always a mistake.

I asked to see the letter from her admirer, so that I might get a list of the tasks to be accomplished. I thought, from all the details in her story, that it must certainly have been a very long letter, or perhaps an entire series of correspondence. However, she responded that she had received just a note and she thought she had left it in her suite. She remembered it quite well, however, and went over with me the prodigious list of chores I needed to perform to secure our passage. The oddest of these was arranging for the disinterment of Lost-Cause Lawson from his tomb and his transport to the steamer.

This I determined to tackle the following day. I got a rather late start. I left Sasha Devine during the wee hours Sunday morning, when it was not yet light and the fog made the alley look like the smoking aftermath of a great fire. I have traveled the streets of my native city in what I fondly believed was perfect safety for most of my life, but in these early hours, I felt ill at ease. The rain finished its demolition work on my mourning bonnet, which had not been especially crisp to begin with. My one good woolen coat had used the warmth of Sasha's dressing room to finish permeating its fibers with damp, so that I was now chilled through. My spine was already curling itself into tight ringlets when the black carriage flashed past the alley entrance, drenching me to the waist as the wheels splashed through a puddle.

I shouted a few of the more colorful epithets I had learned in Texas at the denizens of the carriage, little expecting response, for half of my remarks were in Spanish, the vernacular being particularly suited for self-expression of that sort.

To my dismay, the carriage stopped abruptly and swung around in the middle of the street, the lamps gleaming off the coats of the horses and the polished ebony of the coach. Shadows shrouded the interior, but as the vehicle drew even with my dripping form, a low and melodious voice from within said softly, "*Se lo reuego usted que mi disculpas con todo sinceridad, senora.*"

"Oh, dear, excuse me," I sputtered, wringing out my hem. Evidently, I had just had the honor of being splattered by a member of our local Spanish nobility. "I mean, I didn't think you'd under—oh, never mind . . ."

"Ah, you are American, despite your bilingual fluency." The voice sounded pleased. Its accent was foreign but not, I thought, Spanish after all. "Please, madam, permit me to offer the services of my carriage to your quarters, where you may change your attire and present your other clothing to my man for cleaning or replacement, if the damage is too extensive."

I peered into the shadows and alternated between feeling like a perfect fool and feeling very cautious about this disembodied voice. The man sounded like a gentlemen, but many gentlemen, I had found, were anything but gentle and had attained their wealth and high station by taking the position that everyone else was inferior to themselves and, therefore, fair game.

"Don't trouble yourself, sir," I said, inching away. "My lodgings are not far and my landlady and her family, who are waiting up for me, operate a laundry. Jade Fan will have my costume good as new tomorrow at no expense to me."

And before he could say any more or possibly leap from his carriage and drag me in, as my overheated imagination began to suggest, I sprinted—or splashed—away.

I bounded up the outside steps that were my private entrance above the laundry and slammed the door behind me, throwing the bolt. As soon as my heart stopped pounding, I began to feel extremely silly. The man hadn't even gotten out of his carriage, for heaven's sake! And he certainly was polite. And my best mourning costume, which was not all that good in the first place and might have inspired him to replace it, was certainly the worse for its drenching. I removed it and toweled my hide briskly before slipping into my nightshift and between the covers. The laundry opened an hour later than usual on Saturdays, so I would have a little while to sleep without having to combat the noise and heat rising from below.

Jade Fan and her family did not sleep below, as I had insinuated to the man in the carriage. The laundry had become prosperous enough for the family to occupy the entire first floor of the hotel owned by Fanny's eldest daughter. I occupied their previous quarters, a space far too cramped for the family of fifteen. My room had a dormer ceiling and was furnished with a narrow iron bed, a writing desk salvaged from the newspaper with the help of Wy Mi and father, and a Chinese lacquer chest, a loan from Fanny, for my clothing. These meager possessions occupied all floor space save a narrow pathway. The room did have a large window on each end, under the peaks of the roof. Beneath one of these I had situated the head of my bed. Beneath the other stood my writing desk.

I could not sleep immediately, despite the late hour, for I kept seeing visions of myself in the gold fields, swirling water in a pan with glittering chunks at the bottom, interviewing the newly wealthy, eating moose, and fending off wild bears. How uncharacteristically kind of Sasha Devine to think of me. Whereas I had always admired her for many other traits, her toughness, her beauty, her talent—for over the years she had shown herself to be a fine actress as well as an energetic dancer and versatile chanteuse—and her skill at managing people, kindness had never been one of her more obvious qualities.

Well, I mused, all of those stories about tarnished angels with hearts of gold surely had to have some basis, and perhaps I was finally discovering it in the character of my new employer. Anyway, travel, adventure, and much needed revenue aside, it would be worth accepting the position just to imagine the expression on the Widow Hig's face when she heard that her stepdaughter was traveling in the employ of a woman of virtue that had not even the benefit of being questionable.

With that happy thought I drifted off. Unfortunately, happy thoughts did not linger *after* I drifted off. I dreamed again of the dragon, Quetzacoatl, that great fire-breathing lizard and self-proclaimed fountain of divine wisdom I had encountered in Texas and whom I had delivered by a narrow margin from the clutches of unscrupulous worshippers. The dragon now safely reposed, to the best of my knowledge, in the rocky vastnesses of the Texas desert, but in my dreams I saw him, wings spread in pointed scallops, eyes gleaming darkly, every movement causing avalanches of small stones that rumbled like the sound of carriage wheels over cobbles.

And then I became confused, unable to decide if it was the dragon I was hearing or if it really *was* carriage wheels on cobbles. But surely day was not dawning already?

Then there came a scratching at my door. Another emergency cleaning job for Jade Fan, the client no doubt mistaken about the location of her quarters. I tried to convey the information, but I was much too fast asleep, and the harder I tried to waken, the further back into slumber I plummeted. The scratching moved to the window over my head and changed to a thumping—throwing rocks now, were they? Some people had no sense of proportion. How bad could it be anyway?

Blood stains on a bridal dress? Now, what made me think of that, I wondered—one thinks the strangest things in dreams.

Even today I am not entirely sure that I truly opened my eyes. I kept dreaming that I woke and went to the door, but then I would wake just enough to know that I still slept. When I tried to rise then, I could not and fell into another dream. But finally it did seem that I opened my eyes to backlit darkness—I could make out the gray outlines of furnishings. Outside the window, the murkiness roiled. I was awakened this time not so much by the noise over my head as by its cessation. I waited, my breath coming shallowly, without knowing quite what I waited for.

Then it struck, a point of blackness penetrating the fog for a moment to rap the window, withdraw, and rap again. I discerned no shape. I tried to sit up, and heard my heart pounding in my ears, magnified until it sounded like the jungle drums Mr. Haggard mentions so dramatically. My limbs were suddenly gelatinous, too much so to reach the derringer in the bag beside my bed.

The rapping was accompanied by a rustling sound now and came ever more furiously. I saw the outline of wings—wings like those of Quetzacoatl from my dream—which made me think I must be dreaming again. I had half risen onto my elbow, I think, but all at once the assault at the window crescendoed into ferocity, and I fell back against the bedhead, sending into a pendulumlike swing the wooden rosary given to me by my old friend Mariquilla. One of my braids became tangled with the beads, but I remember laying back very quietly, telling myself not to panic, that it was only a dream, but that nevertheless it would not do to pull my hair so that I cried out or break the string between the beads.

As I struggled, the thing at my window grew quieter. The rapping and rustling ceased, and I heard a sliding noise and a soft thud. I twisted my head as far as the beads would allow and saw a black shape outlined in the gray of the fog. My professional curiosity piqued, I broke the tangled hairs one by one and rose to see what it was. I could not make it out and felt the strongest urge to go to the window and raise it, to let the thing in so that I could study it. While I was deciding, I nibbled on garlic almond duck pieces, as is my habit while pondering.

By the time the pieces were gone, I was no longer able to resist the compulsion to open the window. I bent low and shoved, to no avail, for as usual the frame stuck in the sill. Instead of giving up, I grew oddly frantic, even trying to break the glass. Then I tried once more.

So forceful was I that not only did the sash fly up, but my elbows cracked painfully on the desk and my head shot out the window. My braids and crucifix dangled over the street as I hung there, panting. The thing, which was by now practically perched on my head, shrieked and, with a slap of wings against my scalp, flew away before I could see any more of it.

Shutting the window in one disgusted slam, I eventually settled back into repose, but not before I had done as Wy Mi had instructed me since girlhood—I wrote down the dream, not sure whether I was still within it or whether I would wake on the morrow to find my pages blank.

In China, the printer had told me, people ask about one's dreams and one's family's dreams almost before they ask how one is doing when conscious. This had so impressed me that for my entire life I have kept a dream journal, and should I ever visit China, I expect to be a stunning conversationalist.

# CHAPTER II

·····•◦❦◗‖◖❦◦•·····

*THANKS TO MY* diligence and competence and Sasha Devine's money, we departed in early August.

The arrangements were expedited by a number of factors. Chief among these, of course, was being in the right place at the right time. On July 15, the day before Papa's demise, the excitement had begun when the *Excelsior* steamed into port carrying $750,000 in gold dust from the Klondike strike. This event served to convince the more perspicacious that a northern clime would be healthy for one's personal economy. Two days later in Seattle, the arrival of the *Portland*, bearing an additional $800,000, assured the start of a gold rush even more phenomenal than the one that had figured so prominently in California history. I wondered fleetingly at the fortunate timing of these events, for surely the message from Sasha Devine's admirer must have come on the *Excelsior*, just in time to prevent me from getting maudlin over Papa's demise.

I almost did anyway while booking our passage, for I was reminded of Papa's sociability and popularity over and over again. The drinks bought with the money needed to support us over the years were well remembered by the seafaring men of the San Francisco docks. Most also knew me, of course, since I had frequently appeared in the optimistic hope that my presence would remind them all not to drink me out of house, home, and employment. To no avail, of course.

But now when I appeared in my second-best mourning suit, begging a favor that did not require the restitution of funds, I was met with enthusiasm. More important, I received a wealth of information that eventually led me to seek out a certain Mr. Eustace Flannery, a villainous looking specimen who, I believe, came up in the world Horatio Alger fashion, from pirate to purser of a large steamship, flagship of the line.

The ship, formerly named the *Myrtle Marthe*, after the mother of the line's owner, had been rechristened the *Golden Queen*. Old signs were going down or being painted out all over town, their labels and advertisements replaced with new ones that prominently proclaimed their establishment, enterprise, service, vehicle, or product to be the "golden" this, the "Klondike" that, or the "Yukon" something else.

Once assured that I had not come to foreclose on the gambling debt owed by Mr. Flannery to Papa, the scarred face with its mashed nose, single ear, and one half-closed eye took on an expression that could almost be described as jovial. When I told him I required immediate passage for myself, another lady, and a coffin, the joviality turned into wheezing laughter.

"A coffin? Takin' old Patrick along, are you?"

"Not exactly," I said guilefully. For Sasha Devine had instructed me that she and Mr. Lawson would need to travel incognito. For her part, she wished to avoid advertising her departure until she had informed her employer, which she intended to do the day we left. Mr. Lawson would need to pose as a Canadian subject in order to cross the border without undue fuss or customs. I had already picked up the papers from a local artist friend of Sasha's, who also specialized in portraits of presidents done in shades of green.

Flannery had been flimflammed by better flimmers and flammers than myself, however. He winked with his drooping eye and put a finger to his lips. "I hear you, Miss Pelly. Never let it be said ol' Flan asked too many questions. The space is yours for a hundred dollars apiece for you ladies, a hundred fifty for the coffin."

"Why more for the coffin? That's passenger rate, not cargo and Mr. Law—the departed—won't be moving around or using your facilities."

"Just so, mum. But he will be lyin' down, takin' up maximum space. And there's no cargo space to be had, so he'll need to ride in the cabin with you ladies and the other passengers. I do hope he don't stink much by now?"

I hoped not either. My impression was that Mr. Lawson was among the more recent additions to the heavenly choir.

My next errand was to stop at the address Sasha had given me for an undertaker who would remove our charge from his tomb and deliver him to the docks on the apppropriate day at the appropriate hour. I did not recognize the address, and little wonder. It took me to a part of town I did not frequent, the section where the grandees and their descendents still dwelt sequestered within their haciendas.

I knocked at the iron-bound door of a stucco cottage adjoining a graveyard. The door opened only a fraction. Two dark feral eyes set in a swarthy face all planes and hollows peered at me from around the door, but I was not invited in, nor was the door opened wider. No wonder Sasha and my father got along so well. They both had the strangest taste in friends.

I delivered my message, and the recipient grunted. "Tell me," I said in my most sociable tone, "when did Mr. Lawson die? That is, how much in your expert opinion might remain of him? Quarters will be rather close on the ship, you see, and we're somewhat concerned about the quality of the air—"

"No stink," the man said, and slammed the door in my face.

I knocked on it angrily, then pounded, and finally gave it a kick, which did the door no damage, although I cannot say as much for my foot.

I had had a long day by then, a baffling one that filled me with a certain anxiety. I had awakened hung over from the nightmares of the previous sleep period. Then Flannery had provided me with a new worry, that of sharing a long voyage with a possibly extremely fragrant companion. And though the piratical purser had promised us first-class accommodations, I had a feeling that our ideas of first class might differ. Then to top it all off, here I was, afoot and alone on the edge of a strange part of town, having been forced to spend many hours to speak to what proved to be a secretive person whose comprehension was doubtful, whose reliability was improbable, and whose manners were negligible.

Though my foot was rather tender, I could not control my temper enough to stop myself from stomping down on it as I strode past the graveyard. Or I think it was the graveyard I strode past. Fog was settling thick as smoker's pall in a saloon on Saturday night, and I could see but a foot or two in front of me. And, figuratively speaking, everything I saw was red anyway. I was fuming, and when I fume, I fume. As I walked I gave the rude undertaker a piece of my mind, after the fact, as it were. My angry mumbling to myself ceased only when a small prickling part of my consciousness recognized that my footsteps had acquired an echo. I stopped in midmumble. The echo continued.

"Now what?" I asked myself aloud, exasperated.

I twisted this way and that, my fists balled. I wanted to challenge my unseen companion to come out and show himself like a man, and fight me if he dared. So incensed was I that at that moment I felt fully capable of defeating at fisticuffs someone of even Mr. Flannery's size and expertise. But I never issued the challenge, realizing how foolish I would have felt if the footsteps proved to be those of some perfect innocent, trapped in the fog as I was.

As I stood poised what had seemed the echo of my footfalls drew even with me, and, with a cool rush of air, swirled the fog toward me, and passed me to recede into the grayness enshrouding us both.

For a moment I remained still, then I drew my shawl tightly about my shoulders and continued, more cautiously, toward town. The street passed in front of a row of rowdy waterfront saloons, but I had been in and around these off and on for most of my life. Compared to the tunnel of fog-wrapped road from the graveyard, the lighted bars with their noise and stench seemed cozy.

I whisked along now, anxious lest I be late meeting Sasha Devine for dinner in the small restaurant adjoining the opera house. Two men rolled out into the street in front of me, fighting, and I sidestepped to avoid them, backing into the alley between buildings.

I was watching the fight instead of where I was going, when something caught me behind the knees and I fell backward, flailing to catch at the wall and stepping all over whatever it was that tripped me. The impediment was solid but yielding, and it yielded several more times as I danced across it, my soles seeking pavement, my hands scratched by paint flakes and splinters. When finally I had both my balance and my breath, I looked down—into the sleeping but beatifically happy face of my dead father.

\* \* \*

"But surely you knew it could not be Patrick," Sasha Devine said casually. She was unimpressed by what I considered a magnificent excuse for tardiness. Tardiness in others was inexcusable, she implied, although according to father and the papers that kept track of the affairs of the theatrical crowd, she herself was always fashionably late.

We sat together in the little restaurant, me devouring a plate of beans and she toying with what remained of a disgustingly rare steak. This was her day off and she had, characteristically, slept through most of it. Many stage entertainers of my acquaintance have similarly nocturnal habits. Her face was still innocent of makeup, but the gaslight flattered it, and it seemed to me that her color was better now, although she still appeared somewhat languorous. That was no doubt due to the fact that she was not yet fully awake.

"I suppose so, but I'm not used to him being gone yet. I keep expecting to run into him in just such a setting. It must have been the expression, of course—you know, I don't believe I ever saw him look so happy about anything while he was alive—did you?"

"Ummm, yes, several times," she said.

Realizing what she meant, I gave my attention to my food for a moment. The corpse *had* worn the same expression as my father. But more than that, it was as if, as I was focusing on it, my father's features were superimposed on those of the man who looked very different from him. My father was a middle-sized man, clean shaven but for a mustache, and his hair was still distinguishably red despite the gray and the ever-loftier forehead. This man was large, with a black beard and shaggy black hair. I felt as foolish about the mistake as I had about the squeal I let out when I made it. The two combatants had even stopped fighting, and one of them, good citizen that he was, fetched the constable. But even as the men disentangled to see what made me screech and possibly to see if there was any benefit to be had by them, either from the cause or the effect of that screech, I saw Papa's features melt away from those of the man on the ground—and it seemed to me that one eye opened and closed again in a wink.

What possessed me to confess these private hallucinations to Sasha Devine I don't know, except that I was sure she'd heard things even crazier.

"Hmm, well, perhaps you are being haunted, Vahlenteena.

Or you are missing your papa a little maybe. You have bad dreams, too?" I confessed that I did, and she patted my hand peremptorially. "Well then, it is a very good thing, is it not, that we are leaving this sad place? That busying yourself with such arrangements leaves you less time for gloom."

"I suppose," I admitted reluctantly. I felt she was taking all too lightly the rigors of my tasks, and I went into some detail about the difficulties with Mr. Flannery and expressed my chagrin at the behavior of the undertaker entrusted with Mr. Lawson's remains.

Sasha Devine looked unexpectedly uncomfortable and tugged at the prim lace collar petaling up under her chin. A wide blue satin ribbon fastened the lace above a sheer bodice, which plunged dangerously into periwinkle tucks. The dress seemed too hot for her, despite the flimsiness of the fashionable fabric.

"Never mind the undertaker. All he must do is deliver the coffin, and that he will do. And you handled Flannery very well—I suppose I could have gotten the passage for us much more easily by using my contacts, but my contacts might have expected payment in coin that would be inconvenient, if you understand me. While I am still a better dancer, a better singer, a better commedienne, a better actress, and also better at— other things—than any woman in San Francisco, one must think of the future. After twenty-five . . ."

She shrugged so that I could imagine what happened after twenty-five, which I didn't have to since I had been over twenty-five for many years, as had she, if she cared to admit it.

Then she sighed elaborately and twiddled her fingers in the air beneath her ear. "I want a place of my own, a fortune of my own, where I call the shots, do you see? Where no one else says, 'Sasha, you will dance now,' or 'Sasha, tonight you will be the comic relief.' I will answer to no one. Once we are in the Klondike and I have received the payment promised me, I will make my own fortune."

I thought that for a woman in her business, she was showing incredible optimism about her patron's reliability. "And if the payment isn't forthcoming?" I asked.

"Oh, it will be," she said and smiled a rather smug and somewhat nasty little smile. "Never fear. It will be."

# CHAPTER III

*I HAD THE* rest of the week to gather provisions, our "outfit," and to acquire suitable clothing for the journey and afterward. For these things it was necessary that I stand in line for hours and borrow a wheelbarrow in which I hauled my acquisitions—a tent, a tarpulin, blanket rolls, sheet metal stove (rapidly becoming known as a Yukon stove), food stuffs too inaccessible or expensive to obtain in Skagway (our first stop), a lantern, and numerous other items.

Sasha Devine had commissioned me to buy her traveling clothes. Normally, I was sure, she would no sooner let another female purchase items for her wardrobe than she would consider taking second billing in a program, but in this case she needed, she said, my expertise. She would journey as a respectable widow recently bereaved, and had no idea what such a creature might wear. Since all the good little widows were home counting out their pittances prior to crawling into their lonely beds before Sasha Devine even got up for the day, I saw her point. She did not, she assured me, wish to look dowdy, merely dauntingly decent.

For most of my life, merely clothing my body in enough attire to go about in society without comment had been a strain on my pocketbook, so I had to give the matter some study. That was when I had the brilliant idea that allowed me to perform my commission, settle a score, and have enough of the clothing allowance left to make my own purchases.

I could not have done it, of course, had our boat not been leaving the next morning. The idea blossomed of its own accord when it occurred to me that the only place I knew of to purchase widow's weeds was the one frequented by the Widow Higgenbotham for her various black costumes, first celebrating her widowhood from Mr. Higgenbotham, and lately from Papa. I suspect she just felt she looked good in black. It certainly became her nature.

So it was with a sense of innocent investigativeness that I entered the dressmaking establishment and inquired of the rather snooty proprietor if perhaps Mrs. Harper had a recent order that had not yet been delivered. I merely wanted to look at it, to give myself and the woman some idea of my requirements for Sasha. Although of totally different personality types, the women were rather similar physically, statuesque, wide-shouldered, deep-bosomed, and narrow-waisted. My father's taste was consistent in that respect. Austere though she was by nature, the Widow Hig would never have dreamed of wearing something unbecoming.

The proprietor glared at me, but she bustled to the back of the shop and bustled back carrying three costumes, among them a walking suit. While I was reflecting that just such an ensemble would be perfect for Sasha Devine, the shopkeeper began wrapping all three outfits.

"Please tell Mrs. Harper that if she insists on sending someone round for purchases before I am able to hang them properly, I can't be held responsible for the consequences. Only the walking costume is complete with chapeau at this time, I'm afraid. She'll simply have to wait until tomorrow as we agreed for the other accessories." And she plopped them into my arms, assuming that I was my stepmama's errand girl.

What was I to do? I do so hate to disappoint people in their expectations of me. I assured the woman that tomorrow would be fine for the hats, although in the future if things could not be in complete readiness within the time the widow had specified, she might be tempted to take her business elsewhere. And I walked out of the shop with Sasha Devine's wardrobe, paid for by the Widow Higgenbotham with, I felt, the money she had bilked me of for the serialization of my last novel.

The clothing money given me by Sasha Devine was, therefore, now mine to spend. And spend it I did, going straightaway to the ladies' riding outfitter and buying myself a divided riding skirt of the sort favored by Little Sure-Shot, Annie Oakley, sharpshooting female star of Buffalo Bill Cody's famed Wild West Show. At various other places I also purchased long-handled red woolen underwear, red plaid flannel men's shirts, a pair of men's trousers and suspenders, a pair of fur-lined leather boots, a pair of galoshes, a wide leather belt, four pairs of woolen socks, and a hat with flaps to keep one's ears warm that was said to be very fashionable in the Yukon. A warm coat made of a Hudson Bay blanket and ruffed with wolverine completed my purchases, with money left over. A man's toilette, I learned some years ago, goes for considerably less than a lady's and is on the whole far more practical, particularly for adventuring. By combining my new purchases with the clothing I already owned, I could present a more or less genteely feminine appearance and still be warm and comfortable.

A small grizzled man watching me from the end of the counter remarked, "You look like you're loaded for bear, little lady."

"Indeed, I am, sir," I told him. "I'm told there are bears aplenty in the Klondike."

"That's for damn sure, ma'am. That's for damn sure. But say, I just come down from the Klondike, and if you're going to go after bears up there, you'll be needin' you a bear gun. I just happen to have one here—"   •

And the upshot, if you will pardon my choice of expression, was that I bought for a pittance not only his rifle, but also a pistol, which he assured me was just the thing to take berry picking or wildflower gathering in the northern forests.

The merchant's wife, a canny woman not overly pleased to find someone else making a profit off her customers on her premises, said, "Pshaw, honey, you ain't likely to need no hardware with thousands of big strong men all around to protect you from bears and everything else. I got me a friend up in Dawson. *She* says what you need up there is dancin' dresses."

So I acquired my first ball gown as well, down the street where the lady who ran the shop was having a clearance sale and going home to Chicago because her husband had lost his mind and was heading north with the hordes.

Feeling quite plucky at having obtained two wardrobes for the price, to me, of one, I headed for my room. To my surprise I saw Jade Fan, her eldest boy, and two men ascending the stairs with what seemed to be packs.

I dropped my purchases at the foot of the steps and followed them up. "Fanny, what's going on here?"

"New tenants," she said tightly. "You go. They stay. They need. You don't. Vely simple."

"But I am not leaving till tomorrow morning," I protested.

"Pelly, you been with that woman. Mai saw you. She no good you papa. She no good you, too. Wy Mi at that place when he killed. You no pay two month now."

"But one more night, Fanny . . ." I said.

"No. You need place to sleep, you come my house. But I need money. They got. Get stuff and get out."

There was nothing to do for the time being but comply. I rescued our new outfit, my old wardrobe, already packed, my writing materials, and an indispensible box of books, flouncing down the stairs and back up again until all of my belongings were removed. I was hurt by Fanny's attitude, but not really baffled. Jade Fan had always considered Papa and me to be extensions of her family. She did not like for him and Wy Mi to drink, and she did not like it that he associated with Sasha Devine. As a newly arrived bond servant, Jade Fan had narrowly missed being in a profession even lower on the social scale than Sasha's, and this made her touchy about such matters. She was determinedly middle-class aspiring to upper-middle-class, and I gathered she felt that I had fallen in with evil companions and was disgracing her lodgings, and that I was no longer to be trusted on my own, sweet young thing of thirty-six that I was.

Worst of all, I had not consulted her before deciding to go to the Yukon. She ruled her household with an iron fist, and I was not obeying rules. Therefore, I must either go or fit myself in with the rest of the children. Cursing to myself and sighing with exasperation at her lack of insight into the artistic soul, I reloaded the wheelbarrow to precarious proportions and trundled off to await Sasha Devine at her lodgings.

The landlord, indulgent of his theatrical clientele, recognized me from my photographs in the paper as my father's daughter and let me in, even assisting me with my bundles.

"Miss Devine is engaged in a performance right now, Miss Harper, but she'll be home later on. You just make yourself comfortable and I'll send word over to the theatre that you're here." I wondered what he thought, that we were going to be roommates? But I didn't wonder long. Totally exhausted from the day's exertions, I found her fainting couch irresistibly alluring. No sooner had the packages fallen from my weary fingers than I curled up on the luxurious red velvet upholstery and fell asleep.

I have no idea what time it was when I awoke, chilled by a sudden draft. Even before my eyes opened, I experienced a feeling of oppression, as if something loomed over me. I lay facing Sasha's private terrace, the doors to which now hung open. My hand was raised above my forehead, as if to shield myself from attack, and I recalled that I had been having a dream, no doubt prophetic of my journey, of swatting at the largest mosquito I had ever seen.

Although no insect now shared my shelter, someone else did. As I sat up, I felt him withdraw to the darkness that veiled most of the room, stepping a few feet back into the deeper gloom surrounding Sasha's canopied bed.

"But how stupid of me," a cultured voice with a pronounced foreign accent said. "You are not Sasha."

"No," I said a little regretfully.

"No, no, I see that now, but you seem very nice all the same. Are you a new servant girl perhaps? Or a coworker?" He asked, his tone hopeful, and took a step or two forward again.

"No—nothing like that," I replied, smothering a yawn, for I suddenly felt sleepier than ever. He drew close enough that I could almost discern features in the shadows shrouding his face. "Are you from the same place as Sasha?" I asked. "Your accent—"

"Yes, yes, the same place. And you, my dear, where are you from?"

"Here," I said. "Here in town." And then, ridiculously, for had I not been so sleepy I would have found it quite threatening to be in extended conversation with an unknown man in the middle of the night in a courtesan's bedroom, I added, "I used to work with my father, you know, before he married someone I disliked. Then he died and I was alone when Sasha—"

"Ah," he said sympathetically, stepping near enough now that light reflected from his eyes, which stared intently at me. "How sad it is that those we love cannot stay with us always. I myself have been very unfortunate in that respect. So few women are really willing to commit to a full and diversified lifetime such as I—"

"That's what I think, too," I agreed, lying back down on the comfortable couch as the gentleman inched his way closer. As I lay down he was to one side and somewhat behind me, but for some reason I didn't mind. It was not exactly that I trusted him, but that I felt, in my stupor, that he had a *right* to be there, that whatever he did or did not do was his entitlement. "And Sasha does, too. That's why we're going to the Klondike," I finished drowsily.

"You—you are going to—excuse me, my dear, are you by any chance called Valentine Lovelace?"

"Yes, how did you know?"

"Ah—how? My little secret. Mine and Sasha's. Well, my dear, this has been very pleasant, but I really must be going—do be more careful about whom you speak to in the future, will you?" He stepped toward the terrace, and I got the oddest feeling he was about to jump off it. "Sasha will need much help on her journey and we're—I mean, I know that she is counting on you. Sleep well."

His admonishment was redundant. Despite my excitement over the trip on the morrow, my exertions of the day and the spate of nocturnal chitchat must have exhausted me more than I imagined. I did not even see the gentleman actually leave, but I did hear the terrace doors close even as my eyes did likewise. I have no idea when Sasha Devine came home. When she woke me, she was already wearing her new widow's weeds. The bundles she had plowed through to find them had to be repacked before we disembarked.

I boarded the boat wearing the same dress I had slept in, for all of our new purchases had been loaded into our cabin by the time we got there. I was not alert enough to ask why, and Sasha did not explain. She could not have if she'd wanted to. The docks and all the streets leading to them were so crowded and noisy that it made traffic nearly impossible, and I feared lest we prove unable to knee and gouge our way through in time to secure our berth. The first-class accommodations for which I had paid so dearly turned out to have everything they should—berths, for instance—but also a couple of unanticipated extras—a tinhorn gambler and lady friend, who had already taken the lower bunk. Our goods and those of the couple were piled against the walls.

I was pawing through one of my valises when I heard Sasha Devine say, "This way, and be careful about it."

"Light sleeper, eh?" asked the crewman on one end of the casket. The gambler and his girlfriend looked daggers at him, casting significant looks at our mourning clothes. At the other end of the casket was a tall swarthy man, obviously an Indian of some sort, but quite unlike the Comanches and Apaches I had met in Texas, or any of the local tribal peoples one occasionally encountered in the city.

As soon as the coffin was lowered, taking up what little space we had left, the Indian backed away, and the crew member sprinted over the coffin to follow.

"That's very inconvenient," I said. "Wait!"

I, too, hopped across the coffin and out onto the deck, where it was impossible to progress any farther because the people were packed together so tightly. A few other women and a child or two could be seen in the crowd, but mainly the company was masculine. I wiggled through to the railing, where people were waving good-bye, and saw the Indian clamor down the gangplank, mount the driver's box of a shiny black carriage, and urge the equally shiny black horses onward.

When I returned to the cabin, Sasha Devine and the gambler's lady were already making do by piling some of the other things atop Mr. Lawson, whose receptacle had been mightily shoved by the gambler into the corner farthest from the door. Once more we had a footpath, which was fortunate since the gambler was ill for the duration of the journey and needed quick access to the rail.

The ship stuck to the coast for the two days it took to reach Seattle, where we boarded more firewood and squeezed in one or two passengers and a team of oxen. Another day at open sea, and then we were within the Inside Passage, a twisted skein of sea running between mountains and among the islands and peninsulas in the waters intertwining the land masses of Alaska and Canada.

The *Golden Queen* was a splendid ship, compared to most of the ones that were hastily rehabilitated for the trip north. She was seaworthy and her captain had not been drunk for almost three days when we started the voyage. I saw Flannery once, but he didn't see me. The ship was not large, but it was extremely congested, with men sleeping in the dining and forward saloons, both of which were piled high with freight. Horses, oxen, dogs, and mules also abounded, and I thought I saw a cat sitting high above the confusion. Gambling and drinking were rife, as were wild parties. Sasha Devine was hard put to maintain her image as a grieving widow, but trooper that she was, she stayed in character whenever anyone was around. And whenever that anyone might have been someone she knew, she kept the black net veil down over her face. It had the additional advantage of deflecting mosquitos.

Some jocular souls claimed the mosquitos were also responsible for the occasional disappearance of a passenger, but most of us figured the missing parties got drunk and fell overboard when the noise was too loud for the splash to be noticed. All but one seemed to be drifters, with no one to care much that they were no longer in this world. The exception was a young Norwegian with a wild streak no doubt harkening back to his Viking ancestors. He left behind a comrade who insisted his friend had been lured on deck by a man in evening dress. Even when it was pointed out that none of the gentlemen on board had come quite so formally attired, the man ranted on, and finally sat sullenly staring out to sea, his head drooping and his raw-knuckled hands clenching and unclenching.

He was still sitting there after dinner, and I hunkered down beside him, drawing my shawl close against the breeze of our passing. I almost told him about Papa's death, but I was afraid I'd start him up again, so I didn't say anything. He seemed to relax almost imperceptibly, but said nothing, and when I left he was still sitting there.

Despite the noise and excitement, I slept well and deeply every night, as did the others in my compartment, even the seasick gambler. My dreams were vivid and full of foreboding, as well as images. I kept feeling like something or someone was biding their time, waiting in ambush for me. And I kept seeing Papa's face on Sasha Devine, on the corpse in the alley, on a big mosquito carrying a miner who looked like me, but when I twisted up to say hello, retreated into the shadows. While I wanted to run, and in some of the dreams did, I also felt like I was missing something, and if I just could make contact with whatever it was or whomever it was everything would be all right and I would receive something better than I had ever had from anyone. I often awakened teary and retired reluctant to sleep and return to such dreams. My good spirits returned only after my first cup of tea.

But on the whole it was a good trip. The food wasn't bad, the berths were not buggy, and Mr. Lawson, as advertised, did not stink. He did, however, almost get wet.

Dyea had yet to build a dock. Common practice was for passengers to wade ashore and goods to be dumped overboard. The weather was fair and I had no objection to wading. We had been warned of the eventuality of our goods being dumped into the tide and had accordingly bound them in oilskins. Strangely, it was neither the goods nor her own person that Sasha Devine feared to dampen. She set up a howl only when a pair of crewmen offered to toss Mr. Lawson overboard with the other items, which we were hoping would hit one of the small boats that ferried the more precious belongings, including a piano, ashore. The livestock swam, their owners jumping overboard with them. Altogether the scene was as lively as a fully clothed and much diversified beach party, with much the same spirit since everyone was elated to have finally arrived at the entrance to the goldfields.

But Sasha was not about to let Mr. Lawson get wet, and to preserve his aridity, she gave the two crewmen the full benefit of her dramatic skills. "Ah, how can you be so cruel to a poor widow woman?" she cried, throwing herself across the casket.

"Lady, if you can think of another way, fine. Otherwise, pay up for a ticket back for the mister here and we'll be on our way," one of the crewmen told her.

"And have you bury poor Henri at sea against his specific requests? Never! Did I tell you, dear Miss Lovelace, that Mr. Lamour had a particular aversion to water?"

The Norwegian mourner, who had been standing apart from us but close enough to hear the commotion, shouldered his way to the casket. He patted Sasha awkwardly on the shoulder. "You wait here, lady. Too many lost at sea dis time, I tink. Egil Larsson will get your boat and take your man ashore."

Small though our deception was, his concern shamed me. So I was very glad when a boat with a pair of Indians seemed oblivious to the other passengers shouting for their attention and rowed straight to the rail beneath us, indicating with sign language that we were to load Mr. Lawson aboard.

These miraculous Indians also owned a sledge and oxen and, without instructions or the payment of extra funds, began, once ashore, to load our belongings along with Mr. Lawson aboard their sledge.

Sasha Devine lowered her eyes at the stares of our fellow former passengers who envied our good luck. But the smile beneath she gave me was smug. "My admirer seems to have foreseen our difficulties," she said.

"How do you know it is he who sent them? Perhaps they simply picked us out as two lone women in desperate straits," I said. Though my nature is as charitable as the next person's,

I felt it unwise to be unduly trusting so soon after arriving in a new country.

"Dahling, what do you think? That they will take advantage of us in the middle of this crowd? Burdened like that?"

"They *could* rob us," I said, now feeling foolish at realizing how silly my suspicions sounded. Still, there was something too pat and too convenient about them showing up so suddenly when everyone else was having to rough it.

"If they tried such a thing, we wouldn't even have to resort to the Royal Canadian Northwest Mounted Police, with whom no one, forgive me, fornicates. You see these boys? I personally could organize a lynch mob in two shakings of a sheep's tail—"

"Three shakes of a lamb's tail—" I muttered.

"No matter. As I say, they must have been sent by Mr. Lawson's partner. And even if not, packing is a very good business here from the looks of it. Why ruin a good thing? It makes no sense to steal a few dresses and things from inbound travelers when miners rich with gold are coming the other way and could be robbed so much more profitably." She sounded almost as if the notion was giving her inspiration for business opportunities.

She insisted that the packers lash the coffin round several times with rope lest they fall and Mr. Lawson be dislodged from his resting place. I couldn't see what difference it would make—of all the people in our party who might be damaged in a fall, Mr. Lawson was the least likely to suffer. But he was our ticket to Dawson, so Sasha was as solicitous of him as if he were a first-class passenger on a luxury liner. The Indians were very responsive to her manner, being positively reverent in the way they handled the casket.

I had taken time to repack my belongings, extracting my riding skirt, boots, and a few other items. The stove and groceries stayed packed. Neither of us knew how to cook anyway.

I carried my valise strapped to my back and Sasha Devine had a similar small pack. She also produced one additional item for the journey. "My alpenstock," she said, wielding a canelike wooden stick with an elaborate silver handle.

The packers left hours ahead of us while we partook of nourishment in the form of beans and cornbread served from a tent kitchen. We then got in line for the long trek up the Chilkoot trail.

Even my by no means modest narrative skills cannot sufficiently explain how demoralizing it was to tramp behind Sasha Devine up the steep incline of the Chilkoot Pass, where men and women had died before us, where the less surefooted horses all but filled the valley with their rotting carcasses. The wheelbarrowing I had done up and down the hills of home while procuring our goods had hardened my sturdy San Francisco calves and ankles to iron. Many of the men fared less well, used to flat cities and lesser burdens than they now bore. But Sasha Devine put us all to shame. Restored to the full bloom of radiant good health, she climbed surefootedly, even after dark, when we were a third of the way up the mountain and others turned back. She all but danced up that pass, and little wonder, I suppose. Not only did she live and walk in San Francisco, she danced the cancan three shows a night, six nights a week, besides her other terpsichorial activities.

I was glad I had brought the extra clothing, for we were almost at the top of the pass when an avalanche occurred, injuring two men and killing three others who had left three hours ahead of us. We waited, nearly freezing, for night was upon us now. The only consolation was that night would at least be a short one. Even in late August the nights are foreshortened compared to San Francisco. We still had light as late as nine P.M. We should have it again by five in the morning.

Meanwhile, a path was carefully cleared by those nearest the tragedy, and though it seemed like forever, it was really only about three hours before we were able to pick our way past the debris. I tried to look neither to the right or left, but as the sun rose, it glinted off a metal object. I bent to one side to investigate.

A crucifix—silver but much worn and inscribed on the back with initials—perhaps a confirmation gift or a graduation present. Another Roman Catholic had died here then —perhaps a fellow child of Erin. Nothing else remained of the wearer, who was probably pushed over the steep edge of the precipice by the force of the slide. I could throw the crucifix over the side, or I could keep it with me until I could learn the identity of the victims and perhaps by surname or description decide to whom my discovery belonged and return it to the family. I stuck the sad artifact into my pocket, and the line moved on.

When we began the descent, I wished ardently that we had arrived in winter, when it might have been possible to slide to the bottom—the pressure of my body against my toes was torture. Sasha Devine hummed a little song under her breath until I reminded her that she was supposed to be in mourning. She switched to a lament, but kept humming.

The trip from Dyea to Lake Bennett took four days altogether. Two of them were spent ascending and two descending the pass to the lake. Although our packers carried the bulk of our equipment, we maintained our bedding, our coats, some extra clothing, and those things dearest to us— Sasha had her ivory-backed mirror and brush set with the etchings of mermaids on their backs, and I had a picture of Papa, my journal and pen, and the latest Sherlock Holmes story by Sir Arthur Conan Doyle.

I found it hard to read, sleep, or to concentrate, however, the entire four days. It must be the proximity of the goldfields, I thought, for I had slept like a babe on the boat. Everywhere outside the canvas walls of the tent "hotel" room at Lake Lindeman, men talked, drank, hauled, swore, and dropped whole outfits on their feet from the sound of it.

The next morning it was raining, but gently enough so that the Petersboro canoe that ferried us to the portage, three-quarters of a mile from the head of Lake Bennett, did so without difficulty. We walked along the ridge while ropes guided the canoe down the narrow, crooked stream that emptied into the lake.

The scene that met us at the lake was a daunting one. Men in teams carried huge logs, while other teams of men whipsawed more logs. The nearby forest was practically denuded already, and rafts and boats were banged together hourly. Thousands of tents lined the shore. We hoped ours was there, too, for we were both weary from lack of sleep and Sasha Devine was quite snappish, although I maintained my usual pleasant demeanor despite the increasingly stupid remarks and irrational actions of those about me.

But the rain was growing colder and the wind stronger. We were actually looking for a cup of coffee when we spotted our own distinctive cargo—Mr. Lawson's coffin sat upon a well-made raft with sail unfurled and tent pitched on board, while our packers, plus one other of their kind, busied themselves distributing the cargo.

"How fortunate we are to have been chosen by such an enterprising tribe of Indians as their primary customers," I said. "Have you noticed how little these fellows look like the Chilkats packers? Obviously they are of another people well versed in the travel industry and have discovered already how to make this arduous journey as worry-free for the client as possible."

"I have noticed," Sasha Devine said, "that our warm dry tent stands empty aboard the wherewithal to make our departure while *we* stand in the rain making conversation."

Although she didn't have to put it so snidely, her point was well taken. We availed ourselves of the facilities with all possible dispatch, and set sail for the Yukon that very hour.

# CHAPTER IV

·····•··━❦◗‖◖❦━··•·····

*I FOUND IT* oddly comforting to be back in the company of Mr. Lawson. Our previous companions, now boatless, had offered kindly to join us and protect us from any possible designs that our packers might have upon our persons and our belongings, but we demurred.

We were not exactly unescorted, however, since there were from eight to twelve other boats on the river most of the time. Our guides were the ones who skillfully led the others down the right-hand channel when the raft hit the first series of rapids, expertly steering through and setting an example that meant success for all who followed us. If any boat was foolish enough to ignore our guidance, I fortunately did not witness what became of it.

In view of what happened there, I feel rather foolish to admit how glad I was to see the Lake Tagish customhouse. But the river journey, for all the grandeur one could glimpse when the sky cleared, which was approximately two woefully short periods during our five-day journey, was a silent and frustrating one.

Although an author and as full of deep literary musings as others of my calling, I am a sociable sort of person by nature. I had hoped to use the journey to learn more about Sasha Devine, who I presumed wanted my company since she had asked me along. I also hoped to learn by means of sign language more about our remarkable native guides. Neither was to be. What I learned about instead was sweepers—trees half-up-rooted that bowed low over the riverbank with the express purpose of knocking tent, mast, and crew into the river. I also learned about snags—piles of deadwood that lurked around every turn to snatch the edges of our raft and try to dismantle it to add its logs to their number. And, of course, there were all the sandbars and shallow spots Mr. Twain is so fond of describing.

I spent most of the trip watching the river anxiously for these obstacles, though for the most part our crew avoided them. I did read some of my Sherlock Holmes book but found it difficult to concentrate—inside the tent the light was insufficient. Outside the tent it was raining.

The use of stove and lanterns inside the tent was imprudent anyway, due to the danger of fire. My single attempt at lighting the stove nearly met with disaster when we hit a gravel bar and the boat lurched, opening the door and spilling embers onto the logs. I hastily ran to the edge of the raft to fetch water to extinguish the ensuing flames, at which time the raft lurched once more as the Indians dislodged it. I, too, was dislodged, and fell into the river. I might have drowned except that the water was only shin high at that point. The fire was doused and the cookstove nearly washed overboard with the waves I made. Already wet, I assisted the men in prying our craft loose and was rewarded afterward with a piece of dried salmon.

From then on, the salmon was the mainstay of our diet, the rest of which consisted of dried fruit. I began to wonder why I had thought writing western adventure novels preferable to writing the society page, which at least offered the fringe benefit of tasty hors d'oeuvres.

The exchange of my labor for salmon turned out to be the height of my social season on the Yukon. Throughout the rest of the trip, the Indians exchanged only the briefest administrative communication with me and did not respond to my questions or statements. I assumed they could not understand the same sign language I had learned in Texas, or perhaps were not interested in communicating with women, a trait common to many of their Caucasian brethern.

Nor did Sasha Devine prove a stimulating companion. She slept almost the entire trip, and I thought that despite her seeming energy throughout our hike, she must have been more fatigued than she admitted. Soon I realized, however, that she simply was maintaining her customary nocturnal schedule—she was only truly awake after I fell asleep. She kept watch with the pilot, and once or twice I heard her cursing as we drifted too near an impediment. But overall, I felt no dimunition of social contact when I crept into my bedroll beside Mr. Lawson. Once one got over the macabre aspects of sleeping next to a coffin, it was quite convivial, compared to the rest of the company.

Thus, after five days of smoked fish and silence, I was looking forward to answering any sort of questions that the mounties at Tagish had to ask, just for the sake of conversation.

Five other crafts of various sorts were tied up to trees along the bank while the water-logged Canadian flag drooped overhead in the fading twilight. A few of our fellow travelers had made camp ashore for the night, and their tents glowed softly from within, though their goods were strewn about, half-opened to the rain. Several men blundered about in the twilight, trying to reassemble their outfits after they had been inspected and taxed.

A constable strode over to our raft and climbed aboard, entering the tent and, as he thought, surprising Sasha Devine in dishabille, which he ignored. "Who's in the coffin?" he demanded in a flat, official voice.

I intercepted him at the tent flap, my indignation aroused. "See here, Constable, we will present ourselves for proper inspection momentarily . . ."

"Eeek!" Sasha Devine squeaked, sounding extremely modest and refined. "Oh, officer, sir, how you startled me! Why, I feel quite faint—"

She flicked her eyes, signaling me, and I led a rather confused constable away from the tent opening and onto the shore.

"My poor friend was only recently tragically widowed, and her nerves are still a shambles."

The flustered officer blustered and glared red faced at the register book he brandished as if it were his weapon, "Well, just get this unloaded and be quick about it. The light is nearly gone." He sounded as if I were personally responsible.

From the cabin another mountie called in a voice thick with a Scottish burr replete with r's rolling like moors full of heather. "Constable Williams, I would be verra grateful if you could see fit to exercise the authority vested in us without undue alarm to ladies, causin' them to shriek and scare awah yon fish I was plannin' to apprehend for our breakfast."

"Yes, Constable," I chimed in. "Really, I am surprised at your lack of sensibility for the bereaved and defenseless—"

"It iss alright, my dear Vahlenteena. I haf not soffered—" Sasha Devine said, emerging with her shirtwaist buttoned almost far enough to cover her chemise, her black walking skirt accidentally tucked up to show a flash of petticoat and a trim ankle encased in a boot. Her hair was a work of art—the artificial curls were arranged so that they appeared absolutely real, but in charming disarray as if she had just risen from sleep. Her pallor fit the rainy evening, and her eyes, bright with the challenge of bamboozling the authorities, seemed feverish with grief.

"As to your question, Constable, the—coffin—contains my beloffed hosband." She sniffed elaborately into a lace handkerchief. Her voice was even huskier than usual and her accent far more exotic than twenty years in San Francisco had allowed it to remain. "He 'wass Canadian citizen. Vahlenteena, hiss documents? He 'wass gold miner. Found notink. Before he die he say to me, 'Sasha, my beloffed, you take me back to Klondike. I must be there for the big strike.' "

I fished out the papers from their oilskin packet while Sasha heaved her remarkable bosom with a not-quite-stifled sob. The mountie's eyes widened. Sasha's lashes fluttered and dropped to half mast. She took the papers from me, her fingers caressing them as if they were flesh, and her hands trembled delicately as she proffered the packet to the constable, her fingertips brushing his. The mountie started as if she had handed him the lit end of a cigar. He looked faintly alarmed and rather indignant.

"These are all very well, but you must open the coffin, madam. We are checking for contraband here."

"Oh, certainly, officer, certainly," she said a little sadly, and turned, lifting her hand as if to motion to the packers. Then she seemed to have an afterthought. "But, oh, my goodness, officer, please first to tell me. You haff had mumps as small boy, yes?"

"I can't precisely recall, madam," he said stiffly.

I was sure he hadn't. It had clearly been a long time since he had suffered the indignities of childhood, if ever. He seemed to have been born in uniform, with his hat on, probably with the register in his hand.

"But, officer! Iss very important. You must try. My poor Henri, he did not recall either, but you see, he had not had them at all. First he swells up, you know, not just in the jaws but down there?" She brushed her skirt lightly in the region of her lap to indicate where and the constable's eyebrows disappeared beneath the brim of his hat. "It was horrible. Truly. Very painful, I think, especially when he burst."

"He—burst?"

Overcome, the Widow Lamour sobbed into the lace-edged handkerchief she untucked from her conveniently bared decolletage.

"Constable Faversham, will you no mind what I told you aboot the fish, mon?" exclaimed the other mountie from the doorway of the cabin that constituted their official outpost. "Eh, beggin' your pardon, ladies," he said, "but what seems to be the nature of your problem?"

Constable Faversham turned to him as if he was water in the desert. "Sergeant Destin, sir, these ladies are bringing a corpse into the territory, sir. But he had mumps and—er— burst, sir."

"Burst? From the mumps?"

"Oh, yes, officer," Sasha replied, wide-eyed, "It was shocking, he soffered so. And for many months before, you know, because the disease took him—down there—" She repeated her previous gesture for his benefit, and he was much more receptive and appreciative, his eyes following her hand at her lap with keen interest. "He was—how do you say—ah well, suffice it to say I was very lonely." Another sniffle, but over the handkerchief she gave the sergeant a long look during which her tears and the rain virtually turned to steam on her cheeks.

"Ah, were you now? You puir puir dear," he said, taking her arm and brushing past his constable with a jerk of his head that wheeled the subordinate into an about-face and a smart trot toward the woodpile.

I was not the least bit sure the sergeant was taken in by Sasha, but he certainly was taken with her, from the lingering way he kept patting her sleeve.

"Do come inside," he said, "while I have a wee look at these papers of yours and you can have a nice cup of tea while your raft is unloaded."

I stood there in the rain for a moment and didn't even notice that, without translation or sign language, our guides began unpacking the tent and dragging the coffin ashore. I, too, wanted a cup of tea, quite desperately at that moment.

Belatedly, the sergeant remembered his manners and turned back to me. "And your companion, madam, is she perhaps a kinswoman travelin' with you as chaperone?" He regarded my bedraggled form kindly. "Your mother perhaps, or a maiden aunt?"

Mother indeed! Just because her blond hair concealed the silver better than did my brown. At least all of mine was real. I felt mortified that a sturdy man such as the sergeant, with that solid square build, those reliable shoulders, and those otherwise intelligent blue eyes, should be so blinded to my worth by the more obvious charms of my resplendent partner. During our journey I had begun to get used to such reactions, however. Not all of the preferential treatment given to Sasha was on account of her alleged widowhood. Nevertheless, I felt it only self-respecting to embellish our cover story.

"As you will see from our papers, Sergeant, I am Miss Valentine Lovelace, novelist, journalist, and public lecturer currently on assignment for the *San Francisco Herald*, covering the human interest aspects of the new El Dorado for our readers. My editor and I feel that Mrs. Lamour's touching story of a wife's devotion to making her husband's lifelong dream pan out, as it were, even after death will add a poignant note to the rather overwhelmingly male essence of this event."

"Verra wise, madam. But I fear you ladies will find conditions here rough on your delicate constitutions."

"On the contrary, Sergeant, I have found it invigorating," I said, and thereby overplayed my hand.

"Ah, then, you're a hearty lass, Miss Lovelace. Puir Mrs. Lamour looks about to swoon. I think she must rest inside for a wee bit, perhaps even take the constable's bunk. I will be on hand to guard the door. Come now, dear lady, time enough for official matters in the mornin'. Rest is what you need—" he said and kindly led Sasha inside, to hot tea and a fire newly warmed by the wood with which the disgruntled constable had just stoked the stove before being summarily evicted.

The door closed firmly behind him, and Faversham turned toward the woods, from whence for several hours issued the sound of wood being hacked to pieces.

\* \* \*

I wandered to the edge of the woods, too, although I did not see the constable. Nor was I looking for him. I was searching for some deadfall with which to build a small fire and make myself a cup of tea. I also considered inquiring at one of the tents farther down the shore, but the rather raucous sounds issuing from those still lit from within deterred me.

By the time I returned to our raft, the packers had finished their task and disappeared, leaving our worldly goods huddled under the frail covering of oilcloth that spared them the worst depredations of the rain. Too tired and disgusted to bother with finding the wherewithal necessary for the insurmountable task of brewing that longed-for cup of tea, I crept back inside the tent.

It was still pitched on the raft, the view of the mountie post from within partially blocked by the coffin, which rested about a foot beyond the waterline. I wondered at Sasha's elaborate deception to prevent the sergeant from looking in the coffin. No native to deception myself, I was surprised that she would go to such lengths over what seemed to me an unimportant matter. Of course, perhaps she was being pragmatic. Possibly she knew from her broader experience that once the coffin was opened, Mr. Lawson *would* stink, and we, not the constable, would have to smell him the rest of the way to Dawson.

While that reasoning might sound lame to me, I realized that Sasha Devine took a rather more casual attitude than I about lying to the authorities.

My musings receded as darkness encroached, clear thought giving way to a vague awareness of the clatter of utensils, the whimper and yelp of dogs, the stamping of horses, the sound of men's voices, the sonorous snore of someone very nearby. Perhaps it was my own snore, I thought, and I had simply neglected to realize that I had fallen asleep. Certainly that was more likely than the alternative—that the snore could be issuing from Mr. Lawson's casket.

It must be my own noise, for it sounded familiar—I had heard it every night on the boat and thought it was the gambler—well, it did have a masculine sort of quality about it, although with snores that was hardly reliable. I felt myself rise up out of myself and glide toward the coffin, for all the world like something out of one of Sir Walter Scott's ghost stories. But as my dream self gently wafted casketward, it came face-

to-face with yet another apparition. Constable Faversham, a
fanatic gleam in his eye, his ledger clutched to his uniformed
breast like Moses clutching the tablets—assuming stone tablets
lent themselves to that sort of thing—stood glaring down at
the casket. My dream self beat a hasty retreat back into my
shivering body, and I sat up.

"Constable, what is the meaning of this?" I demanded. "Up
until now I had a good opinion of the much-vaunted valor and
courtesy of men in your service, but you, sir, try my patience.
Do you never go off duty?"

"That, madam, is precisely the point," he said. "We always
get our man. Or whatever. The sergeant may be taken in by
your story, but I'm not easily swayed from *my* duty. There is
something suspicious about the way you women act, and the
widow has an air about her I have noted in a great many other
women who prey upon the baser instincts of mankind. I think
that you are transporting liquor in that casket, madam, and I
mean to have it opened and impounded."

At least I could be honest in denying this particular charge.
"Constable, that is nonsense."

"Very well, if you insist. But even if, as your fine friend
claims, this is her husband dead of a contagious disease, he'll
have to be buried here or hauled back where he came from.
Can't have diseased corpses entering the country."

I sighed. If not opening the casket meant so much to Sasha
Devine, *she* could sleep nearby and guard it. I did not intend
to get into trouble with the authorities so near to our goal,
having gone through so much to get this far.

"Of course, you must do as you think best, Constable," I
said wearily.

He made another smart about-face and returned with a
crowbar before I could get cozy again. He cut the ropes Sasha
Devine had tied around the coffin and inserted the crowbar
into the sealed rim of the lid. It slipped on the damp metal and
gouged him in the chin. He fell back, flinging the crowbar onto
the coffin lid with such a great clangor that I was surprised it
did not rouse the sergeant or the other men camped nearby. I
recall seeing the constable standing there, holding his bleeding
chin while looking at the casket as if he would kick it open.

I could see nothing but the coffin and his angry, bleeding
face, which he turned on me, his back to the coffin. "All right
then, madam. What's the trick?" he asked unreasonably. "How
do you get it open? Be quick and it will go easier on you."

"Constable, your accusations are ridiculous and unfounded. Perhaps if you are so convinced we are desperate criminals carrying contraband cargo, you should await the arrival of your superior to continue your investigation. I intend to go to sleep now. Good night to you, sir."

His mouth opened and closed, but no sound came out. I watched from between slitted eyelids, pretending to settle into sleep. He backed toward the coffin, crowbar in hand, and was still backing when the mist that had been coming from the river seemed suddenly to boil out of the coffin lid, through the crack that the iron wedge had been unable to penetrate. It seeped quickly through and surrounded the constable before he knew it, enveloping him in swirling gray that abruptly darkened to blackness, thoroughly engulfing him. Or was it only that sleep thoroughly engulfed me then, that my pretense suddenly became dire necessity as I sank helplessly into slumber?

The lethargy that exacerbated my own exhaustion swept through me like fire. But still, as my lashes fell and my mouth and nostrils breathed in the rags of mist, imprinted on the insides of my eyelids was a last sight of the constable being swallowed by blackness. The whimpering sound he made as it took him was the last thing I heard before I lost consciousness.

# CHAPTER V

SOMETHING COLD AND wet pressed against my cheek, and I opened my eye in time to have it licked. I groped upward and my hands encountered coarse fur. Panting and bad breath confirmed the rest of my suspicions even before I faced the canine entity so intent upon awakening me. One of the sled dogs, I thought, had gotten loose. Fortunately, it seemed to be one of the friendly ones, though its eyes bore a distinctly feral expression. It whined and turned and licked me again. I sat up and banged my head on the tent pole. It was dark outside and raining, a slow cold drizzle that reminded me heartwarmingly of home. For a moment I thought I had dreamed the whole incident, and then my eyes adjusted sufficiently that I made out the body, its boots grazing the water, its trunk lolling against the side of the coffin.

I crawled through the tent flap as the dog leaped from the raft and onto the shore, heading, as I thought, for the woods. I knelt before the body and looked down into the face of the constable, a man who had, I thought, gone out with a whimper. Perhaps it was a giggle. For this straight-laced officer, who I would have sworn was incapable of pleasure, bore the same blissful smile I had seen before. Shock and the dregs of whatever had caused me to lose consciousness before knocked me off my haunches onto the ground before the body. I ground my hands into my eyelids and tried to re-examine the situation with some sort of objectivity. To no avail. When I looked up again, my father lolled there, in that uniform, lending the late constable a sort of gauzy phosphorescence. His eyes opened and the smile changed briefly into a frown, as if I'd done or said something very stupid, before the glaze of ghostliness evaporated from the body, and I was left once more with an inconvenient corpse.

Whatever the apparition had to say, it would have to wait until more practical matters pertaining to the living and the more recently dead were addressed. For although it seemed to me that an epidemic of smiling deaths was following me around, I could only believe that grief somehow made me see my father's face superimposed on those of the victims. And this was no time for me to give in to the tricks my mind had played on me.

Had it not been for my canine friend, I would have been found with the body in the morning. Then Sasha Devine and I would be arrested or deported, and Sasha would never get her saloon, Lost-Cause would never be buried on his partner's claim, and I would never get the story I had come for. What we might get would be a jail term. Or executed. Who knew what sort of justice was meted out on the northern frontier? I felt sure I would never be able to convince the sergeant of the truth of my tale. He would not believe that the constable had managed to die without assistance from me. I would need to get rid of the body. But just putting it in the river would not guarantee that it would float away on the current—with our luck it would get caught in an eddy or snag and be discovered.

Nearby, a wolf howled like a cross between a sobbing child and a scream of a freight train. Not to be outdone, the sled dogs tethered behind the outpost joined in. I shot an anxious glance at the cabin. No light blossomed. No one stirred.

But as the howling continued, the bumps that rose on my skin were not entirely from the wind or rain. Perhaps Mr. Lawson did contain some sort of contagion that had been loosened by the constable's assault on the casket and had escaped to kill the officer. In that case, I was in grave danger myself. Still, I had laid out my father for his funeral and practically waltzed all over one other corpse bearing the same signature. I could, I supposed, scream and pretend I had just discovered the body. Surely that would look less incriminating than trying to dispose of it. Surely. The choice was snatched from me suddenly as the last light in the last tent went out, and a group of men spewed forth.

"Hooboy, lady luck was with me tonight," I heard one voice, the only happy one among the throng, say.

I looked up sharply and tried to see through the darkness. A man swaggered toward me, ostentatiously counting money aloud. But it was the Texas drawl with which he counted that interested me, and the familiarity of the voice behind the drawl.

"Purdy?" I half whispered.

"Huh? Shhhhh!" he said, and all but stumbled over me. "Pardon me, ma'am, sir," he said to me and the constable's corpse as he disentangled himself from us. "I'll just dust myself off and leave you young folks alone."

"Alonso Purdy, identify yourself," I hissed.

"Don't know no such person. Wait a minute. Purdy? Ain't he the fella got in trouble with a mountie inspector's wife? Why, I don't know no scum like that. Name of Petrie, ma'am. Slim Petrie. Yes'm. Petrie's my name. Poker's my game."

"You can't fool me, Dr. Purdy," I said, for now I could see that it was indeed he—somewhat paunchier, and he had grown a beard, but the same rainmaker I had known in Texas.

"Miz Valentine, darlin', that you?" he asked, as if I had been raised from the dead. "Well, I'll be hung."

"Precisely," I said. "Dr. Purdy, it is very fortunate that you happened along just now for that very thing may happen to me soon if you cannot advise me what to do about the constable."

"Why me? I'm a gambler, not an advice writer for the lovelorn."

"We are not discussing love here, Dr. Purdy. The constable is dead."

Purdy immediately dropped his spurious air of jovial drunkenness. "You kill him, ma'am?"

"I did not. But that sergeant is going to think so if he finds us like this."

"No, he won't. He'll get to checkin' closer and find out who I am and decide I done it, just to accommodate that inspector."

"But couldn't you leave?"

"Not without gettin' chased clear across the Yukon, which is not my intention, which is to get rich, not dead. These boys don't give up, Miss Valentine. You may have heard."

"But what can we do?" I asked, shamelessly linking his

precarious position to my own. Shamelessly because I knew that for all his lack of moral fiber, Purdy was a good man in life and death crises. Just now, however, it was his known criminal tendencies that would come in handy.

My trust was not misplaced. Before the wet gray sky lightened to biliousness, we had very discreetly weighted the constable with stones and dumped him into the river, along whose banks we went for a stroll, looking like a courting couple, but in reality guiding the body by means of a length of the rope cut from the coffin. When we came to a spot well overhung with sweepers, where the water was deep but the current swift, we released the constable.

The two of us separated then, for Purdy wished to draw no attention to himself by being associated with the only two women at the post at the time. And I felt the presence of a gambler in our party would arouse associations with her profession that Sasha Devine had been strenuously trying to avoid.

I was walking back to camp when the door to the mountie post opened, and Sasha Devine and the sergeant, half in and half out of uniform, emerged.

The packers had silently returned while Purdy and I disposed of the body. Perhaps they had been wiped out in the card game my old friend had won.

At any rate, when Sasha and the sergeant arrived, she looked refreshed and wide awake, while he looked sleepy and mildly disgruntled and also a bit abashed. After the most cursory look at our belongings, he said, "Duty's twenty dollars. I'd feel much better if you had a wee bit more food. Food is gettin' scarce in Dawson, I hear. Word is it may not last through the winter."

But he declared us legal and even helped us load the coffin back aboard the raft. "There you are, dearie," he said to the Widow Lamour. "There's yer mon, now. You be lettin' me know when ye need someone livelier."

Sasha Devine, playing her role with a fine subtlety, took both of his hands in hers while gazing soulfully into his eyes, and then stepped aboard the raft, ducking into the tent like Cleopatra saying farewell to Mark Anthony. I could not bear to look at the man.

The wind was high, the waters of Lake Tagish blowing wild and choppy as we set forth. The trees sighed and creaked. As we pulled away I saw Purdy approach the sergeant and indicate his gear. The sergeant looked around, undoubtedly for his recently departed subordinate, and then with a shrug of his brawny shoulders, followed the gambler. I watched apprehensively as Purdy led the mountie downstream, afraid he might betray me. I had no illusions about whom the former rainmaker looked after, first and foremost.

"Really, Vahlenteena, you should have let me know you were so interested in that little soldier," Sasha Devine said laughingly, reclining on her bedroll as if Nubian slaves ought to be fanning her with peacock feathers. "But you hardly can expect him to notice you when you look so like a drowned rat. You should fix your hair—"

That was too much for me. Now that I fancied we were safe, I had begun trembling like a drunk three days after his last refreshment. "I should fix what's *under* my hair for ever becoming involved with you and this scheme. While you were flirting with the mountie and having a nice rest and a cup of tea, I became an accessory to murder. If it hadn't been for a friendly dog, your nice sergeant would probably be locking me up right now."

"Murder?" she asked. She looked alarmed. "What murder? What dog?"

"The one that howled the whole damned night," I snapped. "And furthermore, I saw Papa's ghost again. On the face of the constable. And mist coming from Mr. Lawson's coffin that seemed to envelope the constable, who died of the same thing father did."

"No!" she said, with insufficient incredulity to convince me. I suddenly realized that my news was not entirely unexpected.

I told her all that I had gone through that night, and by the time I had finished, I realized that I had not *quite* finished.

"Miss Devine—Sasha," I said, "I sense there is something about our mission you have not confided in me. What *did* Mr. Lawson die from, anyway? Was it the same thing that killed Papa? *Are* we transmitting a deadly, albeit seemingly gleeful, disease into Canada? If so, what has prompted you to commit such a hideous act? I want you to know I deeply resent you involving me in any such scheme and intend to turn myself in at the next outpost. I cannot think why I have cooperated this far—why I hid the body—"

She smiled engagingly at me. "And you did it very well, I'm sure. Really, dahling, I do not think I would have done any better myself—well, perhaps a little better. I might have been able to get that man—what did you say his name was? —to help me without letting him know quite so many of the unpleasant details. But on the whole you were wonderful, my dear girl."

"So wonderful I've incriminated myself for something I—"

Sasha looked bored, her eyes turned skyward—or rather, canvasward. "Vahlenteena, I asked you to come along because I hoped you would not be so dull as most women. Not so stupid. Did you think there would be no price to pay? You sit and write about your petty little adventures, but do you not realize one must *dare* to live? To take risks, to break rules, to cross borders, to smuggle perhaps, and to involve oneself with people your wretched stepmother would disapprove. You've done well. Don't turn into a prig on me now."

"But the mist and all those bodies and Papa's ghost—"

"My friend, listen to me. You act as if you do not care about your papa, but me, I know better. All your life you sought him out, no matter which bar, which alley, which opium den he inhabited. Do you suppose you can stop looking for him so easily just because he is no longer alive? I had hoped this trip would give you some time to get used to that. You have not been fooling anyone else with your pretence of nonchalance about Patrick as well as you have fooled yourself. I understand. My whole family was murdered when I was little girl. My nurse smuggled me out of the old country or I would also have been killed. I travel from this place to that one, hide here, hide there, take this train and that ferry, and *finally* the ship to San Francisco. When at last I have my first job as a great operatic actress, I cannot wait to write and tell my papa and mama. Not until then did I remember that they were not there any longer, to be ashamed or to be proud. That what I did was of no consequence to anyone but me. So—I think you see Patrick on dead men's faces because you look for him and maybe you see mist coming out of coffins, too. As for the deaths—life is full of death. How many died in the avalanches? How many ships did not make it to Skagway from Seattle? How many rafts did not make it past the rapids? We all die, dahling. And if it is true that you die as you live, consider that the constable was an obstructive and awkward young man who chose to die at a time that was obstructive and awkward for us all. You merely outmaneuvered the wretched fellow. And I say good for you. Enough of this breast-beating."

* * *

Later, it occurred to me that Sasha Devine could have made a fine career for herself in politics. Although she had given me no direct answers to any of my questions, I felt much better and also far too confused to ask any more. Anyone who can dodge a trained journalist such as myself in that fashion has a real calling for public office.

Still, I could hardly be so blase as she concerning the event at Lake Tagish. Not being able to discuss the matter with Sasha merely drove my thoughts inward, so that it preyed on my mind all the more.

I regret that I was so preoccupied with my trepidations that I saw little of the now-historic scenic landmarks that have so often been rhapsodized when others speak of the Klondike gold rush. I spent the time on Lake Laberge looking backward for pursuit from the mountie sergeant, and held grimly on through the various rapids, all but daring drowning in my bleak mood, and feeling that it would keep my good name from disgrace if I were to die here.

In retrospect, that was an unrealistic concern, for in what way even the direst charge might have disgraced me I cannot rightly tell. Ned Buntline, Edgar Poe, and many others of my profession had greatly enhanced their literary reputations with various incarcerations and addictions. Being arrested for murder most likely would create an instant revival of my work. As for my family, at least on Papa's side, it was expected of offspring that they would come to precious little, and if one of us made a name for ourselves by being hanged, then any later generations would at least have a colorful ancestor to decorate the family tree.

Sasha Devine grew quite chatty during this interval—partially, I think, to keep me from brooding too much on the questions I had asked her before. Also, she was probably trying to keep herself awake. With the gradual onset of colder weather and longer hours of darkness, nights on the river were more hazardous and less comfortable than ever, so we began spending them ashore, forcing Sasha to a daytime schedule. She asked me many penetrating questions about the dragon, Fort Draco, and how I felt about those experiences, what they meant in terms of my life. She herself did not answer any questions or allow herself or our trip to become a topic of conversation.

The day we left Tagish, we hit the White Horse Rapids. The river is broad and deep at the head of the rapids, but constricts to a mere forty feet at the foot, where the pent-up waters burst through the narrowed channel in a white spume that rages for about seven miles before resuming its formerly well-mannered ways. Along the banks hundreds of men had carved their names and legends into bare tree trunks. Our guides once more proved skillful in riding the foam, and we had a wild trip through towering waters that bucked worse than any of my old friend E.F. Ledbetter's Texas cayuses.

From there we entered Lake Laberge. While on the lake, we passed three men in a poling boat going the other direction. I watched this craft closely, looking for lawmen, and also for possible means of escape, should I need them. The boat was propelled by means of a twelve-foot pole and had to be kept close to the shore to keep contact with the bottom and out of swifter currents. A good poler, I later learned, sometimes made twenty miles a day. The men aboard the boat I saw hollered that there had been a rich strike on the Stewart River, and that they hoped we had plenty of grub with us as none was to be had farther up the river.

Later that day we shot more rapids and passed the mouth of the Teslin River. The next morning our water bucket had a layer of ice as thick as the first knuckle of my little finger. The surrounding hills were frosted with a thin coating of snow, and Sasha Devine dug out her warm coat, scattering many of the other provisions heedlessly around the tent.

The ice was yet thicker the following morning. After landing on a rocky beach, we pulled the raft ashore and built a fire. I decided that I was going to grow gills if I didn't have something other than smoked salmon to eat. Cups of coffee and tea also held irresistible appeal in this harsh weather.

I searched the gear for our groceries and new cooking utensils. I had only opened these packages partially to show the contents to the sergeant. He had not searched them, but had passed everything with a nod. Therefore, I was surprised to find that my cast iron frying pan had been replaced by a Chinese wok. Also, dried Chinese mushrooms, dried ginger root, canned water chestnuts, and a string of garlic, Fanny's favorite spice, had been added to my other provisions, along with a bag of rice. My heart was warmed by more than heartburn. She hadn't kicked me out without any concern for my well-being then, bless her!

I stirred together some of everything as I had so often seen Fanny do, and even threw in a bit of salmon, to prepare the first hot meal we had had in two weeks. Our guides were grateful at first, but after a mouthful or two retreated from camp and were violently ill. Sasha Devine barely whiffed at it and said her stomach was feeling rather nervous that evening. I was forced to enjoy in solitude a splendid repast of the sort to which I had become accustomed over the years as Fanny's lodger. That night I slept more soundly than I had at any time since leaving the ship at Skagway, my dreams broken only by the howling of wolves.

And though they didn't care for my cooking, the Indians apparently thought hot meals a noteworthy idea, for when I awakened, they were butchering a moose carcass. A very good thing, too, for we needed all the strength we could get that day, when we shot Five Finger Rapids shortly after noon.

We found Fort Selkirk all but deserted. A sign on the trading post door, no doubt put there because the trader was weary of being asked the same futile questions and of having to supply the same discouraging answer, said, "Parties contemplating going out this season take notice that no provisions of any kind can be obtained here except, possibly, a little moose meat and dog salmon in small quantities for dog feed. No steamer has been here for two years. No flour can be had." The trader and his Indian wife were there, but, as advertised, the shelves were empty. I made another forage through our provisions to find a bit of flour so the couple could bake themselves some biscuits.

We spent three more long, cold, tense days on the river. I was glad the nights ashore were no longer, for when I slept there, I slept that helplessly deep sleep that I had experienced intermittently since leaving home. It puzzled and frightened me, and I worried that I had caught some rare ailment of which this strange comatose sleep was an initial symptom. Never before in my life had I been a heavy sleeper, oblivion being my father's department. But now, each night I seemed plunged into another world where I stayed until roused by one of my companions or by the packs of wolves whose howling enlivened the night. I wondered if the stories we'd been hearing about the lack of food in Dawson were understated. It seemed the wolves were already at the city's door.

The last night before Dawson, when we had tugged the raft ashore and built our fire, I cut up some of the moose meat and prepared a celebratory feast. Despite the cold, the meat was getting a little ripe, and I mourned my garlic, which had been lost overboard with a few other things when a sweeper brushed our bow. At least, that was what Sasha said must have happened to it.

As I cooked, the men were hunkered down, staring upriver, conferring among themselves. Suddenly they stood, as from the woods a party of their fellow Indians appeared. These people bore a distinct family resemblance to our companions, unlike any Indians we had seen so far. Tall, long-boned, and fine-featured, the lot of them conversed in their own language, while Sasha Devine made lists of what she would need for her saloon. I tried to tell from facial expressions the tone, if not the topic, under discussion. Except for wearing moose hide moccasins and perhaps a bandanna for a headwrap, all of the men wore western dress, trousers, suspenders, and plaid shirts—the woman among the newcomers wore a skirt three sizes too big for her, pinned together at the waist, and a man's shirt for a bodice. Our guides, whose faces were so blank when in our company, were quite expressive when conversing with their visitors.

As the shadows grew longer and I grew sleepier, it became increasingly difficult to keep my eyes open enough to watch their faces, which grew darker and darker. I no longer heard whole exchanges, just snatches, which sounded to me oddly like German or Russian—certainly like no Indian language I had ever heard before.

Their voices droned on as I drifted into sleep. Once I felt the woman turn toward Mr. Lawson's coffin and gesture, her outflung arm throwing the scent of woodsmoke across my nostrils. Another time I roused briefly as I heard what I thought was Sasha Devine's voice join into the conversation. Later I heard her skirts rustle as she rose from her place to the left of my head. For a moment her skirts blocked the warmth of the fire, which popped and hissed as if receiving new fuel.

Then I felt long cold fingers at my neck, fumbling beneath my collar, and the rasp of metal against my skin as the crucifix given me by my mother was drawn forth. I tried to lift my hand toward my throat to pull it back, but the effort was too much for me. Suddenly I felt the prickly wool of her traveling skirt against my cheek and shoulder as she slid down, Sasha's weight resting against the arm I was trying to raise. Before I could think or do anything else, sleep billowed over me once more.

# CHAPTER VI

••••••◦❀◦❘❘❘❖❀❀❖❘❘❘◦❀◦••••••

*I SURFACED ABRUPTLY* from a snug spell of sleep to cold and emptiness and a vague feeling of panic. Every muscle in my body was clenched fist-tight against the freezing night. The fire that had warmed my feet when I fell asleep was nothing but embers, a few sparks echoing the pale specks of stars blinking from behind flying scraps of navy cloud. The moon was bloated and blurred, its light spilt into the river and washed away. From within the black spruces, other mysterious chips of light flared in pairs, and vanished. Wispy trails of woodsmoke tickled my nose, the promise of warmth taunting.

But here, in the camp, I was utterly alone. No Indians muttering among themselves. Not the faintest hint of Sasha's dainty snore. The blanket draped around my shoulders was coated with frost, as were the gravel and dead leaves under me. The hair at my nape curled without the benefit of a cosmetic appliance.

I rose on the balls of my feet and stood very quietly, not realizing even then that I was listening for something specific. A sharpness stung my neck as I swung my head toward the raft. I grabbed my collar and found it open—mother's little crucifix, biting like ice, nipped my hand as I pulled it away from my skin. I crept to the boat. Sasha's bedroll was still neatly rolled and the interior of the tent looked oddly spacious, even in the darkness. It took me a moment to realize that the coffin was gone.

I looked stupidly back toward the woods. The woodsmoke—a settlement perhaps. But not Dawson, not yet. Maybe an Indian village or a fort, which might have explained why I had been left behind, though if so the ruse was less than crafty, leaving me out in the open like that beside a perfectly visible tent.

I was working up a good warming case of righteous indignation when I heard the rumbling growl. I stopped dead and listened, aware suddenly that I had heard it only seconds ago in my sleep and had since been waiting for a repetition. The river picked up the sound, magnified it, and carried it its length so that I could not tell where it came from. A bear maybe, sniffing out our supplies? I smartly removed myself as far from the boat as possible. Just then the growl escalated to a full-fledged snarl, challenged almost at once by a bellow, both noises erupting into a cacophony of bestial fury.

A rifle cracked. And just as I was feeling some sense of relief that other people were nearby and had the wild animals under apparent control, someone screamed. The scream was long and jerky and gargling, not just an expression of fear but of horrible pain.

In my place, Natty Bumppo undoubtedly would have stayed cool, melting silently into the woods, ferreting out the location of the commotion and its cause. Sneaking takes time, however, and I felt justified in assuming that time was a commodity of which the screamer had precious little. So the course I took was not only the most practical, but the one most natural to my inquiring and impetuous nature.

Heedless of the thorns and underbrush tearing at my skirts and flesh, I knotted the blanket capelike around my shoulders and plunged into the woods, uttering fierce banshee cries while thrashing my arms madly at anything foolish enough to get in my way. I wanted whatever it was that caused the screamer to scream to know that something large, loud, and determined was headed its way, so it would have ample opportunity to choose the better part of valor while the screamer—I hoped—had time to reload.

Thus, I ran full tilt upon a scene that those of a scientific nature might say perfectly illustrated the balance of nature, the survival of the fittest. But even Mr. Darwin himself would have had a difficult time deciding who was the fittest of the three bodies in various states of disrepair that littered the clearing before me.

The least fit was easy to decide. That was the poor little animal that had literally had the stuffings knocked out of it, making the footing slippery as well as lending the vicinity a certain nauseating air. The other two, their bellies dragging the ground, squared off just in front of a fire pit that cast a demonic glow onto the bloodied features of a man, on the left, and a moose, on the right. The moose, a cow, had only two good legs—the back legs were torn and dragged uselessly behind her. She braced on her front hooves to lunge toward the man, who tottered on his knees and elbows, but met each of her lunges with one of his own, battering her muzzle with the stock of his rifle. Neither man nor moose seemed aware of me, which was odd, because I had certainly made enough racket. Also, even absorbed as I was by the drama before me, I still had the crawly feeling that *some*thing watched me very closely indeed.

The moose lunged, her breath pluming opaque whiteness into the man's face, her nose missing him by about a foot. He whacked feebly with his rifle, missing her by about the same distance and falling over to one side with the effort.

"Dumb moose," he panted in an aggrieved tone. "Crazy moose. I was tryin' to help ya, ya dumb moose."

The moose responded only by lunging again, doggedly lurching for him as he doggedly whapped at her. The determination in the set of his jaw and the thrust of his pale head more than equaled her own hardheaded stubbornness.

As I drew nearer, the details of the man's appearance alarmed me. The top of his union suit was soaked with blood, one suspender hung broken from his waist, and his pants were soaked through with blood and mud. The moose was not in much better shape. One side of her throat had been torn open, the wound pumping great quantities of blood every second.

"See here, sir," I said to the man as kindly as possible, "I hardly think that's the ideal way to moose hunt. Of course, I've only seen it done once, but I believe it's customary to use the other end of the gun."

As if to make a liar out of me, the moose lunged a final time and fell heavily to her side, her great dark eyes rolling up in her head, her front legs sticking straight out.

The man gazed at her wonderingly and held his gun stock aloft again, the barrel digging into the ground, before looking up to notice me, after which he, too, fell over. I skirted the fire pit, approaching him cautiously, armed and undoubtedly demented as he was. But as he continued to mutter, I looked him full in the face and recognized both his visage and that stricken voice with which he had once confounded a whole ship with his grief.

"Dumb moose," Egil Larsson mourned. "She was a dumb moose. I was gonna help her. Dumb moose."

"Help her what, silly fellow, commit suicide?" I chided. I tried to get him to his feet, but though he groaned he would not rise, but lay still, very wet and sticky and cold, and I grew afraid that something in him was seriously damaged.

"Wolf," he answered me as though we were carrying on a perfectly reasonable conversation. "I was gonna help her with the wolf. Killed her baby. But the darn wolf ran away and she got me insteada him. Dumb moose."

As he spoke I looked elsewhere, searching for help, for some device with which to move him, for details of the clearing, for something to carry water from the creek which I had barely noticed before, what with everything else happening. I was, in fact, looking everywhere but at his wounds and his face, from which the life was surely going to depart unless I could find a way to aid him, and quickly. I scanned the clearing, the creek, the distance to the open-doored cabin about a hundred yards away from us. Thinking of splints, I looked to the woods, and saw twin red points looking back at me.

"W—wolf. Did you say wolf?" I asked. The points seemed to grow larger, and I thought, even in the nighttime shadows of the trees, I could make out a deeper blackness over there.

"Dumb moose—" he muttered less intelligibly than before.

"You're sure it wasn't, perhaps, a sled dog looking for a handout? They look very similar to one another, as I'm sure you may have noted."

Still, I didn't think a sled dog could be trusted amidst all this blood either. By that time Larsson was expressing no opinions whatsoever, either on the relative menace of sled dogs versus wolves, or on the mental capabilities of moose. I unknotted the blanket from my shoulders and spread it over him. Leaves rustled behind me, four times in quick succession, and I whirled to see a distinctly lupine outline studded with red eyes and gleaming teeth, several feet away on the other side of the moose.

Wild animals, as I know from my extensive study of the subject in the Leatherstocking series and the works of several other authors knowledgeable on the subject, are mostly afraid of fire. I say mostly to except the dragon, who generated fire himself and so was not, but then, he was a minor deity of alien origin and not, properly speaking, a wild animal at all. The fire pit contained little more than brightly burning coals now, buried too deeply to produce wolf-intimidating flames.

If I was unable to frighten the beast away with fire, I would have to try another method. Larsson's grasp on his gun was slack enough that I easily pried it from his fingers. My own fingers all but refused to cooperate as I pressed their cold-numbed surfaces lightly over the icy metal, seeking the release that would allow me to examine the cartridge chamber. I found it and the rifle broke open with a clank like rusting armor. No shells remained and a hasty pat-down of Larsson's accessible pockets failed to produce extras.

I peered down the barrel, but saw no light through the other end, even when I pointed it at the fire pit. Clogged then, and useless. Even if I had shells, I would rather risk my luck with what was actually little more than a wild dog, for all of its terrifying press in fairy tales, than blow myself up with a dirty rifle. I have a healthy respect for technology. I preferred taking my chances with flesh and blood, however hairy.

I congratulated myself on my decision when, glancing toward where the wolf had been, I saw now only moonlit woods, heard only the slurp of the creek.

Larsson moaned and I quickly returned my attention to him. Sweat matted his colorless hair and ran into his staring, pale eyes. I had not realized, on the boat, what a large man he was. I could not leave him to go for help nor, I felt, could the two of us stay in that clearing all night. The best thing to do would be to get him inside that cabin. That way, even if the wolf went for friends, we'd have solid walls between us and it. And it could huff and puff all it liked. Probably though, it would just forget about us and devour the moose instead. Glutton. How could it move with half of the calf still in its belly?

I glimpsed a fast flash of blackness from the corner of my eye, but when I tried to pinpoint it, saw nothing. Animals are popularly supposed to be able to tell when one fears them and to attack on that basis. Therefore, I held my breath to keep my limbs steady and scanned the woods as if I were simply admiring the scenery. Amazing, how many things in a nighttime spruce forest resemble a wolf when you are looking for one. The true identity of the objects that stopped my heart every few seconds

I will never know, but none of them bore the flaming eyes and glittering teeth that suddenly, as I finished my perusal, faced me, just a few yards beyond the fire pit.

It didn't like what it saw any better than I did, for it let forth a roar like an open blast furnace.

"Oh, Jesus, Mary, and Joseph!" I cried, and before I knew that I was too small and unmuscular to do so, I had flipped Larsson over in the blanket, wrapping him up like a hand-rolled cigar, and was dragging him toward the cabin.

The wolf leapt an impossibly large leap, and I dropped Larsson and brought up the useless gun. The wolf sailed over my head, twisted sideways in midair, and landed back on the other side of the moose.

"You great glutton," I yelled. "Why don't you eat what you've killed already and let us be!"

It lifted its head and howled, just as if it was laughing at my helplessness.

That infuriated me. The best way to handle bullies, in my experience, is with belligerence. Leaving poor Larsson on the ground for a moment and facing the wolf so it couldn't surprise me with another of its acrobatic stunts, I tore off a section of my petticoat, wrapping it around the stock of the gun, which I then thrust into the fire.

"There," I told the wolf. "Put that to the hair of your chinny-chin-chin and smoke it, confound you!"

The wolf howled again as all my petticoat burned up and fell off the stock, and I was forced to drop the gun to avoid being burned by the debris.

Then casually, slowly, the beast started walking—almost sauntering—toward me, its teeth strong and glistening, its eyes blazing. I didn't look at it, but I grabbed the blanket and hauled at Larsson. He groaned and the blanket snagged under him.

The wolf kept coming. "Stay, damn you," I ordered.

Black lips peeled away from begored fangs, and another blast-furnace snarl told me what it thought of my order. The eyes bored into me, and I knew all at once that this beast hated me. It was not merely hungry. It was not afraid. It hated me.

Ridiculously, I was as much wounded as frightened. The animal's attitude was singularly vindictive on such short acquaintance. I usually have a way with animals. Hadn't I written that well-received series of articles calling for legislation to abolish dogfights and prohibit cruelty to mules and packhorses? It was very unfair for that beast to glare at me with such mad

malevolence, its eyes transmitting visions of my dismember-
ment and mutilation. Mad? *Could* it be mad? Though no foam
flecked its jaws, it did have a strange malformed look to it—
massive shoulders, a snout broad enough for a pig instead of
a wolf. An unnatural look, but, I thought and fervently hoped
for Larsson's sake, not a rabid one.

It hunkered down and poised to spring, then suddenly
stopped, its ears pricking, as a long howl that sounded like a
screaming woman ululated through the night. I leaned down
and scooped up the rifle. The wolf's flat gray head snaked back,
snarling. The howl rose again, like an extension of the wind
cowing the trees and scattering ash and smoke from the fire
pit.

The wolf rose and turned, whimpering in a frustrated fashion.

"Whoo! Listen to that!" a voice exclaimed mildly from behind me.

I turned to look. The words issued from the woods up-
stream.

"Get yer darn claws out of my neck, ya darn cat. You heard
wolves before."

The admonition came as another howl rose, urgent and
compelling. From the corner of my eye, I saw a flash of movement. Our tormenter had vanished, growl, teeth, red eyeballs,
and all.

# CHAPTER VII

————⟡◦⟡————

*LABORED PANTING RASPED* in my ears. I twisted frantically, looking for the wolf, then realized my own ragged respiration was making the racket. Frozen leaves crunched, and the fuzzy full moon outlined a hunchbacked man as he stepped out of the woods, above the cabin. For a step and a half he strode blithely toward me. Within the course of the second step, his hunch expanded until it overshadowed his head, then sprang from his shoulders, and with a steam engine's worth of hiss and eyes glittering red as the lamps in a bawdy house, it bounded past me, skidding to a stop between Larsson's feet and the moose's nose.

By the glow of the fire pit, the self-propelled deformity was revealed as a very large, highly discommoded mottle-furred cat, puffed up to three times its size. With its lips curled back from its teeth, it sniffed the moose, extended a stiff paw to dab at the carcass, made a sound like a consumptive old man hawking up sidewalk slime, jumped back three feet, executed a sixty-degree turn in midair, and with tail rigid, streaked like a Chinese rocket for the open door of the cabin.

The man watched the performance of his companion before continuing his journey toward me. "Ahoy there, stranger. You seem to be runnin' up a distress flag."

"I'd prefer to be runnin' up to the cabin right behind

your cat, but I have an injured man here. Can you give me a hand?"

"An injured—?" And he very sensibly stopped asking questions and started running.

"Migosh, nephew, if you wanted to get outta work that bad, you shoulda just said so. This lady coulda hurt herself tryin' to drag you around." The former hunchback, who by the lantern light in the cabin now more closely resembled a svelte edition of the popular conception of St. Nicholas, spoke softly in a gruff tone belied by the concern clouding his countenance. A hand as large as his nephew's smoothed a canvas sheet across a bed of spruce boughs and laid a heavy Hudson Bay blanket over the casualty, who shivered and sweated but made no verbal response. Poor Larsson had suffered in the transfer from mooseside to cabin, although once his uncle came, the two of us had been able to carry the young man with relative gentleness.

"Wolf attacked him, was that it?" the uncle asked when he had built a fire in the rectangular sheet-iron stove and filled the kettle sitting on top. He seated himself on an upended birch log and faced me across the stove.

I sat slumped on another example of his Yukon Chippendale furnishings and watched with vision blurred by the frost of my own breath as he poked a pipe in his mouth and lit it with one hand, the same with which he did everything. The other, except while hoisting Larsson, he kept in the pocket of his peacoat. Which didn't seem too peculiar for a man who wore a cat around his neck like a ruff. The cat, after a thorough wash and judicious arrangement of its various deep plush multicolored mottles and stripes, with extra attention for the tufts on its ears, impersonated a boudoir bolster and rumbled itself to sleep.

"No," I said. "It was the moose. Larsson told me before he passed out that he had tried to aid her against the wolf, and she attacked him. They were locked in combat when I found them."

"The wolf and the moose?"

"The moose and your nephew. As you can see, your nephew won."

"Well, blow me down and salt me for a herring," he said with satisfaction. "Darned if he didn't. That's the Larsson side of the family for you, okay. Don't know enough to keep outta arguments with mooses. Then *you* fought the wolf, eh?" He raised a furred white eyebrow above startlingly keen eyes that sparked like blue flames through the pipe smoke. "Between the two of you, the huntin' won't be worth much around here. Scarin' off all the wildlife. Likely that wolf didn't know what it was gettin' into."

"I'm so sorry about that," I said sweetly, picking absently at one of the moldy yellow leaves that yet clung to my costume after what this man seemed to think was my lighthearted little fracas in the clearing. "Actually, as a conscientious member of the Society for the Prevention of Cruelty to Animals, I was just trying to save the moose from your nephew. The wolf misunderstood the situation. In fact, if its mate hadn't called it into the woods for a little chat, it probably would have misunderstood you to death, too."

"Do tell? Wonder why the other wolf didn't just come out and join your friend for supper?"

The little stove crackled, sighed, and throbbed forth shimmering waves of blessed warmth. The kettle burbled for attention, and he rose and lifted it from the stove, pouring water into a basin and dumping a rag in it, which he placed beside Larsson's pallet.

"Ahoy there, son," he said quietly. "You've lolligagged around enough for a spell. Got to clean you up now. We've got company, you know. Best bib and tucker and all that."

I followed him to see if there was anything I could do, but he firmly shielded his patient from my view. I turned my attention to examining the decor. It was decidedly rustic. I have already described the sleeping and sitting accommodations, tastefully assembled from native products, and the hot little sheet metal stove. Other than the eclectic assortment of crates and boxes of foodstuffs and cooking supplies, that was about it. Overall the cat was the only grace note in the whole establishment. Except, perhaps, for the library, which flanked the makeshift bed. It was a row of books, but a long row of books. The bookshelves, two wooden crates nailed end-to-end to the moss-chinked log wall, proclaimed in faded red letters that they had formerly held ACME PREMIUM PACKED SARDINES. There was a certain symmetry in that, since many of the books were of a seagoing nature: *Moby Dick*, *Treasure Island*, and a few more obscure exploratory sea journals among them. Others involved red herrings, being the collected mystery stories of Edgar Allan Poe, and at least one of Sir Arthur Conan Doyle's novels that I had not read.

"I have a new Sherlock Holmes on the raft," I said.

"Hmmm . . . she didn't open anything up too bad, boy, but she gnawed on you some," the man muttered. A gasp from the patient. "Pour yourself a cup of tea while the water's hot, why don't you, lady, and make yourself at home?"

I did so, finding the tea tin on the window ledge, the window itself being a small aperture covered with a piece of semitransluscent greased cotton. Above the upright box on which the basin had rested, two nails, driven precisely in line with each other on either side of the window, held two slick promotional gimmicks—coffee cans with tin handles attached to them, so they could be used as cups after the coffee was gone.

Footsteps crunched toward the cabin and the door swung ponderously open. "Heey, Lomax," the visitor called as he entered, "I heard shootin'. Come by to see if you was all right. Them people I was tellin' you about? Somebody seen them tonight around here and Mary thought there might be trouble."

The voice, deep and slow with a sort of sing-song cadence to it, broke off as the short, wiry-looking Indian man closed the door behind him and saw the two men and the basin of bloody water. "Heeey," he said. "What's goin' on here?"

"Aw, you know boys, Tom. Egil got a little lonesome while I was over visitin' Young Jack and tried to strike up a conversation with a lady moose. Guess she didn't figure he was her type, exactly, and got insulted. You know how testy them mooses get."

"Yeah," Tom said noncommittally, no doubt used to Lomax's nonsense. "Boy, he don't look so good. Think I'd better go get Mary, eh? Have her bring some of her medicine stuff."

Lomax grunted and covered Larsson back up. His apple-cheeked face was grave and he massaged his mustache thoughtfully with his lower lip. "Aye, we'd be grateful for that, Tom. Whew, I tell you, boy, I'm sure awful glad I don't have to explain what happened to him to my sister. If Liv wasn't dead already, this woulda killed her. She'da had my hide for givin' 'im the idea to come up here." He shook his head slowly and stared at his boot.

Tom did likewise for a moment. "Boy, that's rough, eh?" Then, drawing his largely buttonless mackinaw more tightly closed, he headed for the door.

"You watch out for them wolves," Lomax cautioned. "One of 'em got the mooses before the moose got Egil, according to this lady. Then the wolf came back and almost got every-body."

"Sure was some wolf then, if it was by itself. But, hey, you said wolves. Is there a pack around then?" He turned so that, although his mouth was still facing Lomax, I was given to realize I was included in the question.

"One wolf that I saw. I only heard its mate," I said.

"Funny kinda way for a wolf to act, but that's what the stories say, you know, about them people. Animals act funny, people act funny, when *they're* around."

"What people?" I asked.

He avoided looking at me. "I'll go get Mary."

"Who's Mary?" I asked when he had gone.

"Mary? She's a medicine woman. Best thing this side of Father Judge."

"Well, it certainly is neighborly of that man to check in on you that way," I said, although still puzzled by the Indian's evasiveness.

"Aye, Tom and me, we get along pretty good now. Too bad Lucy didn't live to see it. She'da gotten a kick out of it. Lucy, she was my wife. She was close to her kinfolks, real close, but ol' Tagish Tom, he's been around white men enough that he wasn't too sure about me. 'Fraid I'd be mean to her, I guess."

"He seems to have revised his opinion."

"Aye, well, it don't matter now. Lucy is gone. She caught chicken pox up to Fort Yukon last fall. Was real sick by the time we got home. Mary wanted to take care of her, but things that just make a white kid sick, they'll kill an Indian, even a grown-up. I nursed her for a week and she was gettin' better, I thought, till one day I come in from choppin' wood and found her lyin' by the stove. I asked Tom and Mary how they wanted her buried. 'Bout this time last year, it was. Ground sure is hard, right about now. Tom, he come and helped me thaw out a space for the grave. Since then, he's sorta been in the habit of comin' by when he's in this neck of the woods." This my host primarily confided to his stove as he fed it more kindling, adjusted the draft, and put more water on to boil.

I murmured sympathetic noises, but he continued gazing at the stove as if it were an object of deep fascination. "Well," I finally managed, "you must have been up here quite a while. Your cabin all built, relatives in the neighborhood."

"Quite a while," he agreed, and swung back to face me. "How 'bout you?"

"Only just arrived," I said. "Actually, that was why I was wondering about the people your—er—brother-in-law mentioned. You see, my companions seem to have wandered away from me while I was dozing. Three Indian gentlemen, not of the same people as your relations, I would guess, and a blond lady."

"Didn't notice 'em. Young Jack didn't mention anybody like that neither. 'Course, *might* not have noticed, though a blond lady—"

"They might have been a wee bit more noticeable than that," I said. "They were probably carrying a coffin."

He scratched his head thoughtfully. "This has been one unusual night and that's a sure thing. Mighty unusual. A coffin, you say?"

"Yes. It was Mr. Lawson, you see—" And I told him the whole story, except for the incident at the river, which was still inexplicable, even to me. It passed the time while we waited for his in-laws to return to care for the boy. My continued interest in Larsson's condition was enhanced by my reluctance to venture forth alone. When I faced the area into which the Big Bad Wolf (or wolves) had so recently disappeared, I wanted to be accompanied. Preferably by the U.S. Cavalry or a division of armed infantrymen, but failing that, I'd take anybody I could get.

Lomax sipped his tea, wiped his nephew's face, and patted the cat, who rumbled sleepily at him. The purring cat seemed to generate and spread its own boneless relaxation and contentment, calming and slowing Larsson's tortured breathing as a faith healer might by laying on the hands, and filling the cabin with warmth as welcome as that of the stove. Lomax swabbed his nephew's face, chewed on the stem of his pipe, and listened to me, grunting now and then. I had meant to provide him with a brief outline, but every time I stopped he seemed disappointed, and finally I was given to understand that although this fellow had undoubtedly heard many tales of the journeys of newly arrived gold seekers, my own was by far the most engrossing he had ever encountered. Thus convinced that my account was fraught with drama and humor, fascinating detail, and a great depth of human insight, I told him all that had occurred in San Francisco, of the death of Larsson's friend on shipboard, and our adventures on the river. The arrival of Mary and Tom prevented me from having to decide whether or not to disclose the events surrounding the mountie's death, but even so, I was a little sorry to see them.

"Lomax, what happened to that moose out there?" Tom asked as he pushed open the door.

"Nothing. It's still by the fire pit—a cow and part of a calf."

"Not no more it ain't. Come and look." Lomax trudged out after him. The crackle of the stove and the crunch of the leaves under the men's feet were enough to drown out the entrance of the soft-walking Mary, a round young woman with a bulging flour sack over one arm and each hand stuck up the cuff of the opposite sleeve of a man's mackinaw.

Her eyes lingered curiously on me for a moment after she nodded to me, then she went straight to Egil's bedside. She flipped back the covers with none of the regard for modesty Lomax had shown, and examined the wound. After a while she sat back on her heels, her breath sucking in through her teeth.

"That bad?" I asked.

"Pretty bad," she said. "But it's funny. Real funny."

"How's that?" I asked.

"He's hurt inside. I can tell. But he sure does heal fast. He's gettin' better already."

My faith in native healers took a sharp dive. "Already? That's imposs—"

"Look here," she said defiantly, and pointed to his bared stomach. Purple and black coloration spread like a great spider from a double row of enormous tooth marks biting in the shape of a gigantic egg horizontally across his torso. Where the sides of the egg touched his breast and navel, the flesh and what lay under it had been mashed together in a stew of that which belonged inside and that which belonged outside. It was a wonder his heart and lungs were intact.

"What do you mean better?" I said, trying to keep my dried salmon down. "That's horrible. The poor boy probably won't make it through the night."

"Nah, nah," she said, shaking her head so that her black braid flopped back and forth between her shoulders. "Look at that black and blue. That shouldn't be that way till near daybreak, anyway. He oughta be swelled up, red. Real sick. Look at him. That's one hell of a guardian spirit this man has."

That, as it turned out, was an understatement.

Nothing remained of the mooses but a long bloody trail leading into the woods. Snow had started falling sometime during the night, glazing the worst of the gore. The fire pit, freshly re-plenished, glowed like the gateway to hell.

Neither Tom nor Lomax had much to say as we passed the spot on our way back to my boat. Lomax strode along with his hands in his pockets. Loki, draped around his shoulders, looked like a deliberately artistic backdrop for snow crystals. Tom padded along with his head bent, the flaps of his fur cap pulled firmly down over his ears. All of us stiffened a little as we entered the woods, but the only sign of the wolves was the foreleg and hoof of the moose, laying slantwise across the trail. We quickened our pace.

The scene at the clearing on first glance seemed much as I'd left it. The raft still lay beached and deserted on the rapidly whitening shore. It was Tom who first noted the claw marks that had scratched the snow back to thin stripes of lacerated dead leaves.

We stepped carefully around the tracks, and Tom shifted his rifle so it was parallel to the ground. The tent flap was closed and neatly tied, I saw as we drew nearer. I knew I hadn't stopped to do that.

"Unnnhuh."

I jumped back as the groan issued from the raft.

"What was that?" I asked.

"It ain't no wolf," Tom said, and pulled the bow loop with the barrel of his rifle, nudging the icy canvas aside with same. I peered around him and a horrified breath caught in my throat.

The blankets covered a person-sized mound of rippling gray and black fur. I'd seen such fur just the night before. But as Tom drew a bead on the head of the bundle, another groan escaped it. This time I recognized the voice and rushed forward. I had been listening to such moans and groans for most of two months now. The wolf in our bedclothing was none other than Sasha in wolf's clothing, as I proved when I tugged at her shoulder to wake her and she rolled over, the hood to the wolf-fur parka dropping away to reveal her customary spill of golden hair.

Lomax whistled. "Boy, Miss Lovelace, you told me your friend was a pretty spunky lady, but who'da thought she'd have that old wolf skinned out and made a coat of him before morning?"

I grinned back at him, but as I continued attempting to wake Sasha, my grin faded. Her face was clammy and pale as the prevailing climatic condition. Her eyelids were thin shells of white whose golden lashes curled into deep craters of shadow. Her head flopped on her neck as I shook her. As her cheek turned away from me, I saw that the pulsing line of her jugular was once more studded with a pair of inflamed insect bites. "I don't know where she got this coat," I said. "But she was cheated. It has fleas. Or something worse. She seems ill, like she was before, and I can't wake her up."

Lomax handed me his gun. "You keep this. We'll fetch Mary."

And before I could ask if it was really necessary for both of them to go, they went.

I half lay within the tent beside her, watching her face and feeling perspiration I didn't know I was capable of generating at such temperatures slick the gunmetal under my palm. The gun lay within the folds of the mackinaw I'd borrowed from Mary. I wiped my hands on my skirt, left the gun laying in my lap, and following a lifelong habit, looked for something to read. The sun penetrated the white canvas with enough force that if I strained a little, I could read a few pages of my new book to take my mind off the rigors of reality. Unfortunately, Dr. Watson's professional status kept reminding me of my patient and I looked over at Sasha after reading every other word.

I heard Lomax and Mary coming after what seemed like enough time for him to have gone to Seattle and back to fetch her. I crawled outside to meet them.

"How's she doin'?" he asked.

I shrugged. "Maybe Mary should be the judge of that."

Mary, wearing Tom's mackinaw and carrying her flour sack over her arm, crawled into the tent.

"I sorta forgot to thank you for helpin' Egil back there, Miss Lovelace," Lomax said rather formally. "I hope Mary here can help your friend."

I looked down at my feet and felt my face thaw. What could I say? That it was nothing? That I fought wolves every day?

Mary rescued me. I heard her suck in her breath again, and I ducked back into the tent to see her kneeling over Sasha, fingering the puncture wounds.

"What do you make of them, Mary?" I asked. "Infected insect bites, I thought. Perhaps a salve?"

She cast a wild look back over her shoulder at me, as if she thought I had gone completely crazy, and scuttled backward out of the tent. Lomax, who had been staring in, had to jump aside to avoid being run over.

I followed Mary outside. Without a word further to either of us, she took off down the path toward the cabin. Lomax frowned after her and looked to me for explanation. I shook my head and ducked back toward the tent. That was when I saw the police boat gliding toward us. In a moment it had docked, the mountie pilot expertly guiding it so that it blocked the raft, to which he moored his own craft before climbing aboard. I had been so intent on the winter-uniform-muffled policeman that I failed to recognize one of the passengers until he spoke to me.

"Sorry, darlin'," a hangdog handcuffed Purdy apologized. "Seems like that poor little ol' constable got dumped right in the sergeant's favorite fishin' hole. Somebody saw us together walkin' and when this fine representative of Canadian law asked me who was that lady I was seen with, I just thought he wanted to pay his compliments."

It sounded lame, even to me, and cut no ice at all with the mountie.

"Valentine Lovelace," the Scottish sergeant who had fancied Sasha Devine said, "it is my duty to inform you that you are under arrest for the murder of Constable Hamish Faversham, and also that extradition has been requested by this officer." He nodded to a man wearing a black overcoat with a fur collar. Under his thin black mustache, the fellow smiled at me as if he'd just panned a cabbage-size gold nugget. "*His* charge is petty theft."

"Detective Norman of the Pinkerton Detective Agency," the overcoated man announced, just to let me know with whom I was dealing. To Destin he said, "We, too, always apprehend our party, as you mounties say, Sergeant."

Destin wasn't listening. His face was hard and impersonal as he stepped forward with a pair of handcuffs. I took a step or two backward. Lomax stepped in between us, jerking his left hand free of his pocket. Where the hand should be a metal hook protruded from a wooden socket.

"Move aside, Dag. You heard me. This woman murdered one of my men and I'm bound to take her in."

"I think this bears talkin' about, Sergeant Destin. This ain't one of your murderin' barroom hussies you're fixin' to truss up like a Thanksgivin' turkey. This lady is a book writer and she saved Egil's life last night. Wolf attacked him—well, sort of. It's a long story. But if it wasn't for her, he'd be worse off than he is. Which ain't good."

"*Cap*tain Lomax, will ye be steppin' aside, mon, or maun I arrest you, too, for the obstruction of the Queen's justice?"

"Queen's justice be damned. I know a lady when I see one," he said, and thrust his jaw out at the same angle his nephew had done when arguing with the moose. And with about as much effect. I feared the sergeant, clearly in no mood to placate anybody, would arrest the man. I stepped around him and presented my wrists as if I expected him to kiss my hands instead of cuffing them.

"It's perfectly all right, Captain Lomax," I said haughtily, as the metal bracelets snicked shut. "As you pointed out, the sergeant has made a mistake, but he will soon discover it when we've had a chance to discuss the matter in a calm, reasonable fashion."

"You can calmly and reasonably tell it to Inspector Constantine, madam," the mountie said. "In the boat with you."

"Oh, oh no, I can't." I backed away, suddenly remembering Sasha. "My companion, Miss—uh, Mrs. Lamour, has been taken dangerously ill. I can't leave her here on the boat alone. Captain Lomax and his family already have one patient to tend to."

I hadn't even gotten out the last part, however, before the mountie was inside the tent. He scooped up Sasha, wolf fur and all, and lay her tenderly in the boat. The Pinkerton man cradled her hooded head in his lap while Destin returned for me.

"What happened?" Norman asked. "Did you try to kill her, too?"

I glared at him, devoutly hoping the fleas in her wolfskin parka infested him in unscratchable places.

"Well, what about Egil?" Lomax asked in a last-ditch attempt to preserve my honor. "You gonna take a perfectly healthy woman who you just *suspect* of doin' somethin' wrong and leave my nephew here to die?"

"If your nephew was dying, Dag," the mountie said with more patience than I expected, "you wouldna be standin' here arguin' with me, even if this woman was the Queen of bloody Sheba, now, would you? Go back and do the best you can for him. I'll either return for him myself or send someone."

Lomax glared at him and picked up Loki by the front paws,

settling the cat on his neck, where it slapped its tail against his shoulder like a judge rapping the bench and stared at us all as if we were guilty of dog loving.

"Malcom?" Lomax half mumbled Destin's first name as the mountie climbed aboard.

"Aye?"

"I'm right about this lady."

Destin ran his tongue around his teeth and looked at his hands for a moment, and gave a short nod.

As we cast off, Lomax called, "I'll bring your boat up myself, miss, soon as we can move Egil."

I nodded quickly as several yards of water rapidly separated us from shore. "Oh, Mr. Lomax!"

"Ma'am?" he called back.

"Feel free to read the new Holmes. If they hang me before you can return it, consider it your inheritance for your kindness!"

The bow turned and we headed downstream then, and when I turned around he was trudging into the woods. Loki's tail, rising and falling against the back of the blue peacoat, waved a languid farewell.

# CHAPTER VIII

••••━🙥❘❘🙥━••••

"REALLY, SERGEANT, THIS can all be explained—well, most of it can be explained," I said, speaking to Destin's back as he steered us downstream. He was not having an easy time of it. The paddle kept icing up.

"You can make a statement when we reach Fort Herchmer, madam," the Scot replied without turning to look at me. "I ken yer accomplice here has made all the explanation I'll need."

"But I'm not a criminal!" I told him. "I've never—"

I felt the eyes of the Pinkerton man on my back and stopped, dismayed by my luck. Thousands of men toiled for months to make it into the Yukon, many of them dying in the attempt, yet the long arm of the Widow Hig could still wiggle dirty fingers in my pie from thousands of miles away, just when I most needed to leave her ill opinion behind me. Perhaps I should have kept her ill opinion and left her dresses. The Pinkerton man spat into the water. I was sure he wasn't just clearing his throat, but reiterating his opinion of my integrity.

"Give it up, darlin'," Purdy advised. "You know you're tellin' the truth—or most of it, and I know it. But there's people lie better than you can tell the truth and these dedicated officers of the law have heard 'em all."

"Well, you're one of the latter kind of people," I hissed. "Why couldn't you have been a little gallant for a change?"

"Ma'am, I am *always* a perfect Texas gentleman, but my gallantry does not extend to wearin' the kind of necktie in fashion at the fort to the kind of party they're hopin' to make us the guests of honor at. You got me into this, lady. *You* figure a way to get us both out."

There was a bright side to the situation. By being arrested, Purdy and I had secured some of the finest accommodations Dawson had to offer at that time. Hotels and saloons were in the final stages of construction, but almost every other building in the city consisted of canvas tents or rickety lean-tos standing in a sea of rutted frozen mud. Fort Herchmer, on the other hand, was a series of fine log buildings—a barracks, a police hospital, a mess hall, a headquarters building, a warehouse, an outhouse, which was not yet too backed up and which smelled really unbearable only when there was a little breeze, and, of course, the guardroom and stockade, which was where Destin deposited us after summoning two officers to carry Sasha into the hospital.

We arrived at about five o'clock that evening, and were immediately provided with gainful employment (for Purdy) and an active social life (for me.)

For when I was shown to my cell, Purdy was placed in the charge of a burly young policeman and marched off to the police woodpile.

"He'll have another good three hoors yet of steady choppin' before it's fully dark," Destin said, grinning in much the same manner as the grim reaper as he closed the door of my cell behind us. "We find that woodpile a powerful deterrent to lawlessness. While a man is cuttin' oor wood, he's no cuttin' his own nor minin' and as for gamblers and riffraff like your friend, who make their livin' off the sweat of other men, why, they find the work its own punishment enough. If they don't, for you Yanks, we usually just give ye a blue ticket and send you back where you come from. You, however, may force us to use oor imaginations. We've never had a case before, you know, where a female foreign national drooned one of the constabulary."

"But I didn't—" I protested, and most earnestly.

"If you had a motive, woman, I'd appreciate hearin' it, just to keep myself frae flyin' into a rage and doin' aught I might regret. Why did you kill him?" He thrust his jaw forward and lowered his voice two octaves. "Are you goin' to try to tell me he made advances?"

"Not of the sort you imply, no. I very much doubt he could have appreciated even my modest feminine assets without first having them appraised by a second party and figuring the customs due. By that time I could certainly have screamed for help instead of resorting to the kind of desperate measures you accuse . . ."

"You had no reason for killin' him then?"

"I had no reason, nor did I kill him. Be reasonable, Sergeant. He was rather larger than I, used to the outdoors—I presume even your constables on customs duty at some time or other have to lift something heavier than a pen? I am a woman of sedentary occupation and inclination, nearly worn to a frazzle by unaccustomed exertion. How could I have possibly had the strength to drown him even had I earnestly desired to do so?"

If I detected a flicker of doubt in the sergeant's eyes, he managed to keep from his voice anything but determined condemnation.

"Trickery, I suspect," he said, glowering at me from under beetled brow and voicing his charge quietly, the words measured and weighted as an ounce of gold on an assayer's scales. "You lured him to the edge of the water and drooned him then got Purdy to help you move the body."

"Ask Purdy again. He seems to have told you a great deal. I hope he didn't neglect to mention that your constable was dead—and no, not by my hand—and dry when he went into the water. Haven't you a doctor of some sort who could examine the body? An expert in police science, one who employs some of the techniques used by Sherlock Holmes? If you have, that expert could tell you that Faversham certainly did not drown."

"How was it you *did* kill him then?" the sergeant slyly inquired.

"*I* did not kill him. He came to open Mr. Laws—Mr. Lamour's casket, and then—then I passed out—and when I awoke, he was dead, and with no wound I could see. No stab wound, bullet holes, or sign of strangulation."

"And have you had these mysterious blackoots before, madam, when you wake and find you've killed someone?"

I blew out my breath, which emerged in a cloud, and sat down on the edge of my bunk. I reminded myself that to those not suspected of murder, the sergeant had shown himself a kindly and reasonable man. I had to enlist some of that kindliness on my side, but I knew instinctively that nothing would convince him but the truth. If only the truth weren't so unconvincing, even to me.

"Sergeant, please forget for a moment that you think you already know how and by whom your subordinate was killed. I do know more about it, but it will require an open mind on your part to hear me out. I have not yet made sense of it myself, although I have formed a theory."

To indicate his receptiveness, the sergeant stood glaring down at me, arms folded across his chest, one of his heels firmly planted on each side of the doorway.

"You—uh—you see, though I saw no wounds on the constable when I awoke, I did see something else." The sergeant did not nod encouragingly, say "umm humm" or "go on" or any of the other indications that might have made it easier. I twisted my skirt in my hands and stared resolutely at the moisture freezing on my boots. The stove was in the guardroom and the heat did not adequately reach the cells. "I have reason to believe, judging from the man's facial expression and the condition of his body as I found it, that he was killed by the Deadly Miasma that attacked my father and his oldest friend as well as several other people I have seen lately."

"This Deadly Miasma, was it the mumps by any chance?" the sergeant asked without missing a beat and with an unpleasant curl to the side of his mouth.

I ignored the tone and responded to the content of his question. "No, something deadlier, an affliction that, when it kills, leaves its victims with a seraphic smile on their faces. I was under the impression it always killed until I saw Miss Dev—Mrs. Lamour. Perhaps the vector is some insect—though she bore no signs of violence, she did have what might have been insect bites on her throat. I did not inspect the constable for such marks, but it occurs to me that I may have seen them on other victims."

"May have? If you really thought Faversham was killed by an oversize mosquito or some other farfetched beastie, why did you dunk him instead of reportin' his death to me? Could be I might have saved the lad, whether you thought him dead or no."

"I thought you might decide the—uh—the late Mr. Lamour had brought the dis—oh, never mind. I can see I shall have to tell you about the others." Carefully avoiding revealing Sasha Devine's identity, for I was determined not to be a tattletale like Purdy, I described the circumstances surrounding the deaths of Papa, Wy Mi, and the drunk in the alley. I also related the disappearances aboard the *Golden Queen*.

"Tragedy seems to follow you aroond, miss. To be sure, had I known, I'd have sent you back over the pass."

"I thought as much. So surely you can see why I panicked when I awakened next to the policeman's corpse. Dr. Purdy agreed to help me only because he saw what a tight spot I was in. I hope it won't go hard with him."

He shook his head in grudging admiration. "I must say, I didna put much stock in it when you told me you wrote stories for a livin', but hearin' is believin'. Never in all my eighteen years on the force has it been my duty to listen tae such a farfetched, outlandish, lame excuse for an alibi. If anything more creditable occurs to you, the constable can take your statement. The Crown would very much appreciate a believable explanation for yoor murderous conduct on Canadian soil. Now, if you'll excuse me, I'll take my leave before I come down with some of your dead foggy bug bites. Good evenin', miss."

"Sergeant?"

"Yes?"

"I just want you to know—I mean, I know it looks bad, but I'm innocent of that other charge, too. It's a family matter. My late father's wife owed me money, which she refused to pay me. Since poor Mrs. Lamour had nothing appropriate for the journey, and my stepmother's dressmaker thrust the gowns upon me, I took them as payment instead. I—"

"Miss Lovelace? That is what you call yourself, is it not?"

"It is."

"Miss Lovelace, dresses are the least of your problems and mine right now. I suggest you concentrate on Faversham's death and look to the salvation of your soul, woman."

And with that he slammed my cell door behind me. Had I had a guilty conscience, I would have hung myself on the spot out of sheer remorse. It was such a shame to waste an exit like that, in fact, that I almost wished I were guilty of something I *could* repent.

Late that night, when I had settled down for sleep as best I could, I had another visitor. Purdy was snoring boisterously in the next cell, a room like mine with a barred window in the door through which we desperate criminals could be observed.

The poor rainmaker had on his return from the rigors of the woodpile spent considerable time and vocabulary cursing me for involving him in my problems, but he eventually wore himself out.

I, too, had finally fallen asleep, the total darkness of the windowless cell and my own exhaustion from the previous sleepless night overcoming the mill race of if-only-I-hads and no-but-I-couldn't-have-that-wouldn't-have-worked-eithers cycling through my brain. I dreamed of the wolf again, so vividly that I heard its triumphant howl and knew, from the answering howls, that it had brought the pack to finish off all of us— Larsson, Sasha, Papa, the sergeant, Purdy, the dead constable, Lomax, Tom, and Mary. The baying grew so insistent that I sat bolt upright, ready to meet the wolves as they sprang for our throats. Then my eyes flew open and I remembered where I was. The howling continued, though, a mournful "woo-wooing" from the sled dogs tethered behind the barracks. Even as it dawned on me that here, at least, I was safe from wolves, the outer door of the guardroom scraped shut, and the guard's muted voice cursed, followed by a loud yelp and a whine or two.

I did not hear the door open again, but a moment later the fragrance of burning lamp oil reached me, and soft yellow light flooded my cell. Thinking it was the constable, returning in what was probably an unsociable mood to check on us after silencing the dogs, I pretended to sleep. Perhaps if I was a model prisoner, quiet, well-mannered, and untroublesome, the police would conclude a woman of my ladylike bearing was incapable of having drowned one of their brethren.

Then, though I heard no rattle of keys, the light grew brighter and I sensed that I was no longer alone in my cell.

I rolled over rapidly and sat up, shielding my eyes from the lantern light. A tall shadow knelt and set the lamp on the floor. As my eyes adjusted, I saw that the figure was a man, civilian, not a policeman. He wore a well-tailored frock coat and a ruffled shirt, with golfball-sized cufflinks and a stickpin made of gold nuggets twinkling with diamonds. His black boots shone mud-free in the lantern light. With curling dark hair sporting a distinguished white streak in the middle, sorrowful dark eyes, and a dazzling toothy smile, he looked the perfect picture of a riverboat cardsharp, which was what I took him for.

He beamed at me wordlessly, his smile containing an avidity

I hoped I misunderstood. "Excuse me, sir, but I think you've wandered into the wrong cell. There is a free one next to Dr. Purdy."

He chuckled a deep, rich chuckle and wagged a nugget-clad finger at me. "Ah, Miss Lovelace, you make a little joke, even in these so deplorable circumstances. Such spirit! But then, I expected no less from a woman of such remarkable wit and wisdom."

"I beg your pardon? You're not a new prisoner?" I asked a little stupidly. Prisoners and policemen were the only two categories of people I could imagine in the cell at night. It had yet to dawn on me that a fellow prisoner would not likely be carrying a lantern.

"No, no, of course, my dear lady, I am not a prisoner, and neither should you be."

"A lawyer!" I said. "But who retained you—who—"

He made a face. "Dear Miss Lovelace, you insult me. I am an honest businessman, not a lawyer. The solace I am here to bring you is completely free of charge. As it should be since it was I, you might say, who drew you into this predicament. I came as soon as I learned of your arrest, but you understand, with the responsibilities of running a dance hall, it is difficult to extricate oneself quickly, even for such urgent matters. Please rest assured you will be free soon. This business—a free spirit such as yourself imprisoned—it is terrible, terrible! What must you think of my adopted country! I cannot understand how such misfortune could have befallen me."

From his aggrieved tone and lugubrious expression, I had trouble telling whether he was sympathizing with me or expected me to sympathize with him, but the mention of a dance hall gave me a clue to his identity. "You're Sasha's admirer! Lost-Cause Lawson's partner," I exclaimed in a whisper.

"Ah! Ah, yes," he said and swooped down upon my hand like a hawk on a rabbit, kissing it rather more fervently than custom dictated. "It was I who engaged you and the inestimable Miss Devine to escort the casket to Dawson. Permit me to introduce myself. I am Vasily Vladovitch Bledinoff, a boyar in my own country, but here merely a businessman like everyone else. Please be informal and address me as Vasily Vladovitch. Everyone else does. Well, almost everyone."

"Pleased to meet you—oh, dear, I assume you heard what has befallen Sasha, Mr. Ble—?"

"Please, Vasily Vladovitch. Please."

I wasn't trying to be formal. I just wasn't sure I could pronounce his name. His accent was much thicker than Sasha's, for his voice was in a lower register and very melodious, so that the rhythm of it obscured the underlying syllables. The voice sounded almost familiar, but I was growing tired by then, and the impact of recent events was finally overtaking me. I suppose I was in shock, too, and though a little thing like that has never kept me from functioning, it did impair my ability to recall certain past events with my customary lightning speed.

"Yes, oh yes, in fact, I have seen her and she is recovering very quickly. With proper diet and rest, my lovely Sasha should be able to be transferred straight from the police hospital to her new quarters."

I wondered if his lovely Sasha was aware he considered her his. The woman who had spoken to me of wishing to gain independent means would not, I thought, be pleased by such presumption. But then, no doubt she had vast experience at disentangling herself from such situations. I, on the other hand, had no experience at jailbreaking.

"I'm glad she's all right," I said sportingly, wishing that the same could be said for myself.

"There, there, my dear lady, you must not fret. And please also rest assured that I do not consider you remiss for failing to deliver the casket here to me personally. As a matter of fact, I wished only that you facilitate its passage through the legal intricacies at the border. From there on the Indians who accompanied you were perfectly capable of taking it to its proper resting place, as indeed they have already done. You see, those people are relatives by marriage—"

"Of yours or Mr. Lawson's?" I asked.

"Mr.—? Oh, Mr. Lawson. They are Mr. Lawson's relatives to be sure. And mine. A remarkable people, very loyal, very intelligent, very dedicated. They heard from contacts along the river that the policeman was coming and decided to remove the casket to safety—"

"I wish they had moved *me* to safety," I said.

"But it was for you the policeman came. Had you been gone, he would have continued to search and their precautions would have been useless."

"I see—I hadn't thought the Indians understood so much, to be honest, Mr.—uh—anyway, I see I misjudged them. They thought I was guilty of murdering the constable, too, didn't they? My, they are loyal to you. When they feared my supposed little lapse into homicidal mania would jeopardize Mr. Lawson's chance of reaching his resting place, they dumped what they thought was a guilty living person to protect the rights of an innocent dead one. While I admit there's a certain appealing reverence about such logic, I must implore you to believe me. Appearances to the contrary, the police and the Indians are wrong, sir. I did *not* kill that constable."

His soft laugh was kindly and full of genuine amusement. "Why, dear lady, I know that perfectly well. I, of all people, do not need to be convinced of your innocence." He paused for a moment as if the statement was self-evident, then added, "That a lady who has personally conversed with the great god Quetzequoatl should be subjected to such indignity—"

"Why, Vasily Vladovitch, you've read my work!" I said. His name no longer seemed the least bit difficult and, indeed, rolled fluidly off my tongue. For I realized from his last statement that this charming, erudite man of impeccable taste meant to use his keenly insightful and perceptive mind to help me, not because I was a temporary employee of his, but because he was an admirer of mine, one who obviously understood the immense value of my, alas, thus far grossly underrated literary accomplishments.

"Not to have done so would have been a grave omission in the education of a man of my station, my dear lady. And I insist that at a more opportune moment, you will tell me all that passed between you and the Great Dragon, all that minds smaller than ours would have been unable to grasp. Understand, my dear, that it is the same sort of small mind now imprisoning and threatening you over what was truly an insignificant mishap. So, come, let me take you away from all this," he said fervently, and taking me by one hand and the lantern by the other, walked out of the cell and into the guardroom.

He didn't have to ask me twice, and I followed him gratefully. A dismantled rifle and polishing rag lay in disarray upon the duty officer's desk. The kettle on the stove burbled for attention.

I grabbed a rifle from a rack near the door and Vasily Vladovitch, who had paused to hang the lantern on the hook above the desk, removed the gun from my hands and replaced it in the rack.

"Just because you are treated like a criminal, Miss Valentine, does not mean you need act like one. You will have no occasion to use a firearm. Come now, we have much to do and quickly."

He stuck his head outside and watched the courtyard for a few seconds before beckoning me out. "To your left, around the side of the building and behind the woodpile. Under the first tier of logs near the middle, you will find a pair of policeman's trousers, a uniform coat, and hat. Please to don these garments beneath your own."

"But I'll be seen—"

"It is arranged. Go."

Well, if he was going to be snippy about it—but then, he was the boss, and he was delivering me from circumstances from which I had little hope of delivering myself by legal means. I went. And halfway past the building, I went back again, cracking the door. "What about Purdy?" I asked. No answer. I opened it wider. Vasily Vladovitch was not there. He must have circled around the other side of the building. I could unlock Purdy's cell, too—but the keys were not on the hook. Vasily Vladovitch must have them. Purdy would have to wait. I scuttled around the building once more, along a well-worn path, and out to the woodpile.

Vasily Vladovitch had obviously allowed his regard for my work to magnify my stature in his eyes in more ways than one. Purdy had done his punitive task well. The mountie's woodpile, covering a house-sized plot of ground, towered to the roof of the guardroom. How the devil was I supposed to *reach* the second tier of logs, especially toward the middle, where they were pyramided even higher than on the rest of the pile? Why couldn't he have put it toward the end? There, some of the logs had rolled free of the pile. I hefted one of these back to the center and stood it on its end, like one of Lomax's stools. Climbing up on it, using the pile to balance myself, I spotted the little scrap of yellow stripe against the logs. I grabbed for it. As the clothing came free, so did the top logs, rumbling over their fellows and sending them flying. The dogs howled with alarm as the whole woodpile threatened to scatter from the river to the hills beneath which the city huddled. I cringed in the shadows, waiting, my hands over my ears to shut out the rumbling and the howling. Abruptly, the howling ceased. I tugged on the hard-won uniform garments and fluffed my skirt out over the britches. My jacket wouldn't fit over the uniform blouse, however, so I draped the flimsier garment over the shoulders of the mountie coat.

"You are ready?" Vasily Vladovitch hissed from the other side of the woodpile.

"I think so," I hissed back.

"Then come, before this oaf freezes to death and you have to your discredit the death of another policeman."

I rounded the pile to see Vasily Vladovitch standing beside the guard, at whose feet several dogs lay apparently asleep.

"Good heavens, is he . . . ?"

"Do not concern yourself with the constable, Miss Valentine. If he could move, he would prevent you from the so desperate measures you are about to take. Please walk over that bank there, down to the river. No, no, not that way. Walk where you are in full view of the constable. I will supply him with the necessary interpretation of your tragic actions."

I had little alternative but to humor him. His voice murmured softly to the constable as I walked the two yards to the edge of the overhang dropping down to the skein of gravel fronting the Yukon. Beyond what seemed to be a drainage ditch separating the fort from the rest of the town, the beach was covered with tents, but here, within the immediate domain of the police, it was barren of all but police boats tied up along the shore.

"Now then," Vasily Vladovitch said from somewhere just behind me. I jumped forward a foot. Once more, his approach had been soundless.

"I know you can't knock or anything," I said, "but you might stomp a little to let a girl know she's got company."

"Take off your clothes," Vasily Vladovitch said.

"I beg your pardon?" Had I escaped from the hand of justice only to fall into the claws of perversion?

"Take off your clothing—your own clothing, that is. We must make it look as if you drowned."

"Why would I do that?"

"From despair, naturally. In the old country, it is a highly respected motive for drowning oneself."

"But won't that make it look like I'm guilty?" I asked. I asked while stripping off my jacket and skirt, however.

"It will make it look as if you are dead, which will mean that the mounties will believe that they no longer are under the obligation of apprehending you. In a city the size of Dawson, it is very difficult to hide secrets or persons. So we must resort to subterfuge."

"Subterfuge. Got it. Now what?" I asked, standing arrayed as a mountie except for my boots.

"Now, dear lady, you have removed your pitiful little pile

of garments and have plunged into the icy river, where you freeze almost before you drown. Your pathetic corpse is never located, but your garments and that little cross you wear at your neck, of which you must divest yourself along with other remnants of your past identity, bear silent testimony to your terminally desolate state of mind."

"Wait a minute," I said, "I take off my clothes and dive into a freezing river, committing a mortal sin while compounding it by renouncing my faith at the moment of my death, as evidenced by my ditching my crucifix? You must be joking. I'd have to be crazy to do that."

"And you would have to be a criminal, in their eyes at least, to have killed the constable. My dear Miss Valentine, surely you see that these rustic wardens of the peace are at a loss to understand the sensibilities of a woman of your complex and sophisticated nature. Now, please, the crucifix. Oh, and I almost forgot, your shoes."

"My *what*?"

"I see no reason you would take off your other clothing before immersing yourself while leaving on your shoes, do you?"

"None except that it's blessed cold to run around barefoot out here."

For the first time he looked abashed. "Yes, I made an error. I forgot that you would need boots and, anyway, the officers do not keep spares of those." And with unparalleled chivalry, he removed his own boots and tossed them to me. "Here. I have a rather neat foot, so perhaps you will not be too uncomfortable. Now then, attend me well. You must pretend to be an officer on patrol. Walk along this beach until you reach the hospital at the upper end of the city. There you will turn up toward the hills until you see set against them a large building made of logs. This is my home. Await me there. I will rejoin you soon. Later, we can find a way to return the uniform. Be swift. I must release the guard to report the terrible tragedy he has been so helpless to prevent."

I looked back up the hill. The constable still stood motionless, staring over our heads at the river. The overhang hid us from his view, but his eyes did not seem to see anything anyway.

"Mesmerism?" I whispered to my conspirator.

"Something like that," he agreed. "Now, if you don't mind, it is my feet that are cold. Please, go."

I tucked my hair under the winter uniform cap, straightened my jacket, and trudged off, each step sounding like a cannon shot to me. To my chagrin, Vasily Vladovitch's "neat foot" was quite a bit neater than mine and his boots pinched uncomfortably.

Although the hour was quite late, Dawson City remained awake. Lights burned brightly in the saloons along Front Street and from within issued the tinkle of ragtime piano. Miner's gumboots clomped along the boardwalk, which kept the patrons of these superior solid-walled establishments out of the mud. From the tented encampment, conversations, laughter, and quarrels mingled with the familiar plash of the river. The smell was a less colorful and more pungent mixture of unwashed bodies denied the amenity of outhouses and woodsmoke.

Twice men looked out of their tents and wished me a "good evening, Constable," and one asked me if I had heard anything of the supply ships that were supposed to be arriving at any moment. I kept my head lowered and shook it gravely, as if the weight of my official duties was particularly heavy that evening.

The distance from Fort Herchmer, past Princess, Queen, and King streets, which rapidly degenerated into unnamed, tent-strewn, brush-filled semiswampland, seemed interminable. By the time I reached St. Mary's Hospital, three fine log buildings set around a church with its religious symbols, as advertised, prominently displayed, my poor feet felt in need of its healing services. Only my desire to remain at liberty kept me moving, for I was sure I was now suffering from compound blisters, total exhaustion, migraine headaches, and possibly the vapors.

I'm sure that in the time it took me to complete the walk, Sherlock Holmes would have decided how Vasily Vladovitch controlled the dogs and the constable, how he moved so silently, and how he unlocked doors without the apparent benefit of keys. Unfortunately, unlike Sir Arthur's fictional powerhouse of intellectual vigor, I am a real-life, frail, flesh-and-blood creature. I become quite cranky when uncomfortable. When my feet are aching, I can do nothing at all with my head. I was much less interested in my savior's facility with locks, by the time I reached his dwelling, than I was gratified that he had dispensed with locking his own door.

As soon as I stepped into the house, warmth surrounded me, oozing gently from the ornamented iron stove that was the centerpiece of the parlor. Unlike Lomax's rugged cabin, Vasily Vladovitch's contained real furniture—a cherry dining table covered with a damask cloth and claw-footed chairs upholstered in rather dusty red velvet, all sitting on an amber oriental carpet with a wine and lapis border. From a silver candelabra on the table, seven glowing candles shone like pearls. Scattered and stacked over the floors and across the huge cushion-strewn dogsled along one wall were enough sumptuous furs to depopulate the forests between Skagway and Lake Laberge. Deep, silky, and rich as frosting on a birthday cake, they drew me irresistibly into them. First I sat on them, removing the painful boots and tossing the blasted things toward the door. Then I wiggled my toes in them, savoring the voluptuous warmth and softness. And finally, without bothering to drag myself to the divan, I fell asleep on them, my cheek stroked by the luxuriance, my nose tickled by the feathery strands, my slumber blissfully dreamless.

# CHAPTER IX

❖◦◦◦◦•━◁━◈▐▐◈▷━•◦◦◦◦❖

*WHEN I AWOKE,* the room was cold, colder than the outdoors had been, it seemed to me. I wrapped myself in a fur, but even that didn't help. I used the edge of the table to pull myself awkwardly to my feet, for my muscles were stiff and one leg had gone to sleep. The cloth slipped and the candelabra slid toward me. The candles were only an inch or so shorter than they had been when I arrived, so I could not have slept too long. I padded over to the stove. The kindling was in a carved wooden cradle pretty enough for an upper-class baby. When I opened the firebox, however, flames crackled up at me from a healthy supply of logs. I shivered again, even as I closed the stove. Either I had been suddenly stricken with illness or there was a draft from somewhere. Perhaps some of the chinking had fallen from between the logs.

Hoisting the candelabra, I walked toward the walls. The logs on three walls were stripped of bark and polished to a golden sheen. They fit together beautifully. In the few places where they were packed with strips of moss and fur, the packing was tight. The fourth wall was covered with red brocade, over which was a large white bearskin. As I lifted the candles higher, further evidence of Vasily Vladovitch's depredations on the animal kingdom became apparent. The walls were decked with a caribou rack, the skins and heads of bears of all colors, lynx, fox, beaver, an ugly creature with beautiful fur I did not recognize but later learned was a wolverine, and on a small shelf in a gold capped jar, a collection of extremely large dead mosquitos.

As I stared at this last whimsical trophy, the candles guttered to cowering blue sparks at the base of the wicks. The cold draft got colder, carrying on it a faint fragrance of whiskey and smoke. I looked up. One of the moose faces had grown whiter, the snout shorter, the eyes sadder.

"Sweet Jesus, Papa, but you look strange with antlers," I whispered.

The stove roared suddenly, as if devouring a new log, although the room felt no warmer. The hiss and crackle of the fire, however, provided the raw sound material for a voice, at first full of short vowel sounds and a lot of hissing s's, but a voice all the same, shaping distinct words. "Sscat! Get out! Sscram—"

I set the candelabra back on the table and faced the spectre. I supposed I should have been relieved that this time my paternal parent was not inhabiting someone I could be accused of murdering. Still, his melodramatic entrances, no longer novel, were beginning to annoy me. After what I had been through, I was in no mood for ghostly warnings, and I found the incendiary speech defects irritatingly melodramatic.

"For pity's sake, Papa, will you quit the macabre monosyllables? I am half-frozen and totally exhausted. If you've something to tell me, come out with it. Telling me to scat from the only refuge I have, since thanks to the schemes of *your* mistress I am now a wanted woman, is not helpful. I have been scatting all night, as I'm sure you must have observed from whatever other world you inhabit. Surely even you can see that scatting any further is highly impractical under the circumstances. If you insist on haunting me, please try not to make such a hash of it. Proper ghosts are supposed to tell the living how to put them to rest. If you can't do that, I'd appreciate it if you'd just fade back where you came from and put *me* to rest."

"Nag, nag, nag." The fire snapped and Papa grinned a moosewide grin. Then the fire developed a wail, and Papa's voice grew almost recognizable. "Pelly, my girl, for shame, to be blamin' your troubles on a poor dead man such as I am, and me goin' to all this trouble to warn you. Ah, it's sharper than a serpent's tooth, this havin' of an ungrateful child—"

"All very well for you or whoever said it originally to say,

Papa, but I am in a terrible jam," I told him, and had to pause to wipe moisture from my face.

As cold as I felt, I was soaking with perspiration. Papa's image swam before me. My head throbbed and my feet burned, and here I stood arguing with my dead father, who was no doubt of even less use in spectral form than he had been in life. I unsuccessfully tried to stifle a sob of frustration.

"Ah, that you are, daughter, and you don't know the half of it. But there now, you mustn't take on so. Where's the old Harper fighting spirit? You got most of it, y'know. I never had much after your mother died. I see that now, death bein' the sadly soberin' experience that it is."

"But, Papa, I can't fight the entire Royal Canadian Northwest Mounted Police Force," I protested. "I can't even prove my innocence by telling the truth because I honestly am not sure what the truth is."

"Ah, now that's an easy one, me girl. What the truth is, is highly relative, is what it is. You just decide how it's to be with you, you see. Make up your story and stick to it, and if anything or anyone tries to tell you differently, you just make it go away."

"How?"

"Drown it out is what I did."

"I tried that, with Constable Faversham. That's what got me into such a pickle."

"Not at all, Pelly darlin'. What got you into trouble was the same thing as did me in. Ah, the blood suckin' bastard would never have taken me if that killjoy stepmother of yours hadn't shorted me so that I could not afford the extra fortifyin' pint necessary to keep me in fine fightin' shape as Hard-Hittin' Harper, terror of the dockside ring, as I once was called. I tell you, he never would have taken me, never, never never never—"

His image dribbled away as his chanting grew louder.

"Don't carry on so, Papa. Look how draining it is—"

But the chanting grew louder, deepening to a drumming chug that shook the floor. The door flew open, and I twisted to stare dazedly at a stocking-footed, opera-caped Vasily Vladovitch.

"Never mind Papa," I told him. "He's just an hallucination. Has to be. He never talked to me at such length while he was living. No reason to think he would now that he's dead. That's just a moosehead, really."

My host stared at me as if I was insane, then began kicking

hides and rugs away from the stove, which glowed cherry red. Grabbing a poker, he pulled open the firebox door. Flames belched halfway to the ceiling.

"The water bucket!" he cried, and pointed. I picked it up and threw the contents into the fire, which blossomed into a wide explosive ball before wilting back within the confines of the stove.

Bledinoff rammed the door back into place, but the stove still resembled an oversized tomato with a freight train rumbling inside its skin.

He grabbed the bucket from me and dashed outside. I dashed after in time to see him scooping up snow.

"Go back in the cabin," he said, surprisingly calm now. "There is another bucket in the kitchen. I will climb upon the roof and throw this down the chimney. You throw the other bucket of water onto the stove."

As I raced toward the kitchen doorway, I heard a faint slither and scrabble on the roof. The freight train thundered within the red-hot metal. I found the other water bucket and ran back to the parlor, snatching open the door with a hand full of jacket inadequate to prevent me from getting a good singeing.

Flame, steam, and soot hiccoughed with a giant whooshing whoop down the chimney, which crumbled into firey sections on the floor. I poured half of my water into the stove and the other half on the still-burning pipe charring the floorboards.

Suffocating black smoke filled the air. Coughing, I fanned it away from me. From within the stove, the choked flames sizzled themselves to death, hissing "crosssss" and then "crussss-cifixsss" as it died.

Vasily Vladovitch, looking as if he was ready to put on a one-man minstrel show, kicked the door shut behind him and set down the bucket.

"I'm so sorry about your house," I stammered. "I—I hope the furs can be cleaned and the stove, once it cools off, shouldn't be too hard to repair—"

"My very dear Miss Lovelace." Bledinoff clasped my hand in his, his voice throbbing with some intense, unidentifiable emotion. His hands felt cold enough that I feared he had been frostbitten. "Do not apologize. By no *means* must you apologize. If only you knew how thrilling it is to meet once more such a firey woman."

"But the fire wasn't deliberate." He looked as if he did not believe me, and furthermore did not want to. "It was an accident. Although actually—" honesty compelled me to admit with a sidelong glance at the moosehead, "I suppose it might have been Papa."

Vasily Vladovitch had lost interest in pyromaniac supernaturals by that time. He had me backed against the wall right under the caribou rack. His lids drooped heavily over his magnetic brown eyes as they fastened on my person somewhere south of my chin and north-northeast of the high brass-studded collar of the policeman's uniform blouse. His hand cupped my cheek in an extremely familiar fashion, slipping over my ear and down, until his fingers fished inside the collar.

Now, I do not customarily permit liberties to be taken. However, in this case I found myself at a loss. His movements were not threatening, but seductive, as if he himself were now mesmerized. Perhaps he thought I was, too, although actually I was trying to think of what I might say to dissuade him. He had just helped me out of a terrible predicament, he was my employer, and I had been responsible for the ruin of his stove. Furthermore, he was an erudite man of highly sophisticated literary taste, not to be dismissed like some crude ruffian. Then his fingers moved deftly over the top brass buttons and I knew I had better say something, and fast.

"Oh, yes," I said, scooting sideways. "The uniform, of course. You'll want to return it to the fort before its owner discovers it missing. Have you something else I could wear? I hate to impose on you, but old overalls and a mack perhaps, until I can find something suitable?" He edged closer to me as I fiddled with the buttons myself. My little cross fell forward, its delicate chain tangling around the button.

He took a step backward and regarded me reproachfully. "I believe I told you to throw that in the river."

"So you did, but I decided against it," I said. "It is all I have left of my mother's. Besides, I'll want it if they catch me again and somehow I—uh—fail to clear myself." I shivered both at the idea and because the room was rapidly growing truly cold, now that the fire was out and the stove pipe was little more than a large straw for the room to suck in freezing air.

He took my hand in his again. "Please, my dear, do not fear. No matter what happens. *You* will not be permitted to die. I give you my solemn promise on this."

"It is so good of you to believe me," I said, shifting away from him again, pacing for warmth. "But I haven't told you my theory yet—about the Deadly Miasma responsible for the sudden, fatal, and apparently, from the expression on the face of the victims, highly euphoric disease that seems to be at large."

"Why, I know all about that, my dear lady. Believe me, the symptoms are extremely familiar to me. It is a common disorder where I come from. It wreaked great havoc in the Old Country. Let me deal with the policemen. You must not worry yourself. You have higher things to contemplate. You must rest and regain your strength. Poor dear," he breathed, closing on me again. "You are so tired, so cold. Your veins pound blue there, beneath that creamy pallor of yours—"

"Whose creamy pallor is it now, Vasily Vladovitch?" a familiar voice demanded silkily from the doorway. "Can you not contain yourself for even one night?"

Bledinoff whirled around so fast that his opera cape tickled my nose. "Sasha, my darling girl! You are well! You have found me!"

Sasha, wearing the wolfskin parka like a fine mink, slinked slowly over to Bledinoff. Putting a hand on either side of his head, she shook his face gently. "Ah, yes, and now that I have found you, my beloved Vasily Vladovitch, what am I to do with you, eh? You'll frighten poor Vahlenteena carrying on like that, you know. She's not used to our kind—show people, I mean. My God, it's freezing in here! Vasily Vladovitch, have you forgotten that those of us with warm blood in our veins have need of proper heating?"

"A little accident, my darling—" he said, and explained all that had passed between us.

"I hadn't expected you to be well so soon, Sasha," I said. "I'm delighted to see you hale and hearty."

"Likewise, Vahlenteena. More than you can possibly imagine. The police were very kind to me, but as soon as I ate those moose steaks you so thoughtfully had delivered to me, Vasily Vladovitch, I felt much better. When the constable came to the ward to look for you, Vahl, I thought I had better come looking for you myself. I asked the first questionable-looking woman I saw on the streets where was the home of Vasily Vladovitch Bledinoff and, of course, she was able to show me the way immediately. Vahlenteena, that policeman's uniform is not very becoming, dahling. Have you nothing more fashionable for her, Vasily Vladovitch? We shall have to hide her, and I have no doubt that the mounties will notice if they suddenly have a new recruit. In fact, whomever those clothes belong to may already have noticed the sudden poverty of his wardrobe."

"I was thinking to hide her on my claim," he said. "The Metklas will guard her there—"

"No," Sasha said very quickly. "No, that is not a good idea. In an isolated place a strange person, particularly a woman, will be noticeable. We must conceal her by not concealing her, if you see what I mean, by placing her where she would be expected—"

"Yes, yes, of course," I said. "You're referring to the sort of clever ruse used by Mr. Poe in *The Purloined Letter*. However, if you intend that I should return to jail with the other felons, forget it."

"You silly girl. I do not imply that you belong with felons, but with other women. I think that you must come to work with us at the Rich Vein. Where are the police less likely to look for a missing woman than onstage at the opera house?"

So, while the mounties spent that cold September Sunday searching the river for my poor drowned body, I was busy being reincarnated in time for the Monday evening grand opening of the Rich Vein. I would be presented to the public as one of the troupe of girls who had arrived two days ago on a steamer from Alaska, along with the upright piano and a few of the saloon's finer last-minute fixings.

Although Sasha Devine and Vasily Vladovitch concurred almost at once on the wisdom of the plan, I had my doubts. I didn't see why I couldn't continue in men's garb and pose as a miner, surely a more thorough disguise. I could cut my hair and alter my silhouette with appropriate binding, and perhaps add a false beard and mustache made from my own hair. When I suggested this alternative scheme, however, I was roundly and thoroughly pooh-poohed.

"You have no understanding, dear lady, of what life is like here in Dawson. Such a deception would be impossible!" Vasily Vladovitch said sternly as he, Sasha, and I slipped down Second Street, past the tents and log cribs of Paradise Alley, and up to the back door of the newly constructed Rich Vein.

I was swathed from head to foot in Vasily Vladovitch's opera cape, and rather resembled a monk on his way to vespers, another role for which I felt much more suited than that of femme fatale.

Vasily Vladovitch slid the door open and beckoned us inside, where he lit a stubby candle that cast a pool of light no larger than my head. The smell of the place was of new raw wood, polish, and wallpaper paste. All of the windows faced Front Street, and the backstage area was, to use a metaphor appropriate to the premises, black as the ace of spades.

The darkness bothered Vasily Vladovitch not at all. He threaded his way through the rows of chairs, lined up neat as crosses in a military graveyard, past the cat's eye gleam of the bar, and up a set of carpet-cushioned stairs. Behind us, empty theatre boxes stared blankly at an empty stage. He let us through another door, then shielded the candle as he passed us into the little room beyond. He pulled a cord, and the slice of starlight that had striped the floor vanished.

He lit a lamp. Red velvet, gold brocade, and lace trim danced just at the fringe of the halo. "There," he said. "Everything that is not here in this room, makeup, dyes, creams, costumes, you will probably find in the trunks backstage."

"But, Vasily Vladovitch, this is ridiculous! I will run off your business! I'll make a much better gold miner than an opera star."

"Out of the question. Remember, please, that in assisting in your escape, I have become your accomplice, as well as your employer. I have some responsibility for you. My dearest Miss Lovelace, you are a sensitive, scholarly woman with—excuse me —a constitution that does not lend itself to athletic activities. As a man you would be asked to haul wood, to build cabins—"

"Women on the western plains also do those things," I said loftily.

"To thaw frozen ground, to dig mine shafts."

"I suppose I'd be as good at it as any transplanted male bank clerk."

Sasha, seated in her overstuffed velvet upholstered chair with the lace antimacassars at head and wrist rests, smiled indulgently at us both and said, "Nonsense, Vasily Vladovitch, a clever girl like Vahlenteena can, of course, overcome such things. But I think she will have difficulty with those pissing contests of which you so amusingly wrote to me. Do tell her about those, Vasily Vladovitch. About how every man must stake his claim in the same way as a wolf—so primitive, so natural a custom—I found it quite thrilling, but for Vahlenteena, well, it might prove difficult—"

"Sasha Devine, if you think that a line of blarney like that is going to take me in, you're mistaken," I informed her, plopping myself firmly on the straight-backed visitor's chair. "However, I suppose if you believe in this scheme of yours desperately enough to tell such a whopper, I should go along with it for a while, at least. But I warn you I do not intend to remain cooped up in this building. I must investigate this menace that seems to have followed us down the river, and if at all possible discover its source and find a way to clear my own name with the mounted police. Failing that," I added wearily, "I'd very much appreciate being smuggled into Alaska and back down to the states again. This is not exactly turning out as we'd planned, is it?"

"Nonsense," Sasha said. "You'll do marvelously, dahling. What better place to learn secrets than a saloon? You will have a story unlike that of any other journalist. The true tale of what it is like to be an entertainer in these arctic goldfields, to comfort and succor the weary miner. Perhaps we could have you dance the dance of the seven veils," she said, playfully fluttering her fingers under her eyes. "That's good concealment for you— well, most of the time anyway—and will certainly make the boys want to talk to you."

"I have someone for that specifically, my darling," Vasily Vladovitch said regretfully. "Manhattan Maisie and her Vanishing Veils. A class act. However, the flamenco dancer drank from the Yukon and had to be sent back to Spain to recover. Perhaps Miss Lovelace could take her part. She so eloquently described the dancing of the Mexican ladies of Texas in her book, I am sure she could emulate them. She could wear a lace mantilla and a shawl and carry a fan in front of her face much of the time. We could say she came straight from Barcelona and speaks little English. I think," he said with a conspiratorial smile at me that stirred a vaguely uncomfortable recollection, "her Spanish vocabulary will suffice for the role."

Sasha concurred. I watched helplessly as the two of them gathered costume materials and argued over makeup, hair dye, and other details. Sasha Devine won every dispute. Finally, Vasily Vladovitch departed to fix his stove, he said, with a sulky glance at me, and to sleep. But I was not allowed a moment's rest until my pompadour was pulled down, cut in front into little curls around my face, and all my hair was dyed to dead blackness. My rather bushy brows were plucked into a totally different shape, too. The injudicious application of a great deal of makeup provided my exhaustion-reddened eyes with a smoldering appearance and my lips with a carmined luxuriance at odds with nature's plan and society's sanction.

Even without the costume, my overall appearance was, with those small changes, as far from the wan and studious demeanor of a renowned woman of letters as cabbage roses are from regular cabbages. I had to admit, gazing into Sasha's mirror, that in such garb even Papa's ghost would have to look twice to recognize me.

I held the spangled costume to my chest, piled my wet black hair atop my head, and skewered it with a tall tortoiseshell comb. Sasha's reflection winked at me in the mirror, and mine, to my surprise, winked wickedly back, a brilliant scarlet grin spreading across what was formerly my face. Exit Valentine Lovelace née Pelagia Harper. Enter Corazon, the Belle of Barcelone.

# CHAPTER X

*MUCH MORE WORK* was necessary to make me a star before the following night, however. The costume, a constraining creation of crimson satin with black lace sleeves and flounces, had to be let out enough for me to move, as well as breathe. We found a pair of high-heeled dancing shoes that fit me, but overall I felt I was in less danger from the mounties than I was from breaking my neck as I tried to prance around without looking at my feet. I could avoid catching my heel in my hem only by carrying the bottom ruffle up over my head like wings while I stomped in what I sincerely hoped was a passably Hispanic fashion.

I had even less confidence in my ability to charm the customers than I did in my dancing, but Sasha Devine shrugged off my fears.

"To be the fascinating woman is very easy, and very profitable, though at times very very boring," she told me. "Observe me. I simply tilt my head a bit to this side, widen my eyes, and appear to be listening to whatever is said to me, nodding now and then or saying umm hmm or making a delightful face if my customer says something he seems to wish me to find disagreeable. The most important thing to remember is to do your act onstage. When you are offstage, keep your mouth shut and let the customer do his act. *Si, senor* should see you through most situations."

I tilted my head a bit to the side, widened my eyes, nodded, attempted to curtsy my thanks as I said, "Si, senor," and fell off my shoes.

Sasha Devine sighed. "Ah well, great courtesans are not made in an afternoon. And, fortunately, our audience is not composed of dance critics."

Despite the banter and foolishness, we were both exhausted. She was still peaked looking and seemed troubled, besides. We had come such a long way from the times when Papa walked through town with one of us on each arm while gentlemen stared, the ladies stuck up their noses, and I silently cheered each outlandish thing Sasha said and did. I had no doubt outraged every known saint by praying to become just like her. Rather belatedly, it seemed, my prayers were going to be answered. I reached over and took her hand.

"I'll try not to be too bad," I said. "We're great hams, we Harpers. If I don't make it as a romantic dancer, perhaps I'll be a hit as a comedienne."

She patted my hand.

"Sasha?"

"Yes?"

"What happened to you back there on the river? Where were you? Where did the parka come from? What made you so ill?"

"Poor dahling, were you worried about me? It was nothing, really, to cause such a fuss. As Vasily Vladovitch probably explained, the Indians heard the mountie was coming and decided to move poor Mr. Lawson. You were fast asleep, but I was curious to see their camp and went with them. They lent me the wolf coat, and when we reached their camp I dined with them. They fed me a great delicacy, they said, but I'm afraid it did not set delicately on my stomach."

I was beginning to realize that when she explained so much so readily, she was, at least partially, exercising a penchant for creative invention that was the equal of my own. She tried to bat her eyelashes, but they stuck shut on the second bat. She yawned widely.

I tugged the costume off over my head.

"Vahlenteena?"

"Mmph?"

"That little cross you wear? That is a very good touch, you

know, for a flamenco dancer. Make it your trademark. Never take it off, no matter what anyone says."

I pulled the dress all the way off. She already lay fast asleep, curled up on the velvet-covered bed.

It looked like a wonderful idea, but the room was icy and there was only one bed. I decked myself out in a wrapper and the wolfskin parka and braved the cavernous theatre once more. The corridor was even colder than Sasha's room. I trotted down the stairs to the big stove and stuffed in a handful of freshly inked playbills stacked on one of the chairs. Over these I arranged a teepee of kindling, and a log. Then I searched the shadowy bar for matches. Columns of light striped the ground floor of the theatre and cast mini spotlights on the stage. When my kindling ignited and I was quite sure there was nothing that sounded remotely like a train inside *this* stove, I wandered up to the stage. I wanted to remain close to the stove until I was quite sure a controlled, steady warmth rather than a raging conflagration would ensue from my efforts.

The stage occupied about half the width of the room, the remainder being taken up with wings in which to wait. Currently the backstage area also held props, scenery, and unopened cases of liquor. The door through which we had entered the previous night was the backstage door. As long as I had to wait for the fire, I tried blocking out my dance in relation to the space—I could make a lot of noise with my feet but would need mainly to try appearing impressive by executing dramatic turns, throwing my arms over my head and bending over backward. Maybe a rose in my teeth? It would have to be a silk rose here in Dawson at this time of year.

The core of the room was just beginning to thaw when the back door rattled with the thump of a heavy fist.

"Open up in there!" a masculine voice demanded.

Unaccustomed as I was to being a fugitive from justice, I complied without giving the matter much thought. The fact that I had had very little sleep in the last sixty hours probably had something to do with it, too.

A policeman glowered in at me. "What's that smoke for?" he demanded. I scurried back behind the theatre curtain, covering my face to the eyes, shy Spanish maiden that I was.

Now was as good a time as any to get into character. "Por favor, senor," I said, "eeet ees mucho cold." And I shivered graphically until I feared to bring the theatre curtain down around my ears.

"What are you doing in here? This place is closed on the sabbath."

"I—no sabe, senor."

He glowered more deeply and set a booted foot inside the door. I wondered how I was to get out of this one without becoming a lot more eloquent in English than I was properly supposed to be. Sasha Devine, dead to the world, was not an available resource.

"Yoo hoo! Officer, honey, is that Miss Devine you're addressing, by any chance?" A mop of bronze curls appeared to the left of the mountie's elbow and a dark-eyed face bobbed above and below the man's arm in an attempt to see beyond it.

"And who's wanting to know?" the policeman said, turning on this new and seemingly worthier target for his official inquiries.

"Grace Margaret Mary Adanopolis." She beamed up at him, a dimple showing on either side. "Are you one of those handsome mounted policemen I've been hearing about? You know, when Mr. Bledinoff's agent contacted me about coming up to the Klondike, I said to my mama, I said, 'Why, Mama, I'd be scared to death to go way up there with all those gun-toting miners and bears and outlaws and such.' But she said to me, 'Maisie, honey,' she said, 'look here, you'll be safer out there in the Klondike than you will be back home in Manhattan. Why, those mounties won't let any bears even say so much as a naughty word in front of you much less take a bite out of you. Those boys are *good*,' she said. 'They always get their *man*,' she said. Now tell me, officer, is that so? Because now that I see you I understand what she means and I do so hope you don't restrict yourself to getting *men*—"

The policeman was a strong person and did not exactly give in to this spate of effusiveness, but Maisie had visibly softened him up some. "Well, you see, miss, in order to keep the law and order here your mother told you about, we have very strict laws about closing on the sabbath. Gun control, too. Oh, yes, no handguns allowed."

"I'm not armed, officer," she said. "But you can search me."

"I doubt that's necessary. I was just making certain this establishment is obeying the Sunday closing laws. This lady here doesn't seem to speak English very well."

"Oh, then that can't be Miss Devine. She's to be manager. I wasn't coming to see her on business, of course, just to say

hello and introduce myself—a social call, you know. Hi, honey."
She wiggled her fingers at me, and I wiggled mine back. "I'm
Maisie. Who are you?" She pointed to herself when she said
her name and to me when she asked mine.

"Corazon," I said.

"Hi, Cory." She pointed to him.

"Tim O'Bannon," he said. "Constable," he remembered belatedly.

"Hi, Tim. Cory, is Miss Devine around?"

I rested my head on my steepled hands and closed my eyes.

"Oh, she's still asleep, huh? Yeah, I'd be doin' that, too, but
I'm too excited about the opening tomorrow night. Wait till
you hear—well, no, I won't say. That'd be too much like working. I think, if you don't mind my saying so, Constable Tim,
honey, it's okay. I mean, if Miss Devine is sleeping, nobody's
working around here, are they? She has a room upstairs. Most
of us girls are staying over at the Miner's Rest for now, but
there's swell rooms for Miss Devine and Mr. Bledinoff and
some of the imported acts, like maybe Cory here. And it *is* cold!
Maybe we shouldn't stand here in the door and let the heat
out, huh? So tell me, Tim, how long have you been stationed
in Dawson City?" she asked as the door closed behind them.

I poked three more logs onto the fire and closed the door.
As I straightened, elongated silhouettes danced across the light
columns on the floor. One of them stopped and turned full
face, staring in the window. I stepped into the shadow and
peered back, but he straightened and strolled on. Still, there
was something familiar about the way he carried himself, the
way his hat tilted across his head. I had seen the man before,
and the associations were not pleasant ones. It seemed a good
note on which to acquire some much needed rest before Monday officially began and the other girls would be arriving for
instructions, introductions, and rehearsals.

I woke up twisting in the soaking covers of the bed in Vasily
Vladovitch's room, my hair dankly plastered to my neck. I'd
been dreaming of Texas and the desert and swarms of dragons
with golden teeth all smiling at me and breathing insufferably
hot sticky breath upon me. A barrel stove can generate an
impressive amount of heat, especially in a second-story room.
Tropical flowers would have felt right at home there over Dawson City's Front Street in the beginning of winter.

Downstairs bloomed exotic blossoms of another sort, their

mingled perfumes enough to gag a whole hive of bees, their questions, demands, exclamations, and jokes vying cacophonously with each other.

I was still twirling spit curls and tugging at the costume as I stumbled down the stairs to join them around the stage.

Vasily Vladovitch was in his glory, his cape fluttering behind him as he swooped down on hand after hand, murmuring greetings and compliments. Sasha, a little apart from the group, slouched on one elbow against the stage and yawned, patting her mouth with much the same gesture as she might use to powder her nose.

"Hi, there, sweetie!" Familiar curls and dimples and wiggling fingers distinguished their owner from the rest of the flouncing bustles and bosoms. "It's me, Maisie!"

I swung wide of the rest and met her halfway. She had by the arm a pixie-faced girl who looked about twelve years old. "This is Cory, Nellie. Nellie the Kid," she said, pointing at the girl, who looked as if she was about to ask if she could have a cookie before she took a swig from a hip flask whose fumes threatened spontaneous combustion.

"Hi," Nellie said, wiping her mouth with the back of her hand before extending that same hand to be shaken.

"Uh—buenos dias—noches?" I said.

"And that other short girl over there with Mr. Bledinoff, that's Bon Ton Bunny. She plays the piano. Great gal. When I was seasick on the ship from Seattle, she single-handedly kept me from trying to jump off the ship and walk the rest of the way. The one beside her, slapping Mr. Bledinoff's wrist with the black feathered fan? That's Miss Millie the Alabama Fillie. I've heard"—her voice lowered a decibel—"that she is from a family in Mobile, Alabama, that had a big plantation and owned half the state before the war. Can you imagine?" I shook my head. "And that one," she indicated a languid red-lipped person chiefly remarkable for arrogant dark eyes and a cascade of black ringlets, "that is Gin-Mill Giselle. *She* is from New Orleans, Louisiana. Sort of dark and mysterious, don't you think? Millie and she don't get along. Millie calls her a two-bit voodoo queen, but she's always been perfectly nice to me, Giselle, I mean."

"Ladies, it has been such a pleasure to have the good judgment of my agents confirmed once again. Now permit me to introduce my own personal choice as manageress of my establishment and star of our show, as she has been of so many others, the incomparable Miss Sasha Devine."

"Attend me, ladies," Sasha commanded, regal enough to cow Queen Victoria. "We must now have quiet if we are to rehearse, yes? Maisie?"

"Yes, ma'am, Miss Devine!" Maisie cried, waving a lacy hanky as if anxious for parlay.

"You're going to start the lineup with your Vanishing Veils. At least for tonight. Then while you change for your second number, the chorus—that's you, Nellie, and Millie, Giselle, and Jeannine—will do the first cancan. Then Bunny leads the boys in uh—'The Beer Barrel Polka,' Bunny? Yes? No, so all right, in 'A Bicycle Built for Two,' before I do my solo. Nellie is on next singing 'Daddy Wouldn't Buy Me a Bow-Wow,' followed by Millie and Jeannine in the acrobatic duet, after which Jeannine performs the Stephen Foster medley. Then another cancan, Corazon's flamenco, and a cancan finale backing up my closing number. Got it? Now for the second show . . ."

I watched with growing horror as one after the other, the previously unrehearsed acts were performed with skill, exuberance, and sometimes even artistry. Although I'm sure the Widow Hig would have declared the performances shocking, I saw nothing in them excessively immodest. When Maisie's veils vanished, she still wore a costume of harem trousers, a very full skirt, a spangled bodice, and quantities of coined jewelry sufficient to provide armor for half a medieval cavalry squad. Admittedly, the fabric of her costume was rather sheer, but she was quite thoroughly covered. All of the girls were, another edict of the mounted police, as Maisie informed me. Miss Millie wore red ruffles, a sassy bow at her bustle, and long black satin gloves. She sported a jeweled topknot of black feathers and carried a black feather fan, with which she flirted as if it was an extra set of eyelashes. She and Jeannine performed splits, handstands, cartwheels, and handsprings while singing "Camp Town Races" and "Dixie" with extravagant sentiment breathed into each and every lyric. Jeannine with the Light Brown Hair, as she was professionally known, also imparted to Stephen Foster's romantic ballads a smoldering quality they did not usually possess when sung by someone without Jeannine's laughing heavy-lidded eyes and deep-throated gravelly alto.

The cancan exhausted me just watching it. All of those flipping flounces, high kicks, and quick turns left me slightly dizzy. Vasily Vladovitch watched with the same expression I had once seen on Papa's face when we covered a wine-tasting party.

Uncharacteristically intimidated into an acute case of stage fright, I pushed past the shimmering curtain of heat waves surrounding the big stove and bolted toward the front of the saloon. A white-haired man cursed regularly and imaginatively as he unpacked crates of bottles behind the bar. Outside the bay windows, feathery puffs of snow assaulted the building, tumbling through the velvety darkness. I pressed my face against the cold windowpane. The Yukon glided sluggishly beyond the tented beach, while tendrils of smoke from the miner's stoves threaded between the snowflakes. Down Front Street a dog fight was in progress. Heavy footsteps thudded on the wooden boardwalk. A competitor's piano tinkled nearby.

The dogfight restored my confidence. My colleagues might present formidable competition, but the cultural offerings of the rest of Dawson City were reassuringly meager.

I returned to the stage to do my bit to instill or reinforce a false sense of cultural superiority in anyone present who wasn't of Spanish or Mexican origin. The estimable Bunny, unfortunately, was incapable of shoring up my performance. She knew no songs even vaguely Spanish, and improvised by playing one of her regular numbers in a rather staccato style.

Vasily Vladovitch was kind. "It will be much better when the musicians arrive," he reassured me. "I hired a small orchestra, but they are still climbing the pass, I think. Meanwhile, you and Bunny must make do."

"I think I'd prefer the stockade," I said. "Or the river."

Sasha Devine laughed. "You'll improve. It isn't so easy, you see, being a fallen woman, but never mind, my dahling. That's why you're on next to last. By the time you get up there everyone will have had so much to drink that you'll look like Lillie Langtry to them."

Calamity Jane was the more likely comparison, but I didn't argue.

As it turned out, Sasha was correct, although she underestimated the intoxicating effects of opening night on one relatively unaccustomed to show business. When I actually stamped onstage among throngs of cheering miners who had been treating the whole evening as a combination of Christmas and the Fourth of July, *I* thought I was Lillie Langtry. And was received as such, which was more amazing. But so were we all well received, every one of us goddesses.

It was heady to be sought after, plied with champagne (which was actually ginger ale for us girls—house rules). Even though I quickly let it be known that I did not have "mucho eeengleesh, senor," the men talked to me as if I was an expert mining engineer and economic advisor on how vast quantities of soon-to-be-dug-up riches should be spent. I enjoyed this attention right up until the time when the excitement and the ginger ale necessitated a jaunt outside and two of the customers attempted to follow me to the privy. They were cheerfully deterred by Vasily Vladovitch, who popped up behind them.

"No, no, my friends, you must not leave yet! Come and have this round on me, to honor the opening of my new place. I will be deeply hurt, deeply, if you refuse." And though he looked comparatively foppish in his nuggets and diamonds and silken pinstripes, he virtually hefted one of his rugged customers under each arm and bore them both away. I pondered on my dash through the dark, as much as anyone ponders anything under such circumstances, on the depredations that addictive drinks could wreak upon the spirit. I meant the miners, at the time.

The excitement faded as smoke thickened. My previous elation was replaced by a dull ache in my head and burning coals in both shoes. I could have danced unshod, but the boots of our less terpsichorially gifted patrons soon would have crippled me. Too tall to dance with my feet on their toes, as Bunny and Nellie did, I suffered my iron-maidenish footwear. The dances were supposed to be long romantic waltzes but felt more like musical chairs—a brief measure of music, then back to the main bar to guzzle a drink and change partners. The object of the dancing was to encourage the drinking, of course.

The pinnacle of achievement for us sirens of the dance floor was to lure a customer upstairs to one of the theatre boxes, where for only twice the price he would pay if he bought champagne on the first floor, he could order it delivered to us in grand style. I was not fated to accomplish this exalted goal during my term of employment, but that first night Sasha, Millie, Bunny, and Giselle all had well-heeled clients pouring bubbly down on the heads of us commoners. Maisie held court at the bar, her customers buying her twice the drinks and avoiding climbing all those stairs.

I think it was not so much my possible lack of physical charm, which would have been difficult to discern through the flashy clothing and heavy layer of makeup, as my putative language barrier that kept me from excelling in my new career. I found, however, that such cross-cultural muteness made it easier for me to smile, nod, and watch whatever I liked while my customer croaked himself hoarse to make himself heard above the din.

The opulence of the establishment only seemed to make more poignant the worn-out, down-at-the-heels, down-in-the-mouth, and down-on-their-luck men comprising the majority of our clientele. These were the ones who had come to the Klondike hoping for riches, and at the Vein, among elegant surroundings inhabited by cheerful-looking women, they seemed to find at least some semblance of, if not what they had come looking for, what they might have left behind. Smoke pooled in a ghostly sea above the crystal chandelier dangling from the second floor ceiling. The genuine cherry wood bar swarmed with sloshing drinks, grimy hands, and worn elbows. Behind the bar, from waist high to ceiling level, green, brown, and clear bottles in hundreds of shapes stood row upon gleaming row, distorted images bobbling around the labels. From the more fortunate customers, enough nuggets and gold dust to mount the crown jewels of Europe and part of Asia changed hands.

But it seemed to me that the most important element in that room was the stove. Its warmth was essential to the sense of cozy security pervading the saloon, creating the relaxed atmosphere for drinking and gaming. It also allowed both staff and customers to shed four or five layers of garments in the interest of glamor on our part and comfort on theirs. Unfortunately, the grand concerted warmth bore with it an off-key undertone, enhancing as it did the gamey aroma of a multitude of seldom-washed bodies and the barely tanned hides of the winter gear that in many cases literally stood between those bodies and frostbite. Take it from me, it is self-defense rather than poor taste or a love of excess that moves ladies of the demi-monde to cloak themselves in strong perfume.

By two o'clock in the morning, the party had died down to the hard-core drinkers, and we dancing girls were expected to retire for our beauty sleep. Upstairs, Sasha Devine was cajoling a customer to please try to stand, while at the bar, Vasily Vladovitch had Gin-Mill Giselle cornered, or was it the other way around? Though I had not noticed Vasily Vladovitch taking so much as a single drink of water all night, he was far more expansive and careless in his manner than previously. As the others started to leave, he unwound himself from Giselle's boalike grip and hailed me.

"Well, dear lady, how have you enjoyed it, your masquerade? Ah, forgive me, I can see by your face that you are depleted. I regret that my stove remains in disrepair, so I cannot offer you the use of my home, and that I must, in consequence, abide here, making my in-residence apartment unavailable to you as well. The hotel, alas, is already full of your new colleagues. I do not think it wise that you dwell among them. I have always found that people reveal the most embarrassingly personal things in their sleep!" He smiled at me in a tipsy fashion and bundled me into Sasha's wolfskin parka, "Therefore, come. See the little surprise I have for you. I love to surprise people, don't you?"

Sasha leaned down over the edge of one of the boxes as we headed for the back door of the theatre. "Val—Vasily Vladovitch, will no one assist me with this elephantine lout?"

"Mr. Lane!" Bledinoff called, and jerked his head toward Sasha. Johnny Lane, the polar bearish bartender, pulled his hands out of a dishpan tinkling with saloon crystal, wiped his palms on his apron, and wearily rose to the occasion.

The snow had melted as it touched the ground. The sky had cleared and the night air crackled with crispness. As we cleared the corner of the building I stopped in puzzled amazement.

An arc of green light rippled through the sky over the far bank of the Yukon. "What's that?" I asked, thinking it reminded me of a halo of city lights, although, of course, darkened Dawson comprised the height of civilization for hundreds of miles in every direction.

"My dear lady," Vasily Vladovitch said formally, "I have the privilege of introducing you to the aurora borealis. Something to do with a form of electrical current, according to scientists, but my adopted people have a better explanation. They say that like the full moon the aurora possesses supernatural powers, magic that intensifies magic. Ah, look there! You see! They know you are admiring them and they display themselves shamelessly!"

The band pleated and expanded like a concertina, fanning into feathery chains tipped with violet, red, and pink. I stamped my feet, blew on my fingers, and watched, thinking that the aurora's magic power probably had something to do with fascinating onlookers with its shenanigans until its admirers froze to death. I muttered as much to Vasily Vladovitch, who pressed his hand against the back of my neck, stroking the left side of my jaw almost imperceptibly with his thumb. Though the gesture was undeniably exciting, it was also decidedly inappropriate familiarity considering my involuntary dependence on his good will. I hunched the parka up around my chin, gently crowding him out. "Well, after that fanfare, your surprise must be something spectacular," I said. "Lead on."

He laughed and shrugged and led me down Paradise Alley to one of the tiny cabins more accurately referred to as a crib.

"Your pied-a-terre in Dawson City, madam," he said. "You will note that unlike many of its half-canvas neighbors, it is made entirely of logs. And even such a crib, when occupied by a lady, can be a castle."

Apparently its previous occupant hadn't been sufficiently well connected to elevate my new home to the castle category. "Redhot Rosie" read the legend painted on the door. The place was so small that the little pot-bellied stove warmed it to a smothering temperature almost immediately. Kindling and fire logs were neatly stacked to one side of the stove, with a washstand, water basin, and jug comprising the plumbing facilities. The bed was little more than a cot, but a roll of familiar looking and slightly singed hides was piled in its middle. Two raw yellow boards with most of the splinters sanded off were nailed together beneath the single tiny window. An unlit cobwebbed lantern hanging overhead and an upended log completed my office suite, or so I thought, until my foot touched a tin pail. I peered down. "Slop bucket? Waste basket?" I asked.

He waxed imperious with impatience. "Do with the pail whatever you like. The important thing is the *candles* I have acquired for you."

"Oh, oh yes! The candles! Thank you! My goodness, what a lot of them there are! How very considerate," I said, recalling dimly hearing someone remark with a wistful glance at the Rich Vein's gleaming lamps and glowing candelabra chandeliers that he had tried to buy a single taper the other day and was asked to pay two dollars. Another customer, who said he was a newsman from Illinois, had anxiously inquired the whereabouts of the precious item. Lamp oil, he grumbled, was worth more than frankincense and myrrh at the time of Christ.

"Vasily Vladovitch, I really cannot accept this largess," I said firmly. I balked at becoming a dance hall queen *and* a kept woman, in however humble a fashion, in the same night. "It is too much."

"Oh, no. It is not so much. One hundred dollars a month, which you will easily be able to repay from your earnings. I felt that you, a woman of solitary intellectual pursuits, should have first chance at it. It is the least I can do. I will have a few other amenities sent down later this morning from my home —a kettle perhaps, and a china cup." He gazed meaningfully into my eyes, his pupils dilated wide in the dim light and glowing slightly, like a cat's, a little crossed due to our enforced proximity. He was so pleased with himself that his lips split into a funny smile, his upper teeth protruding in an incongruously rabbity fashion, until I noticed that some of the poor fellow's teeth were a bit oversized. He raised his hand to cup my cheek and beseechingly bent his head toward mine.

"Hey, in there, open up!" The door banged open, knocking us toward the bed, and a furry head intruded itself. "Who the devil are you?" he demanded. "Where the tarnation is Rosie? What the dickens is goin' on here?"

"As you see, Rosie no longer lives here," Vasily Vladovitch said, sitting up on the cot and crossing his legs, the very picture of savoir faire. "And I am sorry to say she left no forwarding address."

"Well, then, how long you gonna be?" he asked, with a wink at me.

"I—"

"Forgive the lady, but she speaks no English. She also does not sell the commodity you require. I suggest you check her next-door neighbors. Perhaps, if they are busy, they could provide you with a referral."

"Good idea, sport! Thanks a lot. And—uh—have fun," and he banged back out again.

"I think, if we are to maintain my reputation, which is going to be no mean feat in this neighborhood, perhaps I'd better thank you for your kindness and see you to the door," I suggested, but firmly.

"Yes, I suppose so," he said regretfully. "I merely wanted to see you comfortably settled. And, of course, if there is anything else . . ."

"Well, there is one other little thing," I said, suddenly guilt-stricken to have left it so long.

"Yes?"

"About Purdy? I hate to ask, you've been so kind, and put yourself in so much jeopardy already, but if you could please exert your influence on his behalf? He is a scoundrel in general, but innocent in this particular case."

"I'll see what I can do, but your friend has regrettably succeeded in irritating our uniformed protectors on his own merits, you know. A matter of an inspector's lady? Sometimes these things must take their course, but I guarantee, since you scruple against it, that the course will not take Mr. Purdy as far as the gallows."

"Good," I said. "Thank you and—good-night."

"Good-night, Valentine," he said, bending toward me again. "I may call you Valentine?"

"Not publicly, no," I said, staring at the bridge of his nose to avoid the intensity of his gaze. "I'm Corazon, the Belle of Barcelone, remember?"

"Oh, yes, of course, not publicly. But there will be other occasions—private occasions. We must discuss your work, you and I, particularly concerning the dragon."

He bent over me again, but by this time our former visitor had apparently found refuge, for an enthusiastic thumping, whooping, and screeching emanated from the dwelling to the right of mine.

"Very well, then, good-night," Vasily Vladovitch said. Scooping up Sasha's parka, he melted into the night, his black cloak winging behind him.

Aching and weary of limb though I was, I still felt too restless to sleep. Exploring my small domain, I mentally listed things I would need and those I already had. Candles to write by would do me no good without paper and pen. The hide blankets and the wood would keep me warm indoors, but there was still the problem of what to wear outdoors. I could use one of the hides as a shawl until I could obtain a parka. The lantern had no oil, the water buckets contained no water. If I was to maintain my disguise by use of makeup, I would need a mirror. Rosie must have taken hers with her. More alarming, she also took her chamber pot.

My thoughts turned to water, suddenly, and the need to make my preparations, however belated, for bed. Wrapping a hide around me, I waddled into the alley. While not exactly lively, it still bore more life than my old neighborhood in San Francisco at the same hour. In the cabin on my right, the thumping and laughter were finally dying down. And as I passed the tiny window of the crib to the left, the door cracked open, just a little, and light glinted off something shiny at eye level.

"Hello, there," I said sociably, for I thought the denizen of that hovel had muttered something at me, and I did not wish to get the reputation for being superior or stand-offish. Though some social barrier probably existed between stage entertainers and those who provided what Papa referred to (out of my hearing, as he thought) as "horizontal refreshment," I preferred to behave as if I were unaware of them. After all, I would need the assistance of my neighbors to fend off the advances of Rosie's disappointed suitors.

Behind Paradise Alley ran the set of ruts that formed Second Street. A mere stubble of habitation graced this thoroughfare. Beyond lay muskeg. No outhouses. Anywhere. I headed for the cover of the muskeg's sparse foliage. Dogs howled—or wolves—in the distance. Somewhere nearby, something panted. The aurora winked and wrinkled overhead. I watched it wonderingly as I completed my task and headed back to the cabin.

Maybe this whole Yukon adventure would work out after all. I wished Papa could see it—really see it, I thought, and felt such a throb in my upper torso as I might have felt had I swallowed an anchor. Ghostly apparitions weren't the same thing, somehow. I wanted to talk with him again without risking burning down the house around us. I missed him, but I did not especially want to join him.

I fetched one of the pails from the cabin with the intention of making a trip to the river for water. The back of my would-be guest from earlier in the evening was disappearing toward the tent encampment on the beach. Against the door of the right-hand cabin leaned a very ample lady, clad not-so-amply in a gauzy nightdress and a paisley shawl. Seeing me, she dimpled in a great many places and stuck out a set of well-manicured fingers.

"Hi there, kid, new in town? I'm the whore next door. Call me Lurleen. What's your handle?"

I almost spat it out before remembering my new persona. "No sabe, senorita," I said.

"Oh, don't give me that stuff, kid. See here?" She jerked her thumb indelicately at her roof. "Canvas. Real thin. I can tell you what's going on from Circle City to Whitehorse on a night like this. Saw you go into Rosie's with tall, dark, and devastating. I heard you two talking, so I know you're American as I am. So you don't have to say who you are, you know. I can ask around why a gal who speaks perfectly good English is pretendin' to be some little wetback but—"

"No, don't do that," I said. "It's—well, it's a cover story for an article I'm doing. And I'm having a little trouble sticking with it, so it would help me if you'd just call me Corazon, or Cory, as the girls at the Vein do. I'm dancing there to—um— to gather background on conditions here in Dawson for working girls."

"Great. Expecting a fire?"

"I beg your pardon."

"The bucket, kid. Why are you carryin' it around?"

"I was going after water. To the river."

"Where else? But look, you don't have to do that yourself. There's a kid comes around deliverin' every other afternoon. He's due tomorrow. Meanwhile, I got a little fresh left I can let you have. Professional courtesy, mind you. Thanks for sendin' that fella my way." She patted her ample bosom. "Got almost enough nuggets for my necklace now."

"If you think the—uh—others won't object, I'll just send all of Rosie's friends to you," I suggested. Unfamiliar as I was with the ethics of pimping, I was afraid of upsetting the social order of my street.

Lurleen assured me that she would pass along any business she was too overburdened to take to the other girls, thus providing them with more than they had to begin with, and they ought to be satisfied with that, hadn't they?

"Well, yes, but I noticed the person on the other side watching me," I said. "Won't she be offended?"

"Who? Stella the Stiff? No, ma'am. She only works when she has to. She got forced into this when she was a kid and never did take to it. Her specialty is fellas that want it just like they get it at home with the old lady—"

Some time later, supplied with fresh water, a budding case of chilblains, and a great deal of miscellaneous and unsolicited conversation, I retired to my own cabin, boiled some of the water in the extra bucket, and scrubbed myself down before retiring. Tomorrow I would don my hide again and take a portion of the tips I had earned to purchase writing materials, a mirror, and a chamber pot.

Carrying my candle to the bedside, I saw something flicker from beneath the hem of the quilt. A palm-sized shard of mirror was lodged between bed and wall. I picked it up and examined my face for residual traces of Corazon, and almost smithereened the mirror into smaller, even more useless fragments. Papa's bony hand, filmy white as a wedding veil, played at applying an invisible powder puff to the veiny bulb on the end of his nose, then fluffed the ghost of his thin hair into an imaginary coiffure. His toilet completed, the apparition glared at me.

"Well," I said, forgetting in my annoyance at this other-worldly tail-pulling my earlier longing for my departed parent, "you didn't quite burn down Mr. Bledinoff's house last time. Back for another try? Wouldn't it be simpler to tell me what these haunting histrionics are all about and have done with it?"

Not a word did he utter, by fire, wind, water, or other means, but the face in the mirror shivered into an expression of wounded innocence, then dissolved into a singularly unflattering reflection of my own countenance, which briefly bore an expression of simpering awe and credulity such as it has never been my misfortune to see imprinted upon my features.

I arose at noon the next day, splashed water on my face, and wrapped myself in the hide, a fold carefully concealing most of my face. In this improvised overcoat, I took my meager tips from the night before and went shopping. Although no notepads were available, there was a surplus of wallpaper rolls, which the owner of the little stall let me have, ten rolls for twenty-five cents.

"Ah, ladies," he remarked, sounding gruff but looking shy, an interesting phenomenon I had observed many times since beginning this journey into a land where feminine companionship was almost as scarce as flour. He delicately avoided touching my palm as he counted out my change, but joked gruffly at me instead. "Don't you girls love to dress things up though? Paperin' them old log walls just like you was in Philadelphee or somewheres."

"Ain't though," declared a fur-hatted mountain whose shovel-like hand cradled a single egg. "Herb Clauson got mauled to death by somethin' last night—mounties thought bear at first, but the Chinook say it was wolf or dog, most likely. Not that there's much difference between them. That don't happen much in Philadelphee."

A squarish man with a yellow complexion presided over a collection of items easily identifiable as a typical Klondike outfit. A piece of canvas stretched across it was unevenly lettered in charcoal "Wel trad fr meet or flower." The man spat. I did not turn away quite in time to avoid seeing threads of blood in the tobacco gobbet. "It ain't like anywhere civilized," he said sourly. "Nothin' has et so many young, healthy men since the war. Did you hear about that fellow stepped outside his tent this mornin' to take a leak and found that boy, couldn't a been more than nineteen years old, froze solid, so white you'd a took him for snow, and with a silly da—darned expression on his face, excuse me, ma'am, like he'd single-handed discovered the mother load?"

"Father Judge says it's somethin' in the water," my shop-keeper told him wisely.

The yellow-skinned man's laugh emerged as a painful wheeze superimposed on a grimace. "Not too likely. Didn't look like he'd been drinkin' water. Had two empty bottles of cheap whiskey beside him. They found more hidden in his stuff. Con-traband. Constable confiscated it all. Da—dang, but I wonder if them mounties are havin' a fine party tonight."

*I* wondered whether the drunk and frozen boy hadn't briefly looked as if he was a certain dear departed relative of mine. No, I didn't wonder. I was sure. The Deadly Miasma that had slain the constable before my eyes now stalked Dawson City without so much as a by-your-leave from me.

# CHAPTER XI

······•◦►◄◯││◯►◄◦•······

*BY THE END* of the first week my stage fright had vanished, my dancing had improved slightly, and I felt more relaxed with the customers. I was glad I was not supposed to speak English so that I couldn't possibly be expected to encourage others to do what I wished all my life my father would quit. Not that they needed my encouragement to drink. They had plenty of reasons of their own. They drank because they were excited to be in Dawson and dreamed of getting rich (though, of course, the possibility of them doing it while standing at our or any other bar was extremely remote). They drank because they were smart enough to realize they had arrived in time only to see others get rich, and because without the prospect of making a fortune, they had no excuse not to return to whatever life had driven them so far from home in the first place. The less complex drank simply because there was companionship of sorts as long as they drank, or simply because they liked drinking. Many of them were well educated, had left warm homes and well-paying jobs for an adventure. If they found nothing but hard menial work they would have shunned in their native towns and a diet they wouldn't wish on a charity case, they could always lie when they returned home. Providing they lived that long.

Late Friday night, early Saturday morning, the empty floors puddled with half-melted snow from hundreds of unwiped boots that had tramped it hours before. Downstairs, drafts snuck in from the hastily finished doors and windows, but the boxes upstairs shimmered with heat. The piano was covered with its fringed tablecloth, most of the chairs were upended on their tables. Only two of the lamps and a few scattered candles still lit the interior, which jumped with shadows along the vine-striped wallpaper. Lane had wiped and restored all the glasses except for those still in use by the five or six men at the bar and Giselle.

Vasily Vladovitch was there, too. He had arrived late, even after Sasha Devine retired. Again he acted as if he had had too much to drink, although I had yet to see him lift a glass to his lips.

I had spent the evening listening to a customer tell me of his troubles with filing his claim—the poor man really had been robbed and had just cause to lament his fate—when the other women left for their hotel rooms. I saw him to the door and stood watching snowy globs spit against the panes as he blundered out into the two inches of accumulation already pillowing the street. I almost wished I drank so I'd have an excuse to linger in the bar. I lacked the courage to face the slippery walk to my cabin, the cold ashes in my stove, and the ice on my water bucket.

One of the remaining lamps haloed a tousled golden head bent over a gaming table. The man had insufficient flesh on him to fill out his stocky frame. His face was gaunt and the bony fingers of his right hand scribbled furiously. I limped over and sat down beside him. He didn't look up until he had finished, but his hand shook and spoiled the symmetry of his lines, especially when he coughed, which was often. I leaned back slightly, away from his pungent breath. He raised his head from his work, and I saw him flick a drop of blood from the side of his mouth. His two front teeth were missing and the rest of them were crooked and discolored, which was a shame, for he was otherwise a handsome man, too young for me, of course, but very attractive, with a mocking, perhaps self-mocking, gleam in his eye.

"What's the matter, sweetheart? Didn't you ever see a man write before?" he asked, with an attempt at bravado ruined by another cough.

"Si, senor," I said agreeably.

He relaxed. "Oh yeah, I remember. The Spanish girl."

"Si, senor."

"Did it ever occur to you that your ignorance of local custom is being exploited, at the same time depriving you of your native land and some deserving American trollop of a good job?"

I shrugged and lifted my eyebrows.

"Oh, never mind. You ever been to Alhambra? I read a book about that once when I was a boy." I looked blank. "Never mind. I'm Jack," he said, tapping his chest now as if at last realizing that he was dealing with an authentic European non-English-speaking savage.

"Corazon," I responded, and involuntarily recoiled as he leaned closer.

He caught my expression and wiped his mouth self-consciously. "Sorry about that. Scurvy, maybe, or the beginnings of it. My partners and I have had two outfits among the three of us and we're most out of flour already and out of sugar long before we got here. Captain Lomax, down by the Stewart River, insists that the gold will be there if it's there next spring and we'd be smart to winter in Dawson, but I've heard others say there'll be a famine here. Besides, I'm here to dig gold, and that's what I mean to do."

"Ah, but work is not everything, my dear young man," Vasily Vladovitch said. He had been listening from the bar and now picked up a drink and brought it to our table. "Recreation is also important, is it not? Here. I am told that all night long you nurse one little drink. Perhaps, with a hair more, I can influence you to acquire a more pronounced taste for the entirety of the dog, eh?"

"Sir, that particular dog has been one of my best friends for some time now," Jack said, and knocked back the shot, started coughing, and wiped his mouth again. Vasily Vladovitch smiled beneficently, but his eyes were fastened on Jack's mouth, until the droplet of blood disappeared into the rugged growth of red-golden chin whiskers.

"I thank you, sir," Jack said. "London's the name. Jack London. Maybe this dog of yours will inspire me some. I've been trying for the last two hours to try to think like a dog for this story I'm writing and not having much luck. I keep thinking of what poor old Lomax is going to say when he hears that that murderess he took such a shine to killed herself. I confess, I'm not very happy about it on my own account. Lomax told me who she was—Valentine Lovelace, who used to be on the *Herald* and wrote a couple of terrific dime novels. I wanted to maybe visit with her in jail. I know how bad *that* can be, believe me. I could have taken some of that time off her hands by showing her my stories, seeing what she thought. Of course, I'm here to prospect, you understand, but a man can't help thinking." He stopped, and stared at his pages for a moment. "I guess a woman can't either. Poor kid."

He looked very young then and touchingly disappointed at my untimely demise. Though a youngster like that could hardly be expected to write anything worthwhile for years yet to come, I suspected that if things had worked out as he hoped, I'd have given the lad a break. There was something of the quester in his eyes, something sad and at the same time penetrating, that made me feel he might, after all, have something to say for himself.

"Well, then, you are an artist!" Vasily Vladovitch said admiringly.

"Of sorts," Jack replied. "Though not at prospecting. Actually, I mostly came in for your light. I'm camped out up near the hospital. Waiting for my friend Lomax to bring in his partner. But it's mighty cold and practically too dark to think, much less read, out there now."

"My dear boy, I understand," my employer smiled. "Why, I recall my first winter here."

Three of the customers at the bar departed, and Giselle sauntered over and perched herself on Vasily Vladovitch's knee. She had taken to affecting a wide black velvet band around her throat lately. Millie said it was to keep her head attached to her shoulders, because she was too scatterbrained to remember to do it otherwise. "When *did* you come up here, Vassy?" Giselle asked. "How did you manage to get so many beautiful things up here before anybody else got them?"

"Why, because my excellent agent was able to secure your services, cherie," he replied with a gallantness that I found cloying, especially when it was not directed at me.

She batted him with her fan. "No, silly, I mean really. I really want to know."

"Very well, for you, ma petite chou, I will bore these people with my bragging. You see, I have been in this region longer than any other white man."

"How can that be?" she asked with what I felt sure was a broad exaggeration of her honeyed New Orleans drawl. "Why, old Lem Loudermilke has been heah all his life he says, and he must be neah eighty. You must mean to say your family's been heah that long, surely."

"Must I?" he asked. Then to the rest of us, he said, "These treasures of mine had to be smuggled out of the old country, over the years, as my enemies died off. As soon as I learned the Bonanza strike was imminent, I arranged for the building of my home and business and shipped my belongings upriver."

"Where's your family from, Mr.—?" Jack asked.

"Bledinoff, but call me Vasily Vladovitch, please. Everyone does. We are originally from a little place that is now a part of Romania. You probably have never heard of it. We were of the aristocracy—my father a prince of the old order. From time to time, when I think it will impress someone who can be of use to me, I have used what would have been my title had we remained. So if you hear someone refer to Count Bledinoff, that is me, but you understand, that would not be how I would be called in Romania were I still there, and I am not entirely sure that the title is mine any longer. My family moved to Russia before I was born."

"But if you were aristocrats, why evah did he move away?" Giselle asked, welding her shoulder to his neck, thereby providing him with an unparalleled view of the snowy mounds she seemed inclined to substitute for personality.

Vasily Vladovitch's chin rose defiantly, and his eyes tightened at the corners. The fierce pride blazing out of his eyes froze her lashes in midflutter. "Treachery and petty-mindedness is why. The preference of ungrateful princes with depleted treasure chests for wealthy merchants instead of loyal nobles who had spent their fortunes defending their country's honor."

"But if you were—"

"Even the best of blood can be defamed. Always there is someone who carries the family foibles to excess, someone who is—indiscreet. In our case it was my second cousin, an intemperate woman who committed such crimes against the peasants in her care that eventually she became an embarrassment. The family had to allow her to be walled up in her own castle. Terrible scandal, distasteful for everyone. Especially since the rest of us were, as you Americans might say, tarred with the same brush. Peasants actually came to our castles with torches and attacked us—killed our pets on sight, desecrated our family tomb. But—oh, my dear Gigi, I did not mean to frighten you. Here, here, sit back down now."

And he spent a few moments stroking and comforting the silly thing who had, to my eye, been thoroughly enjoying the drama of the moment, having a wonderful time heaving her bosom and rolling her eyes and otherwise feigning feminine fright at his ferocity. The longer he spoke, the more I felt that his ferocity was more re-enacted than actually felt right now, that the lowering brows and the bitter lupine grin were the ritual expressions of hereditary threats toward deceased enemies. I was too sleepy to fear anything anyway. I raised my fan quickly to hide a yawn and Vasily Vladovitch laughed, his amiable mood restored as quickly as it had vanished.

"You understand that when I speak of these things I am speaking of them to you as my father spoke of them to me, and he was quite naturally incensed, as was my older brother, who stood to inherit his title and riches. I myself was brought up on the steppes, amid half-wild Cossacks with no need for castles or titles. In fact, when I heard my father say that wealthy merchants had beaten the abused nobility, it determined me to become a wealthy merchant, and so I have."

"You must have made a real early strike to have done this good," Giselle said.

"Not gold, my dear Gigi, but furs. When first I came to these shores, the Native peoples plucked fortunes from the forests and the seas. Seal silken as your own skin, marten, lynx, fox—russet, silver, purest ivory, and crossed like a churchman—bears whiter than a newborn baby's soul, wolverine that repells frost of its own accord, and wolf hides thicker and warmer than anything found on our own shores. It was a cold life, but I love the cold, being from a cold country, and loved also the wilderness and the company of free, nomadic people. I am also a man of nocturnal habits and do my best work at night. I see extremely well in darkness. This has obvious advantages for the hunter. The Indians came to trust me—and later became my new family, for none of my old one ever joined me here."

"Still, you must have been mighty lonely without others of your own kind around," Jack said.

"Indeed I was. Though if you mean for other white men, in recent years there have been plenty of those. Before opening this business I ran a similar one in Circle City, though nothing, you understand, so grand. But what of you, my friend? What brought you so far, and when you have done with this land, what are your plans then?"

"My plans don't seem to mean much," Jack said. "I *planned* to be a famous writer, only the editors didn't cooperate. So I came up here to become a rich man. However, so far I've been unable to get the land to cooperate. And after today, when I tried to help a man who has been busting his behind for a year record his claim, I learned that certain blood-sucking officials are even less cooperative. After working his claim in all kinds of weather for all this time, poor Bob Clancy found somebody else's name on his piece of ground. And not a soul would listen to him, or to me when I tried to witness for him. I've only been here three weeks, but plenty of folks out there have seen that he's been the only one working that claim."

He had more to say on the subject, but since Bob Clancy was the name of the customer I had already spent most of my evening with, I wasn't afraid of missing anything when I slipped away. The snowflakes were thick as the hairs on my borrowed bear hide blanket. The wool socks, also borrowed, with which I covered my shoes when walking out-of-doors grew quickly wet. Both Stella's and Lurleen's cabins were dark, which could mean either that they were in business or that they were out of candles. Once inside my own place, I tried to build a fire with the hide wrapped around my hands and succeeded in warming a hole in both the hide and my left hand. After setting the water bucket on the stove to thaw, I plucked two candles from the box and plodded back to the saloon.

"Thought you'd gone home, Cory," Lane grumbled when I walked in. The bartender's shock of white hair almost met his furry white brows and gave him a rather grouchy look. This, coupled with a voice like a rock slide, served to counteract any misapprehension on the part of rowdies that an establishment owned by a seeming dandy and managed by a woman was an appropriate place to misbehave. In fact, the bartender was no ruffian, but a contemplative, if rather critical, college man who hid volumes of poetry behind the bottles and read during slack times. This was one of those times. I had interrupted *A Tale of Two Cities*. Lane was alone with a bottle, a book, and a candle and obviously enjoyed the solitude.

Thumping noises and the crash of broken crockery issued from upstairs, by which I took it that Vasily Vladovitch and Giselle might be enthusiastically indulging in recreational pursuits. That was their business. Mine, as I had decided earlier, was trying to catch up with Jack. Snow blew into my face when I opened the front door. The street seemed deserted. Most of the men were sticking to the relative dryness of their tents at this hour. I stepped onto the boardwalk and looked down its length, but I saw no one. Thinking Jack might have taken a shortcut through a side alley, I walked past our building and down as far as the Alaska Commercial Company's warehouse, on the other side of the street.

The boardwalk was icy and I had been treading carefully to keep my footing, but suddenly, ahead of me, the steady sift of snow parted around a black void. I had been concentrating so hard that actually seeing something took me by surprise, and I missed my footing and fell, cursing. The void spun away like a cyclone. The snow instantly filled it.

"Jack?" I called after it, but it had vanished. A grunt from the direction of the Alaska Commercial Company warehouse drew my attention, however, and I jumped down off the boardwalk and ran across the street as fast as one can go flat-footed and pigeon-toed across a slick irregular surface.

"Jack, is that you?" I asked the crumpled form propped against the ACC wall. I didn't like to think I'd toiled across that street for some drunk I didn't know.

Another grunt. Drawing closer, I saw that it was indeed Jack, but before I reached him he was on his feet.

"I am not a well man. One drink is not enough to lay me so low," he complained, shaking his head.

I was about drop my disguise and ask him if he was all right and to tell me what happened, for I felt sure, after what I had learned of him, that he would keep my secret. He was, after all, a fellow former convict and a friend of Lomax's. But as I laid a hand upon his elbow, firm steps thumped down the boardwalk.

A familiar Scots burr called, "Is everrahthing a'right over there?" Before either of us could answer, Sergeant Destin was upon us.

"Just felt a little faint, Sergeant, thank you," Jack said hastily. "The lady happened along in time to keep me from lying here freezing to death, I reckon."

"The inspector frowns on public drunkenness," Sergeant Destin warned.

"I wasn't drunk—couldn't afford to be. I haven't been feeling well lately, still tired from the trip down, probably."

The sergeant leaned forward and gave him a houndlike sniff. "Hmph. Aye, well, you seem to be right enough. You want to let the night sister at St. Mary's have a look at you?"

Jack shook his head. "I doubt she'd like what she sees any better than you do. No, I'll just take it easy and I'll make it back to my tent soon enough."

"You still look a bit off to me, lad," the Sergeant said more kindly. "I'll walk along with you and make sure you've a fire before you crawl into your bedroll. We had a lad freeze to death the other night and I'll not have that happen on my beat, first night."

"Aren't you the sergeant I met at Dag Lomax's cabin? Jack London, remember? I thought you were assigned the Tagish post."

"Oh, aye, young Jack, is it? I didn't recognize you what with the hat and the snow. Aye, I'm on the town now. Lost a man at Tagish. Not that this is a punishment post, mind you. I asked for it. A few things I'm wantin' to acquaint myself with more fully concernin' that case, if you'll keep it under your hat."

"Oh?"

The sergeant almost steered him away before I had time to press the candles into his hand, something difficult to do while holding the bearskin well over my face with the other and trying to keep both hands warmly covered. He looked at the tapers absently for a moment, then recognized the nature of my gift. "Candles? But how did you—never mind, thanks!" And he planted a grateful if disrespectful kiss on top of my befurred head. Then with no further notice of me, he and the sergeant resumed their conversation and trudged into the darkness.

I turned back toward the Vein, planning to cut through to Paradise Alley at the end of the block. But I met another familiar figure coming the other way, staggering slightly. "Vasily Vladovitch," I said, then remembered that I was in public and lowered my voice. "Are you well?"

"Miss Val—Corazon?" His voice was as shakey as his gait. "I am well, yes, except for the mischance of being in the path of a flying chamberpot. A difficult skill, the managing of diverse artistic personalities. But I am learning," he ruefully assured me, rubbing his head. "I would love to stand and talk to you longer, but I have pressing business elsewhere." He swooped down onto my frozen hand to kiss it, but when he observed its stiff and frozen condition, he tucked it back into the bearskin instead. Then with a meaningful look into my eyes, he said, "Another night, my dear, I will not let you go so readily."

With a flourish of his cape, he strode past me. But I was barely two paces on my own way when he turned back to me, his face indistinguishable in the darkness. "Valentina? You will go straight home? There have been men attacked by animals lately. These sled dogs, they may seem tame, but many are part wolf. Even those that are not, when unleashed, form packs. I—"

"Straight home," I promised, wishing his solicitousness extended to paying me my wages for delivering the coffin so that I might purchase appropriate outer clothing to replace what I had lost. I started to say something, but his last footfall hit the boardwalk, and he vanished into the storm. Through chattering teeth I muttered imprecations that would have frightened off any wolfpack in its right mind.

The creaking of Lurleen's bed welcomed me back to my cabin as wind chimes on a front porch or a light (even a red one) in the window might welcome one in a more conventional setting. From my stovepipe, a plume of woodsmoke rose, but woodsmoke was not all I smelled. I recognized the scent at once. Evening in Budapest—Sasha Devine's signature fragrance. But before I put my hand to the wooden protruberance that served as a door handle, I heard the sobs.

"Vahl, oh Vahl, come in quickly and close the door," Sasha Devine sniffed. She lay curled at the head of my bed, her face half buried in clenched fists. "Oh, you will think me such a fool, but truly, I had no where else to go. I refuse to remain under the same roof as that, as that—"

"Giselle?" I asked, lighting a candle, then shaking the snow from my bearskin and hanging it on a nail. I would have to sleep under the smaller, thinner hides tonight, and unfortunately I was longer than most foxes. But sleeping under that bearskin would be about as warm and dry as sleeping under the surface of the Yukon. I regarded my bed with proprietory alarm. I am a hospitable person by nature, but that bed was very small, and Sasha Devine looked as if she was very comfortable and intended to stay that way.

"I'm sorry, Sasha," I said wearily, sitting down at the end of the bed and prying the frozen woolen socks off of the dancing shoes that I then pried from my swollen feet. "And frankly, I'm a little surprised at how things are going. I wouldn't have thought the flower of the bayou would be a match for you."

"She's twenty years younger!" Sasha cried indignantly. "And totally unprincipled."

"Well, that *would* appeal to most men," I acknowledged. "But I thought Vasily Vladovitch higher minded. Forgive me, but I would think your twenty years would be an asset."

"It's probably only fifteen years," she said. "Have you ever noticed how thick her makeup is? Now myself, I use only the barest glaze of skin cream, and look at my face. If you can find a wrinkle—not a laugh line, you understand, but a real wrinkle—why, I'll—"

"I didn't think he was as concerned with your age as he was with your talent and your brains," I said.

"Pah! Men! What do they know of brains?" she asked and started to weep again. "Oh, to think I threw over your dear papa, my sweet Patrick, to come here and follow this—this—philanderer!"

"Papa was dead, Sasha."

"That's beside the point. He's dead, and I took up with his—with Vasily Vladovitch, and now he has forsaken me for that hussy!"

Talk about the pot calling the kettle black. But I kept such observations to myself. She, whom I had once thought invulnerable, particularly in matters concerning men, was rapidly disabusing me of my childish notions. To say she was deeply distressed was an understatement. Vasily Vladovitch should be ashamed of himself, I thought.

"I hope he at least keeps his promise to give you your partnership in the Vein," I said. "I think you more than earned it. For that matter, so did I."

"Oh, yes, of course, he will keep his promise. Have you any idea how many lawyers there are waiting to dig gold in Dawson right now? Besides, I—I know he loves me. But why has he taken to her? Why will he not give me the—oh, never mind, my friend. It is far too complicated to explain. And I might shock you."

Could Vasily Vladovitch be some sort of perverted monster? Though I had secondhand knowledge of a great many intimate practices taking place between man and woman that could have been considered linked to procreation only by the wildest stretch of the imagination, I was not unshockable. Anything above and beyond what I already knew about had to be dreadful indeed. Just thinking about it was going to make it difficult for me to meet my employer's eye. But what seemed stranger to me was that Sasha Devine seemed convinced that he was practicing whatever practice it was upon Giselle instead of her and was deeply disappointed and feeling wronged. Shouldn't she feel delivered instead? Now, I am trained to ask rude and embarrassing questions, but, naturally, we of the press do not stoop to *that* sort of topic. Had we done so, we would have enraged the churches and the Women's Temperance Union and enlarged our circulation beyond our wildest dreams.

"And I don't even have my new c-clothes," she said. "They were all on the raft—"

"Mine were, too," I reminded her. "And I don't have a lovely coat and a nice luxurious room I don't have to go outside to get to. And may the saints preserve me if, if I did, I let some two-bit floozy move into it because I had my feelings hurt. The room, as I understand it, goes with your job, not with your position as Vasily Vladovitch's mistress. Stick to your rights, woman."

I paused for breath. My Irish had, unaccountably, gotten up. "In fact, if you intend to take over my bed because you're too busy feeling sorry for yourself to throw her out, I'll go do it myself and take over your place."

But to Sasha's credit, her moment of romantic weakness was short. Her eyes slitted and glittered, she straightened the mess of hay her iron-curled hair had become at some point during the night, and pulled on the parka.

I felt a little ashamed of myself. "I really didn't mean it," I said. "I'm flattered that you confided in me and, of course, you're welcome to stay, it's just that—"

"Vahlenteena, dahling," she said with a trace of her old smile, "you said I possess admirable intelligence, and this quality enables me to understand good sense when I hear it. I go to reclaim my stronghold. Adieu." And she ceremoniously bussed me on each cheek and, flinging the door open against the wind, swept imperiously out into the storm.

# CHAPTER XII

••••••◄══╣║╠══►••••••

*HAVING SOLVED SASHA'S* problems, I spent valuable sleep time upbraiding myself for failing to solve my own. I was not writing, I was not discovering a way to explain the constable's murder, and most of the time I was not even keeping warm. My assumed language barrier kept me as isolated as if my new persona had been deliberately designed to do so. I could do nothing but listen to random conversation, could ask no incisive questions, and without proper clothing, could not move about town except in cases of dire necessity. There were only three people with whom I could discuss this sad state of affairs, and two of them I had already met tonight, both so preoccupied with their own affairs that they had succeeded somehow in totally occupying me with them as well.

Lurleen was unavailable, not because she was selfish but because she was so giving that she nearly always had company while I was awake and in the cabin. The rest of the time she seemed to be sleeping. Nevertheless, I vowed to myself, punching up one of the hides to form a pillow, this sad state of affairs would not continue much longer. I had had a bellyful of practicing the ta-ra-boom-de-ays in the drafty backstage area simply to keep warm while the other girls performed. I would confront Vasily Vladovitch on the morrow and demand the salary promised me for my assistance in the journey north. And if he used my misfortune as a pretext to refuse, I would enlist Sasha's aid.

But, as the Scottish mountie, Destin, might have told me, my plans, like the best-laid schemes of mice and men aft do, were to gang agley.

The least of my problems manifested itsself as soon as I entered the Vein. Sasha was waiting for me. "The cancan steps, you know them?" And before I could deny it, she added slyly, "Maisie tells me your kick has become quite as high as hers this week."

Wondering if there was a law against a spinster on the wintry side of thirty-five attempting feats intended only for eighteen-year-old girl athletes, I nodded cautiously.

"That Giselle is not only a slut and a witch, she is also a lazy malingerer. She pretends to be ill tonight, so the chorus line is short. I myself must oversee the house. You will take her place, yes?"

And without waiting for my response, she handed me just what I'd been wanting, another costume, Giselle's cancan frock. In what strange ways our prayers are answered. I struggled out of my costume and into this new one. It was not as hard as I thought. I had dropped an inch or so during the week. I started to look daggers at Maisie, but she grinned and squeezed my arm.

"Isn't this just like those stories about the theatre, where the star breaks her ankle and the understudy has to go on in her place?" she asked breathlessly. "Oh, honey, I just know you'll do great!"

Realizing that Maisie was a frustrated legitimate actress who thought she was doing me a favor, I could hardly snub her. So I flounced out with the rest of the girls and did my best to outkick them, no doubt causing permanent damage to several of my joints in the process. By the time I had unhooked myself from the cancan costume and resumed my red satin and black flounces, my abortive flamenco seemed easy by comparison, which, of course, it was.

The final change back into the cancan costume, however, undid me. Literally. As I pulled Corazon's only plumage off over my head, I heard the sinister snap of overstrained threads. The costume flopped away from my hair. The entire right side was split from sleeve to waist, and the left side sported new ventilation at the shoulder. My poor theatre costume, not made for twenty-four-hour duty as a hostess gown, walking dress, wrapper, and ball gown, had finally taken the course of the abused old cart horse. With this last intolerable flogging, it died.

The material was so strained around the seams that it split in several directions, so even resewing the seam would require the use of a new piece.

I couldn't very well be expected to continue like this, could I, with my clothes falling off me? Now I had a legitimate, tangible complaint with which to confront Vasily Vladovitch, one that he could not ignore. I triumphantly donned the cancan costume and outkicked all but Nellie, who overcompensated for her small stature by snapping her tiny feet to chin level with the other girls.

On the final kick, just before we turned around and gave the audience the benefit of our posterior ruffles, Jack London blew in, followed by the familiar hunchbacked shape of Lomax and Loki. Changing back into my ripped Spanish costume and pulling the black fringed shawl over the rips, I clattered down the steps, brushing aside patrons in my beeline for the bar.

Vasily Vladovitch had not yet arrived. Sasha Devine was in conference with Lurleen who, like others of her profession, frequented the saloon occasionally to meet new and interested people and thereby stimulate business. London and Lomax greeted Lane and Wild Miles Mahoney.

The light in the main part of the saloon was unusually dim, and I noted that only half as many candles and lamps were lit as usual, populating the bar with as many jumping, writhing shadows as people. Even in this light, it seemed to me that London's experience of the previous night had done him great harm. He looked pale and ill, his eyes unnaturally bright and his voice forced to a shriller pitch than it had been the previous night.

"Why's it so dark in here, Mr. Lane?" he asked.

"V.V.'s orders. You kinda reminded him last night that our supplies aren't going to last forever. What can I get for you boys?"

"Whiskey," Jack said.

"Saspar—"

"I know, Cap'n. Sarsaparilla. Sorry we got no cherry left. But I saved a little something for the cat," and he set an ashtray with a quarter inch of tomato juice in the bottom on the bar. Loki leaned down and sniffed, then dropped lightly off his master's shoulders and started lapping up Lane's tribute.

The front door banged open and the wind gusted in, followed closely by three bundled figures, one of whom wore the uniform coat of the mounties. When he lifted his head, Destin's ruddy Scots face was set in an expression of dogged dutifulness. He marched toward the little cluster at the bar as if into a council of war.

"Good evening, gentlemen," he said formally. "Captain Lomax, sir, I'll take this opportunity to inform you that your cargo has been inventoried, and, as you requested, your right to salvage has been established, barring one or two exceptions. Half of that property still belongs to the Widow Lamour, and we will hold that pending her return. And—uh—this man here has aught to say to you as well."

Detective Norman, leading with his nose, which must have been a professional hazard, drew unnecessarily close to Lomax. "Several of the gowns formerly in the possession of the Widow Lamour are actually stolen property, taken by Pelagia Harper, alias Valentine Lovelace. I have taken those gowns into custody for return to their proper owner, except for the one worn by the widow prior to her disappearance from the Mounted Police Hospital. When you make contact with Mrs. Lamour, inform her that the frock is to be returned to me for delivery to my client, and that if it is in anything but prime condition, she must replace it. Otherwise, my client will be forced to press charges, implicating Mrs. Lamour as an accomplice."

Lomax stroked his cat and tried to read the labels of the bottles stacked behind the bar.

"You realize that by rights all of those goods should be confiscated to repay my client for her grievous losses," Norman continued. "Were it not for the lack of cooperation of the Canadian Mounted Police—"

"Now, now, Detective," a new voice, odiously familiar, interrupted. I stared so hard I almost forgot to raise my fan in time. Before me was the face of a man I had thought long dead. The tall, lanky shape was the same, but the leathery face had a network of fine lines and the once tawny hair was now silver. Gone were the Mexican cowboy clothes, though. In their place was a dove gray triple button cutaway frock suit of wool cashmere that almost matched his hair.

"Let's not have any of that," Frank Drake, the former master of Fort Draco, chided the Pinkerton. "You're just peeved a might because that fool woman went and killed herself before you could lynch her for stealin' a few dresses. The sergeant here has been the very model of cooperativeness and we 'Mericans appreciate it mightily, don't we now?"

"Yes, Mr. Blake, of course," Norman said.

"You're Blake, the American consul?" Jack asked.

"Assistant consul, yes," Drake said smiling. "But the acting one. The consul is away on a prolonged journey, reporting to Washington."

"Whatever," Jack said. "What can you do to help Bob Clancy? The recorder's office is tryin' to jump his claim and—"

"Oh, my goodness, Sergeant. Perhaps you'd better tell them."

"Tell us what?" London demanded.

"The investigation is not completed, Mr. Blake, sir, and I'll thank you not to be tellin' me how to do my duty."

"No, no, Sergeant, you're perfectly right. I'll take the matter up with Inspector Constantine. But I do feel that these gentlemen have a right to know about Mr. Clancy's untimely death."

Jack seemed to sway, and his shadow lurched across the faces of the men at the tables behind us. "Who found him?"

"I did," Destin said. "On my way back from your tent. He died easy, from the look of it. Had a big smile on his face." Puzzlement washed over the sergeant's features, crimping the tight set of his lips and sending the eyebrows, which met in a V over his nose, toward his hairline. Could he be remembering a similar smile on the dead face of the mirthless Constable Faversham?

Jack groped behind him for an empty chair, dragged it half to him and himself half to it, and sat down abruptly. "Another drink," he whispered.

Destin was no longer watching him. Instead, the mountie stared across the room at Sasha Devine, who was listening to an animated Maisie. Bon-Ton Bunny played the piano and bawled the lyrics to "Who Threw the Overalls in Mistress Murphy's Chowder?" while Nellie danced with a miner three times her size. Miss Millie led Sawyers from the recorder's office up the stairs.

"Excuse me a moment, I wish to speak to that woman," the Pinkerton said, and rushed toward the steps, knocking a deck of cards from one of the dealer's hands and revealing an extra ace in the pack, causing the dealer to produce some rapid and truly imaginative explanations.

I squirmed in closer to Lomax and felt Drake's eyes sweep

over me. There wasn't much to see. Black mantilla, black shawl, and the hem of my tattered costume. I kept my face toward the bar, grateful it did not boast a mirror.

"Terrible thing about that lady reporter, eh, Mr. Lomax?" Drake remarked. "I knew her slightly, long ago. Lovely woman. Though too inquisitive for her own good. I understand from Mr. Norman that you were quite gallant in her defense. Mustn't be taken in by someone just because she's female, Mr. Lomax. Why, there's some as wonder if she's dead at all. Perhaps she had an accomplice spirit her up the river to Alaska. What do you think?"

Wild Miles burped. "What *I* think is it's just like a fool woman to do somethin' like that, ain't it? I mean, here half the people comin' up here gotta bust their butts not to get killed on the trail and once they get here gotta fight wild bears, starvation, and cold that fair freezes the pee right inside of you, just to stay alive, and what does she do? She voluntarily, mind you, jumps in the river and dirties up our drinkin' water. Scandalous, I call it. Oughta haul her outa there next spring and hang her, just on principle."

"I'll bear your recommendation in mind, friend," Drake said, and backed hastily away, toward the gaming tables, by which he suddenly seemed to be fascinated.

"How's that nephew of yours doin', Lomax?" Miles asked pleasantly, his tirade over. I began to wonder if the explosion of nonsensical sentiments hadn't been solely for Drake's benefit. Miles had not shown himself to be an ignorant or loudmouthed sort of man before. With the so-called guardian of American justice out of earshot, he reverted to the thoughtful if occasionally wildly enthusiastic gumbooter I had begun to grow used to.

"Bad," Lomax said.

"At Saint Mary's with the sisters now?"

"Aye," Lomax said shortly. "Whiskey, Mr. Lane. One for young Jack and one for me."

"You sure about that, Cap'n?" Lane asked. "I know it's none of my business, but you don't drink and—"

"You're right. It's none of your business. Whiskey."

"You buyin' for Corazon there, too?" Lane winked at me. Jack looked up. "Buy her one, Cap'n Lomax. I'll pay you back. She did me a favor last night."

But the torn costume, the fact of Drake's inexplicable presence, and the mystery of poor Clancy's death and its certain link to the Deadly Miasma and Papa's ghost all fled when the glass of amber liquid was set before Egil Larsson's kindly uncle. It suddenly occurred to me that with the possible exception of Vasily Vladovitch, every man I had cared for or even remotely taken a shine to had fallen victim to liquor and ultimately to the smiling Deadly Miasma. Poor Lomax, grieving for his injured nephew, for his wife, for Clancy, and apparently for me, was about to succumb. For all I knew, he was a reformed drinker himself, and for my sake was about to fall off the wagon into degradation, and, in this time and place, certain doom. I could not let it happen. I snatched the glass from in front of him as he turned to hand the other to London.

He saw me with the glass and glared at me fiercely. I glared back and did the only thing a well-brought-up Latin dance hall girl could do. I knocked back the shot myself. Halfway to my tonsils it ignited, and quite independent of any desire of mine, spewed back from my lips like the flames from the mouth of the dragon. Lomax's shirt front had the misfortune to be in the way. He raised his hand and Maisie rushed to my side.

"Don't you hit her, mister," she said. "She just doesn't understand our ways yet. She's a foreigner and just got here and she didn't mean to spill that drink on you."

Lane tossed me a bar towel and I began to sponge Lomax's front, not an easy thing to do while trying to keep my shawl together so my rips didn't show. Lomax's grim silence was broken, however, and he smiled, a tight painful smile, but a smile, and lowered his raised hand to wipe his shirt front, which was what I personally had thought he was going to do with it all along.

"Belay that now," he said to Maisie. "I wasn't going to hit her. Where else can a man get a pretty girl to give him a shower in whiskey? The owner ought to advertise it. Some of these boys could use it even worse than me." He dug in his pocket and handed us each a quarter, as if we were small children. "Buy yourself a replacement, missy, if you're that thirsty. Me and Young Jack here got business at St. Mary's. Evenin', ladies, Lane," and he hoisted the cat upon his shoulder once more and nodded to Jack, who was too sick to argue.

"Evenin', Cap'n. Evenin', Jack," Lane replied and waved his bar rag at them.

Maisie dusted her hands together as if she had just saved

me from a fate worse than death. Miss Millie stalked over to us.

"Maisie, what in the devil was that all about? Did you go tellin' that man or anybody else things about Cory?"

Maisie, who always spoke admiringly of Millie, looked as if her pet lap dog had just taken a chunk out of her. "Gracious. No. I have plenty of things of my own to do without mixin' in somebody else's business. I just saw the look on that man's face and thought, well, I'd better smooth things over."

Millie snorted and hiked a black-stockinged leg up on the brass rail. "Somebody's been tellin' tales. That little sharp-nosed private copper said he'd heard all us girls didn't arrive together, that he'd heard Miss Devine was already here and that the original Spanish dancer was Prancing Pilar. I wonder which little swamp-stompin' Leesiana water moccasin could have told him somethin' like that?"

As Maisie sputtered a reiteration of her innocence, I bent down to adjust my stocking. Drake caught my eye as neatly as if I had looked directly at him. I could almost see his ears prick forward, taking in every word. He rose and started toward us.

Sasha, parting the customers like Moses on a seagoing stroll, swept between him and us and planted her fists on her hips. "You think perhaps, ladies, that I pay you to sit and talk to one another? We have another show to do. To work with you." And she clapped her hands once sharply and with a graceful gesture indicated the stage.

I have seldom felt so exposed in my life. Bad enough, during the cancan choruses, to have my labored movements scrutinized, as I felt, by the three men who were my sworn foes. Worse, there was no time between numbers for so much as a quick patch job, and I had to do my solo with my shawl wrapped diagonally around my shoulder.

Twice I forgot my footing, for even in the darkened theatre I could feel Drake's gaze penetrating my disguise. Of course, that was no guarantee he knew it was a disguise. It had always been Drake's custom to penetrate with his gaze the clothing of persons of my gender. But some new element was within that steady stare. No longer did he emanate what had been, until one knew him for the utter cad he was, a rather charming lechery. Nor was what so disturbed me his previous desire for dominance over all he surveyed, for the *desire* for dominance was a thing of the past. His whole demeanor now suggested that total control was within his power, that he was the puppeteer moving everyone around him and had only to pull a string to make one jump.

Even more frightening was the whispered undertone of torment, suggesting that this new power had been dearly bought. For I could not imagine what could possibly have been so important to Frank Drake that the loss of it would cause him any degree of suffering once he had what he desired within his grasp. Of course, when last seen, according to my correspondents in the Despoblado, Drake had been wandering, crazed, through the deserts of Mexico. Perhaps all I was feeling was the remnants of that lunacy. But I no more believed that than I believed that the dragon Kukulkan was only a giant gila monster. Drake's pale eyes, cold as a glacial crevice, burned more brightly in that scantily lit room than any lamp.

I surpassed my customary awkwardness and finished the ruin of my costume by ripping the bottom flounce halfway off. I had turned, not because it was part of the dance but to escape that gaze. That was when the flounce ripped. As I pranced back to the right to conceal the rip, I spied Detective Norman, beaming smugly to himself, dart out the back door.

I didn't have to fake my need for fresh air. I pawed through that last number in a fog, and when it was over bolted through the back door without bothering to pull my wool socks on over my shoes. Once the cold air hit me, I revived and cursed myself for being such an idiot. Just because some fool senator had been dumb enough to appoint a scoundrel like Drake to the consulate didn't mean I had to freeze my feet off. I had outwitted him before and I could do so again. The trouble was, if he decided he was homesick to talk Spanish with someone, he would penetrate my masquerade with more than his eyes. His Spanish was fluent and mine was all but nonexistent. Next time I went incognito, I'd have to remember to be something a little less common, say, a Turk perhaps, or an overgrown Bantu pygmy.

I could worry about triumphing over evil later. Right now I needed the warmth of my cabin and a restoring cup of tea. At least Giselle's cancan costume was not so thoroughly ventilated as Corazon's rags, but I felt ill-prepared to face Drake in anything less than full costume. The clients would have to drink themselves to death without me tonight.

The back steps were crude and without a railing, and the footing was more slippery than the entire city council of San

Francisco combined. Using my cancan flounces to protect my posterior, I descended the steps in a seated position. Wood smoke perfumed the air, that and the sharp tingling of the nostrils, the absence of lesser odors, that is the essence of arctic cold. The sky was hazy beyond the humps of Dawson's guardian hills, its steel gray and navy gradations vaguely backlit with a dull wash of pulsing crimson. The crusted ice and snow outlined the buildings and made the protruding bare brush look like sheaves of bone stuck upright in the drifts. Wings flapped overhead, and something large and black swooped past me, down the alley. A raven, I thought, or an owl. Regaining my feet, I ice skated down Paradise Alley toward my little crib, which seemed to me just then to be the next best thing to the real paradise.

Something was amiss. The cabin door was ajar, light spilling into the long slit between door and jam, the brightness bouncing back from the sheen of a furtive eye watching from Stella's window. I had yet to see the woman's face though I had lived next door to her for almost a week. I gathered my courage and thrust onward. Of course, the intruder could be merely another of Rosie's misguided former clients who had gone in and made himself at home with *my* candles, and if so he would soon find himself summarily ejected into the snow. I was not in a mood to trifle with boors. I feared, however, a more sinister guest.

But just as I was mentally girding my frosted loins, the light in my cabin abruptly died. I started to run, slipped, and fell heavily on the ice, and half crawled, half limped the last few yards. My door swings both ways and I tried to open it by falling against it. To no avail. Something blocked it from within. I thought I heard a hiss, as of dampness touching the hot metal of the stove.

Frantically, I tugged the door toward me. It caught on a bump of ice and would not pull any farther. I was forced to squeeze past it. The illumination I had seen from the street vanished, leaving only the firelight seeping around the closed stove door. My fire would not have lasted so long. The intruder must have built one to keep himself warm while doing whatever it was he was doing in my cabin.

The darkness expanded to cloak the room absolutely for a moment, and something hissed again. Then the little rectangle of firelight reappeared and snagged on two white, sharp teeth, and ignited a pair of red eyes, which I barely glimpsed before something heavy shoved me backward. Claws raked my upraised arms, searing the cold-sensitized flesh, and I was overwhelmed with the stench of decay and the faintly metallic scent of blood. I twisted on the icy ground and looked behind me as the flag of a retreating tail rounded the corner of Stella's cabin.

Assuming the intruder gone, I fell gratefully into my cabin, and across something soft, yielding, and bearing the faintly phosphorescent image of father's face, its expression as reproving and pruney as that of his widow. I did not even need for the image to fade before I knew the true identity of the dead man. The fine woolen coat with the fur collar told me plainly enough that the Pinkerton man had finally poked his nose into one too many places where it didn't belong.

# CHAPTER XIII

·····❖◗⬥II⬥◖❖·····

*SO MUCH FOR* one theory. Papa's ghost was *not* the perpetrator
of these crimes nor the vector of the Deadly Miasma. Some
other creature, the one with the fangs, claws, and glittering
eyes, had attacked Detective Norman and had no doubt attacked the others.

But when a lady clad in a flimsy theatrical costume is lying
wounded in the snow with a killer beast on the prowl on one
hand, a corpse in her cabin, and the mounties hot on her trail
on the other hand, she has a few more pressing concerns that
distract her from the purely logical analyses of the crime at
hand.

To wit, it required no amazing feat of mental dexterity to
tell me that my cabin, warm and inviting, though crowded as
it was, was the least safe place for me in all of the Yukon
Territory, save perhaps within the embrace of a bear. If found
with the Pinkerton, I would be questioned. My disguise would
not hold up to the relentless badgering of the police. If I screamed,
the same thing would ultimately happen. If I did not scream,
the monster was likely to return and attack me. If I tried to
drag the body elsewhere, which I was not sure in my ill-clad
and debilitated condition was feasible, I would probably be
seen, by Stella, if by no one else. Therefore, I did not remain
in my cabin examining the corpse and the premises for clues.

I backed out so quickly I fell over my own feet, then threw myself at Stella's door while emitting small squeaking noises indicative of panic.

In response, Stella was making little babbling noises herself, the only distinguishable words of which were "demons," "spawn of Satan," and "unholy evil." No close examination of her decor was needed to understand her frame of reference. Her room was as liberally plastered with old calendar pictures of Our Lord in as many attitudes of agony and disgruntlement as the average miner's hovel is with pictures of scantily clad women in poses of pleasure. Several wooden crucifixes, their sculptural elements gaudily embellished with gory painted details, added textural interest. Stella's clientele had to be either hardy souls fully ready to enjoy their fair share of guilt, shame, and responsibility for the mortal sin of their illicit passions, or perhaps members of the clergy in need of a home away from home.

For succumbing to such temptation as this creature presented, the gentlemen probably should have consulted one of Dr. Freud's colleagues instead of their local minister. Gaunt and bony, with drab hair skinned back in onion peel fashion from her forehead, her thin mouth writhing with nonsense, her faded eyes gelatinous with terror, Stella was no one for whom I could imagine even the most desperate of men risking the tiniest penance.

We were quite a pair. I had no problem appearing as horrified and tremblous as she. Which was fortunate, in a way. I was more than a little relieved that no witty repartee was required, since I felt in no mood to assume my phony accent.

As we stood there gibbering in unison, I debated the possibility of having Stella scream so that she could explain to the mounties about how she had just cracked her door for a breath of air when she saw this man enter the poor foreign girl's cabin when along came the hideous fanged monster that did him in.

Meanwhile, Stella muttered, "The spawn of Satan stalks us, the antichrist repays us our trespasses and we are doomed, doomed, doomed to damnation and the fires of hell and it serves us right for our sinfulness and—"

And then she shut up, because she wasn't quite as ready for doom as she said and something was scrabbling on the roof, banging at the stovepipe. She grabbed the nearest crucifix and whapped it against the low ceiling. I grabbed two more logs and threw them into her fire. Overhead claws scraped, wings flapped, and something shrieked.

And outside, measured footsteps marched past Stella's door. Inside my head, a whisper told me it wasn't nothin' in this world up there on that roof but a little ol' blackbird with a broken wing tryin' to come in out of the cold and a truly kind, truly good, truly carin' lady would let such a pore harmless little ol' critter inside. Would INVITE it to come inside, 'stead of thumpin' at it with mean ol' crosses.

I was about to lean out the door and take a look at the poor little birdie and see what could be done to fix it. Peculiar as it may seem to be ready to admit something that was clearly, under the circumstances, realistically and validly threatening, I can only say that the voice in my head this time, like the one I had felt urging me to open my window in San Francisco, was overwhelmingly compelling.

But as I looked out the door, I saw Sergeant Destin march into my cabin. The entreaties of the "bird" were overwhelmed by my realization that if Stella was going to scream, now would be a good time to get her to do so. I was considering what would be the most effective and least detectable way to elicit that scream without permanent or unforgivable damage to her person, when the scrabbling on the roof increased for a moment and was followed by a thump. Something dark, something that seemed to swallow the starlight landed behind Destin. It landed on four paws and once more I saw the tail. Then, as gracefully as a dancer, it stood upright in a billowy garment that prohibited my detecting age or sex.

I was still befogged from the hold the creature had had on my mind or I would have yelled a warning at once, of course. I bore the sergeant no malice, just because he had falsely accused, arrested, and imprisoned me. Fortunately, Stella was just crazy and not particularly sensitive. She saw what was happening and screamed the scream she could have used to prevent the situation from deteriorating so rapidly had she only had the good sense to emit it earlier.

At the same time Destin yelled, then moaned, and I was trying to fling open the door again and not having much luck because Stella had planted herself against it murmuring imprecations against evil, monsters, and whatever.

While I was trying to physically reason with her, something else black billowed past the door crack and also lept toward my cabin and the presumably embattled mountie.

I grabbed the weighty wooden crucifix from Stella. It made

a good weapon (from its heft it might have been made of railroad ties), but I couldn't help wishing my hostess had at hand a less symbolically loaded weapon, a broom perhaps. Thus armed, I dislodged Stella and plunged into the fray, much as the early Crusaders might have against the Saracens.

My cabin door was open, the interior boiling with blackness. The Pinkerton's body was halfway out the door, and here and there a flash of a yellow-striped leg or a red sleeve would streak out of the blackness to be snatched back in again. I waded in with a good grip on the cross and bashed at the nearest presenting surface. My intention was to bash repeatedly, until the black things unhanded the sergeant, but I didn't get the chance. With banshee-worthy shrieks, first one and then the other monster shrank from my embattled righteousness into the depths of the room, which wasn't far, where they shriveled and shrank and floundered. The sergeant, who had been suspended in mid-air and whose neck glistened with ominous wetness, toppled, his head diving for the ice. I leaned down to catch him as two screeches of flapping blackness swooped over my head and out the door.

The screams of the monsters were joined by those of Stella, who had followed me into the street and now stood with her hands against her ears, her mouth wide open, performing a veritable opera of alarmed utterances.

Papa looked up at me for a moment, but winked out as the sergeant stirred. All around me, cribs emptied of people wearing everything from quilts to parkas, while the denizens of the saloons spilled into the alley to view the unexpected floor show.

"What in tarnation?" Lurleen scolded from her doorway. "Ain't you people got no respect for other folks? Even if I didn't need my beauty sleep, he sure as the devil does!" I hadn't known she was in, of course, or customer or no customer I would have enlisted her hospitality instead of Stella's.

At the time, I ignored everything and focused exclusively on the sergeant, lying there half pillowed on the dead Pinkerton.

Then I felt someone wrap me in something rather smelly and hairy, but soft and so warm that I realized I had been nearly frozen.

"Take her back to the Vein," Sasha said.

I looked up. Shadowy faces surrounded me as if they were mourners at my funeral and I in my grave. Strong arms lifted me upright.

Sasha knelt beside the sergeant and uttered little crooning noises, which sounded strangely maternal until her head jerked up and she snapped, "What do you stand around for? Someone help me carry him back to the Vein before he, too, dies. Poor boy, poor sweet boy, to think you might have perished to this madness—"

I was trying to make sense of that as the miner, I think it was Miles, half toted me through the circle of vastly entertained bartenders, gamblers, prospectors, and girls.

By the time two miners and Sasha climbed the steps with Destin staggering between them, three more mounties were bursting in the front door, among them Inspector Constantine.

Destin was deposited on a sort of couch made of two chairs shoved together. Sasha bathed the wounds at his neck while the mounties, after reassuring themselves that he was alive, rushed out to retrieve the body of the Pinkerton.

Destin opened his eyes and revived somewhat. "Why, if it isn't the Widow Lamour! You puir lassie, what are you doin' in this place? Have you been so reduced?"

Vasily Vladovitch was there, looking as if he had fallen on the ice and scratched his cheek, which bore a couple of abrasions. He stood over me, kneading my neck and murmuring reassuringly for a moment, then returned to a table where he had apparently been privately entertaining Drake.

"Ah, puir lady," the sergeant said again, oblivious to the fact that it was he who lay wounded and she who ministered. "You fell in with a bad one in that evil woman. Suicide, my *back*side!"

"Shhh," Sasha said.

"Now, woman, don't shush me. 'Twas a woman attacked me tonight and a woman, I'll bet, killed Norman. Who else might it be but the one who was with you? Though I must say, I never thought her to be so old as she is. The biddy who attacked me was verra long in the tooth indeed," and he rubbed his neck thoughtfully.

No one ever said the Scots were flexible people. The sergeant had his preconceived idea of my guilt and, by heavens, he was going to stick with it.

When Constantine returned, his face was grim. Two policemen brought Norman inside and laid him on the bar, which did nothing to discourage the clientele, now gleaned by our superior form of live entertainment from all of the other establishments. They happily ordered drinks all around the deceased and discussed his demise with a verve and enthusiasm probably no one had ever accorded him during his lifetime. The corpse's wide death grin seemed to beam approvingly at them, making the body a tolerable, if dry, drinking companion.

"Now then, miss," the inspector addressed Stella. "Just when would you estimate this attack took place."

"Demons out of hell," Stella hissed at him. "Bloody fang and claw. Evil stalks the—"

"I see. Thank you. Constable Barnstable, I think this woman has sustained a severe shock. Perhaps the sisters of St. Mary's should have a look at her, eh?"

Barnstable saluted smartly and set about executing orders, driving Stella, still babbling, ahead of him.

"Now then, this other lady, I understand, speaks only Spanish?" He stared down at me as if afraid I might, being so strange, mistake him for a tortilla and take a bite out of him.

"Beggin' your pardon, Inspector, but I speak a little Mex myself," Drake said, rising lazily as smoke from his place beside Vasily Vladovitch. "I reckon I can find out what you need to know."

I started to protest and covered it up with a gargle and a cough. After dodging danger all night, was I finally to be caught by the machinations of police procedure?

"Ah, how kind you are, Consul Blake," Vasily Vladovitch intervened suavely, sliding himself between the inspector and me, "but you see, Miss Querida is not actually Spanish, which, at any rate is very different from the Mexican tongue usually spoken on the borders of the United States. She is a Spanish gypsy, and, like all gypsies, her native tongue is an ancient one no longer heard elsewhere upon this earth. Her Spanish is not, perhaps, so good as your own."

"Is that so?" Drake asked a little belligerently.

"Alas, yes."

"I have a question about this lass, since we're on the subject," Destin said. "I happen to know that one of the reasons Norman went to her place was that he'd been told by one of your girls that she didna come wi' the rest of 'em on the boat. If she did not, and she didna pass my border, how did she come then?"

"Ah, how indeed? That is a very good question," Vasily Vladovitch complimented him.

Sasha shrugged charmingly, "But, darling sergeant, did you not just hear Mr. Bledinoff tell you? The girl is a gypsy. I was told by one of her traveling companions when she arrived that her people entrusted her to a nomadic band of Siberian Eskimos, who kayaked her across the Bering Straits to their Alaskan brethren, who then kayaked her down to the Yukon, and further entrusted her to Indians with whom they traded. It was these Indians who delivered her safely to her new employment. She is a very famous artist, of course, and so her people wanted especially to make sure she represented them here in the gold fields of Dawson. Well-traveled people are marvelously ingenious, don't you think?"

The sergeant grunted and fell back heavily against the chair, which made his neck leak again. Sasha's tongue came out briefly, touching the corner of her mouth like a cat's as she mopped the wound. The man was much weakened, though he actually bled very little now.

At that point I started to thaw and everything else faded to relative unimportance. The heat of the stove drove red-hot spikes through my limbs, and I wept while Lurleen patted my shoulder.

During that time the surgeon from Fort Herchmer arrived and examined the body, pronouncing it dead of exsanguination. "Similar, in fact, to the body of Constable Faversham," he added.

"But—" the other young constable said, "but if the same person or persons who killed Faversham also killed Norman, that means the Lovelace woman and that Purdy fellow are cleared, doesn't it?"

"Not necessarily," Destin roused himself to comment. "If the woman is still alive. I never believed she was dead."

"But you must admit it is more likely that you were mistaken, Sergeant," Vasily Vladovitch said with all sweet reasonableness. "And surely, with Mr. Purdy locked in your cell, he can no longer be under suspicion. Perhaps Mr. Blake can undertake whatever legal procedures are necessary. I understand from Miss De—from the Widow Lamour that the poor man is afraid his hands are now too roughened to enable him to work as a dealer. You could assure him I can find some work for him here, even if it is working on *our* woodpile."

Drake's eyes snapped. "Purdy? Alonso Purdy? You think I ought to try to get him freed, do you? That no-good-dirty-double-crossin'-lizard-lovin'-soggy-son-of-a-bitch! I'll see him and everyone in this room in hell before I'll do any such thing. And with all due respect, Inspector, if you and your fine force even look like you plan to turn him loose, I'll raise such an all-fired stink you'll swear there's a polecat convention trottin' through with tails raised all the way between here and Washington, D.C."

"How you doin', honey?" Lurleen asked.

I groaned.

"Any chance of her stayin' here tonight?" she asked.

"Uh—" Sasha began.

"No," Vasily Vladovitch said. "No, she would undoubtedly be most comfortable back in her own cabin—that is, if the police are quite finished with it?"

They were and back I went, bundled off before I had a chance to talk privately with either my employer or Sasha. Vasily Vladovitch left a little ahead of me, in fact, saying that he needed to return home and attend to some urgent business. I wondered what could possibly be more urgent than what had already happened.

Lurleen's customer kindly slid down to my cabin and built up the fire before we left, and someone loaned me some mukluks for the journey and someone else a coat. Lurleen waited with me while my washwater got hot and her customer paced as nervously outside as a first-time father.

As soon as we were alone, I said, "Lurleen, I need your help. I simply have to learn more about what has transpired here, and I can go no further in these ridiculous clothes. I need a set of men's clothing. Can you arrange it?"

"Was Sittin' Bull an Indian? Honey, I been separatin' men from their britches since before you was born. Leave it to Lurleen. How long do you need 'em? I can keep him out of 'em till next week if necessary. You can pay me back later for the time."

"I can have them back before work tomorrow anyway."

"Fair enough."

Bone tired, aching from the unaccustomed exertion of dancing in the chorus, my fingers and toes still nipping with frostbite, I let myself be lulled to sleep by the warmth of my fire until the door opened and a quilt-wrapped figure slung a bundle of clothing in on the foot of the bed.

"Smell ought to keep you awake and anything else away from you, kid. Watch your step, okay? Don't know how I'll explain it to Curly if you bleed all over his Sunday go-to-meetin' suit. Sorry I couldn't get his union suit, but that's a sort of a sacred object."

* * *

One whiff of the clothing was as good as smelling salts. I walked very quickly, for a woman in my condition, the distance from my cabin to Vasily Vladovitch's, simply to keep the odor downwind.

I was a little embarrassed to appear at my employer's house in such array, but its very unsuitability added weight to my argument, I thought with a twinge of satisfaction at finally being able to have *something* in my all-too-wild-and-not-nearly-woolly-enough life under control.

When I had knocked twice without response, I pushed open the door, which was unlocked as it had been the first night. Dawn was still an hour away, but the room was shrouded in darkness. I was about to leave when something white shimmered in the doorway and I beheld, perfectly independent of any underlying structure, the full-length, life-size spectre of papa, beckoning me.

Now, I am not the kind of person who just goes barging uninvited in to a man's home. But Papa's presence naturally, not to say supernaturally, engaged my curiosity and I felt I had to see what it was up to. Also, I felt rather apologetic toward poor Papa. I had been assuming that he was responsible for the murders. After the events of the night, I now knew better.

Whether he went through the doorway to the kitchen or it went through him I couldn't say, but I do know I about bumped my nose on it trying to follow him. It creaked open, and I skinned through just in time to see Papa disappearing through what looked like the pantry curtain. He was still beckoning me to follow. I had taken but a half a step forward when the curtain ballooned as with a gust of wind, and a pair of burning golden eyes appeared.

"Curse you, Papa," I said. "How can you lead me into this and then abandon me?"

The golden eyes blinked. "Miss Valentine?" Vasily Vladovitch's voice asked. "Whatever are you doing here? It's kind of you to accept my invitation at long last, but regrettably I have dined heavily tonight and couldn't possibly eat another drop."

"I didn't come here for food," I told him. "But light would certainly be welcome. Heavens to Betsy, Vasily Vladovitch, however do you keep from injuring yourself bumping around in the darkness like this?"

"Ah, my dear lady, you have discovered my secret. I am too

vain, of course, to say so publicly, but I am quite literally blind as a bat. After so many years of working in dim rooms, I suppose, strong lighting truly does not agree with me. But here, I will kindle a candle in honor of this most unexpected pleasure. If I may be so rude, however, we have not long to converse. I must sleep soon."

"I understand," I said, containing my pique at his brusqueness. I had already been patient a whole week. You'd think if a person took all the trouble to walk over to another person's house in the middle of the night to talk about something that other person should have thought of a long time ago and had, in fact, promised to do, the other person could at least put off his beauty sleep awhile. After all, it was *I* who had fought monsters that night and practically been arrested.

"Well, there are a lot of things, really," I said, hardly knowing where to begin. "But the most important, I suppose—"

"Yes, yes, let us have the most important," he said. From the other side of the pantry curtain, I heard what sounded like a snarl and—slurping sounds.

I tried to look behind him, but he guided me with a steel grip on my elbow back into the living room. "My current lead bitch," he told me. "A difficult creature. I am having problems with her and have been attending her since I came home."

"I'm good with animals. Perhaps I could be of assistance," I volunteered, as the snarl turned to an almost human whimper.

"Your business, Miss Valentine. I must ask you to state it and leave. As I say, you have caught me at an awkward time. The sun will soon be rising and—"

"Well, really! If you must know, Mr. Bledinoff, I wish to be paid for the transport of Mr. Lawson. Miss Devine informed me at the outset I would have to wait until we reached Dawson to receive my salary, but I had no idea that before it occurred to anyone that it was still owed me, I would be reduced to rags and frostbite."

My tone must have been rather more harsh than I intended, for he evidently did not appreciate it. His own voice was cold as he said, "Yes, and the great Valentine Lovelace should not have to endure such hardship, should she? Were she alive, she would no doubt be as upset as you are. Rags are, however, quite appropriate to a gypsy dancing girl."

That did it. "Now you see here, sir. This gypsy dancing girl stuff is your idea, yours and Miss Devine's, and so was getting rid of my own clothing and putting me to a job for which I have no aptitude and less interest. All I asked for initially was a simple set of men's clothing, but it was the two of you who wanted to get fancy. You were too busy entertaining that worthless scalp-hunting coyote-in-consul's-clothing tonight to notice, but I was almost killed and then nearly lost my hands and feet to frostbite while simply returning to the little crib you so kindly, though I must say rather insultingly, chose to rent on my behalf and at my expense. I suppose next you're going to tell me that is what has become of my trail money?"

"As a matter of fact—" he began.

"Aha! A company store, is it? Well, I'll have you know I won't stand for it. You may think you have me over a barrel, but that is blackmail, sir, blackmail plain and simple, and I would rather hang than submit to it!"

"Miss Lovelace, calm yourself. I meant no such thing. I naturally had no idea your circumstances were so hard. Mine is a demanding position, you understand. I had not planned on matters arranging themselves as they have, for you *or* for me. If only you could know the problems I have had to cope with this week, the greed, the jealousy, the avarice, the savagery. I can quite understand why many gentlemen in my position avoid human contact altogether. Better to slink about the perimeter of society than to be forever maligned, forever reviled even by those who know nothing. You try to help people and what does it get you? Trouble. Threats. Nothing but pain. No consideration at all for my feelings. Surely you know perfectly well, madam, after all I have done for you, that I have not purposely neglected you. When first I brought you to my home, I never for a moment intended that you would ever be cold, or hungry, or in want again. I look upon it as a holy duty to protect you from that possibility forever. But I am only one being. Even I cannot handle everything."

"I don't want everything, just my money," I told him.

"Your money! Your money. How can a confidant of the great dragon be so crass? I am becoming disillusioned with you, madam," and he moved closer to me, his voice lower now. Remembering his talents as a mesmerist, I kept my eyes determinedly on the moose above his head.

"Mr. Bledinoff, allow me to repeat. My hands and feet were nearly frozen off tonight. It's well below freezing out there now and getting colder every minute. The Klondike River is solid.

Many of the creeks are frozen. I do not intend to join them, sir. Do I make myself clear?"

"You do, and now I must regretfully respond with similar clarity. Go. At once."

"Mr. Bledinoff, I need a coat. I need boots and a hat. This outfit is borrowed from a man who may make trouble when he's found out he loaned it to me. It is not especially warm— he couldn't be parted from his union suit. I—"

He drew himself up to his full height and, there in that gloomy chamber, was more intimidating than I imagined that courtly and almost foppish man could have been. "Leave me, Miss Lovelace. We will discuss this later, at a time more convenient for me."

And he forcibly cast me into the snow. I charged back toward the door, enraged as a bull, but two things made me reconsider. One, of course, was that such behavior ill-befitted a woman of my maturity and good judgment. I would not demean myself by butting my head against a closed door. I would simply wait patiently and get back at him tonight in any way that seemed handy and dirty. Not that I am a vindictive woman. I am the soul of sweet reason when reasonably treated. Under these circumstances, however, I was ready to live up to my reputation as a murderess. All that stopped me was the face of Papa in Vasily Vladovitch's front door. My dear departed parent was laughing, but when I lunged for the door, he shook his head decisively before fading.

I stared at where he had been, realizing that the sky had drained to dark silver and that I could make out the grain in the wood. More than a week since the constable's death, and heaven only knew how many others, and I still was no closer to the truth than before. I huddled into the borrowed mack and turned away, trotting down the path to the beach until the hospital buildings loomed ahead.

# CHAPTER XIV

·····•◈═╡I╞═◈•·····

St. Mary's Hospital smelled of reused scrub water and alcohol, overlaying the less savory effluvia of sick humanity. Fresh damp swipes streaked the wooden floor and the ends of the white-painted iron bedsteads. Behind ceiling-hung sheets, medicine bottles tinkled. Metal instruments clacked on trays while black woollen robes brushed back and forth, back and forth, briskly in time with the footsteps of their wearers. The men in this ward breathed noisily, their chests rising and falling as if their ribs were called upon to do strenuous lifting just to raise the frail veneer of flesh covering them.

A sister busily engaged with her dressing tray shot me a look so eloquent it made my knuckles ache as I perused the first ward. I failed to see Larsson, so I made speedily for the second building.

My quarry lay directly opposite the sister's desk, which sister fortuitously was not occupying at the time. His face was wet with sweat and bore deep folds, as if it was a sweater that had been stretched out of place and never properly reblocked. A strip of bandage showed above the blanket tucked under his armpits. The top was straight as paper, but the bottom had been shredded and the toes of one foot poked through the tightly tucked bedding. A simple wooden cross hung above his bed. He stared beyond me when I spoke his name.

"Glad to see you're doing better, old fellow," I said with assumed masculine heartiness.

He continued looking through me. His big hands clenched fistfuls of blanket into wads. I stuck my own hand out for him to shake. "Pat Harper. I was with you on the boat when your friend was killed. Just heard what happened to you. Tough luck."

"Uncle Dag?"

"No. No, Pat Harper," I repeated, and changed the subject. "I must say, you don't look half bad for a fellow who was bit by a moose."

"Moose?"

"Of course, moose. The one that bit you. Grow them mean up here, don't they?"

He roused up and twitched in an agitated way, his eyes showing more intelligence now, and a sort of dazed bewilderment. "Ya, but dem was tame mooses. Cow and calf. Uncle Dag fed 'em. Dot wolf, he got the calf. I heard the mama hollerin', but before I could get there with my rifle, the wolf hamstrung her and tore out her t'roat. Then she got me then —then—" holding his head perfectly still, he rolled his eyes downward, toward his bandaged middle.

"Did you see anything else? A man? Or notice anything unusual about the wolf?" I asked eagerly, my voice, I am afraid, rising an octave or two.

He shook his head.

At the doorway, a sister was saying, "I don't care who you are, that animal must remain outside. If I let you bring it in here, half the patients will be demanding we let their sled dogs sleep with them."

"Sister, you're a compassionate woman. Have a heart. If I leave Loki outside on the ground, the dogs might get him."

"That, Mr. Lomax, is why God gave cats claws."

"'Scuse me, buddy, how long you plannin' to be?" I inquired of Lomax, leaving the sick man behind me shaking his head like a broken toy.

"Who are you?"

"Yes, who are you?" sister demanded, crossing her arms on her chest.

"I'm the fella will look after the cat so these sick folks can get some rest around here, that's who," I told them as I ambled over to join them. "That is, if this gent isn't going to stay here all day."

"Matter of fact, I can't stay too long. But Loki don't take to just anyone—"

Loki was already rubbing my hand with his chin. "Takes to me," I said. "I'll wait outside."

Lomax leaned down and Loki leapt lithely onto my shoulders.

My wait was not long, and the cat served as companion, ruff, and mittens while we stood outside the hospital. Though the animal's weight added to the cramps in my back, its vibrating warmth was so welcome that I was almost sorry to see Lomax return. He was shaking his head as he stepped out into the cold.

"Thanks, son. I just want to check that building over there and see how Young Jack is comin' along. Won't be a minute."

"He's not in that one, sir," I said. "I looked there earlier."

But he was already on his way. He had better luck than I, but, of course, I had not been looking specifically for London. "He's haler this morning. Was out haulin' water for the sisters. Got a touch of 'nemia and a touch of scurvy. Nothin' a little decent grub won't fix. Same thing as is wrong with half the men up here." Loki changed shoulders again reluctantly. The ripe smell of my clothing was well worth investigating, from the cat's viewpoint.

"If this country is so hard on cats, Captain Lomax, why did you bring Loki here?" I asked, giving the cat one last stroke.

Lomax shot me a shrewd sideways look. "I didn't. He was up here before me. Ship's cat one of the boys had brought over from Norway had gone into port at Seattle. She, uh, made friends real fast. Loki was born on the trip up. Some of them boys on the *Bear* had a real strange sense of humor. So I took to carryin' the kitten around with me. Saw no reason to change that."

"Was the *Bear* your ship?"

He snorted. "Nah, I was just a passenger." He gave me another sly sideways glance. "What makes you think I *had* a ship?"

"Well, they call you captain and you talk salty and—" I started to mention all of the seagoing books on his wall, but realized I hadn't seen them while in my present role. "And you uh, just look like a sea captain."

"Like Long John Silver, you mean, only fore instead of aft?" He pulled his hook from its pocket. The sun, just rising, tinted it pink. The Yukon was pink, too, sliding sluggishly along beside us between banks encrusted with pink ice.

I shrugged.

"I did lose it while aboard ship, actually, but that was in the war and I was a common seaman, not a captain."

"Oh." For a time we walked in silence together. The sky grew light, the brilliant pink mellowing to a blushing glow, like the inside of a seashell. The flakes fell tickling and wet, starring the cat's fur and Lomax's hair.

"I'm *going* to be a captain though, as soon as we can dig out enough gold to outfit a steamer," Lomax said. "I'll navigate the Yukon. I've read a passle of books on the subject. Don't see why I couldn't learn as easy as anybody. Main thing's gettin' to know the river. If my whiskers and my talk make me a captain instead of an old gaffer to these boys, I figure they're just a little premature. More polite to prove them right than to make liars out of 'em, wouldn't you say?"

Liars out of *them*? Was everybody in this town nothing but a humbug? On second thought, I was not in much of a position to stick my nose in the air on that score.

The snow spiffed up Dawson like a fresh coat of paint. On my one previous daytime foray, the haphazard, slapped-together, temporary and in-progress nature of the town had made it one of the ugliest places I had ever seen, more of an overgrown camp than a city. Plumped with a couple of inches of spanking white snow, however, the rooftops, the ruts, the lean-tos, the shacks, the raw, new log buildings, even the piles of trash and debris, took on a custom-matched elegance, enhanced by pearly plumes of smoke. The frosted spruces on the bluff opposite were washed with gold.

Our footsteps no longer crunched, but sank into muffled silence. As we descended onto Front Street, hunched men padded quickly past us, and what looked like a pair of overgrown twelve-year-olds slid down the street, the slick track of their boots like the wake of the ice worms the sourdoughs invented to torment newcomers. A six-dog team jingled past us, the driver whistling at his dogs to pass "on by, on by."

Ahead, a line of men stretched around the front and down one side of the Alaska Commercial Company's warehouse.

"What's this all about?" I asked.

"There's a ship comin' in from Fort Yukon today. Where you been, boy, out to the creeks? Everybody's waitin' for supplies."

"But not you?"

"Well, no. I seem to have come by some extra, courtesy of that lady who drowned herself last week. You musta heard about it."

"Oh, yes. Miss Lovelace, the novelist. She was on the ship with us. Very sad. A brilliant woman, and one of the great talents of the century."

"Is that so?"

"Yes indeed, I—" I realized I had better control my tendency to eulogize myself since Miss Lovelace, as I very well knew, had had little occasion to get to know much of anybody on the ship. "May she rest in peace," I murmured decorously, and crossed myself.

"Indeed," he said, and buried his face in his hand, his shoulders shaking. Though it may have been snowflakes melting on his lashes, his eyes seemed to sparkle with tears.

"Are you quite all right, Captain Lomax?" I asked.

"To tell you the exact truth, I'm not," he replied. "I am peeved is what I am, and though it wouldn't be a good thing to tell them about it, I'm purely disappointed in the mounties. Here they are, the law of the Yukon, and they can't hang on to one gal, so I'm stuck with all her female doodads. I'd appreciate it, son, if you'd come along and steady me some. I have a powerful temper, and if you was along I'd be less likely to lose it where it would get me kicked out of the country."

"I—well, all right."

"You're sure?"

"I can't think of anything I'd rather do than see mountie headquarters close up," I assured him.

When I saw my outfit spread out on the duty officer's desk, I had to tell myself to be a man and not cry. There it all lay; my practical winter things, the perfect rugged clothing for the tasteful gentleman adventurer, clothing that would look all the more piquant, so I fondly hoped, on a woman of style and dash; my Annie Oakley skirt and my beautiful gown.

My food, parceled between Lomax and the mountie's storehouse, did not torture me with its loss. Vasily Vladovitch had a contract with a small cafe adjoining the saloon, and though the fare was limited, it was better than I could have cooked up from the remaining raw materials.

But, ah, those clothes, so warm and still smelling new, many of them not even worn! My body was numb from the long walk across the length of Dawson, my thighs and arms felt like logs, my hands and feet were without feeling. Oh, my beautiful new sturdy gumboots! Oh, my double-knitted mittens! Oh, my galoshes!

The constable, assuming he was among other men, drew out a pair of Sasha's lacy drawers from under the satiny skirts of the gown, and I snatched them away from him and held them behind my back.

"Some lads got no sense of humor," he said to Lomax.

"Some lads got respect for ladies," Lomax replied. Loki hopped down and investigated the skirts of one of Sasha's fancier gowns, which were piled with my plainer ones but separated from the more masculine items. Lomax thoughtfully lifted my winter coat to his chest, then slipped it over his arms. He was not much taller than I, but barrel-chested and well developed of arm and shoulder. The coat failed to meet in front and pulled over his arms. "Musta been the corpse's stuff," he said. "Can't see why them ladies brought it, but it's too little for me or Egil or Jack. Too bad. Guess I'll sell it or trade it."

"No!" I said, thinking how warm it would have felt last night. "I mean, Captain Lomax, I can't pay you right now, but I have a job and I sure do need clothes and—"

"You sure do," he said, wrinkling his nose at the heat-enhanced aroma of my current wardrobe. "But what makes you think any of this stuff'd fit you?"

"Oh—uh—they just look like my size, I guess. If you could see your way clear to letting me have them, I could pay you later—"

The door scraped open behind us and feet stomped free of snow at the threshold. "Very well, Mr. Purdy, you may be collectin' your personal effects and be on your way."

"Mighty kind of you, Sergeant. Don't know how you boys can bear to lose me since without me to chop your wood you're probably gonna freeze your asses off, but—"

"None o' that. You go see Mr. Bledinoff, like I told you, before we arrest you again for vagrancy, loiterin', and no doubt disturbin' the peace."

"Yes, sir," Purdy agreed. I pulled the collar of my borrowed mack up around my face and sidled past both of them toward the door.

"Day to you, Malcom," Lomax said very cheerfully for a man so full of self-proclaimed indignation.

"Good day yourself, Dag." The sergeant also seemed in

unusually good spirits, considering that he had narrowly escaped being foully and fiendishly murdered the night before.

"If you'll sign here, sir," the constable said.

"What about the groceries and hardware?" Lomax asked him. "There were some books—"

"We'll distribute the supplies to those who have none."

"Then hand them over," Lomax said. "Mine haven't arrived yet, and it doesn't look like they will."

"Only half the goods are salvage, Dag," Destin reminded him. "Naturally the property of the Widow Lamour needs to be duly returned to her, puir lass. If the wee bit the Lovelace woman had doesna do the job, Dag, perhaps you should consider this. I'm just on my way to post it."

Lomax turned toward the door for light, and I was able to read over his shoulder and still not overexpose myself to Destin's scrutiny.

THE UNDERSIGNED, OFFICIALS OF THE CANADIAN GOVERNMENT, HAVING CAREFULLY LOOKED OVER THE PRESENT DISTRESSING SITUATION IN REGARD TO THE SUPPLY OF FOOD FOR THE WINTER, FIND THAT THE STOCK ON HAND IS NOT SUFFICIENT TO MEET THE WANTS OF THE PEOPLE NOW IN THE DISTRICT, AND CAN SEE ONLY ONE WAY OUT OF THE DIFFICULTY, AND THAT IS AN IMMEDIATE MOVE DOWN THE RIVER OF ALL THOSE WHO ARE NOW UNSUPPLIED TO FORT YUKON, WHERE THERE IS A LARGE STOCK OF PROVISIONS. WITHIN A FEW DAYS THE RIVER WILL BE CLOSED, AND THE MOVE MUST BE MADE NOW, IF AT ALL. IT IS ABSOLUTELY HAZARDOUS TO BUILD HOPES UPON THE ARRIVAL OF OTHER BOATS. IT IS ALMOST BEYOND A POSSIBILITY THAT ANY MORE FOOD WILL COME INTO THIS DISTRICT. FOR THOSE WHO HAVE NOT LAID IN A WINTER'S SUPPLY TO REMAIN HERE ANY LONGER IS TO COURT DEATH FROM STARVATION, OR AT LEAST A CERTAINTY OF SICKNESS FROM SCURVY AND OTHER TROUBLES. STARVATION NOW STARES EVERY MAN IN THE FACE WHO IS HOPING AND WAITING FOR OUTSIDE RELIEF. LITTLE EFFORT AND TRIVIAL COST WILL PLACE THEM ALL IN COMFORT AND SAFETY WITHIN A FEW DAYS AT FORT YUKON OR AT OTHER POINTS BELOW, WHERE THERE ARE NOW LARGE STOCKS OF FOOD.

It was signed by Inspector Constantine, D.W. Davies, the collector of customs, and Fred Fawcett, the gold commissioner, and dated September 30. How strange for the dead of winter, with starvation pending, to come so early.

"Aye, well, I hope you can trust me not to rob the lady, Malcom. I'll just take all of this along so she can sort her own from my salvage," Lomax said and bundled the clothing into a blanket and slung it over his shoulder, accentuating his resemblence to Saint Nicholas. Loki jumped onto the bag and clung precariously.

"Here, Purdy, make yourself useful and pack these goods up to the Rich Vein. Follow Lomax."

"From a beaver to a goddamn mule in one day," Purdy grumbled, but shouldered a burden bigger than he was.

When we were well past Fort Herchmer, Lomax gave a deep sigh and set his pack down. "Got to lighten this some," he mumbled, then plucked the men's clothing from the pack and struck me across the chest with it. "Here you go, son. You want to carry this stuff, you can have it."

"I—thanks," I said. "Captain Lomax, I—"

"Forget it," and walked away, Loki's tail tapping the bundled blanket.

I raced down Paradise Alley, bolted into my cabin, stripped off my smelly borrowed raiment, and contemplated my new wealth. Sadly, I realized I could not wear the union suit, trousers, or shirt while in my guise as Corazon, but I could not resist using the wraps. Pulling on the cancan costume, my galoshes, hat, muffler, mittens, and Hudson Bay coat, I crept to the door of Lurleen's cabin and, hearing no noise from within, stealthily opened the door and tossed the smelly borrowed finery in, pitying Lurleen her profession. Stella's door slammed sharply.

I returned to my cabin and swept my new clothes to one side of the cot. I was both very excited by the events of the morning and very weary and sore from the events of the previous night. While I was trying to decide whether to sleep or to join Lomax at the Vein and await news of the steamer, a shadow passed my window and I heard a rap at my door.

Before I could answer, Maisie popped her head in. "Millie and I were just headed over to Madame Tremblay's and thought you might like to come along, honey. I saw how bad off your costume was last night and—"

"Oh, for pity's sakes, Maisie, you know she cain't understand a *word* you're sayin'," Millie said, and swept in and picked up my rumpled costume from the floor. Maisie grabbed my arm and pulled me to my feet and down the street to Madame Tremblay's.

Although I have never been much of a clothes horse, within the dressmaker's emporium surrounded by a prismatic display of ribbons, laces, feathers, beads, bolts of silks, satins, cotton, taffeta, woolens, and imported Paris gowns, I felt like a toothless elder in a chewing gum factory.

I was too exhausted and too full of aches and pains to pay much attention to detail. Maisie fingered the fabrics, held the dresses against her, curled a bit of lace around her wrist. She wore a high-necked red woolen dress with some sort of animal tails for trim. Millie's dress was more summery, with big sleeves that poked through her cloak. She wore a high feathered hat that promptly came off as did her cape while she rushed around scooping up this costume or that one and studying her reflection in Madame's big floor mirror.

The establishment was not large, little more than a two-room cabin, with the store in Madame's sitting room. A curtain separated the store from her sleeping quarters, and from there issued murmurs and the clack and tromp of a treadle machine.

This inspired me to bestir my tortured muscles and inquire through the curtain if my costume could be mended before the evening performance.

A hand reached through the curtain. I deposited the costume. More clacking and tromping and a few moments later a small dark woman, frail as a bird in appearance, flung the curtain aside.

"What have you been doing with this gown?" she asked. "Conducting boxing matches? It will cost you fifty cents for the silk, though I cannot match it and will have to reinforce the red with black, which will give you rather daring stripes down the side, you see?"

I saw. I also saw that I didn't have the fifty cents and started to take the costume back.

Maisie was just then lifting a wide strip of black velvet ribbon to her throat. Millie had already opened her collar and was seeing how much of a bow lent the effect she wanted. Just below the tie, I saw the red mark on her neck.

"Put it on Mr. Bledinoff's bill, please, Madame Marie," Maisie said. "And I think we'll wear these."

Millie was swathed in yards of black organdy trimmed with black ribbons and tiny garnet buttons. "What do you think of this little number, Miss Adanopolis? Think this will be enough to keep ol' alligator-breath bedridden for the rest of the winter?"

"Oh, look here! Madame, how much are these?" cried Maisie as she held forth frothy black silk and lace bloomers, camisole, and a delicate web of a petticoat to match. "Oh, and this! Oh, mercy, do they really wear things like this in Paree?" She tied the red ribbons of the black lace wrapper low on her bosom and swirled, the lace fanning in a circle from her shoulders like the waters of a whirlpool. Her neck ribbon, lightly tied, fell to the floor. The angry red mark above her collar spun before my eyes as she pirouetted.

The shop was dark log, low ceilinged, and cramped, crammed with the headless torsos of mannequins flaunting their finery, the jungle of ribbons and lace squirming like tentacles. The potbellied stove simmered in a thick sauce of perfume and yeasty body smells. Giddy giggles from Maisie and flashing hematite eyes devouring a reflection that wavered and dimmed, wavered and dimmed. Millie danced with the black gown and waggled a red feathered fan over her head.

I had to get out. Half-doubled over, I bolted for the door, but Millie snagged my wrist and cajoled in a babyish voice, "No, no, Cory, don't go. You have to have a new dress, too, Vassy says. New number. Black for everybody. Black and red. Red and black. Right, Madame? Tray oo la la, huh?"

New number my foot! I'd seen those marks on Sasha, on Giselle, and now on these two. At the same time. Two at once. I was virtually in the clutches of a man who not only had weird ideas about how to seduce women, but who had not even the restraint to stick to one at a time. Worse, these girls seemed not to mind that he was after them both. Well, I was not about to be added to the collection. For all practical purposes, this trip had already made me a dance hall girl, a murderess, and a suicide. Even if it had cost me my reputation, it was not going to cost me my honor. Having kept it for over three decades, I'd grown used to it, and if I was going to lose it, it would certainly be to someone more selective than Vasily Vladovitch Bledinoff.

Storming back to my cabin, my head cleared just enough that I realized I was even more confused than I thought. The girls who bore the boss's love bites were not the only ones to sport the marks of such bizarre canoodling. I had seen them on father, on Wy Mi, on other victims of the Deadly Miasma. The necrophiliac implications of that were so disgusting that I simply closed them out and determined to avail myself of the better part of valor. Arraying myself once more in men's attire, this time new and rather cleaner than I was, I returned to the warehouse at about three o'clock in the afternoon, just in time to see the *Bella* appear around the bend below town and battle the floating ice to the landing.

Lomax and a shakey but upright London stood talking together by the corner of the warehouse. A man next to them said, "Well, I'll bet those boys who hightailed it downriver are eatin' their hearts out now. What with the *Weare* comin' in day before yesterday and now this, why, I don't see why we can't all get through the winter."

"Depends," Lomax said.

I lost track of them then, as the ship tied up and the men pressed forward to help in the unloading. The results were disappointing. When all the boxes and bundles were unloaded, only seventy-five tons of freight sat on the dock.

# CHAPTER XV

THE DUTY CONSTABLE, his carroty mustache bristling with frost, strode through the crowd and tacked up a new notice. He was striding away again when a peacoat-clad sailor intercepted him and dropped a bundle at his feet. "Mail. Got hung up in Fort Yukon. Been there a month or so."

With that perfunctory message, the seagoing postman started to return to his ship. But Lomax was standing near the landing, eyeing the steamer with the air of a connoisseur.

"Why, if it isn't Cap'n Lomax!" the sailor said. "Ready to hire me on yet, sir?"

Lomax shook his head. "Not yet. Soon's it pans out, I'll send you word."

"You do that, sir. By the way, that mail? Was a mite scattered when we collected it. Saw a parcel in there from London, England. Had your name on it."

"A book? Was it a book, lad?"

But the sailor was gone.

Lomax, less like Santa now than one of the jolly gent's recipients, accosted the constable at once. I skirted around them and joined the cluster of men around the note.

"What the devil does the damn thing say?" one of them asked.

"Can't you read, Blasingame?"

"Hell no. What does it say?"
"Damned if I know. I never did get the hang of that stuff."

NOTICE IS HEREBY GIVEN THAT ALL PERSONS WHO ARE
NOT SUFFICIENTLY PROVIDED WITH FOOD FOR THE COM-
ING WINTER WILL BE TAKEN OUT FREE OF CHARGE ON
THE STEAMER *BELLA*, WHICH WILL LEAVE TO-MORROW (SIC)
AT NOON. THEY SHOULD REPORT AT THE ALASKA COM-
MERCIAL COMPANY'S STORE TOMORROW MORNING AT 8
O'CLOCK AND SIGN AN AGREEMENT AS TO THEIR TRANS-
PORTATION. THEY ARE ADVISED TO TAKE SUFFICIENT FOOD
WITH THEM TO LAST THEM TO CIRCLE CITY, AS NO MEALS
CAN BE SERVED ON THE STEAMER. SUFFICIENT SUPPLIES
CAN BE OBTAINED AT CIRCLE CITY TO LAST TO FORT YUKON.
THE CANADIAN AUTHORITIES HAVE ARRANGED WITH
THE ALASKA COMMERCIAL COMPANY TO FURNISH FREE
TRANSPORTATION.
     C. CONSTANTINE,
     INSPECTOR NORTHWESTERN MOUNTED POLICE
     DAWSON, SEPTEMBER 30, 1897

There were only two happy faces in the entire crowd. One
was mine, although my feelings were not unmixed, for I hated
abandoning even a web of trouble so seemingly insoluble as
the one in which I had heretofore been ensnared. The other
was Lomax's. He stroked the leather bindings of a large black
book and leafed gleefully through its pages. When the other
men gathered in groups discussing the situation, I sought him
out, but he was drifting down the road and was already deeply
into his book. Had I known what those pages contained, I
would have overtaken him and wrestled him for it, for between
those covers lay many of the answers that had eluded me for
so long.

London drifted into the Vein, along with a knot of other
men exclaiming over the notice, how THEY never would be
quitters and let a little thing like starvation worry them, while
others said that yessireebob, THEY knew enough to come in
out of the rain—or out of forty below, as it were, at least long
enough to get fresh provisions and a trip back to American
soil.

Naturally, each side listened attentively to the arguments of
its opposite number, with much resulting yelling and throwing

about of fists. I slipped through the melee and hurriedly past the bar, for I did not trust my disguise to fool Lane, and took the stairs two at a time. Sasha Devine answered my summons only after repeated knocks.

Her face as it peeked around her door was once more alarmingly pale, but her grip as she reeled me in was as strong as a miser's on his cashbox.

The beaded curtain hung in a shimmering unbroken pattern across the entry to her bedchamber, and the little sitting room was shrouded in gloom.

"Vahlenteena, wherever did you get such a ridiculous costume? You look like a lumpy little boy. Why have you awakened me? I was planning to sleep in."

"Sasha, I require my wages. I spoke to Mr. Bledinoff about the matter this morning and received no satisfaction. Since it was with you I made the arrangements, I expect you to honor them. I cannot abide the goings on around here and can make no progress in clearing my good name while forced into this hideous charade. I will not be classed with women who think so little of themselves as to pursue en masse the same man, and one who returns their affections in such an odious manner at that. Frankly, I am shocked that a woman of your calibre would link yourself to such a man and permit such practices to be inflicted upon you, but that is your lookout. Still, I'd think you'd be alarmed at how unhygienic it all is. Why, I have learned of several people who have died, apparently from contagion from those hideous wounds you all find so appealing. Hell's bells, Sasha, what's wrong with simple kissing?"

Her hand flew to her throat and caressed the side of her neck beneath the midnight velvet flounces of her wrapper. She stared me down, her eyes like molten pennies, and I recalled once more the rumors of her aristocratic birth. She knew how to push people around all right.

"Vahl," she said, "you are sounding priggish again, and it is most unattractive. Who are you, you silly girl, to cast judgment on the cultural practices of people whose existences are so remote from your narrow little world? I will not be awakened only to listen to you babble nonsense. Who are these other women to whom you refer, and what dreadful things are we all supposed to be doing?"

"I—I don't believe I care to go into it with you right now. But after tonight you'll have to find another Spanish dancer. I am sick to death of stomping around and trying to look dramatic to a flamencoed-up version of 'Daisy Bell.' I want the money that is owed me, and we will part with no hard feelings."

"Hah!" she said with a singular lack of eloquence.

"Hah! yourself. By the way, if you want the bar intact, perhaps you should go down and break up the fight that was starting as I came up. Lane can't possibly hold them off forever."

But all was quiet once more as I descended the steps. The factions had broken off into their respective groups. Each group was now drinking and talking with others clever enough to appreciate the correct viewpoint. London sat with another man whose back was to me and concealed by the hood of his parka.

"Yessir, you see, I have been having the damndest time thinking like a dog to get the character of Fang correct. All that sniffing and slavishness. I can't understand why a dog that's half-wild would ever take to a man, no matter how kind."

"Right there's where you're goin' wrong, son. See, a wolf is never slavish, but it does have a deep respect for the pack leader—the dominant wolf—and no matter whether it likes it or not, it will bow to the will of that leader. It's not like an ol' dawg, whufflin' and slobberin'. No sir, a wolf is real special. A lone wolf, of course, doesn't have a leader mostly, but it remembers when it did have—"

"Thank you, Mr. Blake. I never realized bein an American politician in Canada qualified a man to know so much about wolves," Jack said. The funny part was he seemed genuinely to mean it and was scratching his upper lip and writing himself a note.

From an unlit corner a little to my right, Purdy's disembodied voice oozed, "Can't think who'd be *better* qualified than him, though I didn't think even lowdown mangy coyotes went around tellin' their family secrets."

But fortunately at that moment a heated dispute arose in another area of the room and no one heard him. No doubt recalling the rigors of the woodpile, he did not see fit to add to his commentary.

My poor patched costume had been carelessly flung across my bed. I joined it and tried to sleep, but my aching muscles and racing thoughts allowed me no rest.

It occurred to me that I had been much more grief-stricken back in San Francisco than I'd realized. With Papa's sterling example always before me, no one had better cause than I to know the dangers of entering into business propositions with friends. Or the difficulty of collecting from them. And yet I, the victim in early years of many such deals perpetrated by my pater, had fallen into just such a trap myself. What else but the insanity of bereavement could have possibly induced me to plunge penniless into a scheme that would take me thousands of miles into unknown country with an unscrupulous companion on only an unwritten *promise* of payment? Of course, an ironclad contract would have done me no more good in my present circumstances, but that was no excuse. I knew very well from trying to collect from Papa's bosom friends that such collection took every ounce of guile, guilt, and downright bullying a body possessed. In my own case, bullying would obviously not do, and reason and appeal to finer instincts had already failed. Blackmail it was, then.

I pulled on my mended costume and charged through the premature darkness of the late arctic afternoon into the lamplit dance hall. Mr. Lane was alone, polishing the bar with a cloth when I came in. When I started up the stairs, he shook his head and rolled his eyes, but I disregarded the warning.

Whispers came from behind Sasha's door. If it had been shouts I'd have plunged right into the fray, but people whispering obviously don't want to be interrupted. I was sure they'd prefer that I eavesdropped.

"Sasha, my darling, you wrong me. You do not understand that this is all a part of my great plan. Believe me, when I am through this town will be like no other in the history of the world, and our show will be, quite literally, immortal."

"When you are through we will have a town with one less entertainment establishment because the owner cannot learn to keep his teeth out of the till! My God, Vasily Vladovitch, there are a dozen other saloons in town. Why don't you pick on *their* girls and leave my staff alone?"

"Because I don't *know* their girls, and if I am to practice restraint, I must feel something for the girl or I get carried away and—oh, you know how it goes, my love. By the same token I cannot trust myself with great passion such as that I feel for you. So I have a lot of friends. This is so terrible? I told you already that despite my great love and admiration for you, I needed to see other people. So, if we are to have the enduring love I envision for us, must you."

"Yes, but I did not mean you could take every girl in the house and turn her into a lovelorn zombie. It makes me feel such a fool."

"They are happy. What can I say? Why should it bother you? I promise you they will not mind, and neither should you."

"I do, and you know damn good and well they would also if they were not so spellbound by you—" Her voice sank from a hiss to a moan so that I almost heard her melt. "None of them can resist you any more than I—oooh, Vasily Vladovitch, master of my nights—"

"Ah, Natasha Alexandrina, my little blood sausage—"

"Kinda makes your heart go pitty-pat, don't it?" a voice whispered behind me. I whirled.

"Purdy!" I said.

"Howdy, Miss Valentine. Buy a feller a drink?"

I hastily steered him back down the stairs. From his remark, he had heard only the last of their conversation. He was in no position to know as I did that Bledinoff, the great mesmerist, was using his talent to bend innocent—well, of some things anyway—women to his will. Had Purdy known, I'm sure he would have interrupted that private conversation to demand lessons.

"I am so glad to see that my entreaties to Mr. Bledinoff have not been in vain and that he has seen to it that you were freed," I murmured to him at the foot of the stairs.

"Oh, are you? I wish to Pete you'd entreated a little faster, darlin', cause it's going to take my hands a hell of a long time to heal up. Actually, I don't think your friend had much to do with it. Accordin' to Sergeant Destin, ol' Drake—he's callin' himself Blake now and claims to be a politician, which always was the job for which he was best suited, other than 'deceased' if you ask me—threw his weight around in front of the head mountie, and that gentleman didn't cotton to bein' treated like a peon. He got to studyin' on my case real quick and found they really didn't have a goldern thing on me any more. You know, I'm still mad at that-son-of-a-somethin'-I-shouldn't-talk-about-in-front-of-a-person-of-the-female-persuasion, but I should give him a big ol' sloppy kiss. He done me a hell of a favor. Which is more than I can say for you."

"I told you I tried," I said. "And really, we can't go on talking. Everyone here thinks I'm a Spanish gypsy named Corazon. My life depends upon it."

"Does it now?" he asked in a voice that could be heard clear to Skagway.

"Shhh—"

"I am takin' no more raps for you, sweetheart. I—aye yi yi."

Sasha Devine, clad in a gown of black satin with a red high-necked bodice embroidered with spangles of jet prisms, was descending the stairs. "Mr. Purdy, our new dealer. I am delighted to meet you. I am Saaasha. This is my place. You like it?" She was looking deeply into his eyes.

"Yes, *ma'am*," he said fervently, never allowing his gaze to stray from hers.

"Good. Let me see your hands." He held them out as obediently as a small child. "Ahh, the palms are in bad shape. Tell me, Mr. Purdy, may I call you Alonso?" She rolled his name around on her tongue as if it were a fine wine.

# CHAPTER XVI

···••·◄╬►∥◄╬►·••···

"*DARLIN'*, YOU MAY call me Ulysses S. Grant if you take a notion, and I won't bat nary an eyelash."

"Alonso, you look to me like more than a tinhorn gambler. I see in your eyes the sensitive soul of a fellow artiste. I don't suppose you play the guitar?"

"With these paws?"

"Your fingertips are not adversely affected."

"That's true. Hell, just cause my hands are three inches longer on account of the callouses shouldn't stop me. Why, any Texan worth the splinters on the mountie woodpile can play a little Mex'can guitar when he takes a mind to, even if he's been shoving souvenirs of the north woods up his fingernails."

"Then you will play something appropriate behind our star Spanish dancer, Corazon?" She indicated me with a gracious wave of her hand. "I see that you are already becoming friends."

Sasha smiled at me, thereby demonstrating her good faith by trying to solve the smallest of all of my complaints. It wouldn't work, I vowed, as I danced onto the stage for the last time, flirting my ruffles and making wide eyes with the rest of the girls. I was beginning to feel a little conspicuous. As of tonight, I was the only one in the chorus not sporting a black velvet choker.

Maisie explained it between numbers. "We had the funnest little party last night at the hotel. Honey, you shoulda been

there. Vassy was afraid we'd got ourselves upset by all the
excitement, and so he brought a few bottles of this genuine,
authentic, French red wine over, and we played spin the bottle.
I'm not sure if it was the wine or Vassy, but boyoboy, something sure had a kick to it."

"Was that why he authorized the shopping spree?" I asked.

"Yeah, wasn't that swell?"

With no rest, little food, and so many unanswered questions running through my mind, I found the dancing pure
torture, but at least my limbs had gained some flexibility and
strength during the week, although nothing like that of the
other girls. Purdy took his full measure of revenge by setting
a killing pace with his guitar. I stopped right in the middle
once and stomped my foot at him to desist, but he struck
another chord. I stomped again, but he paid no attention,
so I kicked at him, most irritated that I could not tell him
what I thought of him in plain English. When I finished, the
crowd was on its feet, cheering.

"Well, godamighty, she *is* alive," Millie said. "Honey, that
is the most energetic performance I have ever seen you give."

Purdy grinned viciously at me.

I ignored both of them and headed for the bar. During my
number, I had spotted the entrance of what appeared to be a
particularly long-legged humpbacked muskrat. Lomax shed his
fur and met me halfway. He carried something bulky tucked
close to his peacoat as he wound his way through the comradely
crowd, bellowing greetings to those who bellowed first, tweaked
Loki's tail, or inquired about Larsson. I was still two yards
away when he thrust the package at me.

"Here," he said.

Though I would have thought his face was already as red
from the cold as it could get, it grew suddenly redder. Of course,
Lomax apparently had a taste for dark-haired exotic ladies,
judging from his previous marriage, but I had not realized until
then that my theatrical persona had made such an impression
on him. I dipped my eyes beneath my fan and tried to be
surprised, but the oilcloth covering gave the surprise away.
Inside was all of my feminine apparel, old and new.

"Miss Devine says that stuff isn't hers and there's no need
for it to go to waste," he said, and winked. "For some reason,
I just knew this would fit you."

He chuckled and stroked the cat in a self-satisfied way as I
sorted through the packet of warm feminine things, unmen-

tionables without holes in them, and my still-uninitiated ball gown! But the clothing, of which I seemed to be acquiring a great deal in one day after practically parading in Godiva fashion all week, meant far less to me than what I saw in his face. And that was a certain complicity. He no more believed me a Spanish dancing girl than he had believed me a teenage boy. Of course, no one else was as perceptive as he and we had to keep it that way, but still, I was overjoyed to attain attire and an ally in one fell swoop.

As a professional practitioner of words, I could have formed an eloquent verbal expression of my gratitude, had I been able to do so in English. However, for appearance's sake, I could hardly respond in a manner appropriate to Valentine Lovelace, novelist and popular historian, but had to conform to my assumed role. Fortunately, I am quick thinking. I realized immediately what constituted the proper and expected behavior for a dance hall girl of passionate Latin antecedents who speaks no English and must convey a response for a generous and thoughtful gift from an attractive patron.

I threw my arms around his neck and tried to kiss his cheek. To my embarrassment, and I suppose in the privacy of these pages I can admit, pleasure, he spoiled my aim and we ended up in a rather prolonged embrace with decidedly osculatory overtones. Loki sprang from Lomax's shoulders in disgust and sat on the package until we regained our senses.

The first part of that night was as delightful as the rest of it was dreadful. Despite, or perhaps because of, the bizarre attacks of the previous night, business was even livelier and rowdier than usual. Perhaps it was because the weather had suddenly turned quite seriously cold, and word had come with the *Bella* that no more ships would be coming up the Yukon because of the extremely low waters in and around the Yukon flats. Throughout the show, befurred sourdoughs, shivering cheechakos, and a few that fell in a middle category, being newcomers smelling of new winter woolens and hastily acquired furs, kept arriving, some carrying untried snowshoes in case the snow deepened too suddenly for them to return home without that aid. But once inside, with fur hats on hooks or pushed back and boots removed to add pungency to the aroma of the room, everyone made merry.

Between shows, and after the final curtain, Lomax, the cat, and I formed a Siamese trio, the cat on his shoulders and me tucked under his good arm as we coursed the room. Finally, he selected a table near the fire. I had momentarily forgotten my resolution to board the *Bella*, forgotten the murders, forgotten my suspicions of Vasily Vladovitch, had almost forgotten my multiplicity of identities while basking in the glow of this new association. Lomax's preoccupation took a different course, however. When we were seated and I was just beginning to be frustrated because I could not tell him all that had occurred since I left him and what my theories were on the matter, he opened his book and commenced to read as serenely as if he had been in his own cabin.

I tried to read over his shoulder, but Loki's tail kept flipping up in my face, and heaven forbid I should dislodge the beast. I nudged Lomax, but he was so engrossed he didn't seem to notice until London arrived and presented himself in a way that could not possibly be ignored.

"Hey there, Dag, where you been today? I been looking all over for you."

"Been readin' this book. I tell ya, Jack, it's somethin'."

"How about reading it aloud then? I'd like to hear it and I bet some of the boys would, too. Hey, Miles, commere. No-Coat, look here at this book Cap'n Lomax got today. What's it about, Dag?"

" 'Bout a guy meets a bunch of wolves and this rich fella with a lot of nasty habits."

"Like *what*?" Miles asked, leaning forward eagerly.

"Bites folks. Drinks blood. Turns into a bat, all kindsa stuff."

"What's the name of it, Dag?" Lane called. "Read it loud enough and I'll see that you don't get thirsty."

"It's called *Dracula*. Some Irishman named Stoker wrote it. Just came out this year. My sister in London sent it to me. I started reading it this afternoon and can't put it down. Tried to read aloud to Egil some, but he fell asleep and it seemed to upset the sisters."

"Wouldn't upset me. Read it to me. A brand new book, now that's a rare treat. Hey, Herriford, Ladue, Parr! Come on over here and look at this."

That was the end of my chance for a war conference. The aforementioned and several others, including Purdy, crowded around our table while refreshments were provided. Sasha smiled with a rather superior indulgence from across the room and started to undulate toward us, but at that moment Blake entered with Giselle on his arm, and she rapidly recalled something that needed doing elsewhere.

My other preoccupations melted away quickly as Lomax began reading, at first haltingly and in a sort of monotone. His voice quickly picked up color and vibrancy as he continued, though sometimes he read too quickly to be understood. I listened breathlessly, for the longer he read, the more I realized that this book was far more pertinent to my present difficulties than anything I had encountered so far. The rapt faces of the circle of miners, the sinister pulsation of the lamps across their features, and Lomax's voice all faded as my mind's eye recreated the beginnings of a tale of monstrous power and subversion of the human spirit.

Lomax took a swallow of sarsaparilla at the end of the first chapter in which the hero was surrounded by ravening wolves who seemed, in a very familiar way, to be under the control of some force greater than themselves.

Wild Miles shifted uneasily. "The way those wolves are acting. That's not natural," he said.

"Loup garou, Miles," his partner, Emile Piersee put in. "Werewolves, as you say. Oh yes, that is how he act, the loup garou."

"Yessir, that's right," Purdy added. "Not just wolves people turn into either. Why, I used to have me a little Mexican girl-friend whose gramma could turn into a puma."

"Will you shut up so the man can read?"

The last words of chapter four—"At least God's mercy is better than that of these monsters, and the precipice is steep and high. At its feet a man may sleep—as a man. Good-bye, all! Mina!"—died away, and Dag paused to take a sip of one of several more sarsaparillas that had miraculously appeared at his elbow. I had not noticed the approach of Drake, who with Giselle in tow stared at Lomax with undisguised disgust. I turned sideways and scooted protectively closer as Dag began to read from Lucy's letter to Mina.

Drake's voice, which betrayed the amount he had had to drink before he entered our premises, cut through the story. "What you runnin' here, darlin'?" he called across the room to Sasha, "a saloon or a library? These boys gonna go loco mixin' drink with that kinda horseshit. Werewolves, blood-suckin' la-dies trottin' around in their nighties, vampire counts. Hell, ain't no blood-suckers around here 'cept ol' Bleed-Enough hisself."

Vasily Vladovitch chose that inauspicious time to return. Shaking out his cape and placing his fur seal hat on a nail by the door, he asked, "Were you referring to me, Consul Blake?

I fear you mispronounce my name. It has what you would call a short *e*—eh eh. Bledinoff.'"

Drake backed down. "No, no, amigo, not you. Least, not seriously. I was just tellin' your little filly here she shouldn't be havin' this hook-handed codger usin' your establishment for tellin' bedtime stories. Vampires! You ever heard anything so crazy?"

"Vampires?" Vasily Vladovitch asked, his left eyebrow raising and his mouth quirking with amusement. "Captain Lomax, I would see the book, if you please."

He examined it scornfully, then tossed it back so that its pages riffled. "Really, such garbage. And it is quite insulting to my people—my family comes from Transylvania, you know—and my class. I don't know why anyone would print such utter trash."

"We thought it was a good yarn, V.V.," Wild Miles said. "Kind of spooky."

"Hmph," said Vasily Vladovitch and turned his back on us.

Dag shrugged and picked up the book again, and the prospectors resumed their postures.

Drake snarled and swept the lantern from the table, almost immolating Emile and infuriating Loki, who sprang for the raging consul's face. And Vasily Vladovitch turned back toward us, his eyes bugging out and glowing, reflecting the red flames beginning to run through the line of kerosene, his lips retracting in a ghastly grin.

At that moment, Sergeant Destin, whom I had not seen enter, flew forward with a coat in his hands and began trying to smother the flames. The others followed his example and battled the blaze while Lomax and I tried to pull the cat off Drake, who was trying to throttle it. When the flames were extinguished and Loki back on Lomax's shoulders, there was a charred place on the plywood floor in the shape of a giant serpent, a lot of parkas that would need extensive mending, and the sickening odor of singed fur in the air. The new Dracula book had been so badly burned that none of it remained legible save the middle of the pages in the middle of the book.

Drake broke free of the restraining arms of Sasha and Giselle and bolted out the door, snarling, with an outraged London, who still hoped to get in a punch or two, hot on his heels. Again I thought how Drake had changed, the charming veneer that had formerly characterized him even when he was bent on some barbaric deed had become pitted with madness and scored by the man's inner beastliness.

Lomax stooped and gently lifted the ruins of his new treasure. Some of the men who had been listening looked as if they might bawl. Loki licked frantically at a singed spot on his belly. Sasha Devine glared at me as if I'd done something in shockingly bad taste, and Vasily Vladovitch had disappeared without another word.

Only Lane behaved sensibly, appearing with mop in hand to undo as much of the damage as possible. "Next time you bring a book in, Captain, I'd sure as hell appreciate it if it wasn't one that got reviewed in such a goddamn messy way," he growled.

Lomax looked like a child who had spilled his ice cream. I tugged on his arm and led him out the back door. He shook his head in stunned disbelief once we were outside.

"Doggone it," he said angrily. "Pardon me, ma'am, but he didn't have to do that. Claim-jumpin' bastard. Do you know I went into the recorder's office today to witness for a fella and guess whose name was where Bob Clancy's shoulda been? As if that wasn't bad enough, he has to set fire to my book. You know how long I waited for this book? And it was a good story, too."

"I think it was a bit more than that, actually," I told him when I was quite sure we were alone. Lurleen's cabin was dark, but from the noise emanating from the walls, I felt we were in no danger of being overheard from that quarter. Stella's cabin was also dark, and no smoke curled from the chimney. Perhaps she was making a house call. "Didn't it strike you that some of those fictional incidents bore a curious resemblence to the deaths and illnesses that have occurred around here lately?"

"It sure did. That's why I thought everybody'd like it so much. Sorta fun to have a crazy story like that to explain bad food and a touch of typhoid, seemed to me. Who'da thought anybody would get upset over it? What do you suppose the matter is? Don't tell me both that claim-jumpin' politician and that saloonkeeper boss of yours are so religious they don't want anybody readin' anything but the Good Book?"

"No," I said. "I won't tell you that. But I think perhaps the content hit a little close to home. You look like you could use a nice strong cup of tea," I said. "I know I could."

"Wouldn't want to sully your reputation by comin' in, ma'am," he mumbled with more dejection than courtesy.

"As what? A dance hall girl or a murderess? If you won't tell anyone this is perfectly innocent, I assure you I won't."

He clamped his pipe into his teeth and smiled a tight little smile around the stem. The cat's tail flapped rhythmically over his shoulder.

"Your sister in England, is she Egil Larsson's mother?" I asked conversationally while the tea water heated.

"Oh, no, that's my fourth youngest sister, Christina. The one in London's Effie. She married a seagoing man. Met him through my younger brother, Lars. He's gone now, Lars. My fault, probably. Ever since the war, I wanted to go back to sea and I used to talk about it and read to the kids all the time, but when Mama and Papa were killed, I had to stay home and take care of the farm till all the kids was big enough to take care of themselves. That's why I'm a might on the downhill side for a prospector up here. Just right for a steamship skipper though, eh?"

"Indeed, and it would be a pity if you died too young to grow into the title," I said. "I'll need to study that book of yours further, but I believe—"

Footsteps crunched to a stop outside my door.

"Lomax?" London's voice called.

"In here, Jack. What is it?"

"It's Larsson. Tom's with me. He just went up to the hospital to try to find you, and the nuns were in a tizzy. Seems Larsson just walked out without takin' so much as his union suit. Tom tried to track him, what with the fresh snow tonight, but some moose messed up the trail."

"Comin'," he said, and to me, "Watch Loki for me, please, ma'am. He ain't much of a retriever." And he left me to drink the tea alone, with the cat and the charred book for company.

I cursed softly to myself, for I had yet to touch on all I wanted to discuss with Lomax. Besides which, I felt better with him nearby. There was something reassuringly solid and sane about him that filled me with relief. Then, too, there was something endearingly innocent about the dreaminess in his Santa Claus eyes when he spoke of his steamship and his family that made me feel that he really was too nice to be mixed up in all of this. It was bad enough for someone like me who had grown up making her own way amid the streets and saloons of San Francisco searching for her sire in all sorts of seamy situations. Someone who had led the bucolic life of a farmer, nurturing his little brothers and sisters, would be ill-prepared to confront a fiend such as the one in the book. Nor could he be expected to fathom the cunning of a man who seemed benevolent while he waited to prey upon trembling, helpless mortals who were little more than a complicated shot glass from his viewpoint. Of course, on the other hand, Lomax was a veteran who had lost a limb in the service of whichever part of the country he'd fought for (I forgot to ask; as a native San Franciscan of European parentage, I was emotionally untied to either the North or the South) and who had recently buried a wife.

Still, he was no match for the perfidy of an aristocratic vampire like Vasily Vladovitch Bledinoff. And I was convinced that it was my mesmerist boss who was responsible. While that explanation did not quite fit all of the facts, it fit them better than anything else I could come up with. And since such creatures were, according to the book, immortal, I was very glad I was taking the *Bella* the next day.

I would report the situation to the American authorities, who were not trying to convict me of murder, and perhaps the army could send investigators. Or perhaps I could find a better way to disguise myself and re-enter the country. I felt the most important thing was to advise my country of the danger her citizens (and the Canadian subjects, too, of course) faced in this remote territory.

Meanwhile, heaven only knew what Vasily Vladovitch would be up to once he had sated his taste for every dance hall girl and prostitute in Dawson. I would try to get Lomax to bring London and Larsson and come with me on the *Bella*. Failing that, I would convince him that they must remain on their claims throughout the winter and not come to town. If they did, they must at all costs steer clear of the saloons.

I pondered all of this while working furiously at a few chores of my own since, life being what it was, I had been reunited with my clothes just in time to have to pack them. I changed into my boyish apparel and started bundling the rest into a manageable roll. Something unyieldingly hard refused to be rolled. Investigating, I found the silver crucifix from the bottom of the avalanche in the pocket of the Annie Oakley skirt. I pulled it out and thrust it into my trouser pocket instead.

I was rehearsing exactly what I would tell Lomax as I finished rolling up the clothing when the cat suddenly yowled and shot under the bed. Footsteps crunched in the alley. I sprang to the door and tugged it open, thinking that Larsson had been found.

Maisie, dressed in a parka and her cancan costume with long-handled underwear covering her nether limbs from knee to bootop, stared at me in surprise. I motioned her hurriedly inside. She was my favorite among my new colleagues, and I could not simply abandon her without a warning.

"Maisie, tell me, dear, have you been feeling quite yourself lately? A little tired perhaps? Listless? Run down? Er—drained?"

"Cory, just listen to you! Why, you've learned English really well and in such a short time. Just as Mama says, when you really apply yourself—"

"Never mind that. You're in terrible danger. Did you hear anything of the book Captain Lomax was reading tonight?"

She sniffed disdainfully. "Enough. And I must say, Cory, though I'd be the last to criticize ordinarily, that I think that was extremely shoddy of you to let that old man prattle that sort of stuff. I like a good story as well as the next person, but when it's so full of just plain mean lies as that one—"

"Maisie, what if I were to tell you that they weren't lies? What if I were to tell you that those marks on your neck you got playing spin the bottle with Vasily Vladovitch are the trademark of a real vampire just like Count Dracula in the book?"

She giggled. "Like that? Oh, no. Not at all. It's nothing like that." Then she sobered and shook her finger at me. "And I want you to know that I'm real cross with you, honey, for hurting Vassy's feelings like that. He was awfully upset. You know how emotional those foreign guys get, and he's a real creampuff. He likes you and he's done an awful lot for you. He was talking about it upstairs. I don't see how you could take the word of some stupid man you never met who probably just likes to present the bad side of things to sell books without even *asking* a friend of yours how it really is!"

"And how is it, really, Maisie?"

She had been sitting on the edge of my bed and now she leaned forward and clasped my hands, her eyes gleaming with missionary fervor. "Wonderful, that's how! Oh, sure, it hurt a little when he first made the punctures, but no worse than getting your ears pierced. And, oh, honey! What did that book call what he is? The undead? Boy, is that ever right. I never felt less dead in my life!"

"Don't worry," I said dryly. "I'm pretty sure it's just a matter of time."

"You don't know anything about it, do you? You with your prissy little cross. Sorry. Mama would die to hear me talking this way, but believe me, nothing in church ever made me feel so kind of spiritual, you know? And sort of sexy at the same time. And Vassy is so sweet and so tender. He was worried about us bein' weak if he took too much from us and brought juice to put in the champagne and candy for afterward. And he has the most wonderful ideas about how to put this place on the map and maybe take us girls on tour later to Paris and London and Rome! Oh, come on, Cory, wouldn't you love that?"

"The only town I want to see right now is Circle City," I said. "Maisie, I'm glad to hear you are not suffering too many ill effects from your bites, but, believe me, it is not as innocent as you seem to think. I've seen several victims already who are very dead as the result of Vasily Vladovitch's form of affection."

"Is that so, well—"

More footsteps outside, and Maisie jumped up and ran to the door. "In here, Mill!"

"What on earth *for*, sugar?" Millie asked, peeking in just long enough that I caught a cold glint in her eye. "Goodness *knows* I dillydallied so long we're goin' to be late already. So sorry, Cory, wish we could stay and chat, but—" And she hauled Maisie off as the latter tried to explain to her my new and miraculous command of English.

I pulled on my coat and debated for a moment what to do about the cat. The fact that it would not come out from under the bed made my decision for me. I was not about to stay here and be a sitting duck for all sorts of nocturnal visitations while Lomax, London, and a naked, deranged Larsson wandered around in the hills near Bledinoff's lair, heedless of the mortal peril to their immortal souls.

The sky was not navy tonight, but a deep burnished pewter backlit with an eerie glow. A green wave of aurora spanned the Yukon and the moon was high, its sallowness spilling over into a watery haze. I was able to see clearly without a lamp as I climbed the path that wound toward the hospital. Below, the saloons and tents faded into the muskeg, the town marked only by an occasional flicker of a candle, the scent of wood smoke, the echo of a curse carried down the river when some unwary miner barked a shin on someone else's outfit as he left his tent to relieve himself. Otherwise the town in this early morning hour pulled back into the land, and I could easily imagine how it must have been only a year or two before, when no one but Indians lived here.

Something solid stood out against the snow—a man? a tent? It had a broad belly and short, widely spread legs, and as I drew nearer, it shifted. I saw it had been stripping the over-hanging branches and that there were four legs instead of two. There was also a highly efficient looking rack of antlers.

I edged backward. It paced forward. This was the first moose I had encountered since the one that had injured Lars-son. I said a silent prayer that the poor delirious fellow wouldn't blunder into this creature as well. Then I said a prayer for me that the beast would munch on to juicier branches else-where.

Instead, its stiltlike legs carried it toward me, and it forgot the branches entirely. The nearsighted, snoopy look on its long, ugly face reminded me of the Widow Hig. The ludicrousness of the comparison, plus a nervous overload from the events of the night, evening, day, week, month, trip, year, welled up inside of me until I tittered, then guffawed, and finally laughed so hard I fell backward into the brush as the moose charged past. I choked, sputtered, cried, and laughed again to think how silly the moose looked, how silly I must look laughing about how silly it looked. I lay on my back in the snow and rolled with laughter, unable to rise, though I beat the ground with my mittens and my sides ached.

"What the devil's goin' on there?" someone cried and slid past me on the path. I wanted to call to him to look out for the moose, but I couldn't get my breath.

A deeper shadow fell across me and someone crouched down. "You about done with that, or do you want to waller awhile longer? Maybe mark your territory?" Lomax asked.

I looked up at him and hiccoughed.

"Larsson, you bonehead, where do you think you're going, a sauna?" London exclaimed, and then, "Found him. Yell to Tom to bring his clothes."

They got him dressed, back to the hospital, and into bed by about eight-thirty, just as the sun was rising.

"Hope this don't give him pneumonia," Tom said. "Did you see his belly? Can't hardly tell nothin' was there. Sure got better quick. Bet Mary will sure be surprised."

"Never mind h(hic)s abdominal wou(hic)nds, what did his neck look like?" I asked. I had stayed outside while all of this went on since my hiccoughs were so severe that I would have awakened the entire ward.

"Kinda blue, a little frozen, hairy," London said, looking baffled.

"Good," I said. I'd have elaborated, but my hiccoughs were constituting a severe speech impediment.

"*My* neck needs coffee runnin' down its inside," Lomax said.

"And bacon?" Jack asked hopefully.

I joined the boys in the Klondike Cafe, where eggs could be purchased for a month's salary apiece and flapjacks were worth more than nuggets of comparable size, due to the shortage in flour.

"Just think, Lomax, you'll be able to afford 'em soon as you pan some of that out down there to the claim," Tom said.

"What's (hic) this?" I asked, and had to swallow a lot of expensive coffee to overcome further spasms.

"Tom ran a test pan from the pit a couple of days ago and got color," London said. "*Good* color."

"Yessir, I bet you got a paddlewheel already at least outta that one nugget," Tom said.

"Speaking of paddlewheels," I said, rising from the upended log the cafe used for seating, "I'd better see what's happening with the *Bella*."

"I'll come with you—uh—Pat," Lomax said.

"You gonna go with me to get them dogs from Sam, Lomax, or shall I go ahead?"

"I'll be there. Just want to see my buddy Pat here off."

"You're not turnin' tail just when Lomax will be needin' workers are you, young fella?" London asked. I think he was a little confused about me. He had started looking at Lomax rather warily.

"Got to, sir. My—my mother's sick back home in Indiana," I said.

"How'd you find out? That mail from Fort Yukon was six months old."

"Carrier raven," I said. " 'Scuse me."

The door of the Alaska Commercial Company warehouse was beginning to look like a theatre billboard. A fresh layer of notices overlaid those of the previous day. The top one said:

THIS STORE HAS BEEN APPROPRIATED BY THE GOVERN-MENT FOR THE PURPOSE OF REGULATING THE TRANSPOR-TATION OF UNPROVIDED PEOPLE, AND IS DECLARED CLOSED FOR COMMERCIAL PURPOSES FOR THE DAY. C. CONSTANTINE.

Beneath that:

MASS MEETING WILL BE HELD AT TEN A.M., IN FRONT OF
THE ALASKA COMMERCIAL COMPANY'S STORE, TO DISCUSS
FOOD SITUATION AT DAWSON AND THE DEPARTURE OF
UNPROVIDED PEOPLE ON THE *BELLA*.

"You don't have to go," Dag said. "You could come out to
the claim."

"I must get word to the authorities about this heinous menace," I reminded him.

"Oh, yeah. I forgot about that. 'Spect they'll want to send
a squad of cavalry right up here or ask ol' Blake to investigate
the allegation about there bein' vampires on the premises, eh?"

"I'll make them understand somehow," I said. We were back
at my cabin, where I collected my bag and Dag collected his
cat. Loki, knotted beneath the stove, was at first disinclined to
take notice of our arrival but by now had settled back to his
customary place around Lomax's neck. "Oh, Captain—uh—
Mr. Lo—"

"Dag, Pelagia. I think of you by your first name—your real
one. It's a mermaid's name, did you know that? Means 'from
the sea.' "

"And, Dag, that's Scandinavian, isn't it? What does that
mean?"

"Day," he said. "So them vampires had better watch out."

"Just in case they think a day by any other name would be
as tasty, I'd feel better if you had this," I said, taking the silver
crucifix from my pocket. "I found it under an avalanche at the
top of the Chilkoot Pass."

"Thanks," he said, staring at it curiously before pocketing
it. "Us Lutherans don't get a whole lot of these."

"Well, you needn't keep it if you consider it—you know,
papist. I was going to give it to the mounties and ask them to
make inquiries and possibly return it to the family, but then I
rather got off on the wrong foot with them."

"Aye. Well, as to that, I've never been a man to scorn whatever works. I'll carry it while it seems needful and then turn it
in. How's that?"

I nodded and stared at my fingers, which I found I was
twisting together.

He was finding his boot toes fascinating.

"I guess—uh—guess I'd better go get them dogs."

"I guess I'd better go to that meeting and get that grub, since the mounties took mine from you."

"Yeah, well, we won't leave till after you do, I expect."

"No? Well, see you later then," and we gazed longingly into each other's eyes, hungry for the alliance our contact had thus far been all too limited to permit.

"Yeah. Yeah, I guess so," he said and impetuously reached out his hand and pumped mine. "You take it easy, Pelagia. I'll write to you in the states, keep you posted on stuff to tell the cavalry."

"You do that," I said.

The man was blushing. I supposed if we ever met again, I'd have to don my dance hall costume once more if I was to get another kiss. At one time I would have been coy about such things, but at my age, when you meet a man like Lomax, you begin to think about making opportunity feel welcome by installing big brass door knockers.

I watched him stride off toward Front Street. He was kind to animals, generous to the needy, intelligent (if not particularly well-spoken), literate, considerate, had refined taste in female companionship, did not drink, and was reasonably domesticated for a sourdough. Men respected him, and though he had left his family, he did not seem alienated from them. He had lost an arm, but he had most of his teeth and more hair than the vast majority of Civil War veterans. The thought of having met and lost such a man in such a short time because of a few vampires was enough to make me want to go somewhere and throw snowballs at bats.

Instead I attended the meeting. Captain Hansen, the assistant superintendant of the Alaska Commercial Company, urged us all to take advantage of the passage offered by the mounties. His speech seemed a little superfluous to me, since most of us were there to do just that. After the meeting, we presented ourselves at the store to officially say that we wanted to take the steamer. Then in order to draw five days' free rations, we had to sign a special agreement, stating that we would abide by the captain's orders and leave the ship if he asked and that the *Bella* was not responsible for the nonarrival of us or our baggage. A hundred and sixty signed altogether, but I think a great many never set foot on the steamer, but signed solely to draw the free rations. I can honestly say that I, at least, boarded the steamer, though that was, as it turned out, about all the farther I got.

The sky was the texture and consistency of a wool army blanket, the river chopped and chunky with ice. A knifelike north wind tore the first layer of skin off my cheeks as I stood in line waiting while the boxes and bales were boarded. Earlier, the sternwheeler's bow had been encased at the waterline with steel to protect the hull from ice. Now and then the ice struck the hull with a sound like the gnashing of a giant's teeth, and the ship shuddered and groaned.

The banks were crowded with gamblers, gold kings, entertainers of both vertical and horizontal varieties, businessmen and saloonkeepers. Purdy was not there, but Maisie was, and Millie and Bunny, Sasha, and Mr. Lane. I was doubly glad to see them, knowing from the book that despite Maisie's enthusiasm for the profession, neither she nor the others could yet be full-fledged vampires if they could come out even in such pallid sunlight as graced that day.

Lomax sauntered up and stood a little apart, in the back on the edge of the crowd. Slowly he raised his hand and saluted —a sharp naval salute, I presumed. I was starting to wave back when two more figures appeared from the southern end of town, threading their way through the crowd—the fur-hatted, red-coated Destin and Drake, suave once more and elegant in his dove gray. Several of the miners on shore smirked at him, but the ones on the boat shifted uneasily, and I could almost hear them worrying about their claims.

As for myself, I had something else to worry about. I did not wish to be seen by either man. Drake had seen me similarly attired during my youthful foray to Texas. Destin was altogether too astute for me to wish to risk his scrutiny. I passed through the enclosure of the lower deck, strictly outfitted to haul freight, and onto the narrow footing on the lee side, from which the crew could sometimes push off or make fast various lines or whatever it was they customarily did. None of them now occupied this level. I practiced respiratory conservation until we swung into the stream and headed toward Fort Yukon, American soil, and freedom.

The others began finding places to spread their blankets, but I bided my time a while longer, for I wanted to wait until we were far enough downriver that there was no longer any possibility of communicating with those ashore in Dawson. As we rounded the first major bend in the broad ice-choked river, where Moosehide Creek flowed into it, I turned loose of my handhold to go back inside.

The *Bella* chose that particular moment to have a disagreement with a chicken-coop-sized cake of ice. I flailed, lost my footing and plunged, pack and all, into the freezing opaque waters.

Sledgehammers of mind-rending cold slammed straight through my flesh, congealing my blood, splintering my bones. My mouth and nose flooded with freezing water. I pressed my arms to my side and tried for the surface, my scalp screaming. The cold so numbed me that I did not feel the ice cake above until it struck my skull as I broke water, clutching for another drifting chunk.

The *Bella* churned past, the slap of her paddles washing half of the river down upon me. Fighting to stay conscious, I kicked frantically away from the wheel, which loomed nightmarishly large, the flat wooden blades spewing waterfalls. I spun around and around on my ice cake, my screams strangled into gurgles as I swallowed water and choked, while my arms were pulled from their sockets, and my sodden mittens were torn from my hands. My feet seemed no longer attached to me, and my head exploded with one roaring red dynamite blast after another. The last thing I saw clearly was that the water roiling just in front of me was pink with my blood.

# CHAPTER XVII

····•═╬◐║◑╬═•····

*THE TANG OF* wood fire and urine-cured moosehide teased my nostrils to painful life. I felt as though I'd been forced through a giant grater, and for a moment I thought I had probably been pulled into the sternwheel after all and was lying aboard ship dying.

I opened one eye and that hurt, so I yelped and that hurt worse, so I shut up and lay still. But my professional curiosity was stronger than my cowardice, and a short time later I just had to look. Beaded fringe swung from the legs, arms, chests, and backs of tall, copper-skinned people with waving black hair and—and then the swinging of all that fringe made me feel quite ill and I was sick there on my bed of spruce boughs and Hudson Bay blankets.

Fringe swung down upon me, and a man with chiseled cheekbones bent over me.

I felt the need to explain myself. I very cautiously tapped my chest and said in a voice that emerged low enough to cause him to bend further down, but that sounded and felt like an avalanche to me, "Me from big boat."

"Of course you are," he said. "We hardly thought you were a seal swimming around on the ice floe. We're from South Central Alaska originally, but culturally we've come to identify heavily with our venerated Grandfather."

My head was swimming. "Oh, that's very nice," I said weakly. "Excuse me. I think you should move your moccasin now." And I proceeded to demonstrate why.

Later I risked sitting up again. The sun was sinking in one corner of the horizon, the moon rising in another. Both were muffled by a sky dappled gray as an appaloosa's rump. Dimly, I realized that I would never have another opportunity to sound so much like a heroine in a romantic novel.

"Where am I?" I asked in a wispy rasp that nearly blew the top of my head off. "Who are you?"

"How do you like that? She travels that whole way with us and doesn't—"

"Quiet, Igor," said the man I had spoken to previously. At least I think it was him. There was a strong resemblance among these people that would have made me wonder, had I not heard them having conversations, if I was not simply seeing multiples of the same individual. "If you had taken a swim in the great river and then tried to break up an ice cake with your head, you might not remember your name either."

Leaning over me, but keeping his feet somewhere near my knees this time, he said, "I am called Boris. I was one of your guides. Igor was the other."

"No," I said, and sank back into the boughs while the sky whirled above me. The man's face melted away, and my words were swept downriver by the wind. "No, you must be mistaken. Must be thinking of two other women with some other coffin. The men with us only spoke Indian."

"Romanian, actually, o bearer of the sacred earth," he said. "We share the native tongue of the Grandfather, with which he teaches us the paths of lifeafterlife."

I tried to nod because I didn't trust my voice, but nodding was not a good idea either. To say that what part of my brain was functioning was beginning to have very uneasy feelings about my saviors was to understate my position considerably. But whatever dangers or factions these people represented, and I thought I understood all too well exactly what those might be, my physical state was a far more immediate problem. I felt utterly weak and drained. A horrifying thought occurred to me and I lifted my hand to my throat.

Boris laughed. "Not yet, madam. Not yet. Soon, perhaps, when it is night and the Grandfather can see you. Soon."

I fell back into unconciousness then, to be roused I don't know how much later as I was lifted into a sled. Of all the people who had been around the camp, and if I was not suffering from double vision, there must have been more than half a dozen, although I was in no mood to count them or anything else, only Boris remained. He packed furs around me and tied a leather belt from one side of the sled to the other to hold me in. Then he stood on the runners behind me and said something in Romanian, I presume, since it was not English, to the oddly silent team of large and ferocious-looking timber wolves who, in unison, performed a nauseatingly energetic leap forward. The bobbing tails of the bounding beasts before my palpitating pate shattered into a million motes of dancing light.

Warmth, the tickle of fur, eau de Romanian Indian, and Vasily Vladovitch's distinctive cologne infiltrated my various senses as I swam slowly back to life. Voices there were, too, but these mingled softly across the room, murmuring among themselves. I wrestled the room into focus. It was Vasily Vladovitch's furry parlor, the stove repaired and what seemed to be the entire Indian camp having a powwow at the dining table.

What did vampires need with dining tables anyway, I wondered. To maintain appearances, probably, so the neighbors wouldn't talk. And for entertaining. Like Indian powwows. I tried to sit up, since playing dead would do me no good. For one thing, they knew I wasn't, and for another, I would learn nothing from listening to their conversation, my Romanian being less than rudimentary.

"Ah, our guest joins us, my children," Vasily Vladovitch said. "Miss Lovelace, I'm so delighted you dropped in. You forgot the recompense you were so keen to acquire earlier. I had planned to pay you in gold dust, but considering your performance last night, thirty pieces of silver would be more appropriate."

"For a hellish fiend, Vasily Vladovitch, you do muster an incredible amount of righteous indignation."

"For a righteous woman, you have mustered an incredible aptitude for betrayal."

The argument exhausted me immediately, and all I could muster was a stubborn, "Hmph."

"I can't believe that I actually insisted that Sasha invite you. How can I have been so blind? How could I know that a woman who had been so privileged as to converse with the great dragon would be a frumpy, awkward, hysterical prude so full of her own preconceived ideas that she would not know true adventure when it befell her."

"Hah!" I cried, much to my immediate regret. More softly I said, "It is not adventure that has befallen me, alas, but doom."

Vasily Vladovitch raised his arms and I squeezed my eyes shut, fearing the worst. I heard a slap as his arms fell back to his sides. "Miss Lovelace, do you ever ask questions before you begin writing your little articles or do you just make up sufficient libelous allegations to fit the space?"

My voice came out in an uncooperative croak. "Then you deny that you are the infamous Count Dracula of the book by the same name, which chronicles your hideous career and bloodthirsty depredations?"

"Of course, I deny I'm Count Dracula. I could not possibly be. Unlike the barbaric English, our family system does not allow for boy children to be juniors or seconds or thirds. Therefore, rest assured that I am not also Count Dracula, for my father, the last I saw of him, was as undead and well as ever, and *he* is the one and only Count Dracula. *I* am, as I told you, Vasily Vladovitch—that is, Vasily son of Vlad to you— Bledinoff, which is our adopted Russian surname. As for the name of Dracula, you of all people now breathing upon the face of this world should realize what an old and honorable name it is."

"But you admit you're a vampire?"

He looked pained. "I would appreciate it if you would refrain from using these emotionally charged terms. A vampire is, of course, a small South American flying rodent who remains a small South American flying rodent at all times. I, on the other hand, only resemble a small flying rodent when it is expedient. Don't quote me."

I hmphed again.

The door flew open, and for a moment I thought I might be saved, but when the stamping of dainty boots was done, the caller proved to be none other than the perfidious Sasha Devine.

"Oh, Vahlen*teen*a," she said, as if my misfortune was some inconvenience I had purposely chosen to visit upon her.

"Oh, Sasha, how could you?" I asked, my voice needing to be forced ever further to make a sound at all, my head pulsing with pain. "I trusted you. Papa loved you. How could you imagine that I would cooperate with his murderer? That is what his shade has been trying to tell me. That I was in danger. My Papa has tried to protect me even from beyond the pale—"

Sasha patted my hand. "A little late, but sweet nevertheless, I agree."

Vasily Vladovitch raised an inquiring eyebrow.

"Patrick Harper, my dahling. My old love, you know," Sasha said. "He was her father."

"Oh, dear, I didn't know."

"No, of course not. I didn't think it important to tell you. It was all over, and I knew already how badly you felt about Patrick on my account."

"Oh, my love, I did. He should have been yours, but I had no idea he was waiting for you, and it had been so long since I fed. Once it started, he was unexpectedly strong—"

"Nonsense. I'm not ready yet to feed, while you still have business that I need to conduct in the daytime. He would have only gone to waste and—"

"Stop it!" I cried in anguish. "You make Papa sound as if he was the last bonbon on the tray at an afternoon tea party."

"You don't understand, Vahl. It was not Vasily Vladovitch's fault. He is not, as you seem to think, some vulgar sort of Ripper."

"No," I croaked. "He is a refined, titled, aristocratic Ripper. He said so."

He shrugged. "She will not listen."

Sasha stroked my forehead, and I tried vainly to brush her hand away. "Vahlenteena, forgive me. Never would I have brought you had I known this would be so hard for you. But like Vasily Vladovitch, I thought, knowing of your acquaintance with the great dragon—"

"*What* has Kuklukan to do with this?" I asked. Mercifully, this nonsense was receding.

Sasha snapped her fingers by my ear. Footsteps pattered away and pattered back and she bathed my face with snow. I shivered convulsively.

"You are not well enough to hear the answers. Had you your senses about you, you would recognize them yourself without words. For now you must rest, and we must do something about that swelling." Her skirts swished and sparks flew from the fur spread beneath me, sending little shocks into my flaccid hand as she shifted position. "Vasily Vladovitch, if I remove her cross, have I your oath . . . ?"

I felt, rather than saw, the look that passed between them, and he emitted an exasperated sigh. "I suppose."

His pledge to what? I struggled feebly as she unfastened Mama's little cross, and I shuddered as she rolled me over, my head pounding, huge and sloshing as the sea.

"There," she said.

This time when he raised his arms, he loomed above me like death. I screamed when I saw his lips pull back from a set of dentures that would have made a saber-toothed tiger proud. I kept thinking that surely I would finally swoon before the worst happened, but my wounds were oddly uncooperative, and I felt the first moist pressure of his sharpened teeth and screamed again, with the horrified realization that what reverberated through my skull could not be heard any farther than the room. My scream did, apparently, serve to throw his aim off, however, and this much to my pain and chagrin, for the teeth sank like a drilling bit, but not into my throat. Twin lightning bolts plunged into the tenderest spot on my head and I started to shriek again.

Then, before I could quite form the noise, I realized that the fangs had not hurt so much after all, that in fact, the wound felt immensely better. And overall, I felt—wonderful. Euphoria, not pain, shot from the fangs into my bloodstream and buoyed me to the heights of hope and happiness.

What had I been so upset about? All I needed, really, was to sleep, to rest, to snuggle into a blissful dream state and all of my cares would forever disappear. I heard a slow, sipping suction, like a child nursing, and felt the edges of my mouth curl into a smile of unexcelled rapture such as I had never smiled before.

# CHAPTER XVIII

TO: Miss Valentine Lovelace, Circle City, Alaska.
FROM: Dag Lomax, Henderson Creek via Dawson City, Yukon Territories, Canada.

October 15, 1897

*Dear Pelagia,*

I was going to wait to write to you until I heard the *Bella* had arrived safely at Circle City, but a couple of things have happened I thought you ought to know about before you talk to the government.

Tom, Jack, and I left Dawson bright and early the morning after you took off. It was a Sunday. Much as I hated to leave Egil behind, I did. Even though he'd improved a lot, snowshoeing out is pretty rugged and we had too much stuff to take with us on the sled for a passenger.

Tom and I took turns driving the sled and left young Jack blazing trail on snowshoes, though the snow wasn't real deep yet. Even got a little scanty under the trees where they were thickest.

Loki, the lazy bum, slept in the sled the first part of the trip. I think he just likes having dogs haul him around, once he figures they can't get at him.

It got dark around five, but we wanted to make this good campsite Tom knew about, and with the full moon, there was plenty of light, so we kept traveling for a while.

Then all of a sudden the dogs just stopped. They acted like they were listening to something and kind of whined, then one or two of them howled a little.

While we were trying to quiet them, I heard it—a pitiful-sounding moaning and crying coming from up on ahead. "What would you say that was, Tom?" I asked. "An animal or a man?"

"Animal *and* a man," Tom told me, and it turned out he was right.

The three of us left the sled behind and snuck up the trail on foot.

We didn't even have to follow the tracks to find them. Up ahead about a hundred yards there were two things moving. One was Purdy, shinnied so far up a little birch it was bowed right back onto the trail. Right below him, snapping at his hindside, was as big and ugly a wolf as it has ever been my privilege to brag about having seen and having lived afterward to talk about. Its ruff must have stood out, oh, gee, a good foot all the way around and up its back like porky-pine needles. It kept up that whiney-howl like a train on a downhill run with the brakes on all the way. It was bound and determined to shake its dinner down out of that tree.

And Purdy, of course, was just as determined it wasn't going to. When he saw us, he called, "Get his attention, boys, while I finish him off. No goldarn (except he didn't say 'goldarn') overgrown sheepdog is going to pick Alonso Purdy from its teeth."

That wolf howled right back up at him just like it understood. It still didn't pay us any mind. It was after him specifically, like there was no greater wolf delicacy in this whole world than Purdy tail.

It took an extra high leap, and he slipped and screeched and swore something terrible. We made it there just as they tangled. Tom got off to one side trying to draw a bead on the critter while I waded in, thinking I might be able to pull it off with my hook and give Tom a good shot.

Well, I hooked the critter okay, but once I got ahold of it, I didn't know what to do with it. It was bigger than I expected, and heavy. Up close it was more like the size of a pony than an ordinary wolf, and it was fast. And smart. I caught it too far back and just barely hooked through its hide, the fur was

so thick. It turned back on me and bit into my wooden arm.
One of the few times I've ever been glad it was wood. The
wolf was too mad to notice the difference, and it chewed and
snarled, getting more frustrated all the time because it wasn't
drawing blood. Finally, the straps that hold it on my shoulder
broke. When the wolf saw what it had there, it gave me a look
of pure disgust and turned back on Tom.

The wolf jumped just as Tom fired, knocking the gun down,
and the bullet went clean through Tom's leg. Jack dived in to
try to pull the wolf off Tom and get the gun, but the wolf
stood with its back legs on Tom's face and chest and attacked
Jack with its front end. I picked up what was left of my wooden
arm and started beating the wolf with the hook.

It turned and snapped at me, but it had three men down
already and it just didn't seem to take me serious. Jack made
use of the distraction to roll away from the wolf's reach, but
he rolled so hard he rolled right into a tree and knocked himself
out. Tom moaned and dodged and I kept beating.

But while all this was going on, I got to studying on that
wolf, Pelagia. It was not acting natural. A lone wolf away from
the pack might attack one man, but let a bunch come up and
it has sense enough to make itself scarce, if it's able to. And
then I thought, well, maybe it's rabid. It was slavering and
slobbering so that it might as well have been. But there was
something real deliberate about it. It seemed pretty sure it could
take us all on, but it didn't want to just wound anybody. It
wanted to knock the wind out of us and tear out something
necessary. Wasn't going to mess around with maiming us. Now
that is not a real wolfy way of looking at things, any way you
stack it.

But about the time I realized that, the wolf seemed to realize
that I didn't have my total attention on beating the daylights
out of it. I mostly was managing to irritate it, keeping it away
from Tom's neck and leg. But the smell of the bloody leg was
driving it crazy. Crazier. Finally, it decided it would have to
go through me to get to Tom's drumstick. It sprang at my
good shoulder and knocked me down. Stunned me. My hand
went numb and I remember thinking, 'oboy, I farmed and
raised a family for sixteen years with one arm, but I'll be darned
if I can figure out how to work a gold claim without any.' You
can see right there what an optimist I am. I was still figuring
I'd be alive to worry over how many parts I was going to have
to work with.

Out of the corner of my eye I saw Purdy slink back into the woods and try to circle round toward Tom's gun, which would have been encouraging except that Purdy was slinking way over there and here was this wolf dripping wolf slobber down my chin whiskers and daring me to do something about it. The wolf's claws ripped clear through my parka. Seeing them claws up close like that gave me a good idea why the wolf was so sure it could finish us off.

I never have felt so out of luck and ideas all at the same time. I couldn't even reach up and cover my throat since my hand was under my rear end and the wolf was standing on my shoulder, so I just kept hunkering my chin down into my collar like some kind of a darn turtle.

Then Purdy tripped and swore and the wolf looked up and snarled at him, and I yelled and tried to shake it off me. The shaking didn't do me a bit of good, but the yelling did. All of a sudden, before that wolf could turn its head back and bite off my nose, its own nose was full of flying fur and plucking claws and about twenty pounds of angry tomcat.

That cat of mine was all over that wolf, and they spun around and around.

About that time Purdy snatched up Tom's gun. I just about ruined a real good friendship by grabbing Loki by the tail and hauling him off the wolf so Purdy could get a clear shot without killing my cat. Two shots dead center made neat little holes right through the head, and the wolf charged him like nothing happened. I thought for sure it was going to keel over and drop as soon as it realized it was dead.

Then it came to me that maybe I was the one that was mistaken. That no little piddly bullet was going to kill this wolf after all. I may not be a genius, but I catch onto things eventually. I let Loki go and tried to knock Purdy clear and tell him to run, but only managed to knock him under me. Loki didn't get such a good perch the second time he attacked. The wolf shook him off and leaped high as a purebred horse straight at me. I was ready for it this time though. I had finally figured out why this wolf was acting the way it was. It should have been obvious enough after all the reading we'd done about them vampire wolves, loup garous that Canuck called them. Why else would a hungry wolf attack us and then act as picky about taking bites out of us as if he was a girl trying to watch her figure at a smorgasbord, if he didn't have some kind of a reason for it? And your regular wolf is not a critter that is all that big on reasoning.

So I let it come, then at the last minute, held up that silver cross you gave me to give the mounties. You should have seen the look in that thing's eyes as it tried to backpedal in midair. I lunged and managed to brand it on the backside but slipped in the snow and fell over Tom, and I will spare your ears, lady, by not telling you what he called me. That wasn't the worst of it, because the cross flew out of my hand when I fell.

There we were, the wolf licking his rear real fast, Tom screaming in pain from me falling over his leg, Purdy scrabbling around for that gun, Jack out cold, and Loki spoiling for another wolf ride. I dove into the snowdrift and started hunting for that cross, which was the only thing that had done a darn bit of good so far. Without it, we were goners, either now or later on.

We'd have to travel real slow with Tom's leg hurt, and that was always assuming Jack would be able to walk when he came to. There's a lot of places a wolf can pick a man off along the trail if he has a mind to. So I started pawing the snow aside, but I wasn't able to go about it real methodical under the circumstances. But the minute I started looking, the wolf jumped me again, knocking me face down in the snow.

I shook the snow out of my mouth and hollered, "Purdy, get this thing off me!" but Purdy didn't have a chance.

One minute the wolf was on me, snuffling and snarling and ripping at me with its feet, the next it wasn't there anymore. It didn't fall off, it wasn't knocked off. It was just sort of—lifted off.

I got up on my knees and turned around. Purdy was froze in pretty much the same position.

Filling most of the space between us was the biggest, ugliest, antleriest bull moose you ever saw in your life, with the wolf carried on the antlers like it was a baby in a cradle.

Then with a sort of a grunt, the moose flipped its head and flang that wolf clear back to Skagway, from the way it looked. I was sort of afraid it might come after us next, but it just eyeballed us. It looked mean, but anything that big and ugly has trouble looking any other way. Then it strolled on down the path like it had an urgent appointment, and that was the last I saw of it.

Well, I couldn't wait to write and tell you about it, Pelagia, because it's an awful lot similar to what happened the night you saved Egil, isn't it? I wish you were here so I could talk to you about this. That darn Texas gambler is not much help in this kinda thing. Keeps wanting to shoot things. He is a good woodchopper though. After we got Jack back to his cabin and fetched Mary and her people to fix Tom up, Purdy decided to hole up with me for a while.

He says Dawson got kind of unhealthy for him the same night we read the book. I think it had something to do with one of the girls. He started out alone and afoot the night before us, but he slept at JayEllen's boarding house in Grand Forks before pushing on. Said as soon as he was aways up the trail, he started having the feeling something or somebody was following him, and at first he thought his lady friend caught up with him, but, of course, it must have been the wolf right along.

The other thing I think you'd better know before you lay your cards on the table to the government is that I had a visit from Blake. A mighty peculiar visit.

He *said* he'd heard about our strike and I suppose he could have, though Tom didn't let it out a lot, and he *said* he'd heard about Tom's leg and Jack's head and just wanted to come and see that the folks he was there to represent was doing okay. I think he figured we was giving away free samples.

Purdy made himself scarce. He never had said he knew Blake from before, but it was pretty plain he couldn't stand to be in the same room with him long. That was the only reason I let Blake stay, to tell you the truth. I wanted to know what Purdy had against him, so I got him to talk to me. I've had a lot of practice listening, with all those kids I raised, and Blake likes to hear himself talk.

I asked him how he got to be such an important man, and he said it was because he met someone in Washington while they was either fighting or being Mexican bandits (I couldn't exactly make out which it was) down south of the border.

I allowed as how that must have been mighty interesting. He said, yes, it was. Then he changed the subject and asked me if I believed any of what we was reading in that book the other night. He also apologized for making such a donkey out of himself over it but said that was because the book had hit *so close* to the other things he'd learned about in Mexico.

Then he asked if I believe that people, special people with special kinds of powers, could turn themselves into something. I said I knew people who turned themselves into jackasses fairly regularly, but other than that, no, I couldn't say as I did. He just smiled with all his teeth and said he had seen things down in Mexico that would curl my hair.

I'd already had about all the hair-kinkers I could take for one trip, but I shut up and let him rattle on about the wonderful stuff all these broomhos, which are Mexican witches, can do turning into pumas, eagles, jaguars, rattlesnakes, and even wolves, according to Blake. He said he'd spent a lot of time with these people, gotten to know them pretty well, and without quite clobbering me over the head with it, let me know that they thought he was the best thing since bar soap, had they been acquainted with it, which come to think of it they probably weren't.

I said I couldn't think why somebody would want to turn themselves into an animal anyway, as there didn't seem to me to be a whole lot of use in it. He said, oh, sure, there was. He knew some of them broomhos ran villages down in Mexico, some ran whole states or whatever they are. He said some of the leaders were known to practice witchcraft or have a witch on the payroll. Said it was real common down there, because back before the Aztecs and Mayans and those other Indians got civilized, they used to kill folks and feed them to statues of big old feathered lizards and jaguars and animals like that. The head men were these broomhos who knew how to change themselves into animals. Which, I guess, is how they scared everybody else into letting themselves get sacrificed to the statues.

But Blake said being a broomho was a handy thing, since once a person got that power he couldn't be killed by regular means and could use his animal shape to do all kinds of things human beings couldn't do. Like killing people without the law even knowing a person did it. Then he smiled that toothy smile again.

I said that sure was interesting, that I hadn't heard about that before. He said he was surprised to hear that, that he thought you might have mentioned it to me before you killed yourself, since you'd written a book on it.

Anyway, he left when Purdy came in and dumped the wood down by the stove and practically dumped it on his foot. From the stiff, sore way that politician moved, a lame foot was the last thing he needed. He already looked like he had roomatism, artheritis, siaticka, and a touch of sour stomach. And the funny thing was, while he was telling me all that stuff about animals changing, I had a feeling he was not only trying to put the wind up me but was kind of pussyfooting around, testing me like maybe I knew something about something that had him as buffaloed as he was trying to get me. Of course, mainly what it's about is that he's trying to scare me. Since I've been here two years already and have clear title to my claim, nobody can steal it from me unless I get killed or scared off. I'm going to try not to do either one.

Oct. 20, 1897

Just wanted to add a little something before I seal this up. Trial pans are still showing lots of color, and I can tell you this is one man who sure is looking forward to spring.

I also dug that book of yours out of your outfit, Pelagia, and I read it, and now I got a good notion who that Blake is. It's Frank Drake, right? The crazy one? No wonder he and Purdy can't stand each other. You mention in your book about Dolores's grandma being able to turn herself into a jaguar, but you didn't see it and you didn't say if you believed it or not. I just wonder if somebody really can do something like that, what somebody else could do to stop them, being as how bullets obviously don't work. I have been wondering if it might say in the rest of that Dracula book of mine. I guess I must have left it back at your place, and I have a notion I'll leave Purdy in charge out here in a week or so and go on into Dawson and check on Egil and see if I can find that book while I'm at it. I'll leave this at the Vein for you with that Miss Devine, the one that used to be the widow. She'll probably know where to have it forwarded if you've moved on by now.

Cross your fingers for me about this gold that keeps trickling in, and maybe the next time you see me I can give you a ride on my brand new steamship.

*Your sincere friend,*

Dag Lomax

# CHAPTER XIX

"WASN'T THAT FASCINATING? And I should think you would be very cheered to get such a letter from an admirer," Sasha Devine said. She lay aside the letter she had been reading and set the candelabra down at the foot of my coffin.

"Thank you," I said frostily. I would have preferred to read my letter myself, but my eyes were still not focusing properly. Nor was anything else working much better. "Sasha? Am I dead or undead?"

"Why, my darling, you are neither, of course," she said with a shrug. "You're alive. I thought perhaps the letter from the so-attractive Mr. Lomax might convince you of that. How do you feel about him?"

That was just like Sasha. Here she was practically a vampire in a vampire's lair in the middle of the arctic with wolves running around and people striking gold left and right and me sleeping in a coffin in some sort of cave or the other from the look of it, and all she wanted to talk about was men.

"What do you mean, how do I feel about him?" I parried. I actually would have felt very concerned for him were I not so alarmed at my own situation.

"If he were here right now, what would you want to do? Would you want to greet him cordially, shake his hand, kiss him, or bite him?"

"Sasha Devine, even from you, that is an improper and intrusive question!" I snapped.

"Well, then, forget the rest of it. Would you want to bite him?"

"Most certainly not. It sounds like he has quite enough trouble in that department already what with the wolves acting up again and so on. Wait a moment. That letter. When did you get it?"

"He brought it to me this evening at work. He barely spoke to me. He was very agitated to be gone again for he discovered that his nephew had disappeared from the hospital while most of the sisters were seeing the *Bella* off."

I lay back in my coffin, exhausted. Things were starting to swim in front of my face again, but as soon as I rested for a moment, they cleared.

"Let me see the letter," I said. When I had examined it, I added, "I don't know why you're doing this, but this is obviously a forgery. The date is almost three weeks hence. Now I remember quite clearly all those notes stating that the *Bella* left on the first of October and—"

"It did, but the letter is not a forgery. At any time you might have died, except that Vasily Vladovitch was determined that that would not happen to you until you had recovered sufficiently to make the choice."

"Very nice of him. Sasha, I don't understand anything that has happened for a very long time. Where am I?"

"That I will not say except that you must remain here. You are safe, you will be provided for until something can be worked out. But you must rest and grow stronger. Vasily Vladovitch has been very eager to speak with you again. I will fetch him."

And she swirled from the room in a clink and tinkle of the jet crystal beads that dangled from every possible surface of her black gown. A spangled band covered her throat from chin to shoulder blade, leaving only a V of pale bosom exposed in a most dramatic manner. It was a stylish improvement over the black velvet band but indicative of the same thing. I sighed and watched the ceiling whirl above me. Then I wondered why I could. Sasha had taken the candelabra with her.

I had not been awake all that long. I remembered the *Bella* and being bitten, but after that I recalled only a long vague series of rather wild and woolly dreams. Looking around me a little, I realized that a few of them had taken place within this chamber.

It seemed to be a cave of some sort—not the type with icicles dripping in both directions, but a smooth stone surface that might have been scooped out long ago by some immovable force. For a moment I thought of dragon fire, that such an aperture would be just the right size and shape for a serpentine body. But then my attention drifted back once more to the light, of which there was more than there should have been. It was nice not to be completely in the dark, but I wondered if being bitten by Vasily Vladovitch had conferred the sight of bats on me. Was I quite sure, in fact, that I was lying flat instead of upside down? Such was my vertigo that I felt the need to double-check. But as I turned to do so, I discovered the source of light, something so startlingly unexpected that my gasp echoed through the cavern.

A huge, smooth, crystalline window pierced the cave wall behind me, and soft moon and starlight flooded through almost unaltered by the quality of the stone. I had to go investigate at once, naturally, for it was also possible that if the window admitted light, it might provide my egress as well.

Even in gentleman's britches, it is not an easy thing to climb out of a coffin when one's head is unsteady and one's feet are not terribly reliable either. I threw one leg over and hoisted myself up, then lay there turning crazy pirouettes without moving another muscle. Doggedly, however, I threw the other leg over and tried to push myself up. The coffin tipped. I slipped sideways and it tipped further. I teetered crazily on the brink and it toppled.

Then suddenly it righted and I was hoisted to my feet by two abnormally strong hands, my entire weight supported by one of them.

"Ah, Miss Lovelace, I am delighted that you have returned to us in all of your quixotic glory."

"I was trying to see out that window," I said.

"I see. My crystal lens—a natural phenomena. Amazing, isn't it? And very beautiful, with the light of the moon filtering through."

"I am more interested in viewing the topography than the moon, if you must know," I said. "I want to know where I am and how long you intend to keep me here and what exactly are your intentions regarding me. I'll have you know that friends interested in my welfare are even now investigating this whole situation."

"Ah, yes, the worthy Mr. Lomax. I took the liberty of screening his letter before Miss Devine delivered it to you, naturally, since we did not want to convey anything that might impede your recovery. I am surprised at the difference in our interpretations of the message, however. It seems to me that Mr. Lomax is not at all interested in your whereabouts since he thinks you safely elsewhere. Nor is he concerned with little foibles. Rather he occupies himself with the real menace, the one to which you have been so blind, that of the undisciplined and unethical loup garou that hunts among the populace of this country."

"Look who's talking," I said, which was the best I could manage in my weakened condition.

"But, my dear lady, it is precisely because it is me, Vasily Vladovitch Bledinoff, talking, that I can speak with such authority. Surely you do not equate me with that savage thing."

"Sir, I am in no mood for more of your excuses. I know very well that you have murdered and have even, upon occasion, implicated me. I further know that you have corrupted Miss Devine and various members of your own staff to the point where they are unreliable companions. I fear you have done the same to me, and I feel ashamed that you have been able to do so even when the shade of my own dear father bestirred himself from whatever activities he was performing beyond the grave to warn me about you, as I could have seen were I not so blind. Don't try to blow smoke in my face, Mr. Bledinoff. I know very well who is the villain of this piece."

"I refuse to let your pigheadedness exasperate me again, madam. You will retire to your coffin and you will listen to me or I shall be very cross. When I am cross, I find it difficult to behave with restraint. If I behave without restraint, then the realization of your worst fears concerning my vampire nature will be upon your head."

"Or neck, as the case may be," I rejoined. But I did as he said, not only because I was intimidated, which I would have been a great fool not to be, but because I was curious. I would listen, but I intended to ask some hard questions while I did so.

"Now then, about the murders you have mentioned. I confess. I am guilty, although I think murder too harsh a term. You see, I am a special being, by birth, by death, and most particularly by blood—or by the way it is assimilated in my body. You are capable of understanding war, I believe? No? Well, it is not a pleasant concept, but it is the inevitable result of two diverse parties in need of the same resource."

I nodded.

"Miss Lovelace, though you feel compelled to put a moral judgment upon my needs, they are, you know, my needs. I need blood to live, even as you do. I am a friendly fellow. I try to live among others as a comrade, taking only what is necessary, but when I am threatened with death—either by deprivation or by interference—I react as a soldier. I kill before I am myself permanently deprived of what I now experience as life."

"Very well," I said. "I understand that by your own lights you are not a criminal, though the same could undoubtedly be said for many who are indisputably blackguards."

"You as yet understand nothing, and I think that in order to explain it to you, we must discuss my family origins in more depth."

I could see he was settling down to enjoy that. "Please," I said, "you've already explained about the Draculas being descended from the European dragon priests, but I don't see how that applies. The jaguar priests of Mexico had the ability to change themselves into other things, but I don't believe they ever sucked blood."

"No, but they drank it, did they not? And partook of the victims whose hearts they fed to their overlord? Do you not think such a practice might incur a curse or two, maybe even a curse powerful enough to brand a hereditary line of priests with a special—talent?"

"The dragon I met didn't believe in curses," I said. "He was a very scientific sort of creature. Tell me, Vasily Vladovitch, do you read the works of Mr. Jules Verne?"

"I do not believe this is an auspicious time to discuss literature," he said stiffly, somewhat miffed at being sidetracked from regaling me with a recitation of his "begats."

"I thought we were, assuming that your knowledge of the Mexican dragon is gleaned mainly from my book."

"Not only from that. We have teachings, we higher beings, that encompass the philosophies of all five of the great dragons, though, of course, my knowledge of the Northern Wurm is greatest."

"Well, the feathered serpent would be gratified by the works of Mr. Verne. Do your teachings tell you that the worms are scientific missionaries from another world?"

"That much is implied but is couched, of course, in the appropriate beautifully poetic sacred liturgy."

"The better to obscure its meaning," I muttered. "Well, I can add to that. Kukulkan or Quetzalcoatl, as some call him told me that the Jaguar people were, like the dragons, an ancient species, a more assimilated and degenerated life-form, whose special abilities peculiarly fitted them for the priesthood. Might the same not be true of your own forebears?"

"For an artist you have not an ounce of poetry in your soul," he said accusingly.

"I beg your pardon. It is not my theory. It is the dragon's. I don't know about your Wurm, but Kukulkan was in his time a very practical sort of deity. His wings were used for reconnaissance, not flights of fancy."

"Ah, but how does that explain the ability we ancient ones possess to add to our numbers?"

"You have a lot of converts, do you?" I asked, seemingly offhandedly but really with the most avid interest, since I feared I either was one or was about to become one, along with many of my friends and acquaintances.

"Not a lot, no. It is not the sort of life, if you will, for which many are suited. You must understand that our bites can produce a number of results, running the gamut from death to more or less eternal life."

"Pray continue. I confess I have been curious about that."

"Well, there is, first of all, the death bite. I avoid that one, myself, except when I am truly depleted and must have a great infusion immediately to revive myself. This was more or less what happened when the boat docked this summer in San Francisco. You understand that during the daylight hours, I must rest and cannot feed. Although this country has the wonderful property of having nearly continuous night for months on end, the reverse is true in the summer, when daylight reins supreme for almost two and a half months. That is why I chose to go to San Francisco, where it got decently dark and I could live a little. To the best of everyone's knowledge here, I was out working on my claim while my children built my home and my business."

"They aren't vampires then?"

"Not most of them, at least not fully. They are rather all quite fond of being bitten, having developed a hereditary longing for the euphoric secreted by my saliva when I feed."

"That must have been what Maisie was prattling on about," I said.

"Ah, Maisie, yes. Isn't she charming? So enthusiastic. Not everyone has such a positive attitude toward initiation, you know. I had to be quite firm with poor Giselle."

"Did you kill her?" I asked.

"You have the harshest way of looking at things. No, I did not kill her, but I had to restrain her until the euphoric worked its way out of her system. Too bad. She is a particularly succulent sort. But she got carried away and tried to bite others before she herself was fully initiated. Just because she could shift shapes—an ability acquired prematurely as a result of previous indoctrination into the occult—she thought herself my equal. I had to finish off that detective, Norman, myself for she had crushed his jugular in her ardor. I couldn't let the poor fellow, however obnoxious, die like that. Also, her system has not yet begun to produce the euphoric."

"How about the other deaths? The mountie at Tagish? Egil's friend on the boat, the drunk in the alley in San Francisco, the miners around here?"

"That's not so awfully many, you know. You could count them on both hands. And as I said, my relationship to the rest of mankind is similar to war, though no one regrets that more than I."

"But those you condemn to be creatures of the night like yourself?"

"There are not very many of those either. Miss Devine has not yet joined our ranks because of expediency, but she wishes to. What is an actress without youth and beauty, which can be hers forever if she enters into the ultimate embrace?"

"There you go waxing poetic again. You mean if she lets you bite her to death, which you almost have already."

"No, my dear lady, of course not. I mean when she finally bites *me*. She must acquire my transformed blood in order to be herself transformed. So must anyone who would join us."

That came as a tremendous relief to me. I may not have known how often I'd been bitten, but I was pretty sure I had not bitten anyone else—least of all Vasily Vladovitch. I certainly would remember a thing like that.

"Are Maisie and the others going to join you?"

"Oh, I hope so. I wanted to tell you about my plans for an immortal troupe. I think it will be the most exciting thing ever to happen in show business. And through the girls, perhaps we can use Dawson as a source of ongoing wealth, a whole country full of volunteer vampires who can mine tirelessly all winter and either sleep during the summer or vacation in more conventionally illuminated locations."

He spread his arms and his palms as if opening vistas before me. "Imagine, a bevy of eternally beautiful girls, their fame and talent growing over the years, playing all over the United States, Europe, South America. Why, it will be a show business phenomenon such as the stage has never seen! And up here, a haven for us, as this country has been a haven for me. A winter resort for people of my calibre.

"Do you know how lonely this life can be? My father, cooped up all those years in that dreary castle in Transylvania, was not the monster your Mr. Stoker imagines him to be, but he was a bore and a bit of a sourpuss. It ran in the family. I am not surprised in the least that Aunt Elizabeth went over the edge. It is no sort of life for a person, being shut up on lonely prominences while everyone else in the family is off to war, impaling Turks.

"I was fortunate in growing up among the Cossacks on the steppes, free of confinement and free to be the sort of creature that I am and to glory in it, to find a place for it. And then, when I rose in society in Moscow and Berlin, because of my breeding and the family fortune, why, I began to see that the best things in life happen at night anyway. All of the gaiety and glamor, the excitement and mystery of life are enhanced by shadows and moonlight. So, I thought to myself, who needs sunshine anyway? Not I, certainly, but when I heard of this place I knew that there was room to make a whole society beyond the tyranny of sun or summer; an existence cloaked by vast expanses of snow, protected by isolation, but one providing warm camaraderie as well. With wealth, entertainment, fellowship, society, what more would I ever need than this land?" He ran his hands through his hair and stared at me as if his words were inadequate to share the glory of his dream.

"I see. It sounds like a veritable vampire's utopia," I said, humoring him.

"It is. Yes, it is. I am, you see, something of a visionary among my kind, being brought up so differently. And, surely by now, you have discovered that my bite is even better than my bark, when applied with the proper discretion." He wiggled his eyebrows amorously at me and I affected to fail to understand. "Don't you find it dramatic, as an artist, that I am able to deal love and death from this same set of fangs?"

"A fountain of dental passion," I agreed.

"There are, of course—uh—other outlets for the former. My Indian children, for instance, are descendants of a very fruitful union I enjoyed with a lovely Indian woman who bore me fifteen children, only half of them manifesting a vampire nature. The others who travel with me are their descendants. Although it is not readily apparent to you, several generations of my local family are within that little kinship group. Remarkable, isn't it?"

"So one has the choice of becoming a vampire or dying eventually?" I asked.

"If you don't become a vampire, you certainly die eventually," he said. "If you become one of us, it takes a little longer, though I'm not sure how long if you stay away from certain unhealthy articles and conditions. But no, death and conversion aren't the only two choices. We are not the medieval Catholic Church, after all, my dear."

I sat erect in my coffin and stared into his bottomless brown eyes and twirled my thumbs as I had often seen the Widow Hig do. "Ah, yes. And there we come to the crux of the matter, do we not? Your fear of the Church, of crosses, of religious implements?"

"Fear is not the term I would use," he said with a look as if he had just tasted something purported to be blood that was instead tomato sauce. "Avoidance is perhaps more accurate. Religious fanatics who go about brandishing crosses are dangerous to us because of their ill will toward any belief or practice that does not conform to their doctrine. They also make terrible converts. My great uncle Vanya once fell in love with a devout woman and claimed her. Never did she cease tearing both her hair and his and saying 'mea culpas' day and night. He finally had to lock her out of the crypt at dawn to be rid of her."

"Then you are not specifically anti-Christian?" I asked.

"No. Only some Christians. Rising again, you comprehend, is a very routine concept to us. I had hoped you would understand it all better now, having been helped along those lines yourself. Had I not relieved you of an excess of sanguination pressing against your brain, you would have needed full conversion to survive your accident. I could, of course, have exercised that option, but I would never wish to make an unwilling vampire of someone like you, for I am sure that if I did so you would find a way to doom me."

"And what makes you think I will not now?" I asked.

"Because I shall prevent it, of course, and because I think that truly, I have given you little cause for a personal vendetta against me. Unlike a few other extranormal beings in the vicinity, I behave in a principled and disciplined fashion toward prey and acolytes alike and pose no immediate threat to you or those you have reason to care for."

"How about Sasha Devine?"

"You have my permission to ask her if she feels threatened

or imperiled," he said graciously. "You may also keep in mind that without my control, something that is now mostly an annoyance, an occasional hazard, could get completely out of hand, could ravage this territory and bring it under the control of one who is not, like myself, a dreamer, but a despoiler of its riches and the labor of those who would win them."

"Oh, really," I said. "You sound like you think you're some sort of supernatural Wyatt Earp keeping Dodge City safe for women and children."

He looked very pleased and almost preened himself, running his long graceful fingers down the lapels of his embroidered waistcoat. "You do have a way with words, for I think in many ways that is an accurate description. You will recall the night you thought my coffin disappeared at the mouth of Henderson Creek?"

"I am not likely to forget it."

"There was a certain wolf intent on claiming a moose, a man, and you, if it could get you?"

"I recall."

"How were you saved, Miss Lovelace?"

"Dag Lomax and his cat—" I began, but Vasily Vladovitch shook his head and waggled his finger as if correcting a child.

"Dag Lomax and his cat, remarkable as they may be, had nothing to do with it, but would, indeed, have been devoured along with you and Mr. Larsson had it not been for the command of another wolf."

"You are mistaken, sir. The other wolf was not commanding our attacker, but calling to him. Undoubtedly a mating call."

"Oh, is that so, Miss Know-Everything? It so happens, this time, that you are the one who is mistaken," he crowed. "I happen to know for a fact that both wolves were males and that one was dominant. For one of my sort is of a higher order than your mere were-people. They are the children of the night. We are the masters."

"Are you trying to tell me that you are not only a bat and a blood-sucking saloon tycoon, but also a wolf? Really, Vasily Vladovitch!"

"And a mist, don't forget. If you had read the rest of that accursed book, it would have been clear to you. Shape-shifting is a little bonus power we have to make our lives easier. Tell me, my dear, does it excite you that I am a wolf? Does the prospect of being a wolf yourself excite you?"

"The prospect of escaping your clutches for the relative

warmth of the sunlight excites me," I said. "If this is all as benign as you pretend, you will keep me prisoner no longer."

"That's gratitude for you!" his hands exploded outward and jerked expressively in outrage. "We save your life, we offer you the option of extending it indefinitely, no strings attached, and you insult and revile us! You have been our patient, not our prisoner, you stupid girl."

"Then I can go?"

"Of course, you can go! Go! Go fall off another boat and this time drown for all I care!"

"Aren't you afraid I'll tell what I know?"

"Tell who? The mounties? You think they're going to believe such a story from someone who murdered one of their own officers?"

"You framed me."

"Not intentionally, but the situation has had its uses. No, nobody is going to believe you. You'll end up in a madhouse if you try to present this as anything but fiction, and as you can see from Stoker's work, the task of villifying us has already been thoroughly executed. Sorry. Unfortunate choice of words. No, you poor wretch, you have not at this time nor have you ever had anything to fear from Vasily Vladovitch Bledinoff. I would have given you the eminence of someone schooled first-hand in our origins, would have seen to it that you were one of the grande dames of vampire society, accorded the respect and admiration given to—oh, a saint, I suppose would be the best parallel in your narrow conventional terms. If you choose to throw it away, it is your affair, but you cannot hurt me or any of my followers. We are, after all, immortal, and you, you fool, have just abdicated that option."

He glared at me as if I was guilty of something, and I found myself stammering as I might have before an especially severe nun. "I—I'm sorry, but what you want is impossible. I'm afraid I'm mostly a day person."

"Bah!" he said, then fixed me with those mesmerizing eyes, and for a moment I feared that he was going back on his word and would be my ruin after all. "You will remain here, resting, until I send someone to get you. They will lead you from here blindfolded, and you will forget all you know of these chambers once you leave them. This whole incident will be as a dream to you."

That command would have worked precisely as he wanted it had it not been for my old custom of writing down my dreams as soon as I awakened. It was poetic justice, then, that the habit instilled in me by one of his victims should be the ultimate undoing of the vampire.

Looking back upon it, I am rather vexed with Vasily Vladovitch for his handling of the situation. People who are captured by vampires are supposed to be hounded and subjected to nightmares and repeated attacks of various supernatural agencies pressing upon them like so many bill collectors. It really wasn't fair. He had had me in his clutches, and with all the dramatic possibilities, he had chosen simply to give me a bit of a hypnotic preogative and unclutch, as it were.

And then, at the end, they were so clumsy about it. Though I was blindfolded and had my hands tied so I couldn't cheat, if I did not know from whence I was coming, I at least knew with whom. Maisie consoled me on my wisdom the whole long and circuitous journey.

"Of course, you have to do what you think is best, Cory, and I know that this life isn't for everybody, but really, I think you underrate the advantages. You can't go bathing at the beach during the daytime any more, it's true, but then, my goodness, think of getting to sleep in and never having to see eight A.M. the rest of your life! Or—or whatever."

I let her prattle on, though I knew it was my moral duty to try to dissuade her. One always seems to have a moral duty to dissuade people from doing what they enjoy, but in this instance I wasn't yet fully awake anyway, so I felt I could be excused on grounds of incapacitation. Otherwise, despite a bit of weakness that would no doubt be readily remedied by brisk exercise, I felt well enough. I realized suddenly that the deep sleep I had enjoyed while en route from Seattle and later while upon the Yukon was due to some spell of Vasily Vladovitch's similar to the one from which I had just roused.

Long flights of steps and steep slopes had to be negotiated, and on these I concentrated while Maisie regaled me with the joys of semivampiredom. I had become chilly almost as soon as we set out, and from that I guessed that the room in which I had been secreted was equipped with something as prosaic as a stove or at the very least a chimney pipe, though I had seen nothing but a bare room, the crystalline lens, and the coffin—I refuse to call it mine—in which I had apparently rested for more than two weeks.

Abruptly I felt the rush of frigid air seize me, and Maisie

guided me into it. Her chattering was now drowned out by that of my own teeth.

"Just a minute more now, honey, and I'll let you loose and you can put on your hat and coat," she promised.

Finally, in the middle of a snowy field of what had once been muskeg, she kept her promise. Ahead of us lay the raw new facades of the buildings that sparsely graced Second Street. Clearly visible beyond them was the unattractive backside of Paradise Alley, a view as improved by snow as the residents of the area were by their professional warpaint.

Maisie untied my hands and pulled away the blindfold. "Here's your pack—I hope nothing mildewed. It's a little hard to dry so many things out in—well, never mind. I just hope it's all right. And here's your coat." While I was wrapping that around me, she withdrew an envelope. "Vasily Vladovitch says this is your thirty pieces of silver, but it feels like folding money to me. I'd like to stay and chat, but I have to run. I promised to take a pie up for the social at the hospital this afternoon. Bye now!"

And she bustled off, apparently seeing nothing contradictory about wishing to continue good works while leading a secret life as an apprentice vampiress. Well, perhaps there wasn't anything contradictory as long as she didn't bite too deeply and kept away from crosses. Vasily Vladovitch was widely known for being a soft touch for a grubstake or helping someone down on his luck. And despite his aversion to religious fanatics, he had, Lane once told me, donated generously to the hospital building fund in the early spring, presumably before he came to San Francisco and ruined my life.

I was still dwelling on the munificence of my former employer as I reached my former abode. It had obviously acquired a new occupant, as I saw upon opening the door. Her business was evidently doing much better than mine had. Paris gowns and jewels were strewn everywhere, though the bed looked as if someone had nested in it and the fire was cold. My candles were set in profusion around the room, squandered, their wax melting over canning jar lids and crystal holders, crockery, and odds and ends of fine china. A funny arrangement of chicken feathers and a smelly leather bag, no doubt some manifestation of modern art that seemed at odds with the rest of the lady's taste, hung above the bed. The bucket that had held my wallpaper rolls sat near the stove. All but three of the scrolls had evidently fed the fire at some time. I took the remaining three and was turning to go when Lurleen arrived at the doorway.

"Well, hello, there," she said musically.                    "

"Lurleen, for heaven's sakes," I said disgustedly.

"Oh! Cory! I thought you was some guy come to see Madame Giselle. She don't go for the common trade and she ain't home anyway, so I thought I'd just sort of make sure you didn't go away disappointed." She suddenly pinched her fingers over her nose. "Gad, stinks in here, don't it? In spite of that dollar an ounce Paris perfume she wears. Smells like an old wet dog. Come on, honey."

"I was just going to go to the cafe and see—"

"You won't see nothin' there today. It's Sunday. Everything is closed down tight. But a gentleman caller of mine who works the steamships left me some oranges that are just going to go bad if you don't help me eat them. And I've got some bacon and a little tea. Come to think of it, you're lookin' a little peakedy."

While she cooked and talked, I wrote down my dreams, including those I was supposed to forget, and the accident, my rescue, the conversation with Vasily Vladovitch, and all I recalled of the route we followed when I was released. From years of practice, I did not think of these things at all but allowed my hand to do the writing while I listened to Lurleen's gossip, most of it second-hand from the miners. Some of those who had claims up on the creeks had come into town, but some of the claims that had supposedly been abandoned were now haunted by bobbing lights at night and the creaking of equipment. Some of the fellows were claiming that the *Bella* had gone down with all hands and that the ghosts of those men were haunting their old stomping grounds as a way of letting their fellows in Dawson know of the disaster, which, of course, nobody had bothered to report yet because they probably hadn't found out or somebody was trying to keep it from them, probably a politician, probably for economic reasons. Which was silly, because had there been such a disaster, every dog driver in town would have been recruited for a rescue party, and the entire country would have been out searching the banks. Still, in the isolation and growing darkness of the winter, it sounded more plausible than it should have.

"That's about all except for that Giselle decidin' she was too good for the rest of the hussies at the Vein and movin' into your place. Not that you—well, never mind. She's just different. Never refers customers either. That nice old guy with the cat was up here, oh, around noon, looking for something in there. I thought for a minute you was him come back. She didn't give him the book he was lookin' for, but she sounded like she was trying to give him about anything else you could dream up. Some people just got no finesse, you know? Make the rest of us look cheap. If I wasn't a woman who believes in minding my own business, I'd have marched right over there and reminded her that it is Sunday and she has to close like everybody else, even if she's givin' it away."

"Lomax?" I asked her. "He's here?"

"Was earlier. I think I heard him say he was heading out today though. No place much for him to hang out here on a Sunday, unless it would be at one of the boarding houses. You might ask in Grand Forks if they've seen him pass, though mostly the river is solid enough now to support a team right along the shoreline anyhow."

"I wonder if I could catch up with him?"

"You'd better dress warmer than that if you're going to. And take snowshoes. Not much on the ground now, but it looks like there might be more later. You got matches? Coffee? Blankets?" I shook my head at each successive question, and she shook hers, too. "I can loan you a couple of matches, but I don't have any of the other stuff to spare. You'd better send word."

"I can't, Lurleen. I can't stay here. It is urgent that I find Lomax, but I promise you, I'll walk over to Grand Forks, and if they have seen him and he's too far ahead of me, I'll return here."

"You do that, kid. I swear I can't figure out what other problems it is you think you've got, but believe me, none of 'em is as bad as freezing to death. And people aren't the only ones who're hungry this winter. Folks are gettin' attacked by wolves, bears, mooses, and beavers, for all I know. You come back before dark now, you hear?"

Sunday had cast a pall of ghostly silence over Dawson. Those who weren't in church had to be sleeping late—there was nothing else to do. The laws against working on the sabbath were extremely strict. The week before I arrived, a man had been fined for cutting his own firewood on Sunday. The silence, which might have been restful at any other time, was restive instead, and I hastened my steps. Though the sun was only halfway up in the sky, I didn't judge that it could be much past two-thirty. I felt I had a good chance of catching up with Lomax.

# CHAPTER XX

•••◆•⊂⊃I I⊂⊃•◆•••

*DRYDOCKED BOATS CREAKED* with the cold and canvas flapped as someone shifted inside a tent. Dawson on Sunday afternoon made the vampire's lair seem a cheerful, homey sort of place, though perhaps it was only that Vasily Vladovitch's company had had a corrupting influence on my perceptions. Or perhaps I felt ill at ease because, unbeknownst to me, I was being observed. At any rate, I was glad to pass Fort Herchmer and head up the frozen Klondike toward the creeks.

Grand Forks was a little livelier. Men and women were not exactly working on the sabbath, but they were stirring about a little, feeding dogs, dumping slops, doing more normal sorts of things, being a bit removed from the watchful eye of the mounties.

JayEllen herself greeted me. She was a round, busy woman whose usual expression seemed to be resigned tolerance, but whose smile was genuinely both warm and amused. Lomax, she told me, had left scarcely a half hour ago.

"Took him a long time to finish his Sunday dinner, which I fed him in a noncommercial, neighborly sort of way," she told me. "Then he gave me the sweetest little poke of dust— purely as a friendly, neighborly present. The two things were in no way connected, heaven forbid."

Though the few miles between Dawson and Grand Forks

had tired me, I set out with renewed hope. Really, dogs being what they were, Lomax had scarcely any lead at all. What with tangled harnasses, the need for canine irrigation breaks along the trail, if I scurried a little I should be able to catch up. If I didn't within a couple of hours, I would keep my promise to Lurleen and return to Dawson, though the thought was not one that gladdened my heart.

The walk would have been a Sunday stroll had I been a little more on my mettle and not trying to hurry quite so much. It was another of those pastel winter scenes, pretty as a rich child's nursery and about as alarming. The thick tracery of snow over the bare branched alders made them look as if they were sculpted of bone china. The spruces were frosted on every layer of greenery, like a Christmas tree in the yard of a gingerbread house. I almost broke into a skip and thought kind thoughts of granny, whomever and wherever she might be.

If all that wasn't enough to convince me, a benign golden light sat gently as a blessing upon the distant hills, the treetops, the trail ahead. No doubt it would have made a kindly halo for any passing grizzly. I was so charmed and bemused that if I *had* heard footsteps behind me, I would have turned and exclaimed to my pursuer what a glorious day it was.

And though I did not catch up with Lomax, even after an hour and a half of maintaining a pretty good pace, I felt sure that I would at any moment. Sometimes I would stop and think I could hear him just ahead of me, calling to the dogs, or hear one of them "woo woo" that strange husky whining howl that suffices for a bark. I was clearly on his trail—little paw prints and the twin indentations of runner ruts led the way, and a profusion of yellow bushes along the path indicated that his dogs were doing things that would slow him down to where I could catch up eventually. I could surely run as fast as a dog, couldn't I? I did not, at the time, know anything much about dog driving.

Nor did I particularly know why I felt it so urgent to reach Lomax. He was my confidant, but so was Lurleen. He was, perhaps, less publicly occupied than Lurleen and had shown more interest in my problems, but that did not mean he was any better equipped to deal with them. He was as short of supplies as anyone. But then, since he had taken my share, perhaps I did have more of a claim on his attention than on someone else's. That was not it, really, of course. The fact was that I liked the man and trusted his good will toward me, which it seemed to me he had demonstrated repeatedly. I thought that if we could just talk everything over, surely I would find the sensible thing to do in this singularly unsensible situation.

I was probably being entirely too harsh on Vasily Vladovitch, for instance. He, too, had shown his good will, and if he killed people occasionally, he did it less casually than many people who had less realistic need of the blood of their fellow man. Or woman.

The only one of his would-be converts he had been less than courtly to had been Giselle, and maybe he had, despite what he told me, reinstated her in his affections and my cabin. Those Paris gowns had to come from somewhere. Poor Giselle. After longer acquaintance with her dance hall skills, I could see that she was not as good at them as the other girls. There had been no sign, judging from the fact that both Millie and Sasha were walking around unharmed (if you didn't count nibbled necks), that she had any aptitude for being a voodoo queen, as Maisie had suggested. And she had been quite an overeager failure at vampiredom, if Vasily Vladovitch was being truthful, and had had to be drummed out of the corps (corpse?) for exceeding her authority and the length of her fangs.

All of these ruminations ran through my head along with the rhythm of my steps, so that I failed to notice that the sky was growing dimmer, the golden light had turned steely, a wind had come up making the spruces rock like hired mourners and sending a fine dust of snow skimming across the trail ahead of me.

It was time to go back, but I knew it would be dark before I reached Grand Forks again and there was always the chance that if it was growing dark, Lomax would be making camp. If I walked but another half hour, I'd probably stumble over him.

And I was convinced I could hear the dogs howling. I hurried my footsteps and pulled my collar up and my hat down. The wind tingled at the tip of my nose. Perhaps because I had walked into a denser stand of trees, perhaps because I had come into this part of the early winter after a sudden lapse of many days, I was unprepared for the swiftness with which the light failed.

Still, the trail was clear and there was some traffic. From somewhere close by I heard footsteps counterpointing my own. The woods distorted the sound so that I could not at first tell from which direction the sound came. A well-remembered and unloved voice enlightened me almost as soon as I stopped to ponder the matter.

"Hold it right there, little darlin'."

Drake stood behind me in the path. One of his handmade Mexican cigars dangled from a singularly unfriendly grin. I might have tried dissembling except that to the best of my memory Drake was not the sort of man who would address an unknown person in a male miner's togs by one of his quaint regional endearments.

"Why, Mr. Dr—Blake! Whatever are you doing so far from town? Aren't you worried that some beleaguered fellow countryman will come in from the creeks with a rich claim, and you will not be there in time to beat him to the recorder's office?"

"Yes'm, I do indeed worry about that kind of thing a mite, but a good politician needs to learn to delegate authority. I have an assistant to handle the routine matters. I wanted to tend to you personally."

"How kind."

"No, ma'am, I don't believe 'kind' is exactly the word I would use."

"I'm sorry to hear that. I had hoped you'd perhaps come to tell me that after your uncouth behavior on our previous acquaintance, you had seen the light and wished to apologize. Since that is not the case, I'll not take up any more of your valuable time. I'm trying to overtake someone."

"Wouldn't be some old cripple with a mangy cat around his neck and a dog team, would it now?"

"I wouldn't put it that way, no."

"Because if it is, he ain't stayin' healthy all that much longer neither."

"You're very ambitious so late in the day."

"Another new assistant. She'll enjoy chewin' on him more than I would. Enthusiastic type, that Gigi. Finally found the kind of work she's cut out for. But you and me, we'll just wait till the moon shows up. I *like* it when the moon's big and full. Puts hair on my chest."

"I had no idea you were such a romantic, Mr. Drake."

"How well you know me, darlin'. The last time I succumbed to any sentimental horseshit, I lost my ranch. If I had let my old partner feed Claytie and Lovanche to the dragon with the rest of you, Kukulkan would have been pleased with me and let me keep it instead of requirin' me to take up with this new profession."

"I was under the impression you always wanted to be in politics."

"It's not politics I'm talkin' about. It's loboin'. I always was somethin' of a lone wolf, but I never reckoned how complicated it can be."

"Do you intend to continue talking in riddles all night or are you going to explain what on earth you're talking about?" I had a good idea, between the *Dracula* book and Lomax's letter, and at this point I was getting so used to people seeming to be what they weren't or turning into other things without so much as a by-your-leave that I wouldn't have been at all surprised to learn that Queen Victoria, upon contact with salt-water, turned into a mermaid.

"Oh, I'm gonna do better than that, darlin'. I'm gonna show you just exactly what I mean. You just stay right there and be as sweet as you are, and in no time at all you'll get the point."

He grinned again and his teeth seemed somewhat longer. He flexed his hands and it seemed to me that his gloves strained at the fingertips a little. He was too vain, of course, to wear mittens like almost everybody else.

"I have no doubt that I will, but once you begin your explanation, I wonder if I'll have time to fully appreciate its subtleties. Or your accomplishments. Was that you, by any chance, who greeted me at Lomax's camp that first night?"

"It was, and if some other varmint hadn't interfered with me, we would not be havin' this particular conversation."

"But what good can it do you to turn into a wolf?" I asked him.

"Mostly because it's something not everybody *can* do, but you see, a wolf, bein' a critter, can get away with murder and everybody says, 'Hell, that's just a critter.' The most they do about it is try to track it, or wolves in general, down and kill it. But a lobo like me, we're a little harder to kill, man or wolf."

"Oh? And how's that."

"Got any silver on you?"

"Not at the moment."

"Good. That's just hunky-dory." His grin literally split his face, the fangs definitely more pronounced, the end of his straight and rather aristocratic nose starting to look vaguely shiny and wet. His eyebrows sprouted brushy embellishments, and he needed a shave he had not needed ten minutes ago. He pulled off one glove with another and removed the cigar from his mouth long enough to pick his back teeth with a little fingernail like a Chinese mandarin's. "You know, not too many people do have any silver up here. I'm mighty pleased about that. Now, if I was out in Arizona or maybe Colorado, I'd have me a problem, but up here all anybody thinks about or uses or makes pretties for their lady friends out of is shiny yellow gold. Everybody uses it, including me, and by the time I'm done with this place, I'll have it all. See, silver and me don't get along anymore. Can't even wear conchos. Maybe I'll have me some made up of gold, 'cause gold don't bother me any more than tearin' your throat out will, darlin'. Go ahead on and make a run for it if you want to. Won't help you none. I'm FAST and my little compadre, she's gonna be full by the time she finishes with that old man, but she'll be quick enough to catch you."

"Well, I certainly wish you'd done this before we got on the wrong side of each other, Mr. Drake," I said. "This is probably even more fascinating than the dragon. Many people might regard your condition as an affliction or a curse, but you seem to embrace it with the creative and innovative spirit I would expect of you."

"Mighty kind of you to say so, darlin'. See, I've read about these poor suckers who couldn't handle bein' a werewolf, but I learned my lesson when I lost everything by not lettin' the dragon have my kinfolk. You don't get nowhere in this world without, if you'll pardon my sayin' so, dog eatin' dog."

"How wise of you to learn that lesson late in life. Before the incident with the dragon, you were just another sloppy, idealistic scalp-hunter and gun-runner. I'm glad to see you've toughened up."

"I sure as hell hope you haven't. I've been teething on these gumboot miners. A little soft, tender lady would do me a world of good."

He shucked off his jacket and shirt and turned his back slightly to remove his nether garments. The reader may rest assured that even in this extreme a situation, the proprieties were maintained. By now he was so covered with thick gray-black fur that he might as well have been wearing mink unmentionables.

"I guess you acquired your powers rather recently, did you? I mean, I know it's within the last ten years."

"Having met the great dragon and having the hole in my head to prove it, I didn't have a big problem convincing the brujos that are what's left of the Jaguar people to indoctrinate me. It's sort of like magic, but it's a little more like the smallpox. They bite you and then you get to bite everybody else. That's what I meant with the joke about the dogs. You can laugh now, and before I get down on all fours, I'd advise you to take back what you said about me bein' green at this." His voice was by now a low growl that sounded more like a speech defect than what I would have thought a talking wolf would sound like. His hackles were raised and his tail bristled menacingly.

"I only meant that I heard you had some trouble, for a more or less immortal sort of person, killing a few miners the other day. The old cripple among them."

"Shoot, that wasn't nothin'. Only reason they got away was some crazy moose attacked me. I coulda killed it, but that one bite of moose meat I had the first time you and I met up at Lomax's was more than enough for me."

"But you're very ferocious and they weren't apparently even harmed, according to a reliable source," I added quickly.

"Hell, they weren't harmed because I wanted to make sure I killed them with the first bite and none of 'em got away just a little chewed on. Mighta given me some competition. I don't aim to make any werewolves I can't control. I have one more little problem left after I take care of you, the old man and that tinhorn out at what will shortly be my new claim. Other than that, I intend to be strictly in charge here. Now, sweet thing, tell me, what's your best side?" And he sprang for me.

I only meant to duck when Drake, by now fully transformed into a wolf, flew at me, but the exertions of the day, the excitement, the fear I had tried to control by bantering, had cost me too much. My duck became a headlong tumble as I slipped and fell sideways of the path. Drake's body thudded onto the pathway behind me and I started crawling for the woods, thinking perhaps I might hoist myself into a tree somewhere. Wolves, even werewolves, didn't climb trees as far as I knew.

About that time, however, a frightened kiyi-ing rang through the woods, followed by the rapid patter of paws and the howling and yapping of a great number of dogs. I held my breath. The werewolf Giselle had no doubt just encountered Dag, and his trusty dogs were setting up a ruckus. But then the kiyi-ing grew louder, and the dogs seemed to be coming from the direction of Grand Forks. And there was a louder sound on the path, too, the thunder of the hooves of some large animal.

Drake growled, first down the path, then at me, then up the path, sniffing the air and looking more confused than ferocious. All of a sudden, a ball of black fur struck him like one billiard ball striking another, and he rolled nose over tail into the woods while the second wolf tore past us both on the trail.

A giant, angry bull moose pounded down upon her, and she threw her head up and howled as she ran, which was how she avoided seeing the dog team until she ran right into the lead dog. The team howled in panic, the female wolf in fear, and Drake in sheer confusion as he rolled over on the other side of the path, shook the snow from his fur, and saw what was going on. A shot rang out and the female wolf yelped and ran into the woods, apparently forgetting she was invulnerable. The moose turned to follow, saw Drake, and charged him instead. Drake made a speedy exit into the woods.

Sergeant Destin stood on the runners of his sled, stamping on the break, and swearing soothingly in his Scots burr to his dogs, who were snapping, snarling, and strangling themselves in their harnesses trying to get loose. About that time another team of dogs yelped up from the opposite direction, with Lomax running behind them yelling words he must have learned at sea, and possibly some of them from his Indian in-laws, for I had seldom heard such color and variety in one gout of anger.

"Hey, you, get them damn dogs out of the way!" Lomax yelled.

"You clear your animals oot of the path, mon. Ye're interrferin' with due process of the law."

"Malcom?" Lomax stopped dead in the trail, and the dogs promptly tangled themselves around a tree, one hanging himself upside down in his harness. Lomax's voice was barely audible.

"Dag! What're you doin' here? I mean, coomin' roond in this direction? I thought you was well up ahead of me."

"I was, but I got attacked by this wolf that got chased away by this moose. I'm startin' to feel like I've been there before. Did you look through that book like I told you?"

"Aye, but this is no time to discuss lit'ratoor, mon. Help me untangle these beasties."

I kept hoping one of the dogs would swing my way and Lomax would come to free or retrieve it so I could get his attention, but my wait seemed to be in vain. Surely if I just waited long enough, Destin would return to Dawson, and Lomax would continue on to his claim, and I could meet up with him. On the other hand, with Drake and Gigi on the prowl, perhaps we should all return to Dawson. I was in a quandary about whether to add to what Lomax had figured out for himself already and report to Destin what Drake had confessed to me, or to try to form some plan with Dag.

With all I knew now, the mounties could defeat the werewolves, but I was not sure how they would deal with my return from the dead, and I would have to reappear as myself in order to be sufficiently convincing. I wondered if Destin would not still prefer to believe I had killed his comrade rather than face the fact that his death had been due to causes not dealt with in the police manuals.

While I was thus deep in thought, I felt a breath of hot air upon the back of my neck. My immediate fear was that the wolves had returned, but when I rolled my eyes upward, I beheld the moose staring down at me.

I froze and stayed that way until the two men untangled their dogs and Destin turned his and headed back to Dawson. I was too shocked to notice when Lomax commenced to do the same thing. I opened my mouth to yell to him to stop, to wait, that I was there alone in the woods with two werewolves except for a large moose who from my vantage point appeared to be cross-eyed. But the gaze of the moose held me in thrall and I was unable to move, watching helplessly as Lomax gathered his dogs and drove off after the mountie. Then, of course, when it was too late, my voice returned to me.

"Well, I hope you don't mind costing me maybe my life—unless, of course, you're prepared to stay with me until dawn when the wolves go away. I'll probably freeze to death anyway, if you don't stomp me first and—"

I stopped abruptly, for the big animal was kneeling beside me and tossing its head backward. When I looked at it stupidly, it lowered its head as if to butt me. I stood and took a step backward. It lowered its head as if in submission and waited. When I hesitated, it looked back at me impatiently. I could draw only one conclusion from this strange behavior, and that was that it wished me to mount its back. I was very relieved when, upon straddling it, I found that I had interpreted matters correctly.

At a steady and cautious plod, we set out on the trail toward Dawson, always within earshot of the dogs, always with an eye out for the wolves, and now and then, on the part of my steed, with teeth bared to strip the willow branches overhanging the path, in the process dumping snow down the collar of the rider, namely me. It was annoying, but a small enough price to pay for such a large and efficient protector.

During the course of this ride, I became highly appreciative of the handy portion of the adult bull moose known as the rack, or antlers. Broad and flat, they were not only something to hold onto, once the moose got used to the idea that it was absolutely necessary that I do so and no amount of head tossing would dissuade me, but, eventually, something to brace myself against when I succumbed to exhaustion.

I had had an exceptionally busy day and evening for a convalescent. I had a blinding headache that even the gentle pace of the moose meandering through heavy snow joggled excruciatingly. My limbs, too long disused, felt as if hot pokers had replaced my bones. My neck and back felt as if my spine was ready to crack into a thousand jagged pieces, each at right angles to the other.

And on top of all of these was another, more shameful ailment. The little tooth marks where Vasily Vladovitch had drained the blood from my swollen scalp itched, throbbed, and all but made my hair stand out in tendrils grasping for the opportunity to feel those teeth. I craved the release of that sharp crescendo of pain and the accompanying jolt of blessed joyous peacefulness. I visualized those fangs not with horror but with fondness for the first time, and a part of me that seemed to sit somewhere over my left ear looked on clucking its tongue. I remembered the look on Papa's face when he'd been without a bottle for a time, and thought he must have felt the same way. No wonder he had stayed so close to Vasily Vladovitch, even after he died. It was not for my sake alone. The vampire had provided him with the cure he had been looking for all his life, the same sort of thing Purdy once advertised as a panacea for all that ailed a person. The ultimate painkiller.

So that was why Sasha deceived me so readily, why Maisie's outwardly cheerful nature suddenly escalated to manic devotion. I wondered if even after his unnaturally long lifetime, Vasily Vladovitch had any true idea of how his bite effected those he left living. I would certainly have to call on him once I reached Dawson again. I would wear black, of course, my mourning dress for Papa and the hat with the black ostrich plumes, with maybe a dead baby raven perched on the brim, which ought to please the vampire, and maybe I would prick my finger and put a bit of blood in the bottom of a preserve jar and seal the top with a bit of calico and put the whole in a covered basket with my card on top, "With kindest inquiries, Pelagia Harper."

As if it was he who had been ill, not I.

Not until we reached the edge of the woods on the far

side of the Klondike and the moose halted and stood feeding, did I realize that half of my mind's wanderings had been dreams.

Much of the night still remained and here I was, back where I had started from. Across the frozen river lay Fort Herchmer, a candle in the window of the guardroom and one in the window of the little headquarters building. Lomax's dog team, still in harness, rested on pillowed paws while their master was within, probably filling out some sort of police report. I started across the river and the moose hesitated, then crossed with me. There was still a small amount of brush cover around the fort and more in back, though any wood bigger around than one's little finger had long ago been taken for building materials or kindling.

I was about to step up to the door, when from the other side of the building came hurried footsteps, and I shrank back into the shadows and into the moose, who let forth a startled huff of frosty breath.

As soon as the door closed behind the newcomer, I crept to the single window in the small building. The moose crept up behind me. I put my nose cautiously near the bottom of the pane and looked over—straight into two shining eyes. Loki scratched a paw against the pane and made a puzzled mrrowling.

Ignoring the cat, I peered over its rather agitated top half. The newcomer was one of the young constables I had seen before. The pane was thin and I was well able to hear the conversation.

"We'll be needing reinforcements at the Vein, Sergeant Destin," the constable said. "It no sooner opened the doors than Ollie Lindholm mushed up shouting to the bartender to fetch Bledinoff and buy drinks on the house. Seems that claim Bledinoff staked him to has been coughing up more than a small spot of color every day for the last month. Lindholm says he had to bring his poke in now, before it got too heavy for the dogs to haul. It is my considered judgment, Sergeant, that there's going to be a hell of a party."

Destin rose. "Stout lad, Constable, stout lad, indeed. Canna have them havin' more fun than is fittin' without proper supervision of the forces of law and order, eh? Come along, mon," this last to Dag. "And bring yer daft wee beastie wi' you. You might recognize one of the perpetrators at the festivities, now, mightn't you?"

"Not likely," Lomax said, slipping into his coat and setting down his tea cup nonetheless. "They were wolves, like I told you."

"From what Constable Peters here says, there'll be a good bit of howlin' going on over there, too."

Lomax seemed disinclined to argue with that and scooped up Loki without another look out the window. The burned *Dracula* book lay open on the desk. When the three men had trooped out the door and down the river toward town, I poked my hair back into my hat, slipped into the office, and picked up the book, skimming it quickly to try to see if I could find anything about what to do about vampires or werewolves or whatever. There was a space in the spine that didn't seem to have to do with the fire damage and I let the book flop open to that place.

The passage marked was at least partially what I wanted. It told of how Dr. Van Helsing, apparently an expert on vampires by virtue of being Eastern European, persuaded Arthur Holmwood, a friend of the hero Jonathan Harker's, to finish off his fiancee, Lucy Westerna, after she succumbed to the advances of the vampire to such a degree that she had to be entombed. Dr. Van Helsing carried a regular little workshop with him, including a hammer and a sharpened wooden stake, and with this, the book said, "Arthur took the stake and the hammer, and when once his mind was set on action his hands never trembled nor even quivered." While the other two piously read from a missal that the doctor happened to have brought along for that very purpose, "Arthur placed the point over the heart, and as I looked I could see its dint in the white flesh. Then he struck with all his might."

I gagged on the next paragraph, for even though they knew that poor Lucy was in ruddy good health when they'd started their little escapade, Harker went into gorey detail about the poor girl's end. I couldn't help wondering if Holmwood had not been motivated less by altruism, as the lugubrious account of Harker suggested, and more by jealousy. A lot of men would not take kindly to their fiancees allowing themselves to be bitten on the neck by other fellows, no matter how titled or aristocratic.

So engrossed was I in this passage that I had not heard the approaching footsteps, the yowl of the cat, nor the howling of the dogs. When the door swung open, I jumped.

"What are you doin'—Pelagia! I thought you was halfway to Nome by now."

"Captain Lomax, please tell me what you think of this," I said.

"I think it's my poor old book and it's been through a lot. I come back lookin' for it at your old place, but that Louisiana woman was in there already, whatsername, Gigi. Destin come after me earlier today when I left without it. Don't know how he come by it."

"Perhaps this will give you a clue," I said dramatically, holding aloft the wisp of fine bleached cornhusk that had been lodged into the spine of the book.

"Hmph. Didn't know they grew corn up this far north," he said.

"They don't. I have seen this very sort of cornhusk elsewhere, however, and recently. It is what the Mexican cigarerras use to cover their handmade cigars. This evening I saw very similar material wrapped around its smoking contents and dangling from the lips of Assistant Consul Blake—or Frank Drake, as he is more notoriously known farther south—just before he turned into a wolf and attempted to kill me. What have you to say to that, Captain Lomax?"

He scratched his head. "Well, I'll be darned," he said. "He musta been the one sicced the book on Malcom. Mal was plenty steamed up about that. Said some 'party' passed the book on to Constantine, tellin' him that was how the undesirable elements of the town should be handled. I think sometimes Mal underrates Constantine's sense of humor. Pretty gruesome anyway, huh? I've had about all the gruesome I can stand for one day. I got chased darn near clear back to Dawson by wolves. Lucky for me Destin was around—him and that crazy moose. You'd think that thing was a dog."

"No," I said. "I'd think it was a horse. I rode it all the way back to Dawson."

He squinted at me. "Pelagia, you wouldn't take advantage of an amateur liar by tryin' to best him with some of your professional whoppers, would you?" Then he squinted a little harder as I felt the starch in me go limp again. "No, I guess not. So, okay, tell me what is this thing you've got goin' with mooses and wolves anyway?"

I told him as much as I could while he unhitched his dogs, bedded them down, and fed them on the beach before we walked back to the Vein. He chewed his pipe and stroked Loki's tail. I had to take the long way around in telling him about it all because I had to tell him about being rescued from drowning by the vampire Indians, then being bitten by Vasily Vladovitch, recovering in the cavernous lair, and being set free before I told about Drake's attacks, threats, and our past association. "So you can see why that passage upsets me. Why Drake would stage a virtual witch hunt against Vasily Vladovitch just to conceal his own nefarious activities."

"They ain't all that well concealed," Dag pointed out.

"Well, to distract from them then."

"Don't get yourself worked up. Sarsaparilla?"

The saloon looked the same as before but somehow much friendlier than when I had left it. It was about four in the morning when we arrived. The Vein had opened at two, that being as soon as Monday morning as the law allowed following the sabbath closing. The girls performed an impromptu cancan, though no shows were officially scheduled. Sasha Devine, in red satin with black maribou trim, sang something so smokey it was unintelligible, with the general theme of being far from home and, therefore, lonely for mother.

Vasily Vladovitch smiled and pretended to drink the many toasts proposed in his honor. Lane worked like a steam engine fireman shoveling the customers full of drinks. Maisie had her usual crowd around her as she leaned against the rail and waggled her gartered knee back and forth coquettishly as she talked. Jeannine tried to strike up a conversation with us, but Dag explained that I was very shy around girls and awfully young and would have a better time if she didn't tease me. With any of the others that would have been like a red flag at a bull, but Jeannine was the sensitive type and sashayed away to find some other high roller with more gold dust and less reticence.

The smoke, the slosh of drinks in glasses, the heat of the stove, the smells, the music, the press of merrymaking people, all impeded further conversation and lulled half of me to sleep. The other half was keeping a close eye on Vasily Vladovitch. I watched for his departure, which by my calculation should be soon. We still had unfinished business.

Dag left Loki with me while he went over to talk to Malcom Destin, who, I was sure, was far more interested in the conversation he was having with Sasha Devine, who hung onto him as if he were the only law north of the Inside Passage, or maybe it was the only man north of the Inside Passage. Her own black band was gone now, and unless I was mistaken that was *my* cross worn so chastely above her red satin bosom.

I started to get up and go take issue with her about it, when

Vasily Vladovitch, with a rather fixed stare at the last man who tried to detain him and regale him with his latest triumphs in thawing frozen ore, evaporated from the room almost as slickly as if he had turned to mist.

I was closer to the front door and bolted for it, almost closing it on Loki's tail as the cat followed me outside. Risking certain shredding, I slung the animal upon my shoulders and held onto both sets of paws as I ran.

Vasily Vladovitch was disappearing down Paradise Alley when I rounded the building. I almost called to him, but then as I started to pass by Stella's cabin, something stepped out in front of me. I backed into Stella's doorway. Her stove was cold, her bed in disarray, and the cat sniffed in a wild way that confirmed my suspicion that the dark sticky stuff spread around was blood. Vasily Vladovitch was getting faster and messier, perhaps. I had no time to investigate if I was to catch him, however. The thing that had stepped out in front of me planted itself firmly at the door. The cat leaped from my shoulders and scratched at the door, mewing as if asking to be fed. I peeked out the window. The moose stood there, its ugliness not glamorized much by the predawn glow, for it was now close to seven-thirty or eight o'clock in the morning. I opened the door, and the cat began brushing against the beast's feet as if it were a long-lost littermate (assuming that cats are nostalgic about that sort of association).

The moose ignored the cat and simply followed me as I tried once more to catch sight of Vasily Vladovitch. I figured he was heading for his home, so I was not overly concerned about losing him. I would not have minded losing a portion of the small parade I seemed to be leading, however.

This was soon added to when I heard a voice hailing me from Front Street. "Wait up, there!" Lomax called. For the first time, I felt rather annoyed with him. He didn't seem to want to let me out of his sight. In retrospect, this does seem a strange reaction for a woman who had been prepared to walk from Dawson to Henderson Creek only a few hours earlier to be with the man.

But I waited twitchily for him to catch up, then resumed my pace without much further conversation.

We were close to the house when the moose began to shrink. First the back legs seemed to buckle, then the body to draw in on itself both from behind and the side, the muzzle to shrivel, the hide to lighten, and the antlers to suck themselves back into the head, whose mane had paled in an instant.

"My gosh, it's Egil!" Lomax said, and up ahead I saw Vasily Vladovitch disappear into his house.

"Thanks for the ride, Egil," I whispered as Lomax bent over the younger man and I turned back toward the vampire's dwelling.

The house was empty and dark as the stove was cold. Vasily Vladovitch, for a man in store for so much company, was clearly expecting none.

While I stood waiting for my eyes to adjust to the darkness, a familiar pale glimmer sparked in a distant corner of the room. Papa's face changed from an amorphous blob to a semblance of his living features.

"Good evening, Papa. I have finally figured out what you were trying to tell me, and I want you to know that I'm touched by your concern. But I still need to see Vasily Vladovitch again."

The spectre bobbed without changing expression and hovered in front of what I could see upon closer inspection was the pantry curtain I had observed earlier. When the ghost disappeared through it, I followed and walked straight into a can of kerosene.

# CHAPTER XXI

*I DO NOT* customarily open secret passages with my nose, but on this occasion I did. While I was rubbing the injured part, the pantry wall scraped back and Papa squeezed through the crack and back out again to show me where the opening was. Secret panels may work very nicely elsewhere, but in the Yukon the cold and the permafrost that break up the ground every spring and swell it every summer before freezing it again in the winter keep any door from fitting well, no matter how cunningly designed by how supernatural a being. I could barely open it wide enough to squeeze through it. My guess was that Vasily Vladovitch only came through here in mist form.

The passage wound upward steeply as a spiral staircase. I recalled that the house abutted a cliff and guessed that I must now be within it.

Papa lit the way with his ghostly light, playing the will o' wisp for me. I had always secretly suspected he would have preferred the stage to the press, and now as a ghost, he seemed able to branch out a bit. When at last the passage apparently came to a dead end, he hovered by the blank wall for a moment, then folded himself over and through the crack and back out again, as he'd done in the pantry. I pushed where he folded and the wall parted. I was once more in the cylindrical chamber with the crystal window, now curtained against day.

Vasily Vladovitch, natty in a smoking jacket and beaded moccasins for house slippers, did not look particularly surprised to see me.

"Good morning, my dear. I have not much time left for conversation, but it is good to see you again. I must say you're not looking too well."

"Vasily Vladovitch, about your bite—" I began.

He smiled at me tolerantly. "I'm so sorry, my darling girl. I have dined already and you look much too pale as it is."

"You didn't say that to Papa when you killed him," I pointed out.

"Actually, I did, but your Papa was most insistent and refused to let me go. I believe I mentioned that. Also, I did not know him, and I was not as fond of him as I am you, for all the trouble you've caused me."

I had not said I wanted him to bite me again, but he had already divined that and was rejecting me anyway. I felt a flush of shame rise to my cheek. His interest increased slightly.

"I should like to know how long and under what circumstances I will continue to experience this—uh, taste, for being bitten," I said. "According to Mr. Stoker, the wish to be bitten disappears only after the biter is dead."

"How odd that the book should take that viewpoint since according to it I am already dead. As for your own, as you say, taste, I am afraid I cannot help you. I have been the biter since first I came into my fangs. I find it agreeable and most of the people I bite also seem to find it agreeable. I do not understand why you mind having this perfectly natural desire to be bitten. I bit you only once in order to aid you, and now you're acting as if I had done you a disservice and demand that I do you another one! This is a crazy way to act, dear girl."

"For pity's sakes, Vasily Vladovitch, are you really that blind or that callous? You go around biting people against their will, and if you don't inflict death upon them, you inflict instead these inconvenient longings for which you then disclaim any responsibility. If you're not hungry, your victims should not wish to be food. That's not perfectly natural at all, sir. *That* is crazy. I think you should face it, Vasily Vladovitch. All of this ancient-priest-and-wise-grandfather business has gone to your head. You're really no more in control of this situation than I am, than Papa was of his drinking. And one more thing—"

"Only one?" he asked, smiling in a pained sort of way.

"What is between you and Sasha Devine? I thought she was

almost a vampire, and now I'm going around with the bite marks and she's wearing Mama's cross."

"What is between me and the Divine Miss Devine, as you ask so nosily, is over. That is what is between me and Sasha Devine. Her precise words, I believe, were that if she was going to hell she was not going to do it in a crowd. I tried to explain to her, as I am trying to explain to you, that in a short time, when I have arranged matters properly, I will no longer be the only qualified full-fledged vampire here in Dawson. What you both fail to understand is that these things take time.

"I believe that the blood frenzy experienced by my exiled relations, particularly those known for their more obviously gauche self-gratifications, were the result of what Mr. Freud would call a mania. My theory is that because we are rather far removed from our original priestly origins, the longing for blood and its symbiotic companion, the longing to be bitten, alter our emotional and mental controls. I have waited so long to create another such as myself while grooming those candidates most likely to satisfy themselves in a moderate, temperate fashion that will not harm their personalities nor alter their characters by anything more than a desire to go to bed a little later than usual. By choosing subjects judiciously at first and training them properly to assume their new forms, I hope to breed a leadership among Dawson society that will assist in the conversion of the rest of the populace in a more comfortable and natural fashion.

"If you must know, Miss Lovelace, I left home because I had no desire to live among monsters. When, upon landing on these shores, my fellow *promyshlenniks** behaved to the Natives in a manner as barbaric as any of my ill-fated kinsmen, I disposed of them so they would not contaminate this new world. Then I undertook the training and education of a select group of Natives myself. These are the people who rescued you, and I'm sure you saw that they are of high calibre and have their wits about them.

"If ever there was a land where being a vampire could be the normal, acceptable state of being, it is in this place, with its long nights, its shrouded seasons, its frigid temperatures, its riches, and its isolation. Also, it is my belief that because of the ferocity of the mosquitoes during the summer months, the inhabitants in time build a higher blood volume to compensate, and are thus better able to withstand occasional losses.

*Early Russian traders

"So, you see, I have every reason to hope for success. But it needs to be done correctly. Frankly, my dear Miss Lovelace, despite your experiences with the dragon, I don't think you will fit in. You have a tendency to exaggerate and embroider, which tends to imbalance. I am so sorry, but I cannot help but feel perhaps a change of scenery will diminish your craving, although it does seem to be, for some people, nearly irresistable."

"Don't count on it," I said. Perhaps I was asking the wrong person. Sasha Devine had evidently decided that there was more to life and death than biting and being bitten. While I looked into his deep dark eyes and watched his lips curve over those miraculous fangs, Vasily Vladovitch's logic seemed hopelessly irrefutable. But I did realize on some level that there were flaws in his argument, although they weren't occurring to me rapidly enough to articulate them, an unfairness in his attitude, and very possibly several thousand other viewpoints he was overlooking entirely. For somebody who wanted to change a whole society so he'd have somebody to play with, Vasily Vladovitch had very little understanding of the average person.

He placed his cold hand gently on my forearm. "Yes, my dear, you think about it. You surely can see that I am only trying to do what is best for us all. But for now, it will be very much the worse for me if I don't retire at once. Be a sweet, dear girl and close the lid for me?"

I noted with a pang that he occupied the same coffin that had been my sick bed. Thrifty and convenient arrangement, to use a coffin for a sick bed, when you thought about it. Not particularly conducive to sponsoring the much-touted "will to live," but expedient, none the less.

"Ah, that's good. Now then, good day to you, Pelagia. I will give your questions some thought, for I think much of you and can't help feeling there will be some important place for you among us. We will discuss this matter further later, I promise you. But for now—" And he waggled his wrist in a circle for me to shut the lid, then composed himself with his hands on his chest and closed his eyes. The ghostly form of Papa bobbed between us as I drew the coffin lid down, and the apparition smoothed itself across the features of Vasily Vladovitch as it had across his victims. Only this time the ghost seemed to sink in instead of melting away. I gasped and Vasily Vladovitch smiled a fleeting smile. He knew exactly what was going on.

"You see, my dear, when I drink someone dry, they naturally become a part of me. Perhaps you should think that over. Adieu." And the lid finished closing of its own accord.

I turned to leave, unhappy with the mystery, angry, weary, and miserable, and it occurred to me that I could just curl up on the floor and sleep my aches away as I had before. But the chamber was no longer heated and I would surely freeze to death. I was starting to think noble, martyred thoughts about what certain people would say when they found me, about how they should have realized that I was in just as much pain as I had been before, and how I really needed the euphoria of that bite, when the passage door creaked open again.

Why, hello there, darlin'," Drake said when he saw me. "I wondered where you'd gone off to. I found that piece of wallpaper you wrote on back there on the trail and I do appreciate you givin' such detailed directions. The only thing that stopped me from finishin' ol' Bleed-Enough off long ago was I didn't know how to find the bastard when he was nappin'."

I patted my jacket front. The paper was indeed missing.

Drake peered around me at the coffin. "He *is* in there, ain't he?"

"I suppose so. More or less," I amended, recalling how the vampire could ooze forth in mist form. Too bad that seemed to happen only at night.

"There'll sure as hell be less by the time I'm finished with him. You, too, far as that goes. Shall I just shoot you or do you need a stake through your heart, too?" He waved what appeared to be a sharpened piece of firewood and a hammer in the air, and with the other hand drew a revolver on me. "Even if you haven't quite made it to bein' a vampire yet, I guarandamntee one of these suckers through your ticker will do you in good as a bullet."

"It's murder either way, Drake, and I doubt you'll get away with it. I have friends waiting for me."

"If you mean the old man, he and some kid were walkin' toward town just as I arrived. I disguised myself. Wagged my tail and they thought I was a stray dog. No, darlin', it's just you and me and the undead now. Him first though. You're annoyin', but puny by comparison. You know, he really gripes my soul. I tried to do business with him, offered to cut him in on my plans, and he acted like I was callin' his mama names. Snotty damn foreigner. Oh well, bygones should be bygones, and he is by hell going to be gone by the time I'm done with him. You just open that glorified pine box back up and hold the stake while I take a whack at him."

"Certainly," I said in a tone that unfortunately revealed my true meaning all too clearly as I dived for the stake. The headache I had previously enjoyed was nothing to the one I suddenly entertained from the blow he dealt me with the blunt end of the stick. I fell heavily against the coffin and knocked my head against it. I could even hear my skull cracking, I thought wonderingly as I toppled to the ground.

But it wasn't my skull. It was the door scraping open, a sound followed by the soft-shoe shuffling of five pairs of stocking-covered dancing slippers.

"Boy, it just goes to show you really have to watch some people," Millie's voice exclaimed. The boots filed in through the passage door. "That Cory, pretending that she wasn't a bit interested in Vassy, then tryin' to get one up on the rest of us. I don't mind so much except she was just such a little *liar* about it. Who did she think she was foolin' in that silly ol' boy's outfit? God! Give her a drop and she takes a gallon. I—"

"Howdy, ladies," Drake said. "I had no idea so *many* of you would come."

"Why, howdy yourself, Mr. Blake," Millie said. "My, what a big stick you have."

"All the better to beat the horseshit out of anybody who interferes with me. And a gun, too, just in case somebody would seriously like to be dead. Now then, like I was sayin' to that female corpse on the floor before you all came along, somebody hold the lid open. You, curly."

"Who me?" Maisie asked, sounding a little dazed and also somewhat picked on.

"You hold this open for me real careful like and I'll let you live—till tonight anyway. Got about one more night of full moon and we'll see if you girls howl as well as you sing. See, I think you're gonna be looking for a new job real soon." I heard the lid crack, and Drake's shadow fell across me. "Well, there he is himself. Wonder if I ought to scalp him before I do this? Nah, that might wake him up before I'm done. You there, the little one, hold this stake steady while I pound."

"Go to hell," Nellie the Kid told him.

He pointed the gun at her and would have fired, but he made the mistake of having his arm still inside the open coffin. Maisie dropped the lid on his wrist, sending the stake flying. I had enough strength left to grab his ankles, which I did in an excess of group spirit. This was once more an error in judgment on my part, for he still held the gun, although no longer at Nellie.

He kicked at me, and I rolled sideways just in time to see Millie haul up her ruffles, raise a black net clad knee and deliver a cute cancan kick worthy of a mule, sending the gun flying and leaving Drake doubled over, nursing his other wrist.

Nellie, meanwhile, backed up and ran at him full bore, her head lowered like a nanny goat's, butting him into Maisie, who followed Millie's example and executed a high kick in his lower regions. He'd be wearing his tail curled under his legs for the next few full moons.

Bunny grabbed the stake and Jeannine grabbed the gun, while Millie retrieved the hammer and advanced upon their mutual victim, tapping it playfully against her palm.

Drake was a hardened fighter and an old veteran of Civil and Indian wars, but so were the ladies of the Vein. He had only to look into their faces to know he had made a grave miscalculation. "Now, girls, let's talk this over. I can make you an offer. I mean, you know me. I'm a good tipper. I—"

"You cheated Bob Clancy out of his claim and had him killed," Nellie said.

"You robbed half those men that had to leave on the *Bella* because they were starving," Bunny said. "And I'll bet you were the one who bought up the supplies from Alaska Commercial before they arrived. You probably had them offloaded at Fort Yukon, where you sold them so that the boys here would have to leave their diggins for you."

"You liked Giselle better than *me*, you bastard!" Millie cried, and swung her hammer.

Her arm stopped in midair as a large hand clamped firmly around her wrist and another gently removed the hammer from her grasp. "Now, then, lassie, don't go gettin' theatrical with flyin' objects or I'll have to run you in, and that would make poor Miss Devine's show short a verra fetchin' portion."

"Sergeant!" Drake cried. "Boy, am I glad to see you! You're just in time. Arrest these wild women. They're female vampires. They were tryin' to kill me. I was just—"

"Did you *hear* that?" Jeannine demanded in a plaintive tone. "Did you hear what that awful man just said about us? Oh, Sergeant, you've always been kind to us working girls. That man was going to try to kill our boss and when we tried to stop him he tried to—to—well, even if a girl has to do certain things for a living, she has her pride."

"That's right!" Millie said. "He tried to dishonor us, Sergeant. All of us."

"At once," Maisie added.

"It was disgustin', Sergeant, just disgustin'. Why, I have never been so repulsed and insulted in my entire—"

"Oooh! I think I'm gonna faint dead *away*," Bunny said, and tried to do so into the sergeant's arms, but he was too quick for her and left her to the second newcomer—none other than Sasha Devine, who watched the girls with the pride of a mother or a drill sergeant whose troops had performed admirably under fire.

"Quiet!" Destin roared above the continuing squeals and protestations. "I've somewhat to say. Mr. Blake, are these implements of destruction yours, sir?"

"Well—I—I was only doin' what you shoulda done a coon's age ago. Look at this, Sergeant! The man sleeps in a coffin! How much more evidence do you need?"

Millie had half-carried me over to the wall, where I sat up holding my head and watching the proceedings, every word echoing several times through my skull, so that with so much repetition, I remember it all exactly.

"That's irrelevant, Mr. Blake," Destin said. "Inspector Constantine duly passed on to me, as the duty officer in charge, the recommendation that I see you have taken into your own two hands. He did not suggest I implement it, nor was he overly impressed by the evidence, but left it to me to handle the situation. With the assistance of Miss Devine, I am doin' so, and have been takin' under advisement much expert opinion on the matter."

Drake grimaced, but gamely cocked an eyebrow in supercilious inquiry.

"It is my duty to inform you, sir, that the Crown takes no special stand on the matters you refer to. There are no particular laws on the books prohibitin' vampirism per se as long as no other crime is involved. At this time, we have no direct evidence to support your allegation that crimes were committed specifically and exclusively employin' what Mr. Stoker, in the evidence you presented, describes as a vampire's M.O.—that's modus operandi, sir."

"I know that!" Drake snapped.

"Aye, well, further investigation will be necessary to determine the truth of your allegations. Until such time as that investigation is complete, and, in fact, until certain statutes are passed stating that capital crimes of a particular style are punishable by other means than hangin' by the neck, the Crown must take the position that drivin' stakes into the hearts of Dawson citizens is first-degree murder. The inspector checked with the one Canadian barrister we have on hand about this point, sir, and the American lawyers runnin' the new laundry on King Street agreed."

"But lookit there, Sergeant, he sleeps in a *coffin*!"

"That is his own business, sir. Yours is that you were reported by Miss Devine for breaking and entering, and when Mr. Bledinoff is available, he'll be able to press charges. I would just like to add at this time, though, sir, that in view of your interest in this case and of certain other aspects contained in the remnants of that piece of evidence now, incidentally, missin' frae my office, I did take one judicious precaution."

"Sorry, son, I seem to be fresh out of medals," Drake said. "You'll just have to tell me all about it so I can ooh and ah."

His eyes shifted from one of the girls to another, and back to Destin, a fact that was not lost on the mountie.

"Now, you ken I don't believe in all this mumbo-jumbo, sir, but just to be on the safe side, I asked the armorer to pour me a number of silver bullets, with which I have loaded this wee firearm. My intention in askin' him, you see, was to ensure the protection of my fellow officers investigatin' the supposed wild animal attacks on various of the outlyin' residents. I did this at my own expense, meltin' down the Clan Destin candlesticks for the metal, but I figure it is worthwhile if any of this claptrap is true and such a thing as a wee weird wolfie is wanderin' aboot the woods. And if it is, by any chance, just a regular beast or a beastly mon, why, the bullets will stop one of those just as easy. Later on, I'll issue these bullets to the investigatin' officers. For today, I thought I would need them. What do you think, Mr. Blake, sir?"

"I think this is plumb loco. I never said a thing about werewolves. Only vampires. Can't you limeys get anything right?"

"Constable LaBeck suggested that the *wolves* in the book had the same M.O. as mony of the violent deaths we've been seein' of late. They also follow the pattern of the loup garous the Canucks talk aboot."

"Aren't you at least gonna open that coffin?"

"I've got no orders on that matter, sir, and no warrant. Mr. Bledinoff is a prominent citizen. I will say only that if he is indeed sleepin' in there, your allegations are all the more unsupported. For we have certainly been makin' plenty of noise to wake the dead. Now then, I suggest that we all leave before Mr. Bledinoff prefers charges against us for disturbin' the peace. Mr. Blake, you are to keep yourself handy, sir. The next time you go swingin' things, it may be an axe on the police woodpile."

# CHAPTER XXII

·····•➤§◆∥◆§◄•·····

DRAKE WAS THE first out the door. I was the last, keeping as far out of the sight of Sergeant Destin as possible. Sasha Devine was a great help. She held onto the policeman's arm as if she had lost the use of her own legs. When the rest were through the pantry door, I was left to struggle with pulling it shut. That was when I noticed the missing kerosene can.

Even before I went to the door and saw the billows of black smoke belching into the brilliant winter morning, I knew something was wrong.

Lomax and Egil Larsson were running up the path to meet us. "Malcom! I was lookin' for you to go in there and help me find—never mind, there she is. Was Bledinoff in there, too? If so, somebody ought to let him know his place is afire. It's goin' up fast, and unless the boys can get it stopped pretty quick, the whole street will go with it."

"Damn good idea," Drake said, grinning. "Why don't you wake him up?"

Sasha Devine spoke quickly. "That will be impossible, I'm afraid, Malcom dahling. Despite what that horrible man says, Mr. Bledinoff is up at Moosehide on his claim, isn't he, girls?"

Without waiting for their corroboration, she was already half sliding down the path toward town. I lagged behind, and by the time I arrived, it was almost all over, at least for the Vein.

The men who first spotted the fire had done their best to rescue the furnishings. The drapes were gone, but a pile of chairs, some charred, some with singed cushions, lay in the snow. Mr. Lane stood guard over a double armload of assorted bottles. More were scattered around him. The felt-covered gaming table and a couple of trunks of stage props had left a path where they'd been dragged from the building as if they were important. Spittin' Williams stood staring into the fire, hugging a brass spittoon as if it was a baby.

Bucket brigades soaked down the saloons on either side, while flames made the inside of the Vein look like a furnace. Screeches issued from Paradise Alley, where the girls were filing into the street, in case their places caught fire.

Then, abruptly, the screeches turned to real piercing screams. Lurleen, half clad and covered with blood, ran up to Destin and began shaking him. "She's dead. She's dead," she babbled.

"Who's that, ma'am?" Destin asked as if he was about to fill out a form.

"Stella. Poor harmless nut, some bastard ripped her throat out and half ate her. Oh, God!"

Despite the best efforts of the men, three shacks went down with the Vein. The adjoining buildings were badly damaged. The air was so dry, and everything was made of wood. Sasha Devine was at the head of the bucket brigade now and kept trying to save something of the Vein, but when the upper floor collapsed, she was struck down by a piece of flying trim. She stubbornly refused to leave. All of her outfit was in the fire, all of her costumes, and her hopes for her own place.

I sat by her on the riverbank and watched the blaze. At least it kept us warm. The day was one of the coldest yet. Her wet, ash-streaked hands were mittenless, clutching the matted fur sleeves of the wolfskin parka. Her stockings were torn and her hair straggled out from under a borrowed stocking cap. Tears coursed steadily down her cheeks.

I tried to think of something comforting to say but could only stammer.

"Never mind, Vahlenteena. This was not what I promised you. It was not what he promised me. Still, I thought it might be something."

"It was. Something, I mean. Sasha?"

"Yes?"

"You can keep Mama's cross if it helps you." It was all I could think of to say.

"Thank you, Vahlenteena," she said, but unclasped it and dropped it casually back into my hand. "I was only keeping it where I knew I wouldn't lose it, but I must admit it's been helpful."

"Did it, uh, have anything to do with your separation from Vasily Vladovitch? He told me what you said about going to hell in crowds."

"I meant that Vasily Vladovitch has entirely too many little vampiresses in training. I don't mind starting a trend, but I will not be part of a pack."

"But the craving, Sasha. How did you break the craving? He bit you so many times."

"Exactly. I am a woman of the world. All of this thrilling sort of thing pales in time. The things that count may not be thrilling, but they endure."

"Like what?"

"Don't you know?"

"I suppose so, but—"

"Do you feel the urge to be bitten now?"

"Well, come to think of it, no. But I hurt and there's all this excitement and—"

"And you're holding the cross, which even if you are not very devout reminds you of something more important to you than Vasily Vladovitch's dental work, does it not?"

"You mean Mama?"

"I mean anything or anyone that works. But that is really why he dislikes crosses, darling girl. They're competition. It doesn't take training to be a vampire, as he will try to tell you, it takes idiocy. He can take all of someone else's blood if he wants to teach them to be what he considers a credit to a calling that has nothing creditable to recommend it, but as for me, I have better things to do with my blood."

"Well, I'm glad to hear you say that the hold can be so easily broken. I had not realized you were at all religious."

"Easily broken?" Her voice, naturally low, grew raspy. "No, not easily. And also no, I am not religious. But I am Sasha Devine and not some crawling, needy night creature. And though Vasily Vladovitch has taken a part of me I cannot reclaim, as soon as this fire dies down, I damn well mean to reclaim what I can."

I was once more filled with admiration for her spunk. "Sasha Devine, you are an inspiration. I, too, will reclaim what I can."

"What?" she asked, her blue eyes batting with puzzlement. "Did you also have a poke hidden under my mattress?"

The Rich Vein-that-was was well named. By midafternoon the fire had cooled enough that with the application of liberal doses of river water and the careful placement of gumboots, the debris was cleared without serious injury. A town full of previously bored prospectors, lately weary firefighters, once more turned into placer miners, panning the dirt beneath ashes of the floorboards. It was a warm occupation, with heat still rising from the ground to form a little mist above the charry mud. It was also profitable. Over the past month, enough gold dust and small nuggets had sifted down beneath the boards to make panning the Vein more lucrative than panning many of the claims. One of the boys thought he had really struck paydirt when he beat Sasha Devine to locating the contents of her poke. The leather sack had burned away and left her gold all melted together. When she started hunting for it, however, he gallantly returned it to her, emptying his own poke into his cap so that she'd have something to carry the remnants of her treasure in.

But other than a little dust, there was not much left of the best opera house in Dawson. Except for one other grisly discovery, unearthed by Loki while Dag was prowling the ashes looking for anything salvageable.

The fire and the simultaneous investigation of Stella's murder kept the police running all that day. As the townsfolk excavated the Vein, two mounties carried a sheet-wrapped stretcher from Stella's cabin. Destin, who had been interviewing Lurleen, stopped and stood with his hat in his hand when the victim was taken to the ice house to stiffen until spring, along with the other corpses from that winter.

Lomax turned away, eying the ruins moodily. I stood and watched him for a moment. Loki jumped down and padded carefully among the smoldering timbers. He sniffed toward the back of the theatre, near where the stage had been, then laid back his ears and spat at something only he could see on the ground before him.

I picked my way over to him, kicking aside unidentifiable black messes and treading carefully around still-glowing coals. I thought the cat was injured or was stuck.

Dag got to him first. When he found Loki would not be soothed and carried off, but remained rooted, miaowing wildly, to the spot, Dag began pushing aside debris with his mittens.

"Don't come any closer, Pelagia," he said in a strangled voice, and over his shoulder to Destin he called, "Malcom, I think Loki just found your arsonist."

He had told me not to look, but I looked at everything. At Lomax, bent over with his hat down to his brows and his good hand bare, restraining a bristling Loki. The cat was four times his usual enormous size and his fangs rivaled any vampire's.

A round, anemic moon assumed command of the sky over the bluffs. Although most of the Yukon was ice covered, save a thin trickle down the middle, what seemed to be hundreds of hastily chopped bucket brigade holes dotted the near bank. The black water had already clouded over with a new coat of ice. The rest of the river was sliced with the runners of sleds and spattered with the tracks of animals and men. The blackened sides of the buildings abutting the fire loomed accusingly over us. The holes where the burned-out cribs had been lent Paradise Alley the look of a seedy old man's mouth. The snow had stopped the fires there.

Destin marched slowly forward and looked down. Lomax took off his hat and wrapped it around his hook, and with slow and solemn strokes swept away the last of the debris. That was when I looked down. I felt rather than saw Sasha Devine when she came to stand by my side.

It was Giselle, of course, or mostly Giselle. Or most of Giselle. She had not been greatly damaged by the fire, but had been blown by the force of the blast behind a large metal plate. I had no idea what the plate had been, no doubt some interior part of the construction of the building. A lot of the fur was singed off her face, which began returning to human form as we uncovered her. Sasha picked up an oblong of charred ivory and examined more closely the ruins of Giselle's throat.

"My mirror," she said, touching one of the jagged edges, half clear glass, half still silvered. "I suppose the moral to that is never stop to admire yourself while committing arson."

Egil Larsson, who had been poking around silently, watching Dag as warily as a wild animal, which, of course, he soon would be in form at least, leaned over the body, then gave Destin a hard look. "You see what I was tryin' to tell you earlier, Sergeant? Them teeth? All that hair?"

"Aye. And there's less of it than when first I looked, I'll give you that."

"It's the same thing I do, like I said. Yup. It's real, okay." He nodded in agreement with himself—his voice, to my surprise, containing a certain modestly restrained pride.

Destin's face drained and then flushed again, and I forgot to look away as he raised his eyes to meet mine. My disguise clearly no longer fooled him. I doubted that it had since he first got a good look at me that morning. "I owe you an apology and a wee bit of a second comin', madam. Not that I don't have a few questions."

"You're welcome to ask them, Sergeant," I said with a mixture of relief and magnanimity, "I hope you'll find it somewhat easier to believe me this time than you did before."

"I'm beginning to think I'd believe anything," he muttered. The other prospectors had, by that time, noticed something unusual was occurring and had gathered round. As a few of them pulled the metal plate from Giselle, the full moon struck her body, which sprouted and flowed from half human to fully wolf, then back to human again with such rapidity that I feared the sergeant would doubt the evidence before him.

Still, with parts of Egil starting to look a little elongated again, there was plenty of other evidence close to hand to remind him that certain events in Dawson were caused by agencies beyond his ken.

Egil noticed the change in himself, too, and, with a nod of farewell, began walking briskly for the brush.

"Egil," Lomax called, half turning away as Destin laid his jacket over Giselle's face.

"Ya?"

"Stick close. You know."

Egil made a sign of assent with fingers already thickening and hardening into hooves, and bolted away. Still, I was glad to know he would be on guard. As long as nobody went moose hunting with silver bullets, we would all be a little safer.

# CHAPTER XXIII

*····•┅━╾〈◎||◎〉╼━┅•····*

PEOPLE HAD BEEN popping in and out of Jim Ringer's Yukon
Belle saloon all day long, joining periodically in the cleanup
then going back to Jim's for a drink or coffee. Curiosity seekers
had been coming in out of the woods since the first black smoke
signaled the disaster. JayEllen sent in rosehip tea and preserves
from Grand Forks and half a ham she'd been saving for Christmas. I saw her husband unload the food from his sled, along
with his guitar, in front of Ringer's, and started wondering
then.

Even as the mounties carried Giselle away to join Stella,
who had from all appearances been Giselle's last victim, the
darkness began smudging the details of the blackened mess,
and the treasure-seekers wandered away and down toward
Ringer's. Sasha Devine, her skirts kilted up out of the black
mud and her dirty face looking almost its true age, watched
them bitterly. When Ringer, his bartender, and a couple of the
gamblers who hung out at his place came out and began hauling
the chairs and other remains of the Vein inside, her face flared
to anger, and she stalked angrily out into the street.

"Vultures," I said, and started to join her, but Dag took
hold of my wrist, then wrapped his arm around me so that
Loki's tail tickled my cheek.

"Let's see what's goin' on before we fly off half-cocked, eh?" he said.

I tried to shrug him off, remembering that the Vein's owner did not yet know of its sad end. "This is shameful," I said. "Even a vamp—even Vasily Vladovitch does not deserve to be vandalized and scavenged from while he sleeps. Destin might as well have allowed Frank Drake to have his way with him."

Dag raised his eyebrow and looked at me seriously for a moment. "It's who's had his way with you I'm wonderin' about, Pelagia."

"That depends on which way you're talking about," I snapped. I wondered if he guessed the craving I so shamefully entertained—that is, I did, I supposed, when I stopped to think about it. The excitement had pretty much driven it from my mind, veins, and hair. "I'm sorry, Dag, but I'm exhausted, and I hate to think how Vasily Vladovitch will feel when he sees the Vein. It wasn't just a business, it was—well, I can't go into that without getting maudlin on his behalf. But it's a loss."

"Not just to him, Pelagia," Dag said gently, and poked me through the door of Ringer's place, where I tried to elbow my way in far enough to make room for him to follow. Smoke, clinking glasses, and bodies packed the room tighter than I had ever seen a place packed, even on opening night at the Vein. Bunny was taking over for Ringer at the keyboard, while Maisie, Millie, Nellie, and Jeannine sat in front of the stage, trying not to grin. Sasha Devine's chin was quivering, and she kept covering her eyes and mopping the corners with bandannas borrowed from several onlookers delighted to be of service. There was only a little room for anyone to perform on stage, because it was piled with chairs, costumes, brass spittoons, and bottles, all of the detritus of the Vein. One end of the bar was devoted to covered dishes and cold meat, while at the other end drinks were selling briskly.

I had barely taken this all in when the doors blew open as if from a hurricane and I turned to see the ravaged, awful face of Vasily Vladovitch, his eyes red, his fangs bared, his cape blowing back from his shoulders like night invading the snowstorm that had begun outside. His expression was filled with contempt and the pain of betrayal as he glared accusingly at all of his former friends.

Jim Ringer spotted him and signaled to Bunny, who played a little fanfare as Ringer stepped up on the spot on the stage that was bare of salvage. "Ladies and gentlemen, Vasily Vlad-ovitch is at the door now and he looks like he thinks he just came off a hell of a bender and can't think where he mislaid his saloon."

Lubrication-inspired laughter greeted this jibe, laughter not shared by its object, who added puzzlement to the array of expressions already displayed upon his face.

"Well, Vassy, we can't blame you for looking like you'd like to bite somebody. And we knew you'd be sore if we woke you up for a little thing like your place burning down, so we decided to go ahead and do what we wanted to anyway. Boys, make room for the man to sit down, and, Mr. Lane, I think you could start the bidding on this solid gold spittoon here at fifty dollars worth of dust."

Before Lane could take the stage, Lindholm, the man who had made the strike the day before said, "Fifty dollars! That's ridiculous! I'll give you two hundred!"

Lane started to open his mouth, but Ringer jumped up in front of him again. "One more thing, ladies and gentlemen, drink up. It's going to be a long dry night and the Yukon Belle is famous for cutting its drinks with only the finest, the purest, the most sparkling authentic Yukon River water! And exactly half of the price of each and every drink tonight goes to re-building our competition here. Never let it be said that Jim Ringer is not a sporting man!"

The miners cheered. Vasily Vladovitch's face, as four Klon-dikers led him past us, was caving in on itself until he looked fully as old as he claimed to be.

Millie leaped up onstage beside Lane and propped her foot up on a chair, then playfully began to remove her garter, pulling it down over her netted knee and over her shapely ankle with a seductive twist of her wrist, a kick of her heel, and a rolling of her eyes. "How much, Lane, do you think we could get for my little ol' garter?"

It went on like that for some time, but Vasily Vladovitch did not stay very long. He couldn't. People kept plying him with drinks he couldn't drink, reminding him that half the money would go to put him back in business.

I started to go talk to him once and heard him moaning to one of the miners near him. "But this is not necessary. I am a wealthy man."

"Not as wealthy as you once was, buddy, and besides, it's a hell of an excuse to have a party, eh?"

But Vasily Vladovitch couldn't take it. He bolted from the saloon. I thought he was too proud to accept the gesture, and I took it upon myself to take him to task for turning his back on his neighbors. Disentangling myself from Dag, I stepped out into the street, but it was empty. Aside from the noise of the party, the only sound all up and down the Yukon was the howling of wolves from the woods. I thought I saw a pair of glittering eyes watching the bar from over behind Paradise Alley, and though those high, wide-spaced eyes were comforting, the howling chilled me and I went back inside and stayed there.

Purdy showed up sometime around midnight. He and Jack London had mushed in with Tom and Mary, all of them worried when Lomax had failed to return. Though I drank only sarsaparilla, it does seem to me that at one point during the night, after the salvage had been auctioned off, Purdy played his guitar and I, still attired in trousers, my Hudson Bay coat, and gumboots, ended up doing my flamenco number on a table.

Meanwhile, Lurleen auctioned off services to be rendered, Wild Miles donated a stack of furs, and Jack London bid twenty dollars for another pair of candles Ringer put on the dock.

A newsman from Seattle outbid him, but Mr. Ladue, one of Dawson's founding fathers, outbid the newsman, whom he disliked, and presented the candles to Jack as an unsolicited gift.

Sergeant Destin bid a month's pay for a waltz with Sasha Devine, which consisted chiefly of standing still and rocking back and forth, because there was no real room to dance, and besides, the song was a polka, but neither of them seemed to care. Sasha had finally stopped weeping and was laughing and hugging Destin, who didn't seem to mind.

This started a trend. Purdy surprised me by bidding his most recent winnings to squeeze Maisie in time to the music. Since I still looked more or less like one of the boys, Dag did not have to bid anything to dance with me, but threw a poke on the pile anyway. The mounties decided that for the purposes of philanthropy, Mary and Tom were Japanese for the evening instead of Indians, who were not allowed in drinking establishments. Mary whispered something to Lane and he announced the most exquisite item of the night, which fortunately came when everyone was well-oiled enough to bid even more extravagantly than they had to begin with. Mary would make a parka and mukluks out of some of Tom's hides for the highest bidder. I didn't even hear what that went for. Everyone was gasping too loudly, and then there was all that applause.

"Quite a party for a blood-sucking vampire," I said to Dag out of the side of my mouth.

He rubbed his nose with his pipe stem. "Golly, Pelagia, nobody's perfect."

At about four A.M., Lane, Ringer, and Sasha began a final weighing out and counting of the proceeds. When Vasily Vladovitch arrived, clad in a wolfskin parka like the one he had given Sasha, a tall round sealskin hat that pulled over his ears, and knee-high beaded mooseloose mukluks trimmed with beaver, the people on stage greeted him with big smiles and eyes shining with something besides drink for a change—pure greed, in reverse.

"About time you showed up, Bledinoff," Lane bellowed. "We're damn sick and tired of holdin' onto all this heavy gold for you. Miss Devine, honey, you want to tell him?"

"Vas—Vasily Vladovitch," she said with a catch in her voice and an uncharacteristically bashful look at all of the drunks gathered around her. "The people—your neighbors and friends —and—and business associates here would like you to—they have raised for you—five—five—this," she said, thrusting a huge and bulging sack of gold dust in front of her. The crowd parted before her as she walked to the door and held it out to him.

He stopped her by taking her wrists in his hands, not touching the gold sack, and bending her arms back up to her own chest. "My friends," he said. "I—I hoped to bring a certain something here to Dawson with me, to elevate civilization to—"

"Hell, you did that, V.V.," someone hollered. "I ain't never been elevated as high as I been at your place, 'cept for tonight."

"But I—anyway, I must go for a time and—uh, acquire some new materials for building."

"You do that, Mr. Bledinoff," Ladue said. "Come spring those cheechakos are going to be flooding in here and Dawson's going to need all the businesses like yours it can get."

"Thank you. And I, I need to know that there is a Dawson that—ah, never mind. We Bledinoffs are not known to be a sentimental people. Someone hand me a glass." Someone did and he smashed it against the stove, only mildly lacerating the nearest bystanders. "There. That is as emotional as I get. Meanwhile, I must leave this wonderful gold in the hands of Miss

Devine, my business partner, who will be in charge of rebuilding my business and executing my affairs in any other way she sees fit. I have a—business trip—I must take to Alaska."

Loud protests chased him out the door where an Indian sled was hitched to twelve wolvish dogs, all lunging and howling.

"I regret that at the present time my only thanks to you must be not what I bring you, but what I take from you. Some of you, I know, will understand." And he winked a glistening eye at me, kicked off, and yelled, "Marchon!" to the wolvish dogs.

Those behind yelped and tried to surge forward, but the lead dog looked back at Vasily Vladovitch resentfully. Bledinoff braked and strode forward to face the defiant beast, glaring at it until it met his gaze and held it. All around me, the drunken revelers quieted as suddenly as the dog. Then the dog lowered its head and whimpered.

Vasily Vladovitch returned to the runners, released the brake, and yelled again, "Marchon!" And then, as they passed the broken ice to turn onto the river, he called, "Haw, Frank! Haw!"

I stood with my arm around Dag, Loki's tail keeping my neck warm, and watched as they drove to the end of town. There where the brush grew once more along the bank, a moose bounded down off the hill and followed behind them, brown against the moonlit snow. I wondered if anyone else had noticed that the furs on the sled covered a coffin.

# BIOGRAPHER'S
# END NOTE

••••⊷⊱❖⊰ ❙❙⊱❖⊰••••

*MRS. LOMAX'S ACCOUNT* of her early days in the Yukon has long been neglected in favor of her later tales of the exploits she shared with her husband on their steamship, the *Fang*, which many believe to be named for one of the most famous works of their longtime friend, Jack London. The more fanciful elements of this portion of Mrs. Lomax's autobiography have been ascribed by some medical historians to the head injuries she suffered when abruptly disembarking from the *Bella*, as described in these pages. Others blame the recurring bouts of malaria from which she suffered after traveling the rivers of Borneo with Mr. Lomax.

However, in Patricia Coyote's extensively researched collection of oral histories collected from various dance hall queens, *Gold Diggers of the Gold Fields*, Lady Sasha Destin seems to substantiate Mrs. Lomax's story. Lady Destin, who retired with her husband, the former Inspector Malcom Destin, ancestral laird of Clan Destin (of the Hebridean sept), to their estates in Ontario, credits both her turn in fortune and her many philanthropic works to an anonymous benefactor still (according to her) living among Indians in the Brooks Range in Alaska.

The birth and death records that might have substantiated Mrs. Lomax's allegations were unfortunately lost in the fire that swept Dawson City in 1898, and generally this particular set of events is attributed to the famous novelist's overactive imagination and Celtic tendency to embellish even such romantic adventures as gold hunting in the Klondike.

However, it is interesting to note that one of Jack London's most successful works, *White Fang*, was written from the viewpoint of a wolf, displaying the insight into the lupine mind that Mrs. Lomax would have traced directly to London's conversations with the late Assistant Consul Frank Blake, alias Drake. Mr. Blake was reported as missing from his post when his superior, the American consul, returned to Dawson after a prolonged visit to Washington, D.C.

Also of interest concerning the alleged existence of the mythical Vasily Vladovitch Bledinoff and of his contact with the people of Dawson is the fact that it was, in fact, a Yukoner, the much-decorated Joe Boyle, who took it upon himself during World War I to singlehandedly save Romania. Thus, it appears that if Bledinoff did exist outside of Mrs. Lomax's mind and was not actually immortal, he was at least long- and well-remembered by his former neighbors.

## About the Author

ELIZABETH SCARBOROUGH was born in Kansas City, KS. She served as a nurse in the U.S. Army for five years, including a year in Viet Nam. Her interests include weaving and spinning, and playing the guitar and dulcimer. She has previously published light verse as well as six other Bantam novels, *Song of Sorcery*, *The Unicorn Creed*, *Bronwyn's Bane*, *The Harem of Aman Akbar*, *The Christening Quest* and *The Drastic Dragon of Draco, Texas*. She is presently at work on a fantasy trilogy as well as a novel about the war in Viet Nam. She makes her home in Fairbanks, Alaska.